URSA UNEARTHED

SCOURGE SURVIVOR SERIES - BOOK TWO

JL MADORE

To my family: We're one step closer. I love you.
*To my readers: Thank you for loving Blaze Ignites and for blogging, tweeting
and reviewing it so kindly. I hope you love the continuation of our Ambar
Lenn in Ursa Unearthed.*
*To my Writers' Community of Durham Region family: You are without
question, the greatest and most talented community of writers ever
assembled. You energize me. I'm honored every day to be part of the group.
Rock on WCDR!*
*To my editors, Ruth and Gwynn of Writescape: Even when I think I've got
things locked down I know you'll show me places to tighten up and shine.
You're just that good. Thank you.*
*To my writing circle, Critical Realm: Carol, Chris, Dawn, Justin and Sharon,
your critiques are invaluable, your support immeasurable, and your
friendships irreplaceable.*

AMBAR LENN – FATE'S JOURNEY

Alone in the dark, Aust sat at the bottom of the grand staircase of Jade's manse, staring at the cryptic words mounted on the foyer wall. Translated by the Centaur, Chiron of Deleran, the Queen Oracles' prophesy hung opposite the double entrance doors. Aust's Elven brothers and warrior friends boasted thoughts and theories as to its meaning, but theories they remained. And on nights when reverie evaded him—which occurred more oft than not—he sat within the silent stone walls of Jade's new home and tried to glean the prophesy's meaning:

Journey of Fate, two realms to purge
Weapons drawn against the Scourge
Blaze of passion,
Trust unearthed,
Cleansing of past,
Spirit rebirthed,
Fate or free-will, which to choose?
With love to gain and life to lose.
Darkness hides in familiar form
A brother's betrayal, a sister's storm
Empower lost souls or evil shall reign

Noble the child of argenteous mane

Journey of Fate—the first line referred to their *Ambar Lenn,* everyone agreed on that point. Four fortnights past, the inception of his, Galan's and Thamior's journey to manhood had triggered unforeseen events. On that night—the night the exile of his people was lifted —the three of them had set off from the Highborne village to find their path.

Aust had yet to find anything . . . save grief.

His *Eda* had been slain, his *Naneth* left heart-weary, and his people so offended by his goddess-given affinity to communicate with his animal brothers and sisters, they cast him out.

Galan fared well enough, and for at least that much, he rejoiced. Jade was a remarkable female, and to have Recognized with his mate . . . there was no greater blessing. Together, partners in life and purpose, the two now served Castian as Protectors of the Realm of the Fair.

Thamior's journey? Well . . . Tham remained Tham e'ermore. Aust marveled at the strength of spirit the male possessed, his love and wonder of all things, the simple joy he found in living free within the Realm of the Fair. Tham had made no progress in his journey yet paid it no mind.

Weapons drawn against the Scourge—Aust was more than ready to take up arms against the enemy of the realm. He yearned to prove his value, burned to avenge his dead. There were moments, the fury boiled so white-hot in his blood, he almost drowned in the lure of vengeance and pain. He quelled those impulses as best he could.

For the choices made to navigate the journey of the *Ambar Lenn* would determine if he could ever be thought of as a male of worth. And so, he pushed back the anguish and the anger and waited . . ..

CHAPTER ONE

"Ah hell Paige, you're killing me." I shook my head and sighed as my boss steadied her boots on the bench beside me and straightened. Swaying full hips to the bass line of the Goth-rock blaring at us from all sides, she *clinked* her glass with a spoon and waited until my friends raised their glasses.

I glanced across the pitted, wooden table and over the sea of eclectic patrons. Were the exploits of my intimate office soirée registering with the crowd in the anything-goes pub? Nope. High-backed leather booths lined three sides of the dance floor, secluding those of us who were seated in our own little rectangular worlds. Besides, the hedonistic hypnotism of the crowd held everyone's attention locked down tight.

Annnd that is the beauty of Spankz.

"Here's to Mika," Paige said, her mocha cheeks flushed from celebration. "The Nimithic Group may have thought themselves untouchable, but were they?"

"*Nooo,*" my girls chimed in.

"That's right. Thirty-four counts of trading in illegal exotics, five warrants for arrest, three properties searched, and the largest seizure of black-market animal products in Canadian history taught them different."

"*Fucking A!*" Meg placed two fingertips in her mouth and nearly popped my eardrums with the shriek of her whistle.

"Now ladies," Paige continued, "let's down a hearty drink in honor of the most decorated investigative journalist Canada's wildlife has ever seen. A woman who takes warm and fuzzy to a new level, who, quite honestly, could spend a little less time with her pets and a lot more time getting petted, our very own . . . Mika "The Bandit" Silverbrook."

"*Wooo Mika!*"

Focused on the glowing red beacon of the *Exit* sign across the dance floor, I considered my odds of escape. Not good. They'd just drag me back by my hair. "Thanks guys. Oh, for god's sake Paige, get down before you fall." I tugged at her skin-tight jeans until we were all seated around our table. "Really, thank you, but can we get back to the drinking and dancing and stop with the dinner theatre?"

Paige snorted. "Whatever you say, honey. It's your—"

I held up one finger as the vibration changed in the air around us. Fishing into the front pocket of my jeans I grabbed my phone and waited. When my ring tone sounded and the Heartbeat Drum Song started, I answered it. "Grandfather? Everything all right?"

"My question to *you*, Rabbit," Grandfather said, his graveled voice unusually thin. "You were mentioned on the news tonight. Are you safe and well?"

Damn. If I'd been at home tonight, I would have remembered to call him before he saw the eleven o'clock news. I touched my cheek as it tingled beneath his mystical caress and I breathed deep. "I'm fine. I'm sorry. I should have called."

The pause on the other end of the phone tightened my gut. "The destination is not as important as the path, child. The power is in the path."

Grandfather didn't like my path, even so, he supported me. The only thing he asked was that I kept him involved while I worked in the city, so he wouldn't worry. "I'm coming to the reserve next weekend. We have a date with your telescope and a comet, don't we?"

"We do." The rhythmic tap of his cane in the background spoke volumes about his mood. I could picture him sitting in the willow chair at the base of his stairs, his silver braids hanging forward as he leaned over the old walnut phone table. This late, he'd have his threadbare Thunderbird blanket wrapped over his curled shoulders.

"I'm sorry I worried you, Grandfather. It won't happen again."

The tapping stopped and the tightness in my gut eased.

"You make an old man proud, Rabbit. A true guardian of the Earth Mother. Now go back to your evening with your friends. I look forward to seeing you."

After saying goodnight, I flipped my phone shut, then refocused on the scene in front of me. "Sorry. What did I miss?"

Paige wagged her finger toward my phone, her eyes narrowed. "One day you'll tell me how you do that phone trick. I swear you're psychic or something."

Or something.

Paige sputtered mid-swig and lowered her Cosmo, coughing. From our table, near the back hall, we had a clear view of the club's landscape. She cleared her throat and pointed, not-too-discretely toward the front of the pub. "Major stud alert, four o'clock."

Cue the peanut gallery: "Oh, I need me one of those." "Yep. Click, add to cart." "Call my travel agent. I'm eloping."

I laughed, but they weren't wrong. The half-naked sea of dancers parted for two men. Shoulder to shoulder they stood looking like cover models—if GQ ever printed a tall dark and lethal edition. One was about six-foot-four, had ink-black hair, a goatee, guy-liner, and a half dozen platinum piercings. He looked like a Goth hit man, all tone, no fat. His body language said he'd take you down and enjoy the carnage—whether fucking or fighting.

The other stood a little shorter and balanced a perfect blend of bad-boy meets muscle builder. Collar length, medium brown hair fell messy around a chiseled face while shaggy bangs hid his eyes. His worn leather vest covered a crisp white, button-down shirt hanging untucked over blue jeans. *Good gosh, Hugo Boss.* Designer denim hugged thick, muscular thighs. Casual classy was something we didn't see a lot of in this club. The charge in the air shifted, and the hair on my arms stood on end.

"Those hard bodies are making promises for a wild, night." Em breathed.

"And every woman in here knows it." Meg nodded.

I giggled at the estrogen surge in my posse. "Okay, I'm off to the bar. You ladies close your mouths before someone offers to fill them for you." With the next-round list in my head I skirted the dance floor and made my way to the main bar.

"Blender drinks will take a sec, hon," the bartender said. "You mind waiting while I thin out this crowd a bit?"

"Not a problem." I turned toward the dance floor and rested my elbows on the wood rail while the show unfolded. You have to love a place where women in go-go boots and micro mini's jockey with body-painted metro-sexuals for the honor of shaking their junk in cages.

Fifteen minutes of fame.

I chuckled as two Barbie-blondes in thigh-highs and bustiers started sword fighting with their tongues in the cage closest to me. *Always a good time.*

"Here you go, hon." I whirled around, but the bartender wasn't speaking to me. She handed a frosted tumbler to the drop-dead, vest guy with the shaggy hair. "I'll send the bottle and your tab to the back, baby. You boys setting up camp in VIP?"

He emptied his glass and set it up for a refill. "That's the plan. Hey Laney, how's that little girl of yours? Still as stunning as her Mama?"

"More," she replied and topped up his glass, "but she's not so little anymore, Bruin. She turned seventeen last month and boys are lined up around the block."

He arched a brow and leaned over the bar. "If you need a hand beating them off, give me a call. I'd be happy to scare a few dogs out of your yard."

She laughed and shook her head. After popping the caps off two

Coronas, she squeezed quartered limes down the bottle necks and set them on a tray. "That would be a big-ole no thanks. She'd never forgive you, and I'd never hear the end of it. For some reason, she thinks the sun rises and sets on you, Bruin."

He sipped from his glass and shrugged. "The girl's got impeccable taste."

Down the bar, a pink-haired chippie in a seventies, vinyl onesie waved. The bartender chuckled as she headed off. "Duty calls, baby."

Settling back against the rail, I heard the clink and swish of ice cubes grow louder until drop-dead guy leaned in beside me. As my senses tingled, I gave myself a brisk inward shake and stared straight out into the club. He took another swig and gazed into the writhing bodies—maybe taking inventory of the prospects for the night.

There were plenty to pick from and I wondered what a man like him would hunger for. I eyed the after-office flocks unwinding, the usual leather-clad party girls advertising easy pickup, the scary chicks dressed like Dracula with safety pins through their purple painted lips, and the ever-amusing dazed and confused who probably walked in off the street unaware—and now found-themselves lost in the Twilight Zone.

He rested his arms on the rail next to me and his white cotton shirt strained to contain his shoulders and biceps. "Busy tonight."

"*Mhmm.*"

"So, tell me, pretty lady, what band are you with?" The din of the club couldn't drown out the rich, cultured timbre of his voice, but really . . . was that the best he had?

I leaned back a bit to get a good look at him. "Sorry, not a musician."

With a flip of his bangs, his eyes stole my breath. Against the dim light cast by brass and glass sconces, those two turquoise pools practically glowed. He looked me up and down without apology. How many times had he choreographed that move to dazzle a woman?

Full lips eased into a heart-stopping smile. "Not that kind of band," he drawled. "You're First Nations. What band you're from?"

I ignored his cocky smirk and studied his chiseled features. "What gave me away?"

He sipped at the clear liquid in his glass and studied me back. "Well the copper skin, chestnut hair, and deep brown eyes are obvious. More impressive though, is your essence of being one with the Earth. It sets you apart from every other female in this crowd."

It took a minute for my mind to grasp that little tidbit. *Was he kidding, or was that the most original pick up line ever?* He nursed his drink and watched me. Too sexy to be real. He probably had an ego the size of Vancouver Island.

"You're all set, miss." I forced myself to turn and reached for the tray the bartender held out. "Sorry for the wait, hon. It's crazy here tonight."

"It certainly is." I nodded farewell and headed back to my table. After my girls each claimed their libations and sucked back a swig, we moved en masse to the dance floor. Hunk-in-vest still stood at the rail where I'd left him, assessing the sea of leather and denim, muscle, and grind. When he tipped his glass to me, I turned my back and swayed to the music.

Well, if he was looking, I should at least give him something to see. Right?

Releasing the clip in my hair I let it loose to fall down my back. Liane's jaw dropped when Meg sidled up and brushed her hands over my backside in a little girl-on-girl action.

Meg leaned in close and whispered, "He's still looking at you."

Wrap him up. I'll take him to go.

The rest of the sexually charged patrons and the thrum of music melted away. His heated gaze traveled over my body like a physical caress. Warmth tingled down my back, along my curves and paused on my ass. As one song blended into the next, my girls and I kept up the show. The club could've burned to the ground around me and I'd never have noticed. The next song sped the tempo way up, so I opted out and left them to it.

Back at our table, I sipped my Long Island and waited to see if hot-guy nibbled the bait.

"Mika?"

My smile faded as I turned. "Do I know you?"

Three, skull-trimmed, biker types closed in and my inner sense itched like a colony of ants scrambling from the nape of my neck down my back. Mother Earth was never wrong and I never questioned her warnings. I side-stepped to head back to my girls, but not fast enough.

The three shifted to intercept.

"Sorry boys, my dance cards full tonight."

The tallest thug grabbed my wrist and spun me down the back hall. Iron fingers clamped my shoulder and twisted my arm behind my back. A cloth tightened over my mouth and I screamed against the inside of a gag. The noise of the club swallowed the sound. Fabric pulled tight and split the corners of my mouth. My pulse thrummed through my veins. My mind spun. They confiscated my phone and my Taser was in my purse at our booth.

As Curly, Larry and Moe swept me down the dark corridor, I remembered seeing some specialist on Oprah saying, *'never let your enemy take you to a secondary location.'*

"You fucked with the wrong people, bitch." Hot breath washed my cheek, the reek of tobacco and whiskey, assaulting my senses. The old familiar duo made my gut churn.

Shoved from behind, I stumbled down the deserted hall toward the back door. At each washroom door, I prayed someone would step out. No luck.

"You have no idea what you've stepped in."

Moe burst out the back door and dragged me into what the locals called 'heroin alley'. I threw my hands out and clawed to find purchase as the tall guy pushed us forward. Out-weighted and out-muscled I couldn't find a hold. Two hands were no match for six. The heat of the summer night hit me like a wall, and panic rose in my chest. Three strung-out party-goers scrambled and scattered without a second look. The slam of the steel door trapped us out back.

I might be a dead-woman-walking, but I'd go down with a fight.

Think Mika. I sucked in some courage and slammed my boot heel into the top of my captor's foot. Twisting down with all my weight I made a solid grab for his crotch. My hands aren't big, but I grabbed all I could and squeezed like I was juicing an orange.

When he buckled . . . I bolted.

Someone caught a handful of my hair and whiplashed me back. White spots exploded behind my eyes as a fist connected with my face. The smack of knuckles on skin echoed and my cheek caught fire.

"Fucking bitch!" Tall guy palmed himself with the heel of his hand while his buddy used his grip in my hair to force me into the shadows. My skull screamed. I flailed behind my head but couldn't get free from his grasp. "Gimme a minute and then we'll teach this one some manners."

Bile stung the back of my throat as I got shoved down the alley and against the crumbling brick of the next building. Gorilla fingers worked at my button fly as a solid knee forced my thighs open. Another slam and my head cracked against the wall at my back. My head throbbed. My senses sloshed. I twisted and gouged but couldn't get his hands out of my jeans.

"Damn it, grab her arms!"

I screamed behind the gag, my voice useless. Tall guy's meaty hands pinned both my wrists against brick. My shoulders burned like they might pop out of joint.

Thud. Third guy sprawled past and face planted on the damp pavement. *Huh?*

"She needs to work on manners?" The deep husky tone of hunk-in-vest growled beside me. "Three against one seems downright rude."

My head spun as both my captors disappeared, and my body was released. The instant loss of force knocked me off balance. Strong arms caught me before I hit the ground and eased me to sit with my back against the brick wall. My eyes welled, blurring the image of Bruin—I think that's what the bartender called him—coming to my rescue. Gentle fingers made quick work of the knot of my gag and it fell away.

"Don't move, 'kay? Let us handle this." When I nodded, he wheeled around and planted himself in front of me. "How about we even things up a bit, Kobi?"

The black-haired, GQ friend smiled, and I swear his eyes flashed red in the darkness. A trick of the moonlight, maybe. The two moved in graceful tandem. They'd obviously done this before and probably enjoyed it when a fight dropped at their feet.

Bruin loomed large as he tipped his neck from side to side and rolled thickly muscled shoulders. "Care to dance, gentlemen? Or do you only fight women?"

Five men scrambled into a flurry of fists. The thud and slap of flesh on flesh ricocheted from all sides. My teeth started chattering. I pulled my knees up and dropped my head across my arms. I didn't want to be here. I wanted to run, but my body wasn't listening to me at the moment. Someone knelt in front of me and I jumped.

Bruin held his palms up and froze. "You okay?"

No. After a moment, I managed to nod. "Fine. Shaky, but fine. Are they tied up?"

"Nah," he glanced over his shoulder. "They're taking a little nap. They won't wake up until it's time for their meet-and-greet with the boys in blue."

"Speaking of," Kobi said, a few feet away. I lifted my gaze and watched his cigarette glow to life. "I'll get security and call D. Be right back."

After Kobi disappeared into the club, Bruin held my gaze. "Let's get you off the wet ground, shall we?"

He scooped under my knees and eased me against his chest like a weightless child. Though my muscles protested the movement, I draped one arm over his broad, thick shoulder. He set me on a brick retaining wall that bordered the loading dock. With a scowl, he brushed the hair from my face and ran a gentle thumb over the flaming patch of skin on my cheek. "That's going to leave a mark."

Lucky me. "Why do guys do that? Hit a woman square in the face. Do they teach that move in bastard school?"

"Couldn't tell you. I didn't attend that class."

I shuddered as an icy shiver worked down my spine. He shifted closer, letting his body heat seep under my skin.

"Your eyes are really beautiful." I winced as the words rolled off my tongue and wished I could rewind my mouth. *Oh. My. God.* My cheeks flushed hot. They were beautiful—a vibrant turquoise blue, almost electric. Magnetic. But really, *your eyes are really beautiful?*

His laugh was soft and enchanting. "Thank you. How about you take a few deep breaths. I think you're a little shocky. In. Out. In. Out."

His Goth friend returned with the bouncer who'd been rocking the mic and headset at the front door when I arrived. The white 'Security' stretched across his broad-as-a-football-field chest sent a pretty clear message to anyone thinking of stirring up trouble. He glanced down at the three piles of biker-contusion on the asphalt and chuckled. "It's always fun when you boys are in town. Go inside. When Delgato gets here I'll set him up in my office for question period."

"Thanks, man." Bruin helped me from the ledge and walked me inside. When I wobbled in the back hall, he put one hand on my hip and pulled me against him. "We're not dancing here, pretty lady. Give me your weight until your legs steady. Trust me, I can handle it."

I was sure he could.

CHAPTER TWO

I must've looked bad—like train-wreck bad—because when we emerged into the main area of the club my girls swarmed. Bruises would be unavoidable, but not yet noticeable. My cheek, however, had a flaming pulse of its own and felt like it had throbbed to ten times its usual size. After recapping the heroin alley highlight reel, and the fact that I'd pissed someone off, I convinced my friends that I was in good hands and none the worse for wear.

"Take a week or two off, Mika." Paige put up her hand and halted my protest. "If this is fallout from your exposé on the Nimithic Group, keep your head down and visit your granddad for a while. There will be plenty of bad guys for you to persecute when the dust settles."

I smiled, but then winced when my cheek stung. "I might take you up on that."

"I'm not offering. I'm telling."

The thought of spending a week on the reserve sounded beyond perfect. It had been ages since Grandfather and I had taken time to commune with nature together. "Fine, bossy lady. I'll swing by the office and grab some files tomorrow and then take a little vacation."

"Good." Paige hugged me and when she pulled back, she glanced toward the bar where Bruin stood chatting with the bartender. "If you get the chance . . . a little crotch mingling with that one would be a great way to burn off some stress and pass time."

"Classy."

She shrugged. "I'm a poet."

"We better watch out, or Hallmark will be scooping you away from us." I looked back to the bar and Bruin turned, cocked a brow and lifted his glass to his lips.

Someone tapped my shoulder and I gasped.

"Shit, sorry." The security guy frowned. "The cops are almost done outside. Are you ready to talk to them?"

Why was my heart racing? I'd given dozens of statements for work . . . but never as the victim of violence. I didn't want to think about . . ..

My hands started to shake again.

Bruin strode over, and I fumbled for his glass. "You won't like this. Let me get you—"

I arched my brow and he returned the look. Had I ever seen anything cuter? I focused on stilling my hand between us. "Afraid of a little DNA transfer?"

"Not at all." With a shrug, he let his tumbler loose.

I took a deep gulp of the clear liquid and immediately regretted it. Lighter fluid . . . eating down the length of my esophagus . . . *Holy hell.* How could anyone find paint thinner refreshing? Proud that I neither choked nor sputtered, I held out his glass and blinked back tears.

He fought a smile and thankfully took the glass before I dropped it. "It's likely stronger than you're accustomed to. They stock it by request for Kobi and me."

I tried unsuccessfully to regain my composure. "What *is* that?"

His deep throaty laugh made his eyes sparkle. "Everclear. It's vodka, but it's strong."

Strong? "I think it just ate the lining of my stomach."

He caught the attention of a server standing at the bar and she sidled over, beaming. "What can I get you, Bruin?"

He looked down at me seemingly unaware of her affections. I cleared my throat of the last of his killer vodka, but still couldn't find my voice. He chuckled again. "How about a Long Island? That's what you were drinking earlier, right?"

I shook my head but that was a bad idea. "Ginger-ale . . . please."

"Coming up," the server said.

"Uh . . . thanks for the rescue," I mumbled, tilting my head toward the back hall. "I don't want to think about what might have happened if you and your friend hadn't been here."

Bruin cast a gaze to the back hall and his jaw clenched tight. Like the flip of a switch, his easy charm vanished, and a menacing shadow darkened his expression. If I met him on a street looking like that, I would change sides or go the other way.

I stepped back and looked again with an observer's eye. His shirt remained crisp white. Not a mark on him. Aggression oozed out of him. Primitive. Predatory. Who was this guy to take on those thugs and remain pristine? *How is that possible?* Should I feel threatened? Yes. I should. So, why did I find that intriguing and not a giant red flashing warning sign?

When a plain-clothed officer headed our way, I knew I was up. "It was nice almost meeting you. It's Bruin, right?"

He tipped back the last of his drink and nodded. "And you are?"

I slid my hand into his. "Mika Silverbrook."

With a quick smirk, he accepted my drink from the server and set it in the palm of my hand. The cop joined us and the two men shook hands. "Mika, this is Detective Enrique Delgato, or D for short. And D, this is Mika Silverbrook."

Detective Delgato, a distinguished-looking man—despite his nose being broken once too often and its slight dogleg left—was Hispanic, fit, and wore his hair military short. "Seems you've had quite a night, Miss Silverbrook. If you'll come with me. This won't take long."

Walking Detective Delgato through the club to detail the excitement of the night turned out to be easier than I thought. When we were through, he closed his notebook, gave me his card and helped me gather up my things. "I've got a feeling those men aren't first-timers. Once I get back to the station, I'll know better what we're dealing with and what charges we'll be filing."

"Sure, let me know. Can I go now?"

The whole shebang had taken less than two hours. I had been toasted, napped, assaulted, rescued and interrogated and the club still buzzed on. Other than my office crew, no one even seemed aware of what had almost happened out back. When I called it a night, the girls suggested moving the gathering to my place.

No thanks. The thought of being molly-coddled, while worried eyes watched for a meltdown made me itch. It took some arguing, but I was known for being a little stubborn and I wasn't going to budge.

"May I walk you out, Miss Silverbrook?" The detective's warm smile penetrated all the way to his eyes. "I'd feel better if I could at least see you safely to your vehicle."

"It's Mika, and yes, thank you. I'd appreciate that."

He accepted the tangle of gift bag handles and weighted balloon strings from my celebration and waited while I grabbed my purse and said my goodbyes. Placing a hand on the small of my back, he led me toward the door. Detective Delgato had an energy about him. As we walked along the front of the club I looked into the moonlit sky and listened to the Earth Spirits.

Yep. Impression confirmed. True-blue. I smiled and drew a deep breath.

As we rounded the corner of the club for the parking lot, my heart skipped. Bruin, or hunk-in-vest as I liked to think of him, leaned against the side wall, ankles and arms crossed. When our eyes met, he winked.

"You waiting for someone in particular?" I asked.

He pushed off the wall and stalked closer. "Thought I'd ensure you got to your car without incident. There's a dangerous element out tonight. Can't be too careful."

Detective Delgato nodded. "I've been trying to convince her to go home with a friend. She seems to have stirred up a bit of a hail storm at work. It wouldn't be in her best interest to head straight into an empty home."

"I couldn't agree more, D." Bruin stared at me, his intentions obvious.

Awkward.

The detective chuckled and handed Bruin my bags. "Well then, I'll leave you in good hands to discuss your options, Miss Silverbrook. Bruin will see you home safely, whatever you decide. If you have any problems, don't hesitate to contact me, day or night."

"Thank you, Detective."

Bruin inclined his head and stepped next to me.

After a moment, the detective's nondescript burgundy sedan disappeared around the corner and I faced my white knight. "And you waited around out here on the off chance that saving my ass would translate into me falling into your bed?"

He flicked one of my balloons with his finger. His turquoise eyes flashed gold as they caught a beam of headlights and reflected the light. "I won't apologize for knowing what I want."

"And do you always get what you want?"

His arched brow disappeared under shaggy bangs and my pulse quickened. I listened hard to my environment but couldn't get a read on him. *Weird.* I'd gotten more than just my physical traits from my Native ancestors. My grandfather's people had gifts . . . I tried again. Nothing. It seemed mine had currently abandoned me. "So, what is it you want tonight?"

He canted his head to the side as if considering. "Some company in my hotel suite, a little room service, maybe a dip in my jetted soaker tub. I've got a beautiful view of the mountains from my terrace. Play your cards right and I might even massage out those muscles that are going to start turning on you in the next few hours."

I closed my eyes. As insistent as I'd been telling Paige and the Detective that I just wanted to go home, I realize now that I didn't. I hated feeling rattled . . . but I was rattled. I shrugged. "How could a girl say no?"

He wrapped a strand of my hair behind my ear, his knuckle brushing the edge of my jaw. Where flesh met flesh, my skin tingled. "Oh, it's happened."

Yeah, right. No hot-blooded female would shut him down. "All right, you lead the way and I'll follow in my truck. What are you driving?" I scanned the parking lot for something that fit. The night crowd had thinned and, based on what was left between the rows, I'd lay money on one of the two cars in the back: the candy apple red, Shelby Mustang or the silver Audi R8 straddling the lines of two spots. Classic muscle or flashy sport?

"Actually, Kobi headed to the hotel with our rental. Mind driving both of us?"

"Um . . .." For one split second panic rose in my chest. I wasn't a prude or anything. I'd had casual encounters before. But heading out with a total stranger after a night like tonight? He wasn't really a *total* stranger, though. He'd saved me from being raped and abducted and was friendly with the local law enforcement.

That meant he was safe, right?

He crossed his arms and waited for my answer. Safe? No. He was the farthest thing from safe I'd ever come across. But I didn't want to be alone tonight either. Somehow, the idea of sticking close to my buff protector seemed . . . comforting.

Stopping at the front of my truck I scrabbled at the bottom of my purse and pulled out my keys. He whistled through his teeth, his eyes gleaming with the perfect combination of shock and admiration for my black-on-black Humvee. "Your chariot awaits."

CHAPTER THREE

ruin swung my door open and waited while I eased in and tossed my shit behind the seat. Striding around to the passenger side he had his door open and settled in one graceful motion. Most of my tension melted away once the metallic echo of the doors secured us inside. I ran my fingers down the eagle feather hanging from my rear-view mirror and inhaled the power of my truck.

"Nice ride, mystery lady. What's she got?"

I snorted, turned the key and let the throaty rumble of the engine fill the silence. "*She?* Please. *He* is nothing, but raw, unbridled testosterone with cojones the size of Texas. Although, his original 6.5 litre diesel has been slightly neutered to lessen his carbon footprint. Even still, we can go anywhere and crush anything that gets in our way. He's ex-military, armor-plated and don't even get me started on his torque."

Bruin's mouth dropped open and he laughed.

The cloud-laden sky gave up its burden as we pulled out, a misty spit gathering on my windshield. At the edge of the road I flipped on my wipers and waited for the swish and hum to clear my view. "So, where are we headed? And don't say some skeezy motel off the beaten path or I'll hit eject and call it a bad night all the way around."

He chuckled. "Do you know the Wedgewood Hotel? *I* don't consider it skeezy, but I'll leave it to you to decide."

"The Wedgewood?" God he was hard to figure out.

"Yeah, Kobi and I stay there when we're in town. You know it?"

Yes. I knew it. I drove past it every day on my way to work but had never had the guts to go inside. "It's beautiful. Costs a fortune though, doesn't it?"

He shrugged, drumming his fingers on the front dash. "You don't seem to have a problem indulging for something you like."

True. "So how long are you in town?" I dialed up the wipers a notch and slowed to let the car in front of me turn.

Bruin hesitated and ran his fingers along the evening shadow darkening his jaw. "That's up in the air. I'm hiding out for a few days, maybe a week."

"Avoiding something?" The hair on my arms raised as the journalist in me started lining up the possibilities: a wife, the disgruntled husband of an indiscretion, a legal mess, a gang of criminals . . .. I eyed his clothes. He sure made a pair of tight jeans look good. *Oh shit.* "You're not a drug dealer or anything are you?"

He barked out a laugh, his deep, melodic voice filling the cab of the truck. "No. Nothing as sinister as that. One of my adoptive sisters, Jade, is getting married in a few weeks and our household is a little crazy. My other sister, Lexi, is her maid-of-honor and is planning the big event. She's gone completely off the rails."

"And you're hiding? A big, strong hero cowering from a little 'Say Yes to the Dress?'"

"Hell, yeah. Lexi is the biggest little vortex of chaos you could imagine. The entire household is tripping over itself to avoid her. Forget Bridezilla. Lexi is Bridesmaidzilla . . . then cross that with a spoiled princess and add in a whole lotta drill sergeant . . . and then arm her with knives."

He shrugged at my expression, his adorable smile lighting up his face. "I thought it best to pop in for my fittings and then get the hell outta Dodge."

"You live with your sisters?"

He nodded. "They're more than my adopted family, they are my best friends too."

"And is it just the three of you?"

"No. There's our brother, Julian, our father, and some others."

"Others? How big is your house?"

"It's not my house. It was a wedding present for Jade. We just moved in two months ago. It's big enough that we don't need to see anyone we don't want to, but small enough that they always find me when I'm avoiding them." He snickered, staring out the windshield, watching as the swish of the wipers cleared the glistening drops from his view. "They're damn good little trackers, those girls."

I stopped at a red light and glanced sideways at his beautiful profile. "Won't they need your help to get ready for the wedding?"

"No. They have Galan's family and the staff. They won't even notice I'm gone."

Somehow, I doubt that. "And Galan is . . .?"

"The groom."

When the light changed, I pulled forward and indicated my turn onto the parking ramp leading below the hotel. At the unmanned security gate, I lowered the clearance of my truck and rolled down my window. Bruin handed me his key card and I swiped the machine. The digital sign flashed, *'Welcome to the Wedgewood Hotel, Mr. Bruin. Enjoy your stay.'*

After a moment, the gate arm hummed and then lifted, allowing our passage. The garage, a standard maze of concrete pillars and fluorescent lighting, boasted spots wider than public lots. The vehicles parked in them were a car collector's wish list: Jaguar, Mercedes, Audi, Lexus, even a Ferrari. Nothing you'd want to ding accidentally with a military tank of a truck.

"We're over beside the elevators." Bruin pointed ahead of us, to the right and I followed his direction. "The spot should be big enough for your behemoth."

I ignored his snicker and read the plaque on the wall right beside the black Mustang with the Enterprise rental sticker sitting in PH1401. "PH? As in Penthouse?"

"*Yes?* Why do you say it like that?"

I shook my head and pulled in. "No reason. Just getting my bearings."

Trying to unfrazzle my mind was more accurate. If memory served, these penthouse suites went for $1500 a night . . . each. And they had two . . . for an unknown amount of time. A brawny, god of a man, dressed in shabby-chic, saves my virtue, possibly my life and takes me back to his penthouse suite at the Wedgewood.

Where did this guy come from?

He was obviously accustomed to the finer things yet had no air of rich kid superiority or bad-boy-bachelor-with-something-to-prove. It didn't add up. I was missing something, and my journalistic Spidey-senses were tingling like mad. With a turn of my wrist, the rumble of my engine silenced and I withdrew the key.

Bruin slipped out in a blur, opened my door and offered me a hand to step down.

"So, is Bruin your first name or your last? The bartender and the waitress at Spankz called you Bruin, but the security gate has you down as Mr. Bruin."

He shrugged. "It's just Bruin."

I slung my purse over my shoulder as he led me to the elevators and swiped his key card. "Like Beyoncé or Usher or Prince . . . well, until he changed his name into that silly squiggle thing." His blank stare told me I'd lost him on that one. Obviously not an '80s fan. Maybe the one name was an adoption thing and he didn't like talking about it.

"Okay, just Bruin, so where are you from?"

He stepped tight behind me, his cheek brushing against my neck. The rasp of his jaw combined with the warmth of his breath on my throat sent a shiver through me. "Are we going to waste what's left of the evening playing twenty questions?"

The hiss of the elevator doors had my heart jumping. With a

possessive tug, he pulled me inside and pivoted my hips, so we stood face to face. "I can think of a dozen things I'd rather do. How about you?"

Reaching around me, he inserted his card and punched the italic *PH14.*

Of their own volition, my hands traveled up the ridges of corded muscle defining his ribcage. *Wow, this guy had a body.* My skin flushed, and I told myself it had nothing to do with the heat coming off him, the deep timbre of his voice or the sudden hunger in his eyes. I moistened my lips. "I'm open to suggestions."

Bruin drew a deep breath and his nostrils flared. In the enclosed confines of the elevator, he didn't just occupy space . . . he saturated it. He was intensely masculine. He was sexual. And his mouth hovered just inches from mine.

I swallowed hard, my heart beating in my chest like a ceremonial buckskin drum. He fingered a piece of my hair down to where it hung against my damaged cheek. When I flinched, he stiffened, and a muscle leapt in his jaw.

"Don't worry about it," I said raising my fingers to probe the damage. "I'm sure it looks worse than it is."

He laid a gentle kiss on the bruise then nuzzled his way down my neck. When his lips brushed my collarbone, I swear he growled, low in his chest. The primal sound sent my hormones off the charts and I leaned back against the elevator wall for support.

He followed, a predator stalking forward to claim my mouth.

The wait was excruciating, the contact decadent. His lips moved over mine, and though I couldn't get a solid read on him with my gift, I felt the incredible strength he held in reserve. The edge. The power. He tethered something dangerous inside himself. Something fierce. My arms barely reached around his shoulders as he lifted me from the ground and pulled me against his chest. Would he ever use his strength against me like those bastards tonight?

A soft ding accompanied the hiss of the elevator doors. Without breaking our kiss, he grasped both cheeks of my ass and lifted me against his waist. I linked my ankles behind his thighs and we moved as one into the foyer of the fourteenth floor.

Bruin's tongue danced in my mouth as his arousal pressed hard against my belly.

As all my well-cultivated defenses fizzled, I couldn't help wondering what the night would bring. He tasted wild and smelled like the crisp outdoors mixed with Hugo Boss. He hesitated, chuckled into my mouth, and walked us back to the empty elevator. After reaching inside, he pulled his key card from the slot.

Satisfied it had completed its task, the elevator hissed closed and descended.

Bruin fumbled with the card slot outside his suite when the adjacent penthouse door opened. Without setting me down he withdrew from our kiss and inclined his head.

Kobi, stood in the other doorway wearing black Calvins, a dozen piercings and a hell of a lot of tawny tattooed skin. With his nipple ring catching the light and a black, banding tattoo encircling his left shoulder, he rocked the tall-Goth-and-sexy look. But something was off. Regardless of his physical appearance, the man had a haunted look in his dark charcoal eyes.

He gave our situation a once over and raised a bottle of whiskey to his lips. "Glad you're back. Now I can get down to it." He leaned back so we could see into his suite. "You remember the two blondes from the cage."

Oh, the kissy, thigh-high twins.

Bruin laughed. "I do, though I prefer my dance partners free-range."

A sinful smirk crept over Kobi's face as he propped the door open a little wider and we could see a David Beckham look alike inside with the girls. "Tall, dark and sexy was free range. We added him in on the way to the car."

I wondered if the look Bruin flashed his buddy was admiration or disbelief. I hoped for the latter. "So, if you've got a full house what are you doing in the hall?"

"What can I say, I'm that fucking dedicated. Oh, and I like my balls right where they are, fuck-you-very-much. If anything happened to you—"

"Good night, Kobi." Bruin snapped. "We can chit-chat *mañana*."

Kobi gave us a middle finger salute over his shoulder and headed back inside his suite.

"Hey," Bruin called after him. "Keep the noise down tonight."

Kobi laughed and kicked the door shut behind him.

CHAPTER FOUR

 ruin's hand swiped the wall as we stumbled as one into his suite. With the flick of the switch, two lamps clicked on and a soft glow lit our way. Neither of us took in the sights. Bruin set me on my feet, his lips chasing my pulse up my neck. His vest had to go. I pushed the leather over his shoulders, let it flop to the plush beige carpet and made short work of his shirt buttons.

He was a beautifully built man, broad shoulders tapered to a sculpted torso. He even had those fabulous muscle indents on his hips, pointing the way home. *Oh, yeah.*

I ran my hands down the landscape and fingered the dusting of brown hair disappearing under the waistband of his designer jeans. Strong fingers went to work on the top button of my jeans. Electric moment. Explosive potential.

When the first rivet popped free from its mooring I froze. Panic boiled in my gut. My chest constricted, and I staggered back. Leaning against the sofa table, I gasped for oxygen and tried to tame the quakes rocking through me. "I'm sorry. Give me a second."

Bruin didn't move. "Shit. Did I do something?"

I shook my hands out to my sides and paced a quick lap of the room. I felt like an idiot putting distance between us, but a little solitude seemed to help settle my brain cells. "No. I'm totally into you. It's just your fingers tugging at my jeans . . . just an alley flashback."

When the chocolate wall and floor-to-ceiling drapes began to do a fun house sway, I sunk to the overstuffed sofa and dropped my head between my knees.

"Whoa, take a breath." Bruin's soft footfalls crossed the living room.

I focused on breathing. In with the good, out with the bad, in good, out bad. After a moment, he tapped my shoulder with a bottle of water.

"What can I do?" He squatted before me but didn't touch me. "I can take you home . . . or you can stay here. I wasn't kidding when I asked you to keep me company. If you want to veg on the couch and order movies and room service, that's cool with me. Or, if you're getting sore you can soak in the tub then crash in the second bedroom. Whatever you decide."

"You're sweet." I unscrewed the cap and tried to drown my embarrassment.

"Nah, not really. I'd much rather get our horizontal on, but whatever you're up for works." I couldn't help but laugh at his expression, especially when he walked over to the desk in a discreet effort to adjust himself.

"Sorry."

He shrugged, handed me the room service menu and retreated to the other side of the couch. "I'll survive. Let's order some food. You hungry?"

"It's almost 2:30. Isn't the kitchen closed?"

"Kobi and I have an always-open option for room service."

Nice. I thought about the queasy roll of my stomach and wasn't sure if it was nausea or hunger. Knowing me . . . hunger. "Okay, yeah, a cheeseburger and rings would be fantastic. We were supposed to grab a bite at the pub, but with all the excitement, I never got the chance. I could definitely eat."

"Cheeseburger it is. Drink? I've got a stocked bar, or they have milkshakes downstairs."

"Oh, well, if we're going all out, strawberry shake. Definitely."

He smiled, picking up the phone over on the desk. "Nice choice. And FYI, they use real berries not that jam flavor shit."

"Sounds perfect." I rose to my feet, locking my legs just in case. Better. "Mind if I snoop around and walk this off?"

He waved a hand and punched the number pad a few times. "Be my guest. Check out the view from the terrace, if you want some air."

While Bruin ordered more food than a party of eight could eat and gave me a moment, I took a self-guided tour around his suite: vintage antiques, original paintings, heated bathroom floor and every extra indulgence you'd expect for the price. Standing at the glass rail of his terrace I looked out over the tiny, white lights of Robson Square Gardens and let the night breeze centre my energy.

"Was I lying about the view?" Bruin stepped out to join me, still keeping a polite distance. Man, could this guy be the real deal? When he leaned his elbows on the rail beside me, I forced my gaze to return to the stunning Vancouver skyline.

"It's incredible. You could stay out here all night and enjoy a view like this."

"I do. Often." He smiled and pointed over his shoulder at the outdoor furnishings set on the elegant garden patio. "We can enjoy the view more after we eat, if you're up to it."

"Would you mind if I have a quick shower before the food comes? I'd like to wash off the night and freshen up."

Bruin ushered me back to the suite. "There's a pair of robes in the washroom and a basket of complimentary toiletries on the vanity. Take your time."

The combination of hot water hitting my skin and the fancy soaps in Bruin's bathroom reset my senses. So, after sitting on the terrace, wrapped in a luxurious, fluffy robe while Bruin polished off more food than I would have believed possible, the night had pretty much been set right again. Well, other than the aches and pains of my alley brawl catching up.

Bruin pointed a thumb into the suite and stepped toward the jet-tub on the far wall of his suite. "Your muscles turning on you?"

"Isn't there a rule about skinny dipping or hot-tubbing right after you stuff your face?"

Bruin rolled back the sleeves of his white shirt and opened the faucets, testing the flow of the water gathering in the massive tub. "That's swimming and I don't think being naked even comes into play. In a soaker tub you don't sink, so you can get away with more."

I patted my belly. "Good to know. I still shouldn't have eaten so much. I feel like a whale."

With a serious frown he tugged the tie of my robe and eased the two sides open. Cool, night air hit my breasts. As my nipples beaded tight, his eyes swirled with flecks of gold. He studied my curves, sparing nothing for modesty. His brow arched, and a naughty smile spread across his face. "You don't look like a whale. In fact, you look .. . spectacular."

Gentle fingers smoothed over the pendant that hung from my neck. He lifted it, fingered the delicate turquoise beads and bent to inspect the carving. "This is gorgeous."

I dropped my gaze and smiled. "My grandfather carved it. It's my spirit totem."

"A bear?" Bruin stared at the pendant for a few more moments and then set it against my chest. It was unnerving that I couldn't read his expression. Usually, what I didn't gather from facial cues and gut instinct as a journalist, my connection with nature told me.

Tonight, the Earth Mother and her spirits were silent.

A chill raced down my spine as his gaze locked on mine. Strong fingers traced the curves from my hips to my waist and up my ribs to my collarbone. Collecting the bulky fabric resting on my shoulders, he slid my robe off and tossed it to the end of the bed. After one soft kiss to my shoulder, Bruin held his hand out and steadied my descent into the depths of the elegant tub.

I sank into the steamy waters, my stiff body suddenly stinging in protest. Wincing, I closed my eyes and waited for my muscles to ease. Then I waited some more. And kept waiting.

Bruin gave me a dark look. "You okay?"

I waved away his concern. The knots might not be loosening, but the spasms began to back down a bit. "Now, you've seen mine."

A smile played at the sides of his mouth. "Are you asking for a little quid pro quo?"

"That's the idea." I bit my lip and stretched out my shoulders. Leaning back against the molded seat, the scent of the vanilla-cream pillar candle filled my sinuses.

Without fanfare, Bruin tossed his shirt over my robe and let his jeans drop to the carpet. When he turned to toss them onto the bench at the end of the bed, I saw the intricate tattoo that ran down the length of his back from his left shoulder to the dip above his butt cheek. Three inches wide and inked in midnight blue, the series of characters and symbols flowed like Japanese kanji . . . but not. The fact that the ancient script stole my attention from his physique was, in itself, mind boggling.

I'd never seen a man with such perfect lines.

Bruin stepped into the tub and settled in facing me, his long legs bent, his feet resting beside my hips. After laying both arms across the marble ledge behind the tub, he exhaled.

I bit my lip to keep from squealing and making a complete fool of myself. After a few deep breaths, I found I could once again access cognitive thought. "I should have warned you. I'm a safety girl. I slipped condoms in my robe pocket. You okay with that?"

Bruin nodded, turned the dial behind him and set the jets on low. "I'm clean, but have no problem wearing one if you prefer." He lowered his hands, playing with the stream of white water rippling just under the surface. After a moment his turquoise gaze froze on me. "Are you sure you're up for loveplay tonight? You look fried."

His altruism shifted something in me. It was subtle. I couldn't quite pin it down, but the softness in his eyes had sexual energy tingling under my skin. When he opened his arms wide, I didn't know what kind of spell he'd cast over me. It seemed like the most natural thing in the world to go to him. I pushed across the tub.

Gathered into his lap, heat suffused my body and bloomed under my skin. The water swirled and jetted around us and my mind grew woolly. My bruised and aching muscles went languid as our mouths met in drugging sweeps of lips and tongue.

We stayed like that forever, joined in the most exquisite meeting of two mouths imaginable. One of his hands traveled over my back. He touched me, not to hold me in place, but to stroke my flesh, softly, slowly. The world seemed fuzzy and so did I, boneless and numb, floating in the moist, sexually charged air around us.

Bruin slowed our kiss and with a firm grip on my hips, eased me around to face the other direction. Sitting between his thighs, his erection wedged firm against my lower back. The moment his fingers kneaded my shoulders I was lost.

"That's right," he whispered close to my ear. "Just relax. I've got you."

CHAPTER FIVE

he rich, sweet scent of mocha invaded my blissed-out slumber. *Where—*

I cracked one eye open, swiped away the pillow lying across my head and raised my hand in front of my face. "Geez, turn off the sun. Give a girl a chance to wake up before you burn out her retina."

A throaty male laugh moved toward the silky taupe drapes and as the light filtered to a respectable level, I opened my eyes. King size bed, plush antique furniture, spa inspired soaker-tub . . . right, I was in the master bedroom of Bruin's suite.

When the mattress took a major dip beside me, I surveyed the landscape. Yep, just as delicious as I remembered. Long, graceful lines flowed from his shoulder, down his broad, rippled chest, to the waistband of ripped, unbuttoned jeans.

He lifted my knuckle to his lips, his expanse of skin throwing off heat in waves. "Not a morning person?"

"Not until after I'm properly caffeinated."

"Then you're in luck," he said, his smirk nothing but sexy. Turning to the night stand he grabbed two oversized mugs. "You see, living with two women has taught me a few important life lessons. Original Cuban or mocha-vanilla latte?"

I reached for the latte. "How long have you all been together?"

Bruin flipped his bangs out of his eyes and I sucked in my breath. Again. "I was twelve when Maximus Reign, our father, took me in."

"Rain is a powerful element."

"It is. In this case it's R-e-i-g-n. As in sovereign power."

"Strong name."

"Matches the man." He sipped at the rim of his mug and then stared down at the deep brown surface. "Reign has a soft spot for orphans. Jade was his first, then Lexi came to him a few years later. Julian and I arrived in the same summer, two years after that. We're not your typical family, but it works for us."

Passing my latte under my nose I moaned. Nothing rivaled the first coffee of the morning. That rich, sweet smell that nudges you awake, the flavor that spreads down your throat and expands from your stomach to ignite every cell in your body. As I swallowed a long slow sip, I closed my eyes and shifted my legs under the covers.

Stretching brought attention to the tenderness of many of my parts and sparked a flash of memory: the club, the alley—the soaker tub.

"What happened last night? I don't remember anything after you started assaulting me with your magic fingers."

He chuckled and set his mug on the bedside table. "That's because you dissolved into putty the moment I turned on the jets."

My cheeks flared, and I prayed that the lack of light hid my embarrassment. "I fell asleep on you? In the tub?"

He nodded. "Quite a hit to my ego."

"So, we didn't . . .."

Bruin frowned, his brow arced at an adorable angle. "Trust me. When we get together, you'll remember. No. Last night you were in no condition for anything beyond me drying you off and putting you to bed."

"And that's all I missed?"

"Yeah, that and you snoring like a badly tuned band saw all night —" He evaded my hand as I swung, his laughter a deep rumble from his chest.

"I don't snore."

"All right, band saw might be exaggerating."

I sucked in another long swallow of coffee and took a mental inventory of what was happening with me under the fancy, ivory linens. Naked. Definitely still naked. The memory of his fingers touching my skin as his tongue plundered my mouth had my pulse racing. Our bodies made promises last night and I wasn't about to let him off the hook. He had, after all, just said 'when' we get together.

"So white knight, is this savior routine an everyday thing or a new career path for you?"

He eased the mug from my hand and set it next to his. When his gaze met mine, gold flecks glittered in his eyes. "I think of myself as more of an honor driven, black knight."

Interesting. "So, where did you sleep?"

He laid his palm flat beside my hip and leaned close. "I was expecting a call this morning. After I got you settled, I crashed in the other bedroom, so I didn't disturb you."

I swallowed. Man, he smelled good. "You didn't need to do that. After last night, I don't think anything could have disturbed me."

He kissed my good cheek, his scruff-shadowed jaw brushing mine. "Are you very sore?"

I caught the intention in his voice. The current in the air changed and my skin tingled. "After two false starts you're still into getting together?"

"It's all I've thought about since last night. You're under my skin, pretty lady. And I honestly think if I let you walk out of this suite without burying myself inside you—I might die."

Shit, where was all the air in the room?

With a shift of his body, Bruin reached two long fingers into his jeans pocket and came out holding one of the blue foil packets I'd tucked into my robe last night. When he spoke, his voice was even deeper than usual. "Shall we see if the third time really is the charm?"

Hells yes.

Bruin made quick work of his jeans and the fact that he went commando called a mad heat from within me. He laid over me, our bodies touching flesh against flesh from our entwined feet all the way to our shoulders. He kissed his way down my neck, my breastbone, my chest. The sensation of his moist mouth sealed upon my breast made me cry out. And that was before he began to suckle. His touch lowered, brushing over the top of my thigh, down further—

My pelvis arched, urging him on. After the agonizing seconds it took for him to fulfill my safety standards, he rose over me sheathed and poised, a rock-hard body twice the size of my own. Broad, muscled shoulders loomed large over me as the blunt head of his erection probed the heat of my sex. Then he paused.

I laced my fingers into his shaggy hair, cupped his face and nodded.

When he kissed me, the decadence of lust mixed with coffee hit me hard. His tongue twined with mine, penetrating, demanding more. My hips rose off the mattress as I ground my mouth to his and tightened my grip in his hair. I didn't understand the desperate need to have him inside me, but the consuming desire brought a rush of moist heat between my thighs.

I moaned. That was all the encouragement he needed.

He parted my flesh in a slow single thrust that spread my thighs and overloaded my senses. The invasion—it could be considered nothing less—tore through me, filled me, woke places inside me I'd never known. I arced to let him slide all the way in and shifted my palms down his smooth back to the dip at the base of his spine.

Eyes closed, head thrown back, a strangled sound ripped from his throat. As his rhythm built, he clenched his jaw so hard his cheeks hollowed, his face an erotic mask of restraint. With every careful thrust and retreat his pecs shifted.

Seeing him suspended in tortured ecstasy killed me. "You're holding back. Why?"

He kissed the bruise on my cheek. "You're so tiny. I don't want to hurt you."

"I'm not as fragile as I look." When he looked skeptical, I bit his lip and sunk my nails into the flesh of his ass. I didn't wait for a response, I showed him my demands and he met them.

From that moment, our sex took on a life of its own.

Bruin was heavy as a truck on top of me, his body solid muscle and hard edges—I didn't mind a bit. Unhinged and unhindered the man was pure sex. The sheen of sweat covering our bodies increased the slide of skin-on-skin.

"Fuck, you feel amazing." His words brushed my collarbone as his silky hair tickled my cheek. My nails raked his back and his thrusts picked up speed. His hips no longer surged but powered inside me.

"So. Damn. Amazing."

Hard. Fierce. Carnal.

The pinch of his teeth on my neck undid me. My orgasm hit in a devastating blast. He chuckled in dark satisfaction as my body bucked and shuddered beneath him. I screamed something unintelligible against his heaving chest as another wave of moisture slicked our connection. The cry that ripped from my lungs triggered something wild in him. As my inner muscles gripped and squeezed, his breathing hitched, and hips locked against mine.

Bruin's massive body torqued and strained, and as he released, I caught a spectacular glimpse of his ass in the bedroom mirror. Heavy thighs flexed, and the lines of his tattoo stretched tight from his waist to his shoulder as his head tossed back.

He didn't so much roll off me as collapse, panting for breath. When he could speak again, he ran a feather touch up my hip and circled my breast. My nipple gathered to the attention and he smiled. "I didn't mean to lose control like that . . . I wasn't too rough? Was I?"

"No," I said, just as breathless. "No, I'm . . . great. The best. You?"

His brow arced, and it disappeared under his bangs. "As soon as I reacquaint my lungs with oxygen, I'm going to treat you like you've never been treated before. You don't have any plans for the next . . . oh . . . three hours, do you?"

The smirk twisting the corners of his mouth had my core pulsing again. Three hours? He was kidding, right?

CHAPTER SIX

id-afternoon, I stepped through the sliding glass doors on rubber legs and all but crumpled into the lounge chair opposite the terrace rail. The distant hiss of water signalled Bruin's return to the shower—solo this time—and him getting ready to take us for dinner.

Back in my clothes, mug in hand, I tried to sort through the jumble of the past twenty-four hours. There was a hell of a lot to reflect on: the publication of my exposé of the Nimithic Group, the airing of the news coverage, the attack at Spankz and then winding up spending the night at the Wedgewood Hotel with my mysterious honor-bound black knight.

And then there was the sex. Sex? The word didn't even do us justice.

Flipping my phone open I scrolled through eleven missed text messages. Paige, Meg, Em, Paige, Paige, Liane, Meg, Paige and so the list continued. My girls were seriously jonesing for a check in . . . and probably a morning-after-the-night-before update. Selecting them all from my directory I considered what would tide them over. *All is well. Wedgewood hotel penthouse with hunk-in-vest. Sore in girly places I didn't know existed. Will call later. Luv, M.*

"Is this a private party or can I crash?"

I drank in the sight of Bruin's freshly washed body and the way those worn blue jeans hung from his hips. Knowing he protested doing up the top button was one thing. Knowing he went commando underneath—

I hit SEND and buried my phone deep into my pocket. Sweeping my hand to the side, I gestured to the empty chair across the table. "This is your slice of heaven. I'm sure there's room for one more."

Bruin carried a tray heaped with bagels, cheese, crackers, fruit and spreads and set it on the table. "Is this all right? We missed out on a few meals today and our reservation isn't for another couple of hours. I figured we could use refueling."

"Looks delicious." Was I talking about the food or him bending over in front of me wearing those low riding jeans? Tough call.

He caught me ogling and his chest bounced with amusement. My cheeks flushed warm, but I didn't care. Moving opposite me, he grabbed a plate for himself and started filling it. "I wasn't sure what you like, so I asked for a bit of everything."

"Thanks. A bagel and coffee is perfection, but I'll take some fruit too." I picked up half a plain bagel and smeared some strawberry cream cheese on it. It was warm, melting the cream cheese as it spread. "There's a family-owned, coffee shop around the corner from my office called Suzie's. They bake bagels fresh every morning. If you get there early enough, they're warm, like these. Best thing you've ever tasted in your life. Orgasmic really."

Bruin sputtered in his cup and shot me a sideways glance. "Truly? You take one bite and lose yourself right there in the shop?"

I giggled. "Yep. It's a little embarrassing. I make quite a spectacle."

Bruin barked a laugh. "I'll have to go with you. I'd like to catch the show. I've grown fond of watching that particular spectacle."

I looked out over Vancouver and focused on not choking. Rays of sunlight crept around the corner of the building and pooled on the edge of the terrace. In another twenty minutes they would be clouded over by the grey sky rolling in off the Pacific. Until then I'd enjoy the sunshine. We sat in silence for a long while, watching the folks below, out for a Saturday afternoon stroll in Robson's Gardens.

A man and his daughter explored the greenery. The two walked hand in hand, flitting from one flower to another like dragonflies dancing in the sun. The father, totally absorbed in his child's fascination, let the girl's small stride set the pace of their meandering. My bagel sank like a stone in my gut. "Do you ever wonder what their stories are?"

Bruin leaned forward. "Not really. Why?"

I shrugged. "Just a game I play sometimes. It helps keep my observation skills sharp." I pointed to a woman jogging toward our building with a border collie. "Let's call her Jess. She's happy with her life and loves her dog. She's health conscious but isn't afraid to indulge a little. She's open to new people and experiences but likes the comfort of things she's accustomed to."

Bruin looked at me over his cup, one brow cocked and obscured by damp, brown bangs. As good as he looked, he smelled even better. Sandalwood soap mixed with a faint musky scent of clean male and the outdoors. "So, is that a guess or do you actually believe it?"

"Well, it's a guess, but I bet I'm not far from the truth."

Bruin popped a strawberry in his mouth and licked the juice from his bottom lip. "Okay, I'll bite. You know this, how?"

I swallowed the last of my bagel and washed it down with a sip of coffee. "Observation. Take in the visual cues people give off. It's part of my job to observe people and figure out what's going on under the surface."

Bruin stretched his legs out in front of him and crossed his ankles while he studied my expression. "Okay Sherlock, so what kind of read do you get off me?"

I confiscated the strawberry he'd picked up, plucked the stem and took stock. Ignoring the sultry smile and all that taut bronze skin, I looked deeper. "You're passionate and fun, have a strong sense of justice and aren't afraid of conflict. My guess is, you or someone you love was badly hurt and no one stepped in."

Bruin's expression remained passively blank but the tension in the air ratcheted.

I continued. "You're a lethal fighter, but a true and giving lover." I bit the berry in half, juice dribbling down my chin. "Extraordinarily tender actually . . . when the mood strikes you."

Bruin caught my hand as I grabbed for a napkin and knelt in front of me. Sliding his fingers behind my neck, he tugged me forward and kissed the juice from my skin. Slow, warm sweeps of his lips worked their way from my jaw to the corner of my mouth. "What if I said the mood was striking me as we speak?"

His eyes held that sexual glimmer I'd become familiar with a few hours ago. It triggered a Pavlovian bloom and just like that, I lost all reason. What had this guy done to me? "I'd say the terrace is too public in daylight. I'd also say you're relentless."

He nodded and pulled me to my feet. "Insatiable."

"Yeah, you're an animal all right," Kobi said. I jumped and spun to where Bruin's fight-night partner leaned against the frame of the open sliding glass doors. In black jeans and muscle shirt he looked like a really bad idea for a really good night. By the smirk on his face he was enjoying himself a little too much at our expense.

Bruin shot him a glare. "Ever heard of knocking, asshole?"

He shrugged. "Heard of it. You got more java? I need a minute. Reign called."

Bruin sighed as Kobi disappeared into the suite. As he reached the glass door he looked back. "Don't move. I'll get rid of him and we'll finish what we started."

I set my mug on the tray with our plates. "How about I give you two some privacy and make a quick run to my office. I've got a couple file folders I want to grab and have a change of clothes there too. I'll check in with my life and meet you downstairs in say . . . an hour?"

"*Or,* I could get rid of Kobi, finish what we started and then zip you to your office before dinner to grab your clothes." He waggled his brow and sucked me into his lecherous embrace.

I struggled against the cage of his hold, but it was a half-hearted effort at best. "But we'd just end up on the living room floor or the dining room table . . . *again* and the odds of us actually making it to dinner will be out the window."

He flashed me a devilish smile and raised my hand to his kiss.

"And by the way your stomach growled earlier, you need to eat, big guy."

He leaned forward, brushing my ear with his lips as whispered, "I could make a meal of you and die a happy man."

"Yo, Romeo," Kobi said, boomeranging back up the hall, coffee mug in hand. "Cut the cord and let her out the fucking door. I need a minute."

Bruin pulled back and exhaled heavy. "You're a pain in my ass, Kobi. You know that?"

"It's my life's work."

Bruin scowled, walking me to the door. "Well, everyone needs a purpose."

I found my purse where it had landed as we'd stumbled in, and bent down to scoop up my belongings. Bruin met me on the rug and gathered up a pile of business cards and my Taser.

He held up my weapon and chuckled. "Were you planning on using this on me?"

"Only if you got outta hand."

He handed back my stuff and I slipped him one of my cards. "This is my cell number if you need to call about dinner. Or who knows, you might come back to town after this weekend and feel the need to rescue someone."

I pushed onto my tip-toes and kissed him. His lips were warm and soft. With a sigh I slung the straps of my purse over my shoulder. "I'll see you downstairs in an hour."

Bruin fingered the straps of my purse and nodded. "I'll see you to your truck—"

As he scanned the card, his eyes narrowed. "The Vancouver Sun? Wha—You're a reporter?"

"Why do you look like someone just bashed you in the boys with a cricket paddle?"

He scrubbed his palm across his jaw a scowl covering his previously perfect face. "I thought you were some kind of therapist. You said you observe people . . . interpret what they're not saying."

"*Right*. I'm an investigative journalist. I mainly focus on wildlife protection and poaching, but don't discriminate. If another story comes along, I write it."

Bruin's expression blanked right out, and he cast a fleeting glance to Kobi.

"What's the problem?"

He cleared his throat and forced a smile. "No problem. I just remembered why Reign called. I totally spaced. Kobi and I are supposed to meet up with him." He grabbed his key card and opened the door. "I have to bail on dinner. Sorry. Rain check?"

CHAPTER SEVEN

Fifteen minutes later, I backed into one of the reserve spots at the underground parking lot across from my office. What happened with Bruin? Can you say 180? One minute he was begging me to stay and the next, he gave me the bum's rush. The ride down to the parking garage had been eerily quiet, then, after a quick kiss on the cheek, he bolted back to the elevator.

I wasn't expecting sloppy goodbyes or anything—a hook-up was just a hook-up after all—but I thought the potential between us was worth more than a total shut down. I unbuckled my seatbelt harness and slid the straps off my shoulders. "Just because you have hours of life-altering, mind-blowing sex all over a swanky hotel suite doesn't mean you know a guy, geez."

Maybe it had nothing to do with me. Maybe he really did need to get back to his father.

Nah. His expression when he'd read my card said otherwise. The journalist thing threw him. That much was obvious. Maybe he *was* a criminal and thought I'd expose his activities. Well, if he dabbled on the dark side of things it was lucky I found out early so I could steer clear.

He hadn't felt like a criminal though. He'd felt . . ..

I shook the erotic barrage of images from my head and refused to give it another thought. The echo of my truck door slamming bounced around the empty parking garage. I hiked my backpack higher on my shoulder and headed for the Granville Street exit and for the main entrance of The Vancouver Sun.

The air in the business core of the city hung silent. No rhythmic plodding of footsteps or whooshing of cars through the dampened streets. There wasn't even the irate squawk of seagulls or the coo of pigeons. *Weird.*

Was my newfound paranoia a residual from last night's attack? Unzipping my purse, I slipped my hand inside and closed my fingers around the polymer handle of my trusty Taser. Without drawing it, I made a slow, steady sweep, scanning the parking lot and surrounding buildings as I moved. The hair on the nape of my neck stood on end. I ignored the nagging ache in my chest and tried to breathe as I swiped my security card and let myself into the building.

After signing in with the security desk, I headed upstairs.

Geez, my desk looked like the finger of god had touched down: files everywhere, pencils on the floor, stacks of backdated newspapers avalanching across my credenza.

Perfect. Just the way I left it.

After shifting a few files, I excavated two blue folders and piled them with the half-read bodice ripper romance novel from my drawer. When I booted up my computer the vibration in the air shifted. I reached for my cell and waited to check caller ID.

Assistant Crown Attorney Brantfield.

I plunked in my desk chair and stretched my stiff neck. After exchanging the usual greetings, I got right to it. "Do you need me to come in? I'm getting ready to head out of the city for a week or two."

"Two weeks is a problem. The discovery interviews for the Nimithic Group trial are scheduled to start Wednesday. We'll need your formal statement."

"I can come back. When and where?"

"My assistant will let you know the exact date and time as things progress. Can she contact you at this number or by email when I have more information?"

"Of course."

As soon as I snapped my cell shut the battery died and the screen faded to black. I tossed it into my purse and grabbed my USB key from the bottom of my desk drawer. After opening the Nimithic Group files on my laptop I transferred a copy to an encrypted backup on a private cloud server, then saved another onto my key. Once I verified both copies had transferred, I cleared my history, shut down the laptop and slid it from its docking station into my backpack. With the addition of my folders I was zipped up and—

"What the hell?" My legs buckled, and I sank back into my chair. I hissed a foul curse and shook my hand. My palm stung, the flesh searing white hot. It felt like I'd been bitten by a snake and the venom had lit a path up my arm. I opened my fingers, half expecting my hand to burst into flames. "What the—"

A tattoo had emblazoned into my skin, an oval medallion containing a stylized symbol of a bear surrounded by an ancient Sanskrit of some kind. What was it about me that drew this kind of chaos from the universe? I mean really, if anything whacked or weird was going on within a twenty-block radius it would find me like a heat-seeking missile. Guaranteed.

I blew at the seared flesh and studied the tattoo. Another bear clan thing, Earth Mother? After a quick stop at my house I'd head straight to the reserve to show Grandfather. The symbols looked sort of familiar, though I couldn't place them. If not he, then one of the council might know what it was about.

Scrambling through my desk for a pen, I scribbled a Dear Paige letter, pinned it to the board outside her office, grabbed my stuff and locked up.

Back on the street, I drew a deep breath, looked skyward and exhaled.

Apologies Earth Mother. A tickle of mist covered my face and I gathered myself. I held my burning palm open to the cool precipitation. I was of the Ursine Clan. I was of the Earth. I had no business criticizing the ways of the Earth Mother. She was life and energy, creation and evolution. I was her humble servant. I inhaled again. Better.

Vancouver was a wet city, but rain meant nourishment and rebirth. It took filthy smog-filled air, oil-slicked pavement and the grungy streets and washed them clean. It repainted the landscape without anyone even considering what a miracle of nature it was.

The sky belched an ominous grumble which rolled away like ocean waves. Something powerful brewed on the horizon. I could feel it in my marrow. Another rumble, this one, long and with purpose. It gained in strength, blanketing me under a threatening cover.

The breeze lifted my hair and swirled with deliberation. The message whispered on the wind. *Be prepared for what comes.*

Be prepared? That didn't tell me anything. No two ways about it, Earth Spirits were frustrating. I shifted my backpack from my shoulder to my good hand and started jogging. Hustling down the stairs into the parking garage I double-timed it to my truck. After popping the locks, I jumped behind the wheel and dumped my stuff on the passenger's seat. Reaching for the door handle—a hand clasped my arm.

"*Mika.*" Bruin leaned into my view and interrupted the scream pealing from my throat. "Mika, it's me. Calm down."

I closed my gaping mouth and listened to my pulse thunder in my ears. "You scared the crap out of me. *What the hell?*"

"Sorry."

I leaned against the headrest and tried to breathe. When I opened my eyes he was there, standing inside my open door. I inhaled sharply. Just looking at him had every ripe cell within me swelling with need. *Stop it.* "What are you doing here?"

"I need to speak with you."

My laugh held all the *whatever* I could muster. "You didn't have much to say to me an hour ago. In fact, you gave me the old, 'been there, done you, there's the door.'"

Bruin scowled. "It wasn't like that. It's just . . ." He bit his lip and paced to the front of my truck. Leaning both hands on the hood, he stared at me through the windshield. His eyes were almost amber in the reflected light of dusk. "It's complicated."

I laughed again, spilling out of my seat and onto my feet. "Complicated? Environmental science is complicated. World politics is complicated. Hell, shower sex is complicated, but we seemed to manage that. *Complicated* is a cop-out."

"That's not fair."

"No? Then tell me, what's so complicated?"

He clenched his jaw and exhaled. "I wouldn't know where to start."

I laughed. "Right. Don't make this into something it's not, Bruin. We met, we had fun with each other. End of. I don't need this to be anything—"

In a move too fast to believe, he snatched my wrist and flipped up my hand. "Oh, Sweet Shalana. This. Can't. Be."

"What?"

Open mouthed, Bruin held up his palm. He had the same tattoo burned into the skin of his hand as I did. A mirror image of mine.

"But . . . you're not First Nations. Are you?"

His look of bafflement must have matched mine. "What? No. Why?"

"That's what this is, isn't it? A symbol . . . a message from the Earth Mother?"

Bruin laced his fingers with mine and clutched our hands together, palm to palm. I gasped as a current of energy jolted up my arm and through my body. My skin tingled, my heart pounded, and for the first time since it appeared, the tattoo stopped burning.

In all my life, I had never been so lost . . . so uncertain . . . so damned turned on.

I shook my head, trying to clear the muddle clouding my brain. "Bruin, what is going on? This afternoon you all but booted me out of your suite when things seemed to be going really well. And now you .. . what?"

He groaned, his voice rough. "Mika, you need to trust me."

I pulled my hand free. "Trust is not my best event. Why don't you tell me what's going on."

"The Fates have branded us. You can't smell it, but you're giving off a scent. It's like a beacon flashing in the darkness. Any moment we could be surrounded by my enemies."

I stared at him, then scanned the abandoned concrete garage. "Are you punking me?"

"Dammit Mika. I'm trying to keep you alive here."

I stepped back. "You're nuts, you know that?"

"No. I'm not."

"Okay, let's say you're not. I have no interest in your mysterious enemies or your illegal activity or any of your drama. You and I had fun together. End of story. Goodbye."

He shook his head and tightened his grip on my wrist. "That's not your decision, Mika. The Fates have decided."

"Decided what? What do you think these markings mean?"

He opened his mouth, closed it, and cursed. "They're bonding brands. We are to be mated."

I tried not to laugh, even though my brain cramped over the entire situation.

He balled his hands into fists and began pacing. "You are mine. I am yours. That's what it means. Two halves of one heart."

I held up a finger and stepped back. "You. Are. Insane."

The anguish in his expression gave me chills. "My world is different than yours," he said. "It's twisted and dangerous. It's no place for a woman like you—but here you are—mixed up in the mind-fuck that is my reality. There are people who want my line ended. They'll use you as leverage against me . . . kill you before you can bare my young."

Bear his *young*? I watched his eyes, gauged his physical tells. There wasn't one thing to suggest he was lying. He believed what he said. Drugs? Was this whole thing one big psychotic delusion?

He cursed and stepped closer. "Let me explain."

I matched his move and retreated. "Bruin. Look. I'm sorry you're worked up, but I'm done. Forget you met me. Don't call, don't text. And don't show up in my life again."

He grabbed my shoulder as I turned. "You don't get to walk away from this, Mika. They will *kill* you. Like it or not I'm not leaving here without you."

"Take your hands *off* me."

He didn't.

I swung fast with my other hand and smacked his face. Hard. It was like slapping a granite slab. He glared at me, amber flecks surfacing in his eyes, drowning out his usual turquoise. How did his eyes change colour like that? Raising his fingers, he rubbed the pink blush where I struck him. He stretched his jaw, his stare intense.

"Look boys, a lover's spat." The graveled voice had Bruin whirling toward the exit ramp of the garage. Three well-built men dripping menace and dressed in black fatigues blocked our way out. They stalked closer, their extended guns catching the dim fluorescent light from above. "Having troubles controlling your bitch, Bruin?"

In a blurring show of strength and speed, Bruin threw me into the truck, slammed the door and positioned himself at the front bumper. "She's nobody's bitch, Dog. Least of all mine."

The leader of the group lifted his nose to the air and inhaled. His cold sneer grew wider as he stalked closer, raising the barrel of his weapon. "Smells like a bitch in heat to me. You've been on the watch list a long time, Bruin. You don't mind if we drag out the fun a bit, do you?"

"Reign will fry your balls and feed them to Aust's wolves if you attack an innocent."

"You think we're afraid of wolves?" The second guy, a blond brute with a ponytail, chuckled as the three of them fanned out. "Besides she's no innocent. She's your mate."

"Wrong. I met her last night at a bar. She's one hundred percent human."

Human? Of course I'm human. Why would he even say that?

The third guy, an Incredible Hulk type, laughed. "Branding scents don't lie, Alpha. She's your mate and she's not getting out of this alive."

Bruin growled. Not the playful sex-growl from this morning, but a deep guttural warning. "Forget her, it's me you want—and here we are

—three on one. But I bet you still couldn't take me alive without your guns. In fact, I *dare* you to try."

Dog's head cocked to one side as his eyes lit up. "We were told to leave you alive, but now you've gone and dared us." He tucked his gun at the small of his back and signalled his buddies to join him. In a crouch, the three men shifted on the balls of their feet, posturing, circling, ready to lunge, but hesitating.

Bruin chuckled. "So, do you want to fight or are you going to sniff each other's crotches?"

CHAPTER EIGHT

My heart leapt to my throat as Bruin catapulted into the fray. Arms flew. Fists connected. Bodies collided. Bruin grabbed hold of a gun and struggled. Dog caught him around the waist and tried to take him down. Bruin's wide stance remained rooted, but the gun clattered to the pavement. The other two men split and advanced from opposite directions.

Hulk hit fast and low, throwing his weight behind the attack. The three of them grappled, kicked and thrashed. Blood sprayed and oaths sliced the air. Ponytail guy swept the back of Bruin's knee. The contact wheeled him around and he lost his footing. They crashed into the front of my truck as a tangled mob and then dropped to the concrete.

The Humvee bounced and rocked as the fight continued. The noise of the scuffle rose in the air, guttural snarls sounding more like animals than men. Dull thuds of fists to body and curses amplified in the cavernous concrete garage.

I dumped the contents of my purse onto the passenger seat. My belongings rained onto the leather and I scanned the pile. Two options—phone or Taser.

Pressing up against the dash, I strained to see. Bruin launched back to his feet. He grappled Ponytail, grunting and cursing as the others took cracks at him with spiked sticks. *Where did those come from?* I grabbed my phone and flipped it open. Nothing.

I jumped when a silver glint flashed, and Ponytail pointed a gun at Bruin.

I hit the power button again and held it. Nothing. I tossed the thing and grabbed my Taser. The *snap* of bone had my head whiplashing. Ponytail slid from Bruin's grip and fell to the ground with a thud and a vacant stare.

A second later, Dog and Bruin were back at it. Arms, fists and blood spray flew. How the hell was Bruin still standing? I caught the look on the Hulk's face as Ponytail crumpled to the ground. *Hulk mad . . . Hulk kill.*

Flinging the door wide, I rounded the front of the truck at the same moment Bruin dragged the knife across Dog's throat. A scarlet trail gave way to a gush of blood and the body fell to the pavement. Bruin straightened, chest heaving and covered in blood. His? Theirs? It was impossible to tell.

I raised my Taser at the remaining attacker.

Hulk's gaze narrowed as he aimed square into Bruin's chest. "Looks like a standoff, bitch. Except, I have a gun and know how to use it. You ever shoot anyone with your plastic toy?"

I tightened up on my grip and stepped closer. Fifteen feet was maximum range. Closer was better. "It's not too complicated. I just point the laser site where I want to shoot, and electrocuting probes shoot out and knock out your central nervous system."

Hulk adjusted his stance and swept his aim toward me.

Bruin staggered between us. "*No! I'm* the one you want. You have your shot, asshole, right here." He struggled to straighten, slapping a hand against his sternum and broadening his stance. "You got one chance at this, motherfucker. I'm your only shot. Make it mortal or you won't make it home. I promise you that."

I hissed. "Bruin, shut up. What are you doing?"

Bruin ape-smacked his broad, bloody chest. When Hulk gazed at me, he rolled onto the balls of his feed and eased into a crouch. "It's me you want, mutt. Point that thing right here."

Was he crazy? I shifted, and Hulk followed.

Bruin launched. The frenzy of muscle and hard-core determination made it impossible to tell where one man began and the other ended. A shot rang out. I screamed and scrambled for a better position. With my attention locked on the writhing bodies, I tripped and fell to the ground. My palms burned from impact of the concrete and I lost my Taser. Scrambling to regain my footing, I grabbed a weapon.

Another shot.

Who was hit? The entwined struggle went down like a fallen tree. Curses and hisses cut through the violent energy in the air.

I raised my aim, waiting as they steam-rollered back and forth across the cold, hard ground. I couldn't get a bead on who was where until Hulk rolled to his knees and straddled Bruin's heaving torso. Four hands clenched the gun, but Hulk's position gave him the leverage to bull's-eye the muzzle against Bruin's forehead.

A third shot. Time froze.

As my trigger finger released, Hulk's massive frame twisted from the impact of my bullet. Bruin rolled with the falling weight of his attacker, slumping him to the side. I'd never shot anyone before. Targets. Dummies. Bottles.

Never a person.

The *crack* of the shot echoed hollow inside my head a thousand times. Like an endless bang of thunder riding a slow wave across an angry sky. What had I done?

Bruin palmed the barrel of the gun and eased it from my hands. "Shit, you're shaking like a leaf. Here, baby, sit down before you fall down."

My feet weren't listening, but somehow Bruin ushered us around the truck and sat me on the running board. On bended knee he brushed my hair from my face. He was a straight shot of adrenaline. And even beaten and bloodied, I'd bet that was the only thing keeping him vertical.

"You look like hell," I said, my voice thin.

He tilted his face to his shoulder and wiped blood and sweaty filth from his eyes before raising my trembling hands to the warmth of his mouth. After kissing both, he blew on them and held them against his heaving chest. "Are you hurt?"

I shook my head. "You?"

He rubbed his shoulder then winced when his fingers ran down his side. "Swiss-cheesed a bit, but I should live."

I looked at a gun lying on the cement and my head spun. Closing my eyes, I leaned my back against my driver's door. "Good, because I might kill you myself. What the hell did you drag me into? And if you tell me it's complicated, I swear I'll lose it."

His voice was close and deep. "I told you. You just don't believe me."

Bruin traced the bear tattoo on my palm. "We've got a mess to clean up and probably cops on the way. We need to get our asses in gear and clear out."

"What do you mean? We killed three people. The police will want statements and photograph of the scene. We'll probably get taken in and—"

Bruin flashed a tired smile and straightened. "Not an option. Is your tailgate locked? I need to take out the trash."

I shook my head. "I don't know what's happening here, but in my world, we catch bad guys and the police take them away. We don't slit throats or snap necks. And we certainly don't shove dead people into the back of *my truck*."

His stare was dispassionate. "They're not people. Stop feeling guilty."

I cringed. How could I have made such an intimate connection with someone so callous? "Not anymore, but an hour ago they had lives and families and a future. Doesn't that bother you even a little?"

Bruin rounded on me, reached under my arms and marched me to the front of the truck. He set me down hard on my feet and pointed. "No. Like I said, they're not people . . . at least not like you know them."

I looked down and gasped.

In front of my truck lay two very dead, scraggly, Great Dane-sized dogs. I looked over to where I shot Hulk. Same thing, just a bigger heap of matted bloody fur. "Where did the dogs come from?"

"Jackals. They are Weres. Like Werewolves except they're jackals," he said, watching my reaction. "Like I said . . . *complicated.*"

I couldn't breathe. I rubbed my temples, a screamer of a headache taking root in my skull. Sinking onto my bumper, I let my head hang forward. The garage spun, and I didn't relish the idea of revisiting my bagel from lunch. "I'm having a nervous breakdown. Some kind of PTSD from the attack last night."

"No. You're not."

There was no other explanation. At least not a logical one. "I don't know who you are Bruin, but this is way too World of Warcraft for me."

He chuckled.

I failed to see an ounce of humor in the situation. Then it hit me. My head flipped up and I scuttled back along the bumper until I ass-planted on the concrete. "You're one of *them* . . . those animal-people."

"Weres," Bruin corrected, righting me against the truck before stepping back.

"You're a jackal-man?"

Bruin's his face twisted in disgust. "If I were born a jackal, I would have slit my own throat at birth. Jackals are vile, stupid cowards. Honorless mercenaries. Their loyalties lie with whoever pays the highest price for their services. Even then they turn tail. I'm no fucking jackal."

"Then what are you?"

He bit his bottom lip and his stare seared me. Scanning the pavement, he toed a mangled scrap of what used to be his cell phone. "Look, I'll answer all your questions as soon as we're somewhere secure. Right now, we need to make tracks. Give me your cell."

"It's dead."

"Of course it is." His hand grazed his blood drenched hip and he hissed. He leaned against the hood of the Humvee and stared into the darkened sky. "Once you're safe and I'm back on my feet, I'll call for backup."

"Back on your feet? You need help now? Can't you call your Were-people to—"

He growled low in his throat and stiffened. "Neither of us has a phone. Besides, Weres don't tolerate weakness. My animal will rage at being vulnerable if another Were sees me like this. It's too dangerous . . . for everyone. What we need is a place away from the city where we can hunker down for a bit. A natural place where other Weres won't pick up your scent."

"My scent?"

"Technically it's my scent, but you're throwing it off in waves." The quick glance he shot my way was heated and possessive.

Uh huh. I swallowed and reminded myself to avoid eye-contact. "How remote are we talking and why?"

"Remote. An animal scent in the city is out of place, easy to detect. An animal scent in the wilderness—"

"—could be just another wild animal."

"Exactly." He paced around the three bodies dragging them until they lay side-by-side. "Gods, I can't even think. You can't know . . . me . . . a mate . . . it changes everything."

Mate? "Look, Bruin, regardless of what you think, I'm not your mate. That's ridiculous."

He glared, the two of us lost in a whole lotta silence. After a moment he seemed to lock himself down and nodded. "Fine. I'll take care of this, answer your questions, then you can walk away and get yourself killed."

He hauled back and hoofed the dead dog-man and then grabbed it by the scruff. "But FYI, now that you carry my scent they won't stop until you're dead or their prisoner. They think I've got something they want and have been waiting for something to hold over me."

He hefted the mass of fur and blood into the back of my Humvee with a *whump* that bounced the shocks and then held his palm up. "I'm last man standing. The Fates offer one mating opportunity to a Were. *One.* If you're dead, my line dies with me." He wiped his tattooed palm against his jeans and turned away. "Plain and not-so-simple."

Bruin grabbed the next dead jackal by the tail and the third by the hind leg and dragged them to the tailgate of my truck. He tossed them in with a huff and then twisted back to glare at me some more. After gathering my Taser, the remaining guns and some ripped pieces of clothing off the concrete he tossed them in the back seat and grabbed his side.

The growl that tore from his chest had me taking a good look at him. He wiped his scarlet hand against the thigh of his jeans and listed against the truck.

"Shit Bruin, you're really bleeding."

"What else is new?"

I rushed to open the passenger's door. "You need a hospital. Get in."

Bruin belly laughed and cast me a droll stare. "And what will you say when they type my blood and it's not human, or I pass out and return to my base form? They'll call the lab-coats and I'll be a freak in an experiment for the rest of my life. No thanks, I'd rather bleed out."

As I scooped my stuff back into my purse, I got an idea. Punching the console open, I pulled out a roll of duct tape and a Swiss Army knife. From the inside pocket of my purse I snagged three square, yellow packages and unfolded the plastic wrapping. I pointed to the passenger's seat. "Sit."

He tensed at my command but eased himself up into the seat and I went to work cutting off his sopping shirt. Shit, what a mess. Swiss cheese my ass. He was mulch. With all that blood, it was hard to know what to address first.

When I pressed the maxi-pads against the front and back of the biggest hole in his side, he growled low and deep. "You're fucking kidding me, right?"

"Don't give me any macho crap. It's a good idea. Hold here." I bit off two long pieces of tape and secured the makeshift dressing to his skin and unfortunately the hairs on his chest. When his side was covered, I repeated the process for his shoulder and then got into the truck.

Sirens. There were sirens in the distant streets.

"Try not to move," I said, turning the keys. The engine rumbled to life and accelerated in a low growl out onto Granville and toward the highway.

Bruin looked down, his chest vibrating with a steady growl. "Un-fucking-believable."

"Hey. You said no hospital, so shelve the hostility. Do I look like Florence Nightingale? No. But here I am, helping you, despite you totally screwing my life."

"I've screwed *your* life?" he snorted, flipping his bangs and pegging me with a glare. "That's a two-way street, baby. My life was fan-fuck-ing-tastic until we collided: respected warrior, friends I'd die for, a home-life you could never imagine, and enough free time to have fun with the ladies. Now I'm shot, can't access my magic, I'm stuck in the Modern Realm and I'll be lucky to live out the week. Oh, but even if I do, I can forget about the one chance I have for cubs or a family because the woman the Fates bonded me to is human and wants nothing to do with me."

I focused on the road, my mind stumbling on his words. *Cubs?*

When I finally opened my mouth to reply, he held up a bloody palm and let his head drop back. "You're right. Not your problem. Don't even worry about it. I feel like shit. I'll most likely drop dead and you'll be free to resume your life."

"I don't want that, Bruin." Glancing sideways I froze. There was a sheen of sweat on his brow and his colour was sallow. "I don't want you dead . . . but you're a grouchy bastard when you're hurt, and I happen to have my own life too. One I enjoy very much."

He turned his shoulders away from me and groaned low and deep against the window. "Drop it. I haven't got the strength to fight."

I leaned over the steering wheel and tilted my face to the nasty grey sky. The mist from earlier had transformed into droplets and now the droplets were dollops. I turned on the wipers and realized where I was headed. I trusted only one person with life's madness. I pressed harder on the accelerator, turned onto Highway 1 and headed north toward the 97.

usk had relented to dark by the time I blew along the streets of the reserve and arrived at the two-bedroom box-house I grew up in. Despite everything, I smiled as I pulled in. Even the silvery light of the moon could not mask Grandfather's idea of *'vintage'* sitting in the driveway—crappy old beater was more like it.

The laneway spit out pea-gravel as my tires skidded to a crunching halt.

Bruin hadn't moved for—I looked at the clock on the dash—*shit,* too long. Way too long. The only way I knew he remained conscious was because he was still beautifully human. Well, he looked human. I flexed my tattooed palm, but the burning didn't ease.

I cast a sideways glance. "You with me, big guy?"

Nothing. "Okay. I'll be two minutes and then another quick hop and we'll be back-roading into the caverns. Hang in there." I wasn't sure he heard, but he might have stirred a little. I raced inside, my boots clicking out my panic as I burst from room to room searching for Grandfather.

What if he was with the Chief and Council tonight or visiting someone off the reserve? I didn't have time for this. "Dammit!"

"Cursing in my home, Rabbit?" I spun toward the stairs and my breath caught, never so glad to see the man who raised me in all our years. His voice was full of censure, but his faded brown eyes held nothing but love. He eased himself down the last of the steps, his gnarled fingers curled around the newel post of the swaying rail.

"Grandfather," I gasped. Taking his hand, I helped him to the old willow chair, blinked hard and reined myself in. "Forgive me. I have a friend in my truck who is badly hurt. I need you to help me tend to his wounds."

"Why come all this way, child?"

"You'd never believe me if I told you."

Grandfather squeezed my hand and I realized how badly they trembled. He paused until I looked at him. His silver hair, parted in two thick braids, framed his weathered face as he waited for my attention. "I always hear the truth in your words, Mika."

True. But this? He waited.

"Well, Bruin is . . . he's a . . . well, he isn't exactly human. I know it sounds crazy, but I've seen it. Three men attacked us. When Bruin killed them, they turned into jackals. Big, huge, dead dogs."

Violent images from the parking garage flooded my mind. I pinched my eyes shut. "No, he only killed two. I killed the third one. *Oh god.* I killed someone. It was horrible. I was so scared . . . but he shot Bruin . . . twice. He would've killed him. I didn't know what to do—"

Grandfather stilled my flailing hands and his energy eased me. "Focus, Mika. Tell me of your friend's injuries."

"He's been shot. He says he's part animal too. Like a werewolf or something. He needs help, and can't go to a hospital. I did what I could, but I need you."

Grandfather pointed toward his study. "Very well, let us see what we can do to help ease his suffering."

I hurried down the hall and unhooked the worn medicine bundle from its place just inside door. Then I went into his study to gather his pipe and feather and slipped them inside the hide pouch as well. "Bruin said we need to hide somewhere natural and remote."

I kept one hand under Grandfather's elbow as we crossed the

driveway. He grunted as he climbed into the back seat of the Humvee and righted himself. After eyeing the heaped corpses behind his seat, he rolled down his window, closed his eyes and lifted his face to the rising moon. With my hands tight on the steering wheel, I stared into the rear-view mirror and waited for him to tell me the Great Spirit's guidance.

Finally, he nodded. "Take us to frog-mouth cave, Rabbit."

I shifted into drive and headed toward the caverns near the back boundary of the reserve. As we drove through the darkness, I told him everything I could about Bruin and the tattoos appearing on our palms and the men who came after us in the parking garage. "I'm sorry to involve you in this. I didn't know where else to turn."

The wrinkles around his eyes deepened as he smiled. He leaned forward and squeezed my shoulder. "You turned in exactly the right direction. Now let us get him inside."

Bruin rallied enough to hold some of his weight as we shuffled him into the back of the frog-mouth cave. Carrying him would have been impossible. He was built like he'd been carved out of marble. Adonis, on leave from some exotic museum.

I lit two camp lanterns and laid out the blanket from the back of my truck. It wouldn't make it comfortable, but Bruin was in no shape to care either way. Once we got him horizontal, we stripped off his clothes to assess his injuries. I grabbed a half-empty water bottle that had been rolling around in my back seat and tried to get him to drink.

Grandfather touched my wrist and shook his head. "Breathe. Take a moment and think about what you offer."

I looked at the plastic bottle of stale water and exhaled. "I'll be back."

Back in my truck, I rooted through the gift bags from last night at the pub. The burl mug Liane had given me was solid cherry and hand carved. I snatched it from the bag and ran to the edge of the stream. After I said a prayer and made my offering, I dipped the mug into the running current of the stream.

By the time I returned to the cave, Grandfather had removed my makeshift bandages and begun rewrapping the wounds in linen strips.

I lifted Bruin's head into my lap and gave him some water, watching Grandfather smear a pasty poultice over the strips. With the bandaging complete, he began to chant and smudge.

Sage and sweetgrass smoldered in a large shell in the palm of his hand. Like I'd watched him do a thousand times, he drew his eagle feather through the smoke and over Bruin's heart and head, clearing away the negative energies and drawing in the positive.

I knelt beside them and tried to find calm, remembering the times I sat on Grandmother's lap as a child. She loved watching him tend to the sick of our community, so proud of her husband.

After Grandfather finished with Bruin, he smudged me and nodded at the half-empty mug of water in my hand. I took a small sip, the scent of the smudging and Grandfather's chant comforting me like nothing else. I sank cross-legged on the cave floor and absorbed the rhythmic cadences straight into my bones.

What a mess. Blood covered everything. Bruin was minced with bullet holes, gouges, and tears in his flesh that went bone deep in a couple of places. It was like a gory scene in a horror film except that it wasn't a movie. That was real life that had leaked out of him and pooled black into the dirt.

His eyes fluttered, and my insides twisted. The vibrant glow of turquoise was gone, replaced by a dull grey.

Forcing a smile, I tipped the edge of the mug to his swollen lip and let another trickle slide into his mouth. "You're in good hands, Bruin. My grandfather knows about healing with nature."

Bruin managed to swallow once before his head lolled to the side. I fit his marked palm to my own and laced our fingers together. The tattoos lined up perfectly, just as they had in the parking lot, and the instant they connected my palm stopped burning. In truth, size difference aside, our hands fit together like the pieces of a puzzle.

Leaning close to his ear, I repeated the words he'd spoken to me last night in the tub. "Just relax. I've got you."

He squeezed our palms together and smiled. The contact was insanely comforting, like the sensation of slipping into the soaker-tub after the tension of my attack. Bruin half-opened his eyes and his gaze drifted to our hands.

"Don't worry, big guy. Get well. We'll figure out what to do about all this, okay?"

Bruin's eyes fell shut again.

"He has a powerful energy, though his injuries are grave. I removed the bullet from his shoulder. The one on his side traveled straight through. There are many deep wounds which worry me, though, more so because I have no knowledge of how his people heal."

Grandfather's curled fingers tightened the lid on a small jar of citrus liniment he pulled from his satchel. "My ointments will help, but we need the aid of the spirits for him to heal fully."

"Thank you, Grandfather. I'll pray for—"

A surge of energy snapped through Bruin's hand to mine. I released my hold and shuffled back. Bruin's muscular form shimmered. His hulking frame stretched and broadened. It seemed to double in size and then again in mass. An instant later, instead of a man on the cave floor there was a mass of silver-tipped, chestnut fur.

I staggered back.

Part of me wanted to scream, while the other part of me was held transfixed. Though he'd told me he was a Were, part of me hadn't believed it possible until I was staring at his animal form. "A bear. Bruin is a bear."

When I finally tore my eyes from Bruin, I looked at Grandfather. The nonchalance in his weathered face stunned me. He regarded Bruin's colossal form as if it was something he'd seen a thousand times. The mound of fur rose and fell with shallow breath. Grandfather simply nodded as if he was part of some inside joke.

"What? How can you be so calm?"

He smiled the knowing smile I had seen countless times throughout my childhood. "No matter how the ages pass, it remains a marvel to me how the Creator governs our fates."

"What do you mean?"

"Think of your Spirit vision, Rabbit. What was the Great Spirit's message?"

I touched the bear pendant he'd carved for me a decade ago. "I am of the Ursine clan. I must stand amongst the Earth Mother's children and fight the extinction of a great species. What are you getting at? What does this mean?"

"You said he was the last of his kind, did you not?" He waited for my nod and continued. "And he spoke of the Fates marking you as his mate?"

I turned my palm open for him to examine.

He traced his fingers across the design. "I would say that the moment of your destiny has arrived, Rabbit. The question is—will you accept it?"

CHAPTER TEN

*B*ruin was breathtaking. He was massive. He was a bear.

For days I'd been sitting in a cave trying to wrap my cranium around that one. It hadn't really sunk in and I figured I would probably need a decade more before it did. Grandfather, however, had taken to the idea immediately saying, "The Creator's vision can only truly be understood when our relationship to all of earth's kingdoms is embraced with love and acceptance: the animals, the plants, the minerals and the humans."

Under the dim glow of the camping lanterns and the multitude of mineral stars glittering where they hung entombed in stone all around us, those words seemed surreal.

Bruin—a Were-bear, and my supposed mate—fought for his life after being attacked by evil jackal-men trying to wipe out his race.

Even as a journalist I couldn't make this up. I shook my head. Sadly, as much as I tried to be a regular citizen, Earth Mother and her spirits made it difficult.

"It's your path, Rabbit. It weakens your power." Grandfather read my expression and energy as he always had. He completed a sun wise rotation of the stone healing circle he'd created around Bruin's massive bear form and lit his pipe. "You bargain between two worlds, take what suits you from your heritage and contort it to fit your life choices. You use Earth Mother's gifts for good purpose, but act against your heart and spirit. Your energy is out of harmony."

Leaning away from the jagged stone wall, the blood-flow tingled back into my numb posterior. Bruin was deathly still and had been for a while now—a very long while. As each hour passed, it got more difficult to track the minute ebb and flow of his breathing. I had no idea what we'd do if he lost that battle. *Bruin, please don't die.*

"He is a magical creature, Rabbit. Perhaps the Great Spirit is calling him."

I struggled to my feet, knees cracking, arm muscles protesting the reach toward the ceiling as I stretched. Plodding across a pallet of cut boughs, an aromatic wave of fir and spruce released into the cool, damp air. "No. There has to be more we can do for him."

Bruin stirred as I spoke but did not come to consciousness. It happened several times over the past two days . . . as if he fought his way up from the depths of an underwater prison. He seemed to almost break the surface just to drift away, then fight again, and then submerge.

"The only connection I had to his life and his people was his friend Kobi." I rubbed the ache in my chest, trying to remember every moment of conversation we'd had from the club to the hotel. Unfortunately, conversation hadn't been high on the agenda. "I'm sure Kobi knows Bruin is a Were. They fought and sparred like brothers. Yeah, I'm sure he knows."

"And you have no way of contacting this man?"

I shook my head. "Oh . . . *yes* . . . yes, maybe I do." I grabbed the handle of a lantern and moved to my purse. Rummaging through the mess left after the contents-seat-dump, it took a few moments, but I found a mangled business card. Detective Enrique Delgato. "If we had a phone maybe we could get a message to Kobi."

"Where does a police detective come into this story, child?"

Crap. Busted. "I had a little trouble Friday night at the bar. Nothing to worry about. In fact, it was Bruin and his friend Kobi who swooped in and took care of everything. They introduced me to the good detective."

I glanced back at Bruin. "He's a heroic guy . . . and very protective of me."

Grandfather tilted his head to one side and smiled. "Then we must save his life, so I might extend my gratitude. Go. Try to reach his people."

My breath caught at the idea of leaving him. I didn't need to know Were-creature physiology to know he was dying. His breathing was weak and growing weaker. By my guess he wouldn't last more than another day. "How could I possibly be so invested in someone I just met?"

Bruin shifted his head a little.

Grandfather's eyes crinkled with a sad smile. He reached for the business card and patted my hand. "Look beyond reasons. You are a wonderful journalist but needing the '*why*' of every situation doesn't bode well for relationships. Accept what *is*. Now, stay with your bear. I'll venture home and call the officer."

"No . . . I'll go. Bruin doesn't even know I'm here. I'm being ridiculous."

Grandfather pulled my hand and turned me to look at the mass of gorgeous, silver tipped, brown fur. "He knows. See how his face tilts and follows you when you speak? Wherever his journey holds him, he hears your voice and it comforts him. You are the one he needs."

Watching Bruin, the dull ache in my chest grew. Somehow, I knew if I left him, he'd die before I got back. I stood with the keys in my hand and my heart in my throat. "I don't like the idea of you going back alone. What if the people who did this have tracked us down? What if they're waiting for you?"

"Do not worry yourself. The Earth Spirits will warn me if danger is near. Perhaps I'll call from the meeting house instead." He took the keys from my hands and shuffled toward the mouth of the cave.

"Good idea. Be careful," I called. "Ask Delgato to tell Kobi where we are. And if something seems off . . . keep driving until you're safe. And be careful . . .."

Grandfather blew me a kiss on the wind and it warmed my cheek. "Have faith in the Creator's plan, Rabbit. Everything happens as it is meant."

When the beefy rumble of my Humvee's engine faded into the distance, I turned my attention back to the cave interior. Dropping my purse close, I fluffed up the nest of boughs I used as a pallet and curled up next to Bruin. "Well, big guy, Grandfather has gone for the cavalry. Never thought I'd be spooning a bear . . . but it's just you and me here now, and I don't think you mind."

I retrieved Hulk's gun from my where I'd hid it in my purse and slid it under the hoodie I'd been using as my pillow. Grandfather wouldn't approve of the weapon, but no way would Bruin's enemies waltz in and kill any of us.

I brought my arm over his side, careful not to touch his injured hip or shoulder, and let my hand sink into the long, deep fur of his pelt. He was soft, shaggy and smelled of spruce needles and clean outdoors. My fingers kneaded over the thick, course guard hairs and through the sultry underfur beneath. Incredible. The juxtaposition of the two textures reminded me of Bruin himself. Tough and course on the outside, but decadently velvet underneath.

"I thought I *was* living my destiny." I whispered. "That's the whole point of my work. Fight for wildlife preservation. Stop exploitation of animals. Stop extinction due to poaching."

With a languid sweep I drew my face against his fur. It brushed over my cheeks and tickled my lips. I gave him a squeeze. "You know, you're very easy to talk to when you're like this. Maybe when you're better and we start fighting—and you know we will—you should change forms, so I remember that I actually do like you . . . a little."

I kissed the back of his furry, oval ear. It twitched and batted me in the cheek. My heart raced. Had he responded or was the movement involuntary?

"How could this be what the Earth Mother and her spirits had intended, Bruin? How could we be meant for each other and then you die? You can't give up before we figure it out." I closed my eyes and let myself feel him next to me. His strength. His essence.

Nuzzling deep into his scruff, my body grew heavy and relaxed. I yawned, snuggling into the warmth of his fur. Lost to a world of impossibility.

CHAPTER ELEVEN

I woke to my senses bursting to life. The hair on my body stood on end and I launched myself upright. With Hulk's gun raised, I panned the cave before my heart even restarted. I was alone, yet not. The air stirred around me. I scanned every shadow cast against every dark crevice and pock of the stone walls.

The presence grew stronger—a lethal, dangerous essence.

I shifted my aim toward the monolithic man materializing twenty feet from where I guarded Bruin. One instant there was no one, the next a massive male dressed head to toe in black body armor blocked the cave exit. Obsidian black eyes cast a brutal glare, no doubt assessing my worthiness as a threat. The man oozed violence and the cruel expression on his face made it pretty clear his inclination was rising.

He scowled at Bruin lying behind me, his voice slamming me like a physical blow. "Put the gun down, little girl. You get one chance. Do us both a favor and take it."

When he shifted, my adrenaline surged. I widened my stance and tried to steady my aim. "I've got fourteen bullets and I'm a damned good shot, asshole. So, quit twitching and stay back."

Cold air hit me like a gust of a winter storm. When he stepped forward, I squeezed off a round. The shot sunk into the rock of the cave wall, spewing shards and dust bits beside his head. Bile bubbled up from my gut. "Don't even think about it, jackal-man. Crawl back under whatever rock you live under and tell your boss to leave us—"

"*Jackal*—" He spat, the crease in his brow deepened. "I'm no fucking Jackal."

He shook a mane of breathtaking brindle hair and cursed. "It's you who puts Bruin in danger. Now drop the Colt before this gets messy."

No way was this guy the Calvary. How long had I slept? Had Grandfather even had time to find help? No. The man looming large and lethal in front of me didn't act like he was on our side at all. "How'd you find us?"

His stared narrowed and the air crackled. "I don't play twenty questions." He tapped an almost invisible earpiece and a little *beep* sounded. "I've got him and I need Blaze. This location . . . no, he's bad."

"Shut that off." I tightened my grip. "Who the hell do you think you—"

"Bruin's *father*," he roared. "That's who the fuck I am. And you're in my way."

Before the words stopped echoing against the walls, three more bodies appeared beside him. A voluptuous red-head, a tiny woman with black spiky hair and a silver-haired man with strangely pointed ears.

"Bruin!" The two females bolted toward me and I levelled my aim.

"Stop!" I held up my hand and they froze.

The curvy red head stepped forward and I shifted my aim. The air arced.

I didn't see him move. One moment the man claiming to be Bruin's father stood across the cave and the next, a massive hand gripped my throat from behind and his arm banded beneath my breasts. His strength was astonishing. His arm bit into my ribs like reinforced steel, but even still, I could tell he held back. He used only a fraction of the power he held and that was terrifying. His arm tightened. I couldn't breathe.

"Okay, little girl," he said, close to my ear. "Drop the weapon before someone I love gets hurt. Jade is going to heal Bruin before he breathes his last breath. And if you're good, I'll make sure Lexi doesn't kill you. *Got it?*"

Jade? Lexi? Was this really Bruin's family? *Oh, thank you Great Spirit.*

Before I could process that thought, an unnatural vibration filled the cave.

"Do what he says," Jade said. I struggled against the invisible force. Jade's words were hypnotizing, compelling. Wrong. My skin prickled, and I pushed back. Her words tried to weave themselves inside my mind, tiny tendrils squeezing my temples, attempting to usurp control of my actions. Though the mental hold was not vicious, it threatened to hold my will at bay.

I pushed back harder, and the cave began to spin.

The man with the pointed ears stepped forward, his blue eyes piercing and frantic. "Reign, Jade, both of you, enough. Mika is innocent in all this. Her only concern is Bruin's safety. Stop your attack on her and show her we are of like mind."

Reign's grip on my throat lessened and the mental push stopped.

I released the gun. Sinking to my knees I dragged in deep, gulping breaths.

Jade and Lexi barrelled me over as they rushed to the mound of massive brown fur.

Lexi, the tiny one with purple eyes and spiky black hair, drew the dagger strapped to her thigh and twirled it between her fingers and over her wrist again and again. "Who the fuck are you, Mundie? And what have you done to Bruin?"

"Calmly Lexi," the silver-haired man said, canting his head to the side as he watched me. "Mika is worried for Bruin's safety, as we all are. She knew not who we were, or if we deserved her trust. She simply tried to protect . . . her *mate.*"

"What?" Reign growled. "What are you saying, Galan?"

Lexi laughed. "You've got your wires crossed there Highborne. She's not Bruin's *mate. He's* the last of his line. *She's* human."

A wave of hostility heated my blood. Which was insane. Being

Bruin's mate was nothing I wanted, but this snotty pixie-woman denying it made me want to tear through something. My muscles tensed, and I fought the urge to lunge at her. *What is wrong with me?*

Galan's gaze softened. "Nothing. The Fates have bound you to a very powerful Were. Your base instincts—your animal instincts—are heightening to rise to your calling. It is only natural that you perceive Lexi's dismissal as a threat to your place in Bruin's life."

"Bull," I said, "and how did you—"

The silver-haired hottie tapped his temple. "I have a gift or two myself."

I held my hand up between us and frowned. "I don't believe you're reading my mind . . . but if you are. *Stop.* It's rude."

Jade gasped, her gaze focusing on my palm. "Look at her hand."

I fought the urge to tuck my hands into my pockets, but instead, let them see my tattoo.

"A Bonding Brand?" Lexi snapped. "The Fates wouldn't pair Bruin with a Mundie. That's messed on a dozen levels."

"And exactly what they'd do for shits and giggles." Jade dropped her focus back down to Bruin. She was a stunning woman, copper skin, vibrant emerald eyes and carried herself with an ethereal air that hardly seemed real.

And that would make the silver-haired Abercrombie model sporting suede pants and the sexy voice, her fiancé, Galan.

"Castian, can I get him up off the ground?" Jade asked.

A serious surge of energy disturbed the air and then Bruin appeared atop a five-by-eight stainless steel operating table. Jade continued to run her hands over him like nothing had happened. Then she started singing a ballad in a language I'd never heard. The cadence of her voice caused the current in the air to shift again. This time it wasn't hypnotizing. It was—

"Jade is a healer, Mika. What you sense is her gift."

While my brain backfired on that, Galan moved beside me. "You did well as Bruin's champion. Fash not, now that Jade has hands on him, he shall be up and barking out orders in no time. I promise you."

I exhaled. I wasn't sure how I felt about being anyone's mate, but the thought of Bruin surviving stole my breath. I rubbed the ache in my chest, but it didn't ease.

"Easy, sweeting." As the cave tilted and my legs gave way, Galan gathered me against his side. My face rested against the shammy-soft fabric of his old-fashioned tunic. He smelled great, like leather mixed with a summer meadow.

My eyes rolled closed.

I woke as he laid me down on the pallet of boughs. He knelt on the cave floor in front of me and slid my braid behind my shoulder. I couldn't help staring. He had the bluest eyes I'd ever seen. Smooth porcelain skin. He was gorgeous.

"Are you well, little one?"

And he can read minds. I blushed. "Fine . . . uh, sorry . . . but if you could stop spinning the cave that would be great."

My stomach growled long and low.

Galan looked toward Bruin's father standing sentinel near the cave exit. "Reign? Would you mind bringing in some food? Mika is hungry, and Bruin will need sustenance when he regains consciousness."

Reign didn't move. He just glared at me. *Allrighty then.*

When a plastic cup appeared in my hand, I sat up and a carry-out bag from Hamburger Mary's appeared in my lap. My mouth watered as the glorious scent of take-out filled my sinuses. It was my perfect meal from my favorite place. I looked up at Galan. "How?"

He shrugged and glanced up. "Thank you, Castian."

Who or what was this Castian? I lifted my gaze. Nothing but a stone ceiling.

The air stirred once more, and a golden light washed through the cave. The illumination lit the cavern to a level of daylight, the air filling with sweet scents of bergamot and lavender.

The man who appeared this time stood tall and lithe, his features soft yet unmistakably masculine. Wavy chestnut hair framed a square jaw and highlighted the brilliant, emerald green of his eyes. My skin tingled. He was blindingly majestic . . . and definitely not human.

He glided toward me and I had to look down to make sure he was walking and not floating across the cave floor. "I am Castian, Mika. Welcome into the fold."

I was staring. "Uh . . . thank you."

"You must needs eat," Galan said, tapping the paper bag. "And while you do, mayhap you can tell us what ill has befallen you both the past few days."

And so, I did. I ate my bizarre meal and retold everything that happened from Bruin and I meeting at Spankz, through all the jackal death and drama that led us to this cave. Well, not everything. I left out the highlights at the Wedgewood Hotel.

Reign growled. "Was Bruin able to dispose of the bodies before he collapsed?"

"No. They're in the trees behind my truck." I stuffed an onion ring in my mouth. "Oh, sorry, my grandfather took my truck. They're out the cave entrance to the left, hidden under some brush."

Reign left.

That reminded me. "My grandfather? Is he the one who called you? Is he okay?"

Galan threaded long, pale fingers through his hair. The silver of his hair was stunning, but with the burgundy braid that hung down on the side of his face he was absolutely dazzling. "I am not certain how Reign found you, in all honesty. Jade and I were summoned here most unexpectedly, but I shall find word on your grandfather. Fash not."

"*Mika?*"

I shoved the food at Galan, leaped off the ground and raced to where Bruin lay on the stainless steel table. He was naked and in his human form. Still as pasty grey as he'd been in my truck, but awake.

The air sucked from my lungs when I saw the damage to his body now that it was human again . . . scratches and bullet wounds from the jackal attack. The men must have used their claws or something because he was shredded. Why hadn't I seen these before? There were other scars as well, not from the fight in the parking garage. Long lashes and buckled skin detailed a map of injuries past. Had Bruin been tortured?

I searched his face as my stomach rolled. He was as handsome as always, just with the addition of two days' worth of bristling whisker darkening his face. I fingered over a scar through his lip and another which cut through his eyebrow and left a thin line of bare skin where the hair never grew back.

Bruin kissed my palm before lifting his hand and pressing our brands together. My knees buckled a little as the burning pain that had ebbed for days extinguished. His weak smile melted my heart. "Hey. How freaked are you?"

Pretty damned freaked. "You could have given me a heads up that you were Yogi's cousin." As his chest vibrated I pushed a long strand of hair from his face. He looked different covered in scraggly growth, but his eyes were the same.

"Sorry. I was busy taking a header into a coma."

He breathed me in and my nerves started to unravel. "Rather poor timing if you ask me. The lengths some people will go to avoid difficult conversations."

He reached for my neck and pulled my forehead to his lips. "Are you really okay?"

I blinked fast. "Your friends saved the day."

He looked past my shoulder. "Hey guys, thanks for coming. Could one of you throw some clothes on my naked ass, please? My powers are still AWOL." In a flash Bruin wore beat-to-death black jeans and a skin-tight-T that read: *Men have two emotions: Horny and hungry. If you don't see an erection, make him a sandwich.*

Laughter bubbled from my chest. If they were making jokes at Bruin's expense he must be all right, right? I drew a deep breath and realized it was my first in days. "I was so scared. I didn't know what to do." The sting in my eyes grew and I swiped my fingers across my cheeks. "You almost died . . . and I didn't know what to do . . .."

Bruin reached one arm around my waist and hoisted me up to lay beside him on his raised platform. Even in his weakened state he was as strong as . . . well, a bear. I pressed my face into his neck, filling my sinuses his manly spice. As his arms came around me, he spoke over my head. "Guys? Would you give us a minute?"

I didn't hear them walk away, but felt the shift in the cave's energy when we were alone. When Bruin's body shuddered, I pulled away. "Am I too heavy? What's—"

Moisture was building in his eyes. His arms tightened around me, securing me to his side. "I'm sorry, Mika. I wanted to protect you." His voice was ragged, and his hand fisted in my hair. "I should have been there to keep you safe. I let you down."

I smoothed his bangs out of his eyes and scootched up to kiss his cheek. "You did no such thing. You got me out of that parking garage and told me how to stay safe until help came." I laid my forehead against his cheek. It was warm again, thank goodness. "I'm sorry it took me so long to figure out how to get you the help you needed."

His hand slid across my back as he tilted his head and claimed my mouth. Lips met lips, warm and a little salty from the tears. His hand drew up my throat, and his tongue danced with mine. Oh . . . my, this man could kiss.

After a long, quiet moment I pulled back, the sweet flavor of him lingering on my lips. Bear or not, warrior or not, Bruin did something to my insides. Something incredibly powerful. Something I couldn't deny even if I had the gall to try. We stayed like that, linked by our fingers and our eyes. Our palms pressed together. The sting of separation forgotten.

"What would have happened if Reign hadn't found us. What if—"

On a heavy sigh, he whispered, "Don't. You did great. You kept me alive and safe until my family came for me. You couldn't have done better."

"You almost died," I choked.

As my emotional levee crumbled, the flooding ensued. A minute later, it was time to sound the alarm. Bruin secured me against his body and rubbed slow circles on my back while I cried. It all came washing over me: him getting hurt in the fight, me shooting Hulk, the shocked look in his eyes as he slumped to the concrete ground, the powerless rage watching Bruin's life ebb away hour by hour. I thought he would die. But he hadn't.

With my cheek against his chest I listened to the slow, steady beat of his heart.

Bruin was speaking softly in tongues. I had no idea what the words meant, but the tone and the cadence were reassuring, reverent. I lifted my head from his damp neck. "Sorry. I think I'm done that now. I'm not usually such a girl."

"Me neither." He blinked fast, wiped his own eyes and forced a smile. "Thanks for sticking it out for me."

I stiffened. "Bruin . . . I'm glad you're all right, but . . .."

There was a long silent pause before he pulled me back down onto his chest. "What do you say we don't make any decisions right now? I woke up from a coma fifteen minutes ago. Could I enjoy your company for a bit before you tell me we're doomed?"

I ran my hands from his shoulder down to his hip. "Sure. Are you all right?"

"Yeah, a couple more minutes and I'll be on my feet and pissing you off. My magic mojo is coming on-line as we speak." That glorious turquoise sparkle had returned to his eyes and I couldn't help but laugh when he rolled his hips against me. "A couple minutes after that I could flash us somewhere private and you could give me a once over. See how healed I really am."

I laughed and pulled back to look at him. My tears left a dark patch on the neck of his t-shirt. "Sorry about that."

"Any time. It's been a manic couple of days for both of us." What an understatement that was. "Mika, come home with me for a few days so we can work on figuring this out."

I pushed up and out of his arms. "I can't, sorry. I need to be here."

"Surely you can get away for a few days. Your boss told you to take some time off." As the tension rose in his voice, gold flecks began appearing in his eyes. After looking into the amber gaze of his bear, I had a better sense of why they did that. When he was agitated or aggressive, his animal side seemed to gain strength.

"I can't leave Grandfather. If those jackal-men come after me, they'll find him. He's all I have, and I dragged him right into the middle of this."

"Did he see me shift?" Bruin reeled, closing his eyes as I nodded.

"I'm sorry. I needed his help to tend to your wounds. You said no hospitals, and I suck at—"

He shook his head and placed a finger over my lips. "It's fine. We'll speak to Reign about wiping his memories."

"Yeah . . . about Reign. He doesn't like me much."

Bruin frowned. "Why do you say that?"

I chewed at my bottom lip. "I didn't know who he was when he poofed in on me and I'd been carrying the Hulk-guy's gun in case those jackal-men showed up."

"You held a gun on *Reign?*" The newly returned bronze of his skin washed away.

"Yeah, but he seemed to be okay with that. It was when the others got here—"

His eyes popped wide as he scrubbed his palm over his mouth. "*Please* tell me you didn't threaten Jade or Lexi."

"Um . . . yeah, Jade." I winced and hopped off the table, gaining some distance. "Don't look at me like that. I didn't know she was your sister. She *poofed* in here and charged at you when you were unconscious. We got it sorted out, but I think your family hates me."

Galan's rich timbre rang from the mouth of the cave. "No one hates you, sweeting. We were merely concerned for Bruin's wellbeing."

"Speak for yourself, Highborne," Lexi said, pushing past Galan. She only came to my chest, but I had no doubt she could hurt me if she was so inclined. And it was pretty clear she was. She had a knack for spinning her dagger while she spoke and always pointing the business end at me. Her purple eyes were freaky beautiful but sent an icy shiver up my spine. "You ever threaten me or mine again, Mundie and so help me . . . I'll dice you to shreds."

A deep growl tore from behind me and I heard Bruin sliding off the table. "Princess, you don't want a go-round with me right now. I'm cranky and feel like shit. I love you huge, but Mika did her best to protect me. She wasn't born into our world. Give her a chance to learn some of our rules before you kick her out of the game."

"No. I don't think so. If you want your little play toy in one piece keep her the hell away from me." She glared and pointed the dagger at my throat. "I can slaughter you sixty different ways before you know I've even moved, bitch, so think about that the next time you get some bright idea about threatening someone I love."

She meant every word. I read her body language and her visual cues. She would kill for Bruin and relished the idea of going berserker on me.

"*Alexianna Grace.*" Jade joined the party.

Despite the strength of her voice, she looked drained. Her hand followed the contour of the cave wall as she shuffled in. Galan strode to her, gathering her against his side. She laid her cheek against his shoulder and rallied a little. "Lexi, for Bruin's sake we will treat this woman with respect. She may have been wrong in her judgment of us, but her intentions were clear and you know it. She protected our boy. In my book that makes her one of the good guys."

Lexi's eyes widened. "*Fine.* Then you play nice with your new BFF. Maybe the four of you can make it a double wedding."

Bruin lunged. The gust of wind blew my hair as he flipped Lexi over his shoulder and the two of them disappeared into nothingness. I stood, open-mouthed while my mind whirled.

Jade shrugged, brushing her palm over her eyes. "Don't worry, they'll be back. Lexi just needs a time out."

"All this *poofing* in and out is unnerving."

Galan's smile was sad. "You will adjust. We will help you."

I looked into the deep green eyes of Bruin's sister. "I'm sorry our first encounter went so far off the rails. I . . . uh, this has all been a bit overwhelming."

The corners of Jade's mouth inched up as her gaze met Galan's. "Don't worry, Mika. My most treasured relationships started off on the wrong foot."

CHAPTER TWELVE

ormally, the grass clearing and trickling stream outside Frog-mouth cave was the kind of place you'd find in a scene from Bambi, not a ball-busting military incursion. But today, the sun-kissed meadow buzzed with leather-clad warriors wearing handguns either sheathed in a chest harness or tucked in the waistband of their pants. Many men shouldered long-range sniper rifles and some held what could only be described as magic wands.

Were we seizing Hogwarts?

Reign—clearly the man in charge of the operation—stood beneath the awning of a large oak, orchestrating the disposal of jackal corpses, sending men to secure the parking garage and deciding who would canvas any potential witnesses and wipe their memories.

Wipe their memories? Really?

With his hands planted and leaning heavy into massive shoulders, Bruin's father pointed to a holographic map floating and rotating over a large, war-room table. The group of soldiers surrounding him listened and nodded.

Kobi frowned as Galan, Jade and I drew nearer, his eyes flashing red. *Aha, so not a trick of the lighting.* There was nothing mischievous about him this afternoon. His glare left me chilled and after a moment, the entire group joined in. They were huge, intimidating and throwing me a scathing fuck-you vibe palpable from fifty yards.

Well, don't I feel special.

Galan escorted Jade under the awning and I was relieved to see Grandfather sitting there, chatting with Castian. He looked none the worse for the morning's excitement, though I knew how he'd feel about all the guns. In fact, he seemed more animated in his conversation with Castian than I had seen him in years. When Galan kissed Jade's cheek, stooped to pick up a bow and quiver and returned to me, I decided to leave Grandfather to his conversation.

"Is Jade all right?" I asked when we'd stepped far enough away for privacy.

"Extensive healings are exhausting for her. She needs to rest for a time before her strength returns. Fash not, Castian will watch over her."

After slinging the quiver over his shoulder, Galan escorted us past the hub of excitement. I appreciated how he positioned himself between me and the warriors, shielding me from their daggered stares. Soldiers angry about the stupid human who almost got Bruin killed no doubt.

"What's the hostility about?"

"Those are Bruin's brothers-in-arms. He told you he is a warrior, yes?"

"Yes."

"When news spread that he bonded and that he and his intended had been attacked, his comrades rallied. We protect our own, and those we love fall under that protection as well. Any one of these men will give their life to keep another man's mate safe."

"I haven't agreed to be his mate . . . and nobody said anything about love."

Galan shrugged. "And therein lies the source of their hostility. The Fates have paired you and Bruin. In our world, that is immensely significant. It means his brothers will never allow any harm to fall upon you. They will protect you as if you were their own beloved."

I didn't want to argue with Galan, but they looked more like they wanted to tie a weighted bag around my neck and dip me in the creek.

I eyed the intricate carving on the bow Galan carried. "You any good with that?"

A sexy smirk grew as he arched a brow. "I shall do."

"Not really filling me with confidence here, Galan," I said, but I had a feeling that if someone jumped out from behind a tree, Galan would skewer them before I could blink.

He chuckled and placed a hand under my elbow as I stepped over a mossy, fallen log. "Whether you have accepted it or not, you are Bruin's mate and will be protected as such. The Were-Bear species are a great and respected people in this realm. Years ago, the Bear King led a rebellion that kept the Scourge, the criminal faction of our realm, from taking over our lands. The other Were races swore their allegiance to follow the Bears."

"What happened to him, the Bear King?"

"He and every member of Bruin's community were slaughtered."

"Except Bruin."

Galan nodded. "Except Bruin. When they learned of the attack, Bruin and his father were in a distant forest, miles away. He was left there by his sire, to ensure that he survive at all cost."

"Not that I'm complaining, but why him?"

Galan's head tilted slightly to the side, his long silver hair shimmering in the mid-morning sun. "Because he was the Crown Prince .. . and when his father was killed, Bruin became King of the Were kingdoms. You are to be their Queen."

Galan politely ignored my gaping mouth and lifted my hand onto the crook of his elbow. Thankfully, he let that bombshell detonate without further comment. Were Queen? How was I supposed to respond to that little tidbit?

He manoeuvred us beyond the chaos and toward the serenity of the forest before pausing to speak again. "As you may have gathered, we have a warrior-based policing agency. It is called the Talon. They shall dispose of your jackal assailants and ensure that there was no breach of anonymity during their attack on you. If anyone saw anything outside your office or in that parking structure, Talon enforcers will adjust the memories of the witnesses. Our existence must needs remain secret."

My gaze drifted back the way we'd come to where Grandfather sat in a stand of silver birch trees with Castian. My stomach churned. The two of them sat in a tuft of soft ground cover, leaning against a wide trunk, speaking like old friends. They watched the hustle of the soldiers as if it were some sort of sporting event and they had front row seats.

"Is that what they'll do to my grandfather?"

"No. Your grandfather has asked to accompany you into our realm. Castian has agreed, so the two of you will stay in our home as our guests until we can assess the danger."

"Exactly how big is this place?"

Galan laughed. "There is plenty of room. You will go with Bruin and gather belongings for you and your grandfather while we await your return in the Realm of the Fair."

His ocean blue eyes were incredibly soothing, fast becoming a safe place amongst all this craziness. The thought of him leaving me to these other strangers tightened my gut. "Won't you come with me . . . *us*, I mean?"

He patted the top of my hand. "My physical appearance makes exposure more likely. Castian prefers I remain removed from largely populated areas. I am here solely to help you understand our world and protect you from harm. Modern society would not understand about Elves, Pixies and Weres."

"Elves. That's what you are?" His softly pointed ears extended about two inches further than human ears. When they flushed pink, I realized I'd been caught staring. Again. "I'm sorry. I don't mean to be rude."

Galan's expression was full of tenderness. "No offense taken. Yes. There are seven species of Elves in our realm and my family and I are High Elves or Highbornes as we are called. I came to live with Jade, Lexi and the others almost two months ago, after our village was attacked and my younger sister abducted."

"Two months? And you and Jade are already engaged?"

He smiled and walked me under the shade of a large elm. "In truth, we bound as mates within weeks of knowing one another. Our love caught us off guard and changed the course of our lives forever. The wedding is merely a ceremony to include our friends and family in a human celebration for Jade."

"Any excuse for a party." Bruin's deep timbre broke into our conversation. I combed through my hair with my fingers and scanned the trees behind us. Lexi wasn't with him. He leaned in and kissed the top of my head, making me feel dainty and feminine in his wake. "Thanks for watching over her, Galan."

Galan inclined his head. "My deepest pleasure. Blessed be, Mika. Jade and I will prepare your accommodations and look forward to your arrival."

I reached up onto my toes and pressed a kiss to Galan's cheek, his ivory skin soft as silk. "Thank you for everything."

He winked and strode back toward the hustle of the military base with an elegance I'd never encountered before.

Bruin's healthy male glow had returned to his swagger and also to his cheeks. "I leave for twenty minutes and you're taking romantic strolls and kissing my sister's husband?"

I jerked back to look at him. His eyes were turquoise and calm. "Well, Galan is extremely attractive, not to mention charming."

Bruin growled a long, teasing rumble.

I popped my fists on my hips. "You know, Galan and I spoke all that time and he never growled at me once."

Bruin lifted me against his chest, wrapping his arms tight around my waist. While his bristled cheek skimmed up my neck, one of his hands slid down my backside and cupped my ass. His hips rolled sensuously against my belly. "I remember you liking when I growl for you."

I swallowed hard and fought the almost overwhelming urge to wrap my legs around his waist while he carried me into the forest. Communing with nature never seemed so appealing. "Growling *for* me maybe, but not at me."

He chuckled, deep and throaty in my ear, and pinched the skin of my neck between his teeth. "I stand corrected."

Releasing me, he clasped his palm against mine and headed back into the thick of the chaos. After properly introducing Bruin to my Grandfather and assuring myself he was okay, we said our goodbyes and made a beeline for my Humvee.

"Kobi, Cowboy, and Savage you're with us." Bruin strapped on a shoulder harness, checked the gun that was handed to him, and pocketed a replacement phone.

"I'll drive." Kobi held out a hand for the keys.

I snorted. "You wish." After the looks he'd thrown me, he was lucky not to be tied to the roof. Hopping into the driver's seat, I buckled up and turned over the ignition. The beefy rumble took the edge off my mood . . . but only a little.

CHAPTER THIRTEEN

*E*ven though the back seat and the truck bed beyond was wide and open, to wedge the three of them in, they practically needed a shoe horn. Good. Let them feel uncomfortable for a change. Kobi shifted in his seat and lifted my computer bag.

"Careful with that. My life is in that bag," I said.

Scowling, he slid it over to the cowboy who'd drawn the short straw and had wedged himself in the back-back.

"What's our plan?" I asked.

Bruin climbed in beside me, a dozen emotions darkening his gaze. "We'll swing by your grandfather's place for his personal things, then drive to Vancouver. You'll grab what you need from your place, then we'll head to the Gatehouse. If all goes well, we'll be through the Portal and be home before Elora rings her mighty dinner bell."

A low, collective rumble of appreciation filled the truck.

"Wow, that's quite an itinerary."

"What can I say? I'm a planner."

"And what's a Portal?"

"The passageway between our realm and this one."

"Can't we just poof?"

"No." Amusement rang in the baritone of his voice. "Without Castian's help, we can only *Flash* within one realm or the other. To travel between the two we use a Portal gate. Besides, you want your stuff, right?"

He shifted closer and my body reacted before my mind could weigh in. God he smelled good. His nostrils flared and I recognized the look in his eyes.

I swallowed. "*Mhmm*, definitely."

He winked. "Then the Portal gate it is."

Kobi cursed. "If you two are finished with the eye-fucking, we're wedged in back here. A breeze would be nice."

Bruin rolled down his window and gave Castian a wave. As we pulled out, he started the introductions. "Mika, you remember Kobi from the other night. Well, the tattooed sonofabitch beside him is Savage, and the pansy-ass with the drawl and the Garth Brooks hat is Cowboy."

I nodded toward the rear-view mirror then caught sight of my grandfather disappearing behind us. "So Castian will take my grandfather to your home to meet us?"

Bruin squeezed my shoulder. "I guarantee nothing will happen to him while he's with Castian and Reign. He couldn't be in safer hands."

Kobi pierced me with a scarlet glare in the rear-view mirror. "You on the other hand . . . better watch your pretty little ass. You almost got our boy killed, threatened our friends and shot at our boss. You're lucky you're still breathing, Mundie."

Life seriously needed an undo button.

"Actually, I uh . . . didn't shoot *at* him. I fired a warning shot into the cave wall beside him."

That didn't seem to help.

"You won't win friends by making jokes." Cowboy said.

I breathed deep and winced. Reign may have held back when he grabbed me in the cave, but between my ribs and my throat, I was in for another layer of bruises. "Sorry. I didn't mean . . ."

Bruin's eyes flashed a level of compassion that took me by

surprise. "No. Don't apologize. You did what you could. You'll learn the hierarchy of things in time."

In time. I sighed. Three days ago, my life was my own, now I was sucked into a vortex of the unbelievable. What would happen in three more days? I wasn't sure time was really on my side for that one.

Bruin reached to the steering wheel and took my white knuckles to his lips. "This is only your first taste of our world, baby. Trust me, it'll get easier."

Kobi leaned forward. "This is a sweet ride. You sure you don't want me to take the wheel? If we run into trouble—"

"I can handle it." I gripped my steering wheel tighter. "I've been in 4x4 rallies, all-terrain courses and a dozen weekend warrior events. My truck and I are a team. Nobody touches him."

Bruin did that growlly thing again, low in his chest. It vibrated something inside me like a tuning fork to my sex drive. Our eyes locked briefly, and his gaze reached into me. "Mika, you are the sexiest thing alive."

Bastard. He knew exactly what affect he had on me. Man, I was in trouble.

Kobi's curse broke the moment. "All right, Bear, this isn't the Stanley Suites and unless you're sharing, we don't need to be included."

I paid more attention than necessary while we bumped back onto the main trail. It hadn't rained up here in a while and the hard-packed ground threw whirls of dust in our wake.

Bruin patted my thigh and then flipped the backseat a one-fingered salute. "Watch it boys, I've sat through enough of your female sexcapades to not only even the score but bury each and every one of you."

Sitting cramped up in the way back, Cowboy tapped the blue-green stone centered in the medallion of his bolo tie. "How long till we get where we're going, Alpha?" The guy's thick Southern twang filled the back of the truck. He was all Oklahoma ranch-hand meets Channing Tatum. Nice to look at, but with that same, 'snap-someone's-neck-without-a-second-thought' vibe that Bruin had in the parking garage.

In front of him sat a skin-head with tats on his skull. Savage. Apt name. Black, lifeless eyes fixated on me, sizing me up . . . for a nightmare. His brow arched, shifting the piercings over his eye which matched the two labret hoops that contoured his chin.

"Pretty, ain't he?" Cowboy said, his stare hard. "Not much of a conversationalist, but if you like the artwork you should see the rest of him. He's a fucking masterpiece."

I returned my gaze to the road ahead.

Bruin adjusted his seat backward so he could turn to look at them. A long, menacing rumble filled the truck. "Enough. You three will give Mika the courtesy my mate deserves or we *will* have a problem. Cowboy, you especially."

"She says she's not your mate, Alpha. That means she's not my Ursa."

I'd always considered my truck to be spacious, but with these boys and their massive warrior attitude it was more than a little claustrophobic. I drove along, waiting for the staring contest to end and the tension to dial down. "Does Castian seek out humungous men to be warriors or does being warriors make you humungous men?"

"The latter," Bruin said. "Though some of us were physically perfect even before becoming enforcers."

The stone-faced men in the back started to crack.

"Awe, pour some more sugar in my Dixie cup, Alpha. Who's more of a hunk than you?" Cowboy asked.

"Any one of us," Kobi answered.

Cowboy took off his hat and fanned himself batting his sandy lashes. "The way your muscles shimmer in the sun, Alpha, y'all blind me with your manliness."

"And don't get us started on your skill with a sword," Kobi added.

Bruin gave them the finger again. "Yeah, yeah, yuck it up boys, but I'm still the guy who pulls your charbroiled asses from the fire."

Kobi laughed. "That's because you're the only one who will take our calls."

I shook my head. "Are you guys always like this?"

"Worse," Bruin said. "None of the Highbornes are here to really get them going."

I raised a brow and slowed to make the turn into the reservation proper. "Galan seemed perfectly well mannered."

"Galan maybe, but you haven't met Tham or Iadon." Bruin laughed. "They can shovel shit better than anyone and convince you it smells like night-blooming roses."

Cowboy nodded. "Aust is tough to get out of his shell, but when you do, watch out."

Bruin shook with laughter. "True. It's that damn Highborne charisma they all ooze. Women follow them across the grounds, tucking panties in their quivers. It's disgusting."

Cowboy removed his hat and drew his forearm across his brow. "That's why we scope women in the Modern Realm—Elves aren't allowed here. Sadly, Castian doesn't allow guests to be brought into Jade's house, so our options are severely handicapped."

"You *all* live in Jade's house?"

Bruin nodded. "I told you it was large."

Large yes, but was it a house or a city? Buckingham Palace? Vatican City? I had no interest in my seventy-four-year-old grandfather living in a giant frat house filled with oversexed warriors. Man, I regretted dragging him into this.

The gravel crunched as we pulled up beside his old truck. I reached to quiet the rumble of the engine when a cross breeze welcomed us home. All four men stiffened.

Lightning-quick, the camaraderie vanished. Military focus replaced easy humor.

"Comm's." Bruin commanded.

Each warrior dropped a small arm from their earpiece and touched a button by their ears. Four *beeps* chimed as they drew weapons.

Bruin halted my hand on the ignition. "Leave the engine running. Savage you have point. Cowboy . . . perimeter. Kobi you're with Mika and me."

Savage and Cowboy rolled out, moving soundlessly toward the surrounding trees and the side lawn. I tried to follow their movements, but within seconds they were gone, disappeared before I could make sense of what was happening.

"You said this truck is bullet proof, right?" Bruin's voice was hard, but his eyes were gentle.

I nodded.

"Good. Stay here. Lock the doors. If anyone other than one of us comes toward you, hit the gas and run this tank over their ass."

"Is it jackals?"

Bruin nodded. He and Kobi slipped out opposite sides of the vehicle and scanned the treeline along the side of the driveway. Their search didn't take them far, never more than forty or fifty feet before they circled back.

"Clear," Kobi said returning to the truck. Pulling out a package of Parliaments he tapped the end and retrieved one. "How d'you want to play this, Bear?"

Bruin stood at my open window looking across at his friend. "The scents are old, our visitors are vapour. Cowboy stay with the truck. We'll take her in, grab what we need and be out before you even have time to miss us."

"I'll try to control myself," Cowboy deadpanned, approaching silently from behind.

Kobi flicked his thumb against his index finger and his thumb caught fire. He held his cigarette to it and drew a deep inhale. When Cowboy reached across with his own, Kobi lit his too. Who or what was he? I closed my mouth and tried not to stare.

On the floor, between the front seats, I punched the code into the keypad of my console and revealed the jackal guns from the parking garage. Bruin's eyes widened.

"What? I put these in the gun-safe in case we needed them."

Bruin chuckled, grabbing another handgun. "Where did you come from, mystery lady?"

Kobi exhaled a stream of smoke. "More important . . . do you have a sister?"

Savage returned and flipped a few hand signals.

"All clear," Cowboy said. "Your mate is safe to enter."

I frowned at Bruin. He frowned back and shrugged.

Hopping out of the truck, Savage led the way while Bruin and Kobi closed in on me like heavily armed bookends. Tight to my ass and guns raised, we entered Grandfather's house.

"Oh. My. God." My eyes burned as I shuffled through the carnage. "Grandfather will be heartbroken." I picked up what was left of a carving he'd been given from the Mi'kmaq chief in Nova Scotia. A lifetime of working to strengthen our people. Every piece of furniture, every pledge on every shelf was part of him. I set the kitchen chair back on its legs and scanned the destruction. We were in dumpster territory.

A warm hand squeezed my shoulder and turned me. Bruin was quick with the tissue and brushed my cheeks dry. "I'm sorry, Mika, but we have to keep moving. Grab what you need and we'll head to your place. The important thing is that your grandfather is safe."

Kobi made a sweeping gesture in the kitchen and hung a louie down the hall. As he passed through the house the vibration of the air changed and the devastation disappeared. Everywhere I looked things were back in order.

"What's he doing?" I asked Bruin.

"He's throwing up a glamour in case any neighbors come by and look in the windows." He read my blank expression. "It's a magical illusion that changes the appearance of things so if anyone stops by before we get things sorted out, they won't call the Mounties."

Grabbing a pile of clothes from the laundry room and a few things from the front closet, I stuffed Grandfather's old leather duffle. When had our lives become an episode of CSI? "You guys think of everything, don't you?"

Bruin crossed his arms over his broad chest. "Sadly, we've had decades of cleaning up these messes. We'll need you to tell a few of your grandfather's and a few of your neighbors the two of you are going away for a bit. Odds are whoever did this ransacked your place too."

My hand flew to my mouth. "Bruin, I need you to poof us to my place, *now.*"

"What's wrong?" Bruin touched the side of his communicator. "We're moving."

"I don't live alone," I choked, my heart in my throat. "What if they hurt Orville?"

CHAPTER FOURTEEN

*B*ruin flashed us onto my back porch. It took a minute for the buzz-saw in my head to stop whirling and skin to stop crawling, but while it did, we waited for the other three to arrive. "How do they know where we went?"

"They'll follow my energy. It's basic once you get the hang of it."

Oh, of course. "So, how did you know?"

He sighed his gaze narrowing. "Reign pulled together a dossier on you as soon as he learned who you were. Your address is basic info."

I was about to go off about violation of privacy when a burst of black smoke brought Kobi into focus. A second later Savage appeared. Bruin flashed some hand signals and they held their position. Cowboy Flashed in beside us, holding up my backpack.

Thank-you Cowboy.

After setting it on one of the Adirondack chairs, he nodded to Bruin's silent command and disappeared over the railing. Savage slipped behind my hedge and headed up the side of the house, gun drawn. I hoped Mr. Griffiths wasn't watering his herb garden. An armed, tattooed mountain of leather coming at him might just give the old guy a coronary.

"Do you smell jackals here?" I whispered.

"The place is rife with their scent. Older than at your grandfather's. It begs the question, 'how the hell did they find you so soon? There's no way they could have tracked your scent to your identity so fast'." Bruin tapped his comm at his ear and nodded to me. "We're clear."

I reached to the top of the wooden door frame and plucked the hide-away-key.

Bruin frowned. "That is your security . . . a key sitting above the door? Unbelievable."

"No one ever tried to kill me until you came along." I matched his scowl and turned the key as quickly as I could. The ransack hurricane had hit here too. All my stuff ruined. Glass and ceramics crunched under my feet as we tromped over my shattered and shredded life.

Kobi strode into the kitchen, his gun lowered flat against his thigh. "There's no sign of the roommate. Maybe this Orville wasn't home when they came?"

"He's not my roommate." I pushed into what was left of my living-room, scanned the debris and listened. "Orville. Orville baby . . . mommy's here. Come out."

"Mommy?" Kobi swung a look toward Bruin, who missed his bizarre expression because he was already staring at me wide eyed.

"Stop your growling. I can't hear a thing." I broke away from the two of them and tried not to focus on how infuriatingly hot he was when he got possessive. "Orville, baby. Come out."

The scrabbling of claws against hardwood had me bolting down the hall towards my office. I swooped down and scooped Orville into my arms. I examined him from his crazy whiskers, over his long, stocky body, right to the end of his bushy, prehensile tail. It didn't look like he'd been hurt. Nuzzling my face into his fur, I breathed a sigh of relief when he wrapped his tail around my arm and squeezed. "There's my boy. Did those stupid jackal men scare you?"

Kobi snorted. "Okay, I gotta say it. That's the f-ugliest dog ever."

"He's not a *dog*." I brushed Orville's wiry grey fur from his face while they all laughed. "He's a binturong."

"A what?" Bruin tried to hold a straight face but struggled.

"A binturong. And I'd think that you being a loner in the animal world would respect that I'm his only family. Don't make jokes at his expense."

Bruin held up his hands and sobered. "I apologize. Your . . . Orville is charming, in a unique, only-a-mother-could-love sort of way. I wonder how he hid from the jackals?"

"They probably got thrown off by his scent," I said.

Another chorus of laughter erupted.

Bruin quieted his men. "Sorry. It's just, even as stupid as jackals are, any Were can sniff out a bintur-thing, no problem.

"Really? Okay, big-guy, can you or Cowboy tell me what his scent is?"

Cowboy lifted his nose and sniffed, long and deep from over by my overturned sofa. "I've got nothing, Alpha."

Bruin did the same and shook his shaggy head. "All I smell is buttered popcorn. Do you have some kind of weird snack fetish I should know about?"

Now it was my turn to act smug. "No. I have a binturong. Boys, meet Orville Redenbacher."

Bruin leaned in. "He smells like popcorn. Cool. Where'd you find him?"

"Caged in a warehouse on the Canadian side of the border. I followed a lead about the illegal trafficking of bald eagle feathers into the United States and there he was."

"You stole him?" He crossed his arms over his chest and scowled.

"Liberated." I corrected. "I couldn't leave him there with criminals. There was no telling what they would do to him."

Bruin looked at me like I was nuts. "What about what they would do to you? Were you alone in this warehouse of criminals? At least tell, please tell me you had more than a Taser on you."

When I said nothing, he cursed. "We are going to have a discussion about personal safety, you and I."

When he made to reach forward, I raised Orville higher against my chest. "He doesn't like strangers."

"Smart dog," Kobi said. "Probably saved his skin."

"He's not a *dog*. The layman term for binturong is Bearcat."

"So, is he a bear or a cat?"

"Neither." I huffed, my head starting to pound.

Bruin ended Kobi's taunts by bending in front of me. A guttural grumble vibrated from Orville's chest as he sniffed the bear and held Bruin's gaze. Great, a staring contest. Orville stopped grumbling and —moving more like a sloth than usual—rubbed his wiry silver muzzle against Bruin's chest until the two became thoroughly acquainted.

When he uncoiled his tail from my wrist and climbed onto Bruin, I held up my empty hands. "Okay. Stop the ride cause I'm getting off. How did you do that?"

"I'm good with animals."

Kobi snorted. "Sucks with people though. Can't do shit with anyone walking on two legs . . . well, unless he's naked."

The scowl Bruin threw at his Goth friend was interrupted when his phone rang. He barely spoke a word, but by the time he ended the call, he looked like he'd just been nailed in the gut with a Louisville Slugger.

"What?" Kobi asked.

"Lucas and Amy are dead," he said, the animalistic rasp of his bear distorting his words. "They were skinned."

Cowboy reeled. "Son of a bitch. What about the cubs?"

Bruin expression hardened. "I don't have any details. Cowboy, take Orville, Mika's things and the bag from her grandfather's and Flash to the Portal gate. Ask Galan to meet you and have Aust watch Orville until we get there."

"Where are we off to?" Kobi asked.

"African savannah." Bruin moved to hand off Orville who seemed determined not to go. As he grumbled, his tail wrapped tighter around Bruin's wrist. He peeled him off and shoved him at Cowboy. "Luke's place is on the southern tip of the Serengeti. Follow my vapor." He grabbed my hand and tugged me to his side.

"Wait." I straightened and pulled my hand free. "I'll go with Cowboy and Orville and check on my grandfather."

"Not an option. You're with me." He nodded to Cowboy. "Go."

Cowboy didn't even look my way before he disappeared.

"Hey. Don't dismiss me."

Bruin's hand tightened around my wrist and I knew he was about to Flash. I yanked my arm from his grip and came back full throttle at his face. He caught my fist mid-air and gave me a look so scathing I shrunk back. "You struck me once and I allowed it because you weren't aware of who or what I was. That is no longer the case."

Heat burned in my veins and I leaned closer. "Let. Go. Of. Me. If you honestly believe you can bully me into submission, you know nothing about me."

Bruin pulled back, his calm mask as intimidating as his fury. "If you think I'd let you out of my sight when jackals are clawing after you—leave my mate unprotected when you're the only thing I have ever been given by a world that has taken everything from me—you know nothing about *me*."

Well isn't this a party.

I dropped my gaze and looked around. My living room was trashed, my life in chaos, and Kobi and Savage were studiously ignoring our domestic disturbance. My cheeks flared hot. How had this happened? When had I lost the right of choice?

"I don't want this." I swiped at the traitorous tears falling down my cheeks. "I want you to leave. And I want my life back."

Bruin dragged rough fingers across his jaw. "Look, Mika, I've got a slaughter on my hands and need to focus. If not for me, accompany me so that I can help the surviving family of two very dear friends of mine."

I made the mistake of meeting his gaze. Something told me Bruin didn't ask for what he wanted. He demanded. He took. The fact that he asked for my cooperation, no matter how arbitrary, meant something.

He offered me a tired smile. "Please, you have no idea what our enemies are capable of."

I leaned against the back of the couch and studied the debris cluttered hardwood. "Then tell me. You need to go, I get that, but take two minutes and explain it so I understand. All you've done since this tattoo appeared on my palm is growl and boss me around. Maybe if you tried talking to me, we might get somewhere."

"All right." He crossed his arms over his chest and exhaled. "About thirty years ago an evil sorcerer named Abaddon started seducing the vilest of my realm to create an army. They're known as the Scourge and are malignant incarnate, death and hatred and rotting greed."

"So why do they want you dead?"

"Weres are the strongest race of our realm, by strength, by number, and by our sheer animal-based instincts to survive . . . but we're also aggressive and we fight, even amongst ourselves. We're proud, dominant and more often than not—hot-headed. When my father was elected King, it united all Weres against our enemies. Abaddon probably wanted that kind of force off the table before he made his big moves to take over the realm. He had my entire race slaughtered."

"And you believe Abaddon and these Scourge sent the jackals after us?"

He nodded. "Scourge would be very noticeable in the Modern Realm. They can glamour their appearance to blend in, but they can't mask their stench. Once they give themselves over to evil, their souls decay and they reek like fetid death that got sprayed by a skunk."

"Charming."

Bruin lifted my hand and brushed his thumb over my mark. "I don't know how they found you so quickly, but these men are monsters. They brutalized my sisters. They killed my entire species. As a cub I couldn't protect any of them, but I won't let them take you. Please don't fight me on this." He brushed my hair away from my face and cupped my jaw in his palm.

After a long, awkward silence, I set my hand in his. "All right. Let's go."

CHAPTER FIFTEEN

he effects of the Flash lessened the second time round. *By Flash fifty I should be good.*

While the last of the buzz cleared from my head, I looked around the living-room of the sprawling ranch bungalow. The front of the house, constructed entirely from glass, extended the length of the building and a portico extended out from there, shielding the interior from the blinding golden light of the African savannah. With grey slate floors and leather and chrome furnishings, the interior felt surprisingly cool.

Bruin sniffed the air and strode toward a sunken billiards area. "Where?" He demanded of the stalky, thickly muscled man staring out the window wall.

The man turned. His flowing mane of gold and russet hair reached half-way down his back. The bridge of his nose was wide and flat, and his eyes glowed a deep gold with what looked to be a natural Kohl guy-liner. "In there," he rumbled, tilting his head toward the hallway.

Savage Flashed in behind us and followed Bruin.

Kobi appeared in a burst of black smoke, grabbed hold of my elbow and escorted me down the two wide steps, past the pool table and to the man with the beautiful mane. When we stopped, he inclined his head. "Lion."

The two men met chest to chest, thumping backs briefly before stepping apart.

"Kobi, good of you to come." The lion man looked at me, his nose twitching almost imperceptibly. Taking a step closer he lifted my hand to his lips. "Welcome, beautiful lady. I'm sorry to meet under these—" His eyes flared wide as his lips touched my knuckles. Dropping my hand like a hot rock, he clasped his fist to his chest.

"Are you all right?" I asked.

His gaze remained glued to the slate tiles. "Ursa, my informality is unforgivable. I had no idea the Bear King had mated and found his Queen."

Well what do you say to that? "I . . . uh, that's all right. It's all been very recent."

The guy didn't move. I looked to Kobi who obviously had no intention of helping a girl out. *What the hell?* I stared at the Lion-man statue, fist clenched over his heart, eyes fixed on the floor. I swallowed, but my throat remained dry. "Man, I need a drink."

That did the trick. He almost broke into a run as he strode to the kitchen and opened the stainless steel Sub-Zero. "What can I offer you, milady: water, soda or spirits?"

"Water would be fine, thanks." He handed me a glass and I drained it without a breath. It was cold and deliciously wet. I set the glass on the granite counter and realized his gaze had returned to the floor.

Ah balls. "I'm sorry. I'm new to the Were world. Is there something I should be doing?"

He took a step back and cleared his throat. "It is customary for you to address me by my species before I make any direct contact with you, Ursa."

"Oh." I thought about what Kobi did when he walked into the room. I looked at him and tried to project some kind of regal formality. "Lion. Thank you for your kindness."

Amber eyes met mine and his clenched jaw lessened a little. "I am Sloan. It is a great pleasure to meet you, my Queen."

That was going to get old real fast. "Please. Call me Mika."

Sloan shook his head, looking appalled.

Whatever. I set my glass on the counter. "If you'll excuse me, I'd like to join Bruin."

Sloan lunged into my path. "Oh no, milady. What's been left in that bedroom is not for your eyes. Best you stay here until the Alpha returns."

"Thank you for your concern. I'll be fine." Patting his arm as I passed, I headed down the hall toward the angry rumblings of male voices and the smell of old blood. A buzzing sound made me pause outside the door. Flies. I steeled myself and entered.

Oh god. My throat thickened, and my gag reflex started flexing its will. The carcasses of two huge lions laid flayed to the muscle.

As Savage laid a sheet over the bodies, Bruin's fist flew and sunk into the wall. A shower of plaster bits pattered to the stone floor, his growing guttural roar exploding through the house. It vibrated in my chest and made my heart pound and my stomach sour. After the two dressers tumbled like dice across the room Bruin stormed out the patio door. Tipping his head back, he roared at the bluest sky I'd ever seen.

My heart ached for him. I'd discovered kill sites in my job . . . but these were his friends.

Savage pegged me with an obsidian glare, his hands balled in white knuckled fists, the veins in his neck so tight they looked like cables about to snap. It didn't matter that he was mute. His pledge of vengeance echoed in my ears. And I was intruding.

The hair on my nape stood on end. "I'm sorry. I'll wait in the living-room."

As I rejoined Kobi and Sloan, a wall of dust billowed up from the laneway at the front of the estate and then, settled as a Range Rover came to a stop.

Sloan slid the glass door open and we stepped outside. "The quads. They were staying with another pride. It will be difficult for them to understand. They are only cubs yet."

Stifling heat sucked the air from my chest. I pulled deep breaths, but my lungs wouldn't fill. Bruin rounded the corner of the house storming straight toward the driver of the vehicle. Low murmurings of their voices carried, but their words were lost.

After a long moment, Bruin opened the hatch of the SUV and waved me over.

Shielding my eyes from the blinding sun I stepped out from under the covered patio. I squinted and in an instant I wore a pair of dark tinted sunglasses. My footing faltered as I startled. Bruin's expression said everything was fine. Somehow, he'd used Were-magic to give them to me.

Ducking under the open hatch of the truck, I died a little. Four lion cubs the size of chubby house cats, roused in the air-conditioned luggage bed of the truck. Golden balls of stiff fur with bright blue eyes and tiny brown spots on heads and legs, yawned and *mrowlled* as they stretched awake.

"Mika, this is Corin, Dilan, Amra and Kiara." He pointed out each cub as he named them. Dilan trotted clumsily over and stretched his oversized front paws up to knead Bruin's chest. Bruin scooped him up, kissed the top of his head and scrubbed his ears.

I rubbed at the tightness in my chest. Their parents may have looked like lions, but like Bruin, they were people too. And these cubs wouldn't even remember who they were.

As each cub stirred awake, we took them from the truck. Bruin handed two of the boys to Kobi, I took the third and he cradled the sleepy little girl, Kiara, in the crook of his arm. Walking back to the shade of the portico I realized why the temperature of the house remained so cool. It tucked almost completely into the side of a rocky plateau.

"What happens now?" I asked, as we sat in the outdoor lounge.

Bruin stroked Kiara and she drifted back to sleep. "I've contacted the Felidae Prime. He lives on our mountain and will take the cubs for safety sake. Our entire mountain is protected as a sanctuary. They'll be well cared for while we determine what happened."

"What do you think happened?"

"I'm not sure. Sloan says there were rumours of poachers in the area, so Lucus and Amy sent the cubs to stay with another pride. When neither of them called to check on the cubs it set off alarm bells. When they didn't answer the phone or their messages, he came back."

"Do you think it was poachers?"

Bruin scrubbed his hand over the days of bristle covering his jaw. "No. Poachers would have been no danger to Lucas or Amy, only to the cubs. They won't be able to shift forms for another few weeks. Until then, they are defenseless."

"But you said they were skinned. Poachers—"

"—would have killed Lucas and Amy on the grounds somewhere. They were left in the house and their pelts are gone. No. This was someone who knows about Weres."

"Could it be Scourge?"

Bruin shrugged. "Scourge don't come to the Modern Realm. And Lucas and Amy would have picked up their putrid stench long before they got to the house."

"They smell that bad?"

Bruin arched a brow and nodded. "There are no unusual scents in the house. None. Not human, not Were, not Scourge. I can't figure it out. The bedroom is a fucking Saw movie slaughter house, but whoever pelted them didn't leave one clue. I've called in the dogs. Maybe they can find a scent to follow."

I sat up straighter. "Jackals?"

"No. A local pack of African wild dogs." Bruin's voice was neutral, but his expression made me wonder what else had gone wrong.

CHAPTER SIXTEEN

$\mathcal{A}$n hour later, Hugh, the Prime of the Lion species of Weres, and two of his sons left with the four cubs. The local pack arrived, and oversized painted dogs began sniffing through the house and the landscape in animal form. The pack leader, Trace, walked with Bruin and me, calling out commands and directing the two dozen dogs sniffing the grounds.

"It's a fucking waste," Trace said.

Bruin scuffed the toe of his boot through dry, rocky ground. "That it is."

As Trace's men searched the bushes and combed the courtyard, we walked through the out buildings and snooped through the two vehicles parked out front.

"I wish a breeze would pick up." I lifted my hair off my neck and prayed for a break in the oppressive heat.

"It's good that the air is still. Nothing to dilute the scents." Bruin handed me a hair elastic.

I tied my hair up and smiled at his magic trick. He was a handy guy on an outing.

Savage and several men from the lion pride carried out the bodies of Lucas and Amy and set them near a small mound of rocks at the side of the property.

"What are they doing?" I asked.

"The Were custom is for the bodies of our dead to be returned into the cycle of life. At dusk the local wildlife will come, and Luc and Amy will be assimilated back into the food chain." Bruin stretched out his shoulders and rolled his neck for the twentieth time. It didn't take a rocket scientist to see that he wasn't much for waiting around feeling powerless.

I slid a glance to Trace who stepped away to give us some space.

"Hey." I nudged Bruin's elbow and slid against his chest. He took my invitation and wrapped heavy arms around my shoulders. "I'm sorry about your friends."

He blew out a long gust of air. "It shouldn't be like this, Mika. Cubs deserve to know their parents and parents should get the chance to raise their cubs. Luc was so pumped about being a sire. It's all he talked about the entire time Amy was pregnant."

I pulled his stubbled cheek down for a kiss. "I'm sure they would be relieved to know that you're watching out for their cubs."

"Amy would kick my ass if I didn't." He lowered his face and nuzzled my neck. Every now and then Bruin's animal showed in the way he moved. Rooting his nose against my skin I felt his bear close. When he drew a deep breath the tension in his shoulders eased.

Relaxing into his embrace I let him hold me until his phone rang. "Yeah . . . No, we're still at Luc's." He shook his head and ran his fingers through his hair pulling his shaggy brown bangs off his face. "What do you mean missing? How long? Okay, I want a head count. Contact *every* pride, pack, colony and herd. I want *every* member accounted for—"

The hum of the voice on the other end had Bruin's anger and his volume ratcheting with each passing moment. He shook his head, a deep growl rumbling in his chest. "I don't care. *Every fucking member!*" He ended the call and cursed at the afternoon sky.

"What? What's happened?"

He turned to face me but waited until Trace joined us before he spoke. "A wolf pack is down, and nobody can get a hold of the Cougar Prime or any of his den."

"Impossible," Trace said. "Who could possibly get to so many of us at once?"

"I have no clue, but I intend to find out." Bruin laced my fingers with his and spun toward the house. The sensation of ants crawling up my neck made me flinch. I froze, pulling back on Bruin's arm. The instant he saw my face he stiffened and backed me against the door of the SUV. Nostrils flaring he leaned close. "What?"

"I'm not sure—"

The truck mirror beside my face shattered. A blinding heat exploded in my head as the world spun out of focus.

"Gun! I can't Flash. They've got a Pulse." Bruin wrapped himself around me. Another shot and glass pelted my shoulder and rained at my feet. Bruin pulled us to the front of the truck. *"There's a fucking gun on my mate. Find it."*

Trace tightened to my side, barking off commands. A second later, a living shield of men surrounded us. Someone pushed on my shoulders as I tried to rise.

"Stay low, Ursa."

"The shooter is in the rock formation above our position."

"Circle the house."

Bruin's arms stayed tight around me. We moved as a unit, running in a crouch, his growl rumbling in my chest as we swept toward the house. The moment we entered the bungalow, Cowboy and Savage pulled me from Bruin.

"Ursa secured," someone shouted, and Bruin was gone.

We moved through the house in a blur and I landed behind the granite island in the kitchen before I could blink. Half a dozen men took up sentinel while Cowboy crouched next to me and gripped my arms.

"Where's Bruin?" I breathed, dazed and dizzy.

Cowboy touched the button on his earpiece. "I've got audio. Let's see to your injuries."

A piercing whistle above the island brought my attention to

Savage as he passed a damp cloth and a white box down to Cowboy. With steady hands Cowboy worked a pair of long forceps and picked at the bits of glass lodged in my cheek. Piece by tiny, jagged piece.

Tilting me forward, he stared at my shoulder. "I need to take a look under the shirt."

I hated being fussed over, but let him slide my arm from my sleeve. He lifted my shirt off my back so he could get to my shoulder and continue harvesting. *Plink. Plink.* One after another, he dropped shards into a dish. When he wiped a swab dipped in antiseptic across my skin, I pushed him away.

"All right, *enough.*" I tried to get to my feet, but my legs wouldn't hold my weight. "Stop with me and go help Bruin."

"Mika look at me. *Mika!*" Cowboy pulled me back down and brought his fingers into my view. I was stunned to see how much blood covered them. "You have one doozy of a head lac I haven't cleaned. Bruin will tan my hide and cut off my balls if I don't tend to you before runnin' off. Now, sit still and let me do this."

My mind whirled while Cowboy fiddled with every ointment and bandage in his little kit of torture. "What's taking so long?"

A shot rang out.

Strong hands came down on my shoulders as someone knelt behind me. By the way his body curled around mine I knew whoever it was, he was a big one. In the reflection of the stainless-steel dishwasher I saw Savage. Ebony gaze met mine and he curled his lip into a snarl.

"Alpha has the shooter pinned," Cowboy said, pressing his finger to his earpiece. "Lions are in position. Wait. There's a second shooter."

Another shot. My body shuddered. Savage's grip tightened.

"Stay where you are, Mika," Cowboy said, unaffected by my struggle to get up.

"But Bruin . . . he's out there. We should help him."

Savage said nothing. Cowboy said nothing.

I listened, wishing I had the heightened senses of the Weres.

"First shooter down." Cowboy said, focused on what he heard through his comm. He waited. We all waited. The *tick tick tick* of the clock on the wall grated at my last nerve. "Second shooter down. Securing the premises."

More waiting. "Clear. Stand down. The Alpha's mate is to remain secure."

Cowboy lifted me to my feet, then steadied me when I listed. "Sav, grab her a drink."

I heard the sharp pop of the tab and felt the mist of cool bubbles tickle my face as a can of 7-Up appeared in front of me. I sipped at it trying to focus.

Things had gone from bad to worse today and one thought spiralled through my mind. Bruin could be hurt. I needed to see him. I set down my drink and launched myself through the sea of men surrounding me. Out the glass doors and into the scorching afternoon heat. Cowboy and Savage stayed right on my heels.

"Give him a minute. Uh . . . Mika, wait." Cowboy grabbed my arm and jolted me to a halt. "You're out of your depths here, female. Trust me. You need to give him a minute."

Why didn't they want me to see him? Was he hurt? Was he shot again?

My stomach lurched as I pushed forward, the urgency to see him overpowering. It was easy to figure out where to go. I passed two lions and half a dozen dogs coming down from the rocks at the side of the house. They stood aside and lowered their gazes as I passed.

Cowboy cursed. "Mika, give him a chance to clean up and calm down. He's a bonded male in a rage. He won't be able to—"

I spun, fists clenched. "I *will* see that he's all right. I don't care if he's dirty or bloody or in a fit of fury. If I am his mate, then I am also your Queen and you will respect my wishes and stop trying to keep me from him."

Cowboy broke into a broad smile and stepped to the side. "As you wish."

As I came to a little plateau near the rock formation, I heard the unmistakable huff and whine of a bear. Rounding the boulder, my breath caught. Bruin in bear form was more beautiful than I could describe. Unconscious in the cave he stunned me, but I had no sense of his strength or his majesty. Now, standing eye level in front of me, his massive heart-shaped face and golden eyes shook me to my very core.

"Bruin?"

He lumbered forward and pressed his forehead against my chest. I slid my fingers into his muzzle and scrubbed his cheek.

"Hey, big guy." I drank in his strength and size, trembling at how this powerful creature exuded Bruin's essence, yet felt different at the same time.

"It'll take him a minute to shift back." Cowboy shook his head, his voice laced with a trace of amusement. "When Weres are hurt or worked up we tend to retreat into our base selves. His animal instincts will be raw and close to the surface even after he shifts. You should come with us and leave him to himself. You don't know what you're dealing with here."

I shook my head. "I'll be fine."

I didn't watch them go. I nuzzled my face into the fur of Bruin's neck and breathed him in. He smelled good. Pressed against his sturdy frame my skin tingled when he shifted back into a man. A very naked, very aroused man.

He moved with predatory grace and primal sexuality. My feet lifted off the ground. My clothes shredded beneath clawed fingers. Bruin's eyes remained solid gold.

His animal instincts will be raw and close to the surface.

I'd seen the advancing stages of his bear before—in the parking garage while he fought—but this was different. Strong fingers knotted in my hair and I gasped as my head jerked up to look at him. His mouth seized mine, his tongue prying my lips apart and penetrating.

My pulse thrummed through my bloodstream and drummed in my heart.

This was Bruin at his most basic. Bear and man.

When he drew back, his lips curled. "They shot at you. Tried to take my mate from me."

"I'm not your mate—" Electricity crackled in the air.

Before I could qualify my words, he grabbed my shoulders, spun me around and forced me toward a tree. I cried out, shock and arousal warring in my mind. My palms splayed against the rough bark, steadying me against the trunk. "Bruin, what are you doing?"

"Tell me again you're not my mate." The masculine demand in his voice, held an edge that clenched in my womb. He gripped my hips and covered my back, his arousal trapped between us. His hand traced the curves of my chest as his lips brushed against my ear. "Deny me, Mika. *Do it.* It spikes my need to claim you, to cover you with my scent inside and out. It sends a powerful warning. Tells anyone stupid enough to come for you how they'll be facing."

What did I do? This man—this beast was not Bruin. But I did know him. My body knew him—his presence, his possession—and responded. Blood coursed through my veins as my nipples tensed into peaks and my core wept.

Bruin inhaled sharply. "Careful. The man may be patient, but the animal wants what's his. I'm so damned hard for you it hurts."

A shiver chilled my bare skin. Part of me wanted everything he promised. At the same time I was terrified of what it would mean to accept him. Two hundred and fifty pounds of sex and muscle tightened around me.

"I smell your need," he whispered, his words caressing my neck. "Even when you lie to us . . . I smell the truth. *Mate.*"

Yes. "No. It's sexual. I want you. The other stuff . . . me being the Queen, I—"

"Fuck the other stuff," Bruin growled, breathing hard. He bent me forward, holding me in place, running a hand up my back. I couldn't think with him working his tongue down the column of my neck.

Struggling to breathe, I hesitated. Should I protest? Of course I *should.* But I couldn't bring myself to make him stop. I didn't want him to. Rough palms took without invitation. His body, hard and muscled blanketed mine. My head fell forward as his hands travelled over my skin, working in downward strokes from my breast, down my belly, down until his fingers curled between my thighs. "I need inside you, Mika."

A cry slipped through my lips as my knees gave way.

Bruin caught my weight, holding me tight against him. His touch was undeniable. Pure, scalding pleasure. Bruin shifted his stance and filled me.

"You *are* mine," he growled, the guttural vibration baring no resemblance to Bruin's velvet timbre. His foot inside my ankle spread my legs wider as he adjusted behind me, thrusting deeper, driving harder. The clenching muscles of my sex tensed around him. His fingers stroked me, timing, pressure and his ability to read my body, all perfect. The building pressure of my release ratcheted nearer.

My nails dug at the mossy trunk, grasping for purchase to ride out this maelstrom. Bruin was a dominant man. His bear was downright aggressive.

A sharp scrape over my shoulder had my head turning. Bruin's canines had grown, and he gripped the sensitive skin above my collarbone. He bit, not enough to break the skin, but enough to send a message. *I am his.* His face grew tight, savage with lust as he held me captive between his teeth. Watching me watch him, he bit down. White daggers punctured my flesh with a pleasure-pain that scattered my mind. He moaned as his eyes rolled closed.

I'd never felt—never experienced—anything so wildly out of control. Rapture exploded inside me, surged through me, higher, harder. The cry of his name tore from my chest. I was wrong. This was more than sex. This man, this animal . . . possessed me.

He took my body and wanted my soul.

As my orgasm gripped and released, his hips rolled, building from hard and fast to frenetic. Bruin's breathing hitched and caught in short bursts. He thrust inside me, growling, taking, worshipping in a never-ending glide of bodies. Breathing hard and dizzy as hell, I thought the pleasure might destroy me.

With one final growl he pitched forward. Releasing his bite he snarled so loud the echo bounced off the rocks and trees around us. When he collapsed, his heart pounded like a war drum against the bare skin on my back.

It took a few minutes for him to come down from his release and then for him to lift his weight. My legs felt like rubber, my entire body shaking, and Bruin's scent roared in my nostrils. I sensed when the bear receded, and the man regained control. Gentle fingers stroked my shoulder, pausing over the sensitive tissue where he'd bitten me.

"Mika?" His voice fractured. "Oh, gods, what have I done?"

I tried to turn, but he held me in place.

"Don't." From behind me, he licked over the four pinpricks of blood from my shoulder and wiped the insides of my thighs. He flashed clothes on me and let my hair cascade down my back. "I . . . I'm sorry. Shit, Mika, I'm so, sorry. I never wanted to take your choice away. Gods, forgive me."

The warmth of his hands and the strength of his presence disappeared.

And I was mated.

CHAPTER SEVENTEEN

It took half an hour after Bruin disappeared, until Kobi Flashed me to the storage room of an antique store. It was one of the Gatehouses, I'd been told, and the location of one of two dozen ancient Silvers used as Portal Gates. We stood in front of the Silver—a full length mirror, the size of my living-room wall—and waited for it to allow us access to a fantasy realm of Elves, Weres and Faeries. The Realm of the Fair.

I exhaled, no longer sure what was real.

Blinking back the sting burning behind my eyes, I quashed the memory of my sexplosion with Bruin on that plateau. *What happened?* Somehow my protestation had sealed the deal on my mating status. *I never wanted to take your choice away. Forgive me.*

Now I was mated and Bruin was AWOL.

His warrior brothers could downplay Bruin's absence all they wanted, but from what I gathered, no male just up and left his mate. Ever.

"Bet you wish you never went to Spankz that night, don't you?" Kobi asked.

Like I'd answer that. I ran a finger across the dark lead surface of the mirror and touched the heavy gold-gilded frame. "How does it work? I mean, where is your world in relation to say . . . Vancouver?"

Kobi nodded to the beefy guy hovering over the electronics panel. "The Realm of the Fair has pocketed areas of land on each of the continents. Hidden by magic, these areas offer a world which has remained essentially unchanged for millennia—Elves and Weres, witches and wizards, Centaurs and Sprights. When *Mundanes*—that's you—reach the borders of our realm, you are transported across to the opposite side in such a seamless motion you remain as clueless as ever."

"Does anyone in the modern realm know about yours?"

"Sure. We have Haven safe houses in all the major cities. There are also people of our world who choose to live in the Modern Realm over the Realm of the Fair."

"Why?"

He shrugged. "Anonymity. It's easier to come by in a world that doesn't know shit." Kobi's acerbic personality didn't fool me. The guy had lived through something bad, something that made him want to keep people at arm's reach.

"Why didn't Bruin and I go to a safe house when he was hurt? Because I'm human?"

"No. We have lots of humans. I'd guess it was more that you're not from our world. Bruin probably worried you'd be considered an exposure threat and he was too injured to protect you."

"Exposure threat? And if I was, what would happen?"

"Well, because your memories are traumatic, they can't be erased clean, so Savage, Cowboy or another Talon enforcer would have to put you down."

"Kill me?"

He shrugged. "It deters people from taking ads out in the local papers or in your case . . . writing an expose. But when the Enforcer killed you, Bruin would kill him. The Talon would then rank him as a threat and since we outnumber him, he'd be killed. Bad scene all the way around."

Allrighty. That explained Bruin's reaction when he found out I was a journalist. "Kobi, can you try Bruin's phone again."

The coldness in his charcoal eyes knotted my gut. Hell, it was bad enough that I had to come down from the plateau and face Bruin's men alone. Now I had to go to his home without him. What would Jade and Galan think? And the purple-eyed pixie would despise me even more for losing her brother. Layers of questions and intersections of reality pitched and whirled in my head like an out of control helicopter.

Kobi slipped his phone into his leather trench and shook his head. "Still turned off."

I stared at the mirror. How was I supposed to absorb any of this? I felt like Alice except I'd been mule-kicked down the rabbit hole and dragged around Wonderland by my hair. Give me a goddamn cookie so I can eat it and have my life back.

I swiped my cheek and my reflection followed suit. It seemed like a normal, old mirror, but after a few more cleansing breaths, its glassy depths rippled to life. Silver ribbons of light danced from the edges into and across the dark surface. The reflection strobed into the room in a blinding blue-white lightshow.

When the whole surface rippled, Kobi gripped my bicep and pulled us through the mirror. I expected to feel it, feel something as I crossed the threshold. After all, I was moving from one world to another. It was neither hot nor cold; there was no resistance, nor static in the air. It was like walking through an open doorway.

As we reached the other side, Kobi knuckle-bumped a striking black guy wearing khaki's and a navy Polo shirt. He didn't exude the same dominant, intimidating aggression that the other men did. Instead, he gave off a confident charisma. He was actually a very fit, clean-cut, and attractive guy.

"Hey Julian. Have you heard anything from your bro on this side?"

"Yeah. He stormed through in an absolute bitch, scowled, growled and Flashed without a word. I'd guess he took his bike out. What's up his ass, anyway?"

Kobi shrugged. "Mating madness or some shit. Oh, that reminds me, this is Bruin's lucky other half. Julian, this is Mika—Mika, this is Julian, Bruin's brother."

I kept my opinion about my mating status to myself. So far, by clarifying my point, I'd alienated Bruin's friends, gotten myself rutted by a territorial bear and lost all chance at choosing my future. "Nice to meet you."

Julian stood up from the desk and extended a hand. "Welcome to the family. We're dysfunctional at best, lethal at worst, but there's never a dull moment."

"And you're his brother?" The furthest thing from Bruin and his sisters I could have imagined, Julian was lean and preppy with intelligent, mint green eyes.

"I know, the resemblance is freaky, isn't it?" He chuckled and offered me a genuine smile. "We call ourselves the Shitstorm Survivors. I'm the runt of our litter. I leave the warrior stuff to Bruin and the girls."

Kobi shook his head. "That's bullshit. Julian is the brain of this entire realm and more dangerous with a stroke of a keyboard than any one of us with a dagger."

"Flattery will get you everywhere, my friend." Julian chuckled, winked and blew Kobi a kiss. "I love you man . . . deep, deep, man love."

Kobi rubbed the platinum ring piercing his eyebrow with his middle finger.

As they continued, I looked around. This Gatehouse was far more high-tech than the one we'd come from. On the charcoal wall across from Julian's console hung six full-definition, wraparound screens running DebianOS.

Seriously wicked. "Is that the new AMD Phenom?"

Julian's eyebrow shot up. "Actually, it has duel Intel i7 980 quad cores with 48 gig."

"Oh man. What have you got in the back?"

Julian's smirk widened. "Oh, sister-mine, don't tease. Have I finally been blessed with another techno-geek to talk to?"

"No. I'm a wannabe at best, but I'd give my right arm for a setup like this. Geez, it must have cost, what, sixty large?"

Julian snorted. "Eighty, but don't tell anyone. I'm a very creative bookkeeper."

Somewhere beyond the room a door opened and melodic male voices drifted up the hall. "We're in here, boys," Julian called out and resumed his seat.

Galan glided gracefully around the corner, accompanied by another Elf and a silver wolf with ebony points. I stiffened the moment the wolf stalked closer. No one else paid any attention. I dropped my gaze and let her study me without meeting her eye to eye.

Galan and his friend shared the same lithe build, but instead of Galan's poker-straight silver hair, his friend had waves of gold flowing behind his shoulders. He wore the same fitted suede pants and ivory tunic as Galan, but strangely, he also donned a pair of darkly mirrored Ray-Bans and a black embroidered choker around his throat.

"Merry meet, Mika." Galan glided over and kissed my cheek. Yep. Still smelled great. He brushed gentle fingers over my blood matted hair and winced. "We heard about the attack in Africa. Blessed be, you are safe."

"Thank you."

Galan held out his arm and waved his friend closer. "Mika, this is Aust, my Highborne brother and the male who cared for your animal friend since he arrived."

"Really? Oh, thanks. Did he behave for you?"

"Yes. He is fed and rests in your chamber." Aust massaged his fingers through the wolf's ruff, and then, after Galan tipped his head in encouragement, he stepped up and offered his hand. "Merry meet, Mika. Welcome to Haven."

"Thank you." I covered his hand with mine and held it until he raised his gaze. Something about him spoke to me, had my senses tingling. "Would you mind taking off your sunglasses?"

His grip stiffened as a nervous energy built in the air between us.

Galan placed a hand on his friend's shoulder. "Aust, the two of you will become fast friends. I am certain of it. The bond you both share for the natural world and your love of wildlife is remarkably similar. Trust me, brother mine."

Aust seemed to gather himself and then turned toward me. "Most find my eyes unsettling. Apologies." He slid the glasses off his face, folded the arms, and with an agonizing hesitation raised his gaze.

I gasped and moved closer. Stunning. Black pupils pierced ice-blue pools outlined the same black Kohl that the lions had. Cat's eyes— except not the eyes of a lion. Aust had the cool-blue eyes of a white tiger. "They're beautiful."

Aust's jaw relaxed and the pain in his expression lessened. "Gratitude . . . I uh, I am honored by your praise."

"Aust, mayhap you and Faolan would guide Mika this evening. Introduce her to the wolves and get her settled in the room adjacent to Bruin's." Galan waited for Aust to nod and then turned his charm on me. "Your things have been placed in your room and your grandfather is staying directly across the hall from you."

"How is he?"

Galan chuckled. "The male has taken to this world with the vitality of a sapling. He is Castian's guest for dinner this evening, but I would expect he will return before too much longer. I confess, we did not mention today's shooting to him. Jade thought it best that he not fret over you when everything had been resolved."

"Thank you. He worries about me as it is. He'd be frantic if he knew I was almost shot."

"Oh, that reminds me, Mika." Kobi flicked his fingers and lit a cigarette with the flame that burst from thumb. The overhead light glinted off his rings as he inhaled and drew the thing to life. "You have to check that gun you confiscated into a locker. Reign doesn't allow firearms on Haven grounds. He says we are weapons enough by nature without corrupting our Realm."

Julian walked around his desk, punched a code into a keypad and slid open a panel on the wall. I'd never been a fan of guns, and actually, when I took it out of my purse and handed it over, I breathed a little easier. Because of that gun, I had taken a life. Grandfather's words whispered in my head.

"The power is in the path."

When Hulk's Colt was emptied and tucked away in one of the steel cubbies, he closed the locker, twisted the key and handed it to me. "Safe and sound until your next adventure."

I shook my head. "You keep it."

The silver wolf trotted around to Aust's heel and whined.

"She's ready to go, I take it?"

Aust bowed his head looking sheepish. "Apologies, Faolan has yet to learn patience."

Faolan's head dropped and her ebony ears folded back.

I fought not to laugh. "That's okay, girl, being impatient is part of a female's charm."

Golden eyes flashed from beneath frost tipped fur as Faolan's nose twitched and sniffed me up and down and in every private nook. Before I knew it, I was shielding myself from a barrage of sloppy kisses.

"Faolan, enough." Aust offered me a handkerchief and once I'd wiped my face, he held his elbow out to me in an old-fashioned gesture of forgotten chivalry. "If you are ready, I would be honored to escort you."

Crossing a cobblestone courtyard, Aust walked the two of us through the warm August night toward the main house. *House* was a laughable understatement; the place was a castle.

"Good lord," I muttered looking up at the massive stone and iron structure. "And I worried about there not being enough room."

Aust's grin grew into a genuine smile. "In truth, Castian would love nothing better than to have Jade and Galan live in the Palace of the Fae with him, but Jade won't hear of it. She refuses to leave this mountain even for her father."

"Her father? I thought Reign was her father."

"Verily he is as well. At the age of seven, Maximus Reign adopted her. He was the director of the Talon and governed Haven. Castian is her sire separate by circumstance, and though he involved himself in her life, Jade only recently learned of her true paternity."

"So she has two powerful fathers?"

"Correct."

I imagined what that would be like as we took a meandering side path away from the main house and made our way beside a long, stone wall, toward the surrounding forest. Golden light from intermittent lanterns pooled in overlapping circles, lighting our path.

Aust seemed content to let me set the pace. "The original castle is beyond this stand of forest. It is larger than Jade's home and houses an academy for those with affinities. I shall take you there tomorrow if you like."

When I nodded, he lifted a low hanging branch and guided us toward a recessed section of the wall. When we reached an iron gate, he laid his hand flat on a small scanner. When the latch clicked, he led the way in and closed the gate behind us. "Castian wanted something more private for Jade and so created a home for her and her family."

I gazed up at the sprawling stone manse and shook my head. "That's some wedding gift."

Aust stopped walking and clasped his hands behind his back. "Mika, the last thing I want is to frighten you, but it is important that I introduce you to the wolf packs which patrol and secure Jade's private grounds. Once they have your scent they will know you belong here and we will avoid any unpleasant attacks."

I laughed. "Sure, let's avoid an unpleasant attack. That's a great idea."

Aust walked us further into the forested grounds and stopped. "Are you ready? I shall have them come in twos, so you do not find yourself overwhelmed."

Staring off into the darkness of the forest Aust's expression changed. He looked as though he was concentrating on something far away. His hand rose slightly, then he waved his fingers toward us.

When the underbrush rustled, I focused on the shifting darkness before us.

Dozens of golden eyes reflected the lantern light of our trail. Faolan stood to her full height at Aust's flank, ebony tail wagging, while the darkness came alive and wolves approached in an orderly procession.

My mouth dropped open. "Are you communicating with them?"

He dipped his chin, looking wary. "It is the affinity given to me by the Shalana, Goddess of the Woodlands."

"That's the coolest thing I've ever heard. Do you actually speak to them? How does it work?" Distracted by our conversation, I almost forgot about the dozens of wolves sniffing me.

"Imagine it as a series of images and instincts entering your mind. I feel how they see things and I, in turn, am able to think my impressions into their minds as well."

Goosebumps rose on my skin. "That is so much cooler than my gift."

Aust's hair blew in the night breeze as his pale gaze met mine. "What is your ability?"

"It's not as impressive as mind-melding with animals." I was still numb over that one. "My grandfather is a wind-talker and I inherited a bit of that from him. Sometimes I hear things spoken on the breeze, or get feelings from nature, a person's energy whether it's good or bad, truths and lies, warnings of danger, I can sense disturbances in nature and energy."

Aust's jaw fell slack. "Is it the Goddess herself who speaks to you on the breeze?"

"I don't know. I suppose it could be. My people call her the Earth Mother."

"What a fabulous honor."

The velvet reverence in his voice made me realize that I'd never really given myself over to the marvel of it. "Grandfather says there's more that I've never embraced. He hates that I live in the city. He thinks if I surround myself with nature, my affinity will bloom."

The last of the wolves trotted back into the forest and we were left alone. Faolan gave a low whine and brushed against Aust's thigh. "Very well, girl, enjoy your evening."

With Aust's blessing, Faolan barrelled after the other wolves and melted into the night.

As we resumed our walk, the serenity of the moment almost eclipsed the tightness in my chest. Aust covered my hand where it rested in the crook of his elbow. It felt perfectly right. Aust and I seemed to connect on a spiritual level. It wasn't attraction, it was . . . belonging.

"Mika? May I ask you a personal question?"

"Sure. What is it?"

"I smell your confusion and your heartache. How may I aid you?"

I squeezed his hand. "Do you know anything about Were mating?"

He searched my expression and his smile faltered. "Apologies, nothing . . . but mayhap I know someone who does. I have a friend—"

"That's all right." I looked up at Jade's house and my stomach growled long and low. "I think I'm done for tonight. Would you help me find a snack before showing me to my room?"

"I would be delighted."

CHAPTER EIGHTEEN

*S*howered, fed and wearing my yoga pants and Hedley t-shirt, I laid sideways across the queen size bed. My suite was lovely, a small loveseat and club chair by a fireplace, an antique table with two ladder-back chairs and a third tucked under the desk against the bathroom wall. The rich plum of the velvet drapes accented the periwinkle blue walls and was repeated in the bedding and accessories. A ten-foot ceiling rose high over the dark, silky hardwood floor and two pale blue area rugs differentiated the space, one laying under the bed and the other under the sitting area.

I snuggled Orville and wondered if I'd be able to get to sleep. My head spun. My palm burned. And far too much had happened today to just drift off. Orville wasn't afflicted with the same difficulty. His wiry grey fur rose and fell in a lazy rhythm. Down for the count.

My binturong didn't seem to notice the upheaval in our lives, but I still couldn't find anyone who knew where Bruin was. If I were in Vancouver, Meg, Paige and I could track down almost any lead. Stuck here at Haven . . . I didn't even know where to begin.

Where are you Bruin? Damn. My heart actually fluttered when I thought of him.

Sometimes I was such a girl.

His words haunted me. *I never wanted to take your choice away. Forgive me.* I was mated to a Were-bear king. What did that mean? He wasn't in control, granted, but damn him. He did this, then *poofed* off and left me to deal with it.

Muffled voices across the hall had me scurrying over the silky hardwood and out my door. I met him and Jade in the hall as he was retiring into his suite.

"Grandfather, you're back." I closed the distance and wrapped my arms around him. Grandfather's hugs had an almost magical effect on me. My safe place after my mom died. My calm harbour when life's seas were seething. There wasn't the same force or strength behind them like when I was a child, but they still enveloped me in the same sense of security as they always had. "How was your dinner? Are you all right? It's late. Are you tired?"

He pulled back from our embrace and frowned. "I am fine. What happened here, Rabbit?"

I probed the cuts and scratches on the side of my face and shrugged. "A little trouble this afternoon, but I was well taken care of. Don't worry. Tell me about your evening."

Grandfather kissed my sore cheek and smiled. "Tomorrow. I have much to tell but am too tired to even begin to put it to words. If you two beauties will excuse me, I'd like to turn in."

I kissed him back and nodded. "Sweet dreams."

The click of his bedroom door left me standing in the hall with Jade.

Looking at her, I was struck dumb yet again. Knowing that she was at least half goddess made her otherworldly quality easier to comprehend. Standing in the hallway wearing worn jeans, a loose cashmere sweater and bare feet she exuded more beauty than any runway model I'd ever seen. More so, because she had a bit of weight to fill out her curves.

"I'm glad you're still awake. May I come in for a moment and talk?"

I scrubbed my face with my palms and gestured to the door. "Sure. Come on in."

Inside my suite her expression grew deeply troubled. Something bad was coming.

"What?" I asked. "Has something happened to Bruin?"

"Yes . . . and no." Emerald eyes locked on me and a strange energy vibrated in the air. It prickled on my skin and squeezed my eardrums. It was the same invasive sensation I'd felt in the cave, but it was worse now. Stronger. I squirmed and pushed back. Jade was doing this.

She was scanning me somehow. Probing.

I clasped my hands over my ears and stepped away. "*Stop that.* What the hell do you think you're doing?"

Jade looked at me with a mixture of shock and incredulity. "You felt that?"

I nodded, thankful the throbbing had ceased. "I have a few gifts of my own. Now, why don't you tell me why you're really here because obviously it wasn't to check on me."

Jade stood, hands open. "Mika, I'm sorry. I had no idea reading your emotions would bother you. It's never affected anyone that way before. I'm worried about Bruin and trying to figure out what is going on."

"Have you heard from him?"

She moistened her lips. "He called an hour ago and asked how you were. I said I hadn't seen you and he made me promise I would check on you."

"How did he sound?"

"Like shit actually. What the hell happened between you two?"

I turned toward the small sitting area and began to pace. Could I trust her with what happened? Would she answer my questions if I told her? Was it my place to tell her anything about Bruin's private business? God, I wished I could call my girls for advice.

"Mika?" Jade eased onto the loveseat, folded one leg beneath her and patted the second cushion. "I really would like to help. Bruin and I have no secrets. You can trust me."

I opened my mouth. Closed it. Opened it again.

She sighed. "I am truly sorry I tried to read your emotions. I had no idea it would make you uncomfortable and honestly, I wasn't thinking."

"Of me," I said, more curtly than I intended. "You were thinking of Bruin."

"I won't argue that. Bruin is one of the most important people in my life. I was thinking that something is terribly wrong with him and you're involved."

"I'm not the enemy. I'm the one trying to hold on by my fingertips until the ride comes to a complete stop."

A grim smile spread across her face and her eyes brightened with sympathetic warmth. "I know exactly how that feels. It sucks that things got away from the two of you. One thing you can be glad about is that you're bonded to Bruin. You won't find a better man in either realm."

How could I explain so it made sense to her when it didn't even make sense to me? Everything in my head and heart had churned into one giant mash of mixed emotions. "There are moments—incendiary moments—when his touch on my skin, or the tone of his voice saying my name, or a look he gives me, makes the world disappear. In those moments, I wonder what Bruin and I could be together."

"But then . . . ?"

"But then something happens and the fun, sexy man disappears. He becomes this growling, overbearing brute who thinks he's the boss of me. He acts like I'm his property. He's controlling and dismissive and when I refuse to bow down, he just gets more aggressive."

Jade patted my arm. "You're not his property. You're *not*. But try to understand—you are *his*." When I made to argue she held up her hand. "Bruin's bear—his animal-self—has claimed you. When I healed him yesterday, every cell in his body burned with it. To his bear, you are *his*. You belong to him."

"No. I'm *not* and I *don't*. Nothing is settled."

Jade took a moment and waved her palm over the three votive candles sitting on the little coffee table in front of us. As her hand swept through the air, the wicks burst to life. Apparently, Blaze being her call-sign wasn't just about her fiery red hair. She caught my surprise and smiled.

"Being a Were isn't like being a human with extra senses and strength. It's a constant balance between two entities sharing the same space—the man's soul and the animal's instinct. As a dominant, Bruin's bear is as strong as they come and its primary instinct is to protect. Protect you . . . his mate. Even as Bruin struggles to give you time and space, his bear fights to never let you come to harm."

"So, where's *my* choice?" The traitorous burn of unwelcome tears returned.

Jade handed me a tissue. "Aside from the physical changes, bonding brings mood swings and emotional extremes. I know you're confused, but it will continue to build until you claim him, compelling you to accept your destiny."

"What if I don't want this destiny? I had my own plans. What if I want my life back?"

"Bonding is tough for those who grow up with it, but for a Mundie —" Jade blushed as her words cut off. "Sorry. For a human from the Modern Realm, I imagine it's horribly upsetting."

I sighed. "Start with upsetting, then add two different attacks where people shoot at me, my house being trashed and being forced to move to a fantasy world because I'm mated to a man I just met . . . and he turns into a bear . . . and I'm supposed to start popping out bear cubs to save a species on the brink of extinction."

No stopping the tears this time. They rolled in abandon, down my cheeks and dripped onto my shirt. I tasted the salt as a few made it to the corner of my mouth. My head fell loose on my shoulders and I cried until my breathing hitched in sobs and I started to snot.

Jade handed me the whole box of tissues this time. She rubbed my hand and let me fall apart. After a time, I'm not sure how long, a warm soothing sensation moved up my arm and over my skin. My grief eased, the throbbing of my skull and the ringing in my ears replaced by an odd contentment. I looked up.

Jade shrugged. "I'm a healer, remember?"

I scrubbed a hand across my forehead and sighed again. "God, I need a drink. Do you have a liquor store or something around here?" The clock on the mantel said 3:00 am.

Man, could it really be that late?

"I'll ask Nash to stop by in the morning and find out what you'd like."

"Nash?"

"Yes. You'll see an Inuit kid walking the halls with a tribal tattoo encircling his left eye and earrings pierced all up his ears. He's your man. Toiletries, clothes, arrangements, finding someone, avoiding someone, sharpening weapons, anything. He's a bit of a mischievous pain in the ass, but he's the best squire we could ask for. He's a fifth-year wizardry student and he's yours to call on if you need anything."

"Huh. I've never had a beck-and-call-boy before."

"Well you do now." Jade chuckled, her long graceful fingers settling on the silver flower pendant she wore. With delicate silver ribbons wrapped and woven around the stem and teardrop blue-black stones for petals, it was stunning. She noticed me studying it and smiled. "It was a mating gift from Galan. It belonged to his ancestral grand-mother, Castian's half-sister, the exiled Queen Rheagan. An ominous source, but I love it."

"It's beautiful."

Her smile faded as she wiped her brow. She swayed a little then straightened.

"Jade, are you all right?"

"I must be coming down with something. My whole system is off." She waved away my concern and took my hands in hers. "Mika, may I ask you a personal question? I swear I'm not being nosy, but why did you say you were *mated* to a man you just met?"

"That's obvious isn't it?"

She flipped my hand up and studied my palm. "You haven't mated. You've only been branded. What gave you the idea you had?"

I tried to shake the *hubba-wha* from my head while I processed that one. "Well, other than the fact that I don't understand any of it, this afternoon, after the Scourge or whoever tried to assassinate me were contained, Bruin and I . . . I mean—" My cheeks flamed.

"You had sex with Bruin?"

I nodded. "Afterward, he was so upset. He said he was sorry, he never should have taken away my choice and he'd never forgive himself."

Jade frowned and brushed her curls out of her face. "That doesn't make sense. He couldn't mate you without consent. You have to recite a ritual while pressing your mark against his. Did he hold your brands together while you made love?"

My blush deepened as I remember being pinned up against that tree. "Uh . . . no."

"Then what choice did he—" Her eyes grew wide. "Mika, what happened? I know this may be wicked TMI, but it's important. Start at the beginning."

I tried to piece it together, breathing through the ache in my chest. "After the snipers were taken out, Bruin was agitated. Cowboy said he needed to stay in bear form when he's upset."

Jade's gaze remained sharp. "And it was probably worse with his bonding hormones raging and you hurt."

"Well, when he changed back, he was . . . well he was naked and—"

"Ready for you?"

"Right. He said something about not wanting to lose his mate. And when I said I wasn't his mate, his bear got really pissed. He sort of tried to . . . prove me wrong. Physically. It wasn't that I wasn't into it, I totally was. He was just rough and very . . . possessive."

Jade cursed and I understood. He hadn't apologized for mating me at all. "He thinks he raped me? He *didn't*. I was shaken, yes, but I didn't fight him. I never told him to stop. I consented. He wasn't in control."

"No, he wasn't. Bonding stress is volatile, especially with a dominant creature like an Alpha bear. Mika, I have to track him down. You don't understand what this will do to him. With his past—" She shook her head and let the words fall. "He would never take advantage of a woman and if that's what he thinks happened, he will be devastated."

"How will you get in touch with him? His phone is off."

Jade smiled and brushed her hand down my shoulder. "I can reach him."

I followed Jade to the door. "Please tell him I'm not angry. Well I am, but for a million other reasons. Tell him to come back. I don't care what time it is. Tell him I need him here."

CHAPTER NINETEEN

$\mathcal{I}$ woke the next morning afraid to open my eyes. Yesterday had been a disaster, and if today was meant to repeat it, I'd rather play sloth and lay around all day moping. I pulled the covers over my head and hid from the world. Every now and then the dull thud of men in boots trudging heel-toe down the hall stirred me from the depths of exhaustion.

In the end, Orville's raspy snore from the end of the bed teased me from my sleep.

"Orville. What time is it?" I yawned and lifted my quilted shield enough to look at the alarm clock. "Shit buddy, it's almost ten-thirty. Why didn't you wake me up?" Orville grumbled and stretched but didn't rouse. "If you peed on Jade's beautiful bed, I am *so* going to smack you."

I breathed in. Lilacs. "What the—"

The whole suite was filled with vases. Lilacs. Pink ones, mauve ones, deep purple ones and white. "Orville, wake up. A florist shop exploded, and we've been hit by floral fire."

A deep resonant chuckle sounded from the chair in the corner. *Bruin.*

I flew off the bed and across the room before he had a chance to stand. A moment before I jumped into his lap, I skidded to a halt and regained my senses. My fist hit hard and fast, a good one square in the chest. "You asshole. Don't you ever disappear on me again. I didn't know what happened. I spent the whole day thinking I'd been mated, and you were so repulsed you couldn't even look at me."

He stood in a surge. Man, he really was a big boy.

And beautiful—those wide muscled shoulders looming over me, the deep rumble of his voice. My skin prickled in awakening, my nipples tweaked, and my breath caught. Jade said the pull of the Bonding Brand would grow and it was far worse this morning . . . and him looking all apologetic and wounded wasn't helping.

Get a grip. I swallowed. "When you said you took my choice away, I thought you meant we were mated. Then you *poofed* off and I was left crying like an idiot surrounded by warriors who hate my guts." I punched him again but didn't put much into it. "Not cool."

His leaned down and pressed his lips against my forehead. "I'm sorry. My bear, my animal side, has basic impulses. Food, fight, fuck. He doesn't reason, he feels, he acts. It's worse when the moon is close to full and with the bonding raging through me—"

I squeezed his shoulder aware that just yesterday there had been a bullet hole where my fingers pressed. "You and I have two different takes on what went down on that plateau. It was consensual—at least on my side."

He barked a harsh laugh and crossed his arms over his chest. "No, it wasn't."

"Yes, it was."

He shook his head.

I nodded and grabbed his jaw. "Hey. Could you not try to be the boss of me for one minute and listen? The sex was off the hook, true, rougher than I'm used to, but I didn't complain. The thing that upset me was being trapped in a marriage I hadn't agreed to. And you regretting it so much you abandoned me to deal with it."

Bruin's lips tilted with gentle sensuality. "How could I regret mating you? I know *you* don't think so but being branded to you is a miracle. Every female of my species is dead. I never thought I could have a mate."

Those turquoise eyes were too damned hypnotic as he pulled me against his chest. He cleared his throat, but his voice remained husky. "I want this, Mika. And after the way I handled you yesterday, I figured you'd want nothing to do with me."

I glanced around at all the vases of lilacs and stepped away. "I told you before, I'm not that fragile. I decide things for myself. Where'd you bugger off to anyway?"

"I rode my bike 'till I hit the end of the world. When I couldn't go any further, I turned around and headed back."

"Did Jade tell you I wasn't mad?"

He nodded. "I drove like a demon to get back to you."

"You could have *poofed* and saved us both a night of worry."

"Yeah, but I had my bike and still needed to sort out my head."

His heavy-lidded stare had my stomach tightening. Whatever it was between us expanded inside me every time I looked at him. "Mika, I would never force myself on you. It's these damned mating hormones. They're making me crazy."

"I get that, and just so we're clear, Cowboy warned me to back off until you regained control. I didn't. I pushed. The hunger of your bear had me undone. I *am*, however, royally pissed about a few dozen other things, so you better suck it up until I get a handle on what's going on. I'm sick of losing my shit every ten minutes and I need answers."

Bruin's mouth turned up at the corners. *Sexy bastard.*

I glared and continued. "And if you ever *bite* me again, bear or man, you'd better be ready to be bitten back. I don't mind a little kink, but that hurt."

I ran my fingers over the scabs on my collarbone.

Bruin's fingers met mine as he traced the four puncture marks. "I'm trying to control the bonding urges, honestly, but every time you deny I'm your mate, it cuts me to my marrow. I ache with a need to claim you. And even more, to have you claim me. The extra adrenaline and aggression from the attempt on you knocked me for a header."

The pain in his timbre broke my heart. "I don't want to hurt you. Honestly. But at least you understand what us being branded is about. I'd never heard of it. Never wanted it."

He turned and strode to the window. "What about having a family?"

"Why do we have to talk family? I've only known you a few days. Can't we slow things down a little? It's overwhelming."

"What's so overwhelming about how you feel about family?"

I crossed my arms and exhaled. "Well, family didn't work out so well for me. It's not really part of my plan. Men are supposed to be kept at arm's length. Career over marriage. I enjoy working late, sleeping late and sneaking around in people's secrets."

Bruin scrubbed his palm over his cleanly shaven jaw. "You're so focused on what you think you'll give up if you accept me. What about what this could *add* to our lives?"

My face got hot with that one. "Don't say *our* lives because I have nothing to do with it."

"Excuse me?"

"Everywhere I go someone is congratulating me or bowing to me because I'm the new Were Queen. No one cares who *I* am. I'm just a warm body for the Alpha to knock up. A vessel to save your species."

"That's not fair."

"No? Do you consider *me* your miracle or is it that you have a chance to plant your seed and procreate? Any womb would do." The stricken look on his face made me want to stop, but my frustrations of the past few days were escaping faster than I could stop them. "Like you said, feed, fight and fuck, right?"

Bruin's sharp intake of breath broke my fervour. He turned and with long strides ate the distance from my suite to the adjoining door to his. "I'm more than my animal, Mika. What a shame you think so little of the man."

Shit. I launched after him and got to the door just as it was about to slam in my face. "Bruin, wait. Can we back up? *Bruin.*" He turned, and I sighed. "Sorry. I've never been a relationship person and I suck at it. I didn't mean to lash out. I just need to catch my breath."

After a long moment, Bruin exhaled. "Okay. You catch your breath and I'll check in with some of the Weres about missing members. Maybe we can meet up in a few hours and grab a late lunch?"

I nodded. "That sounds good."

An hour later I had showered, dressed and was just pulling my hair back in a ponytail when someone in the hall knocked on my door.

"Good morning," Aust said, holding a small breakfast tray. "Bruin came to the kitchen and asked my mother to send some nourishment for you. I volunteered to bring it up. I hope I am not intruding."

"Not at all." I opened the door wide and he glided in with his wolf at his heels. He set the tray down at the little table and I took a look at the spread.

Though I was generally a bagel and coffee girl, after smelling the egg and pepper casserole thingy Elora prepared, I scooped up the little ceramic dish and settled into one of the two chairs. "Wow, your mom's a talented lady. This is delicious."

Aust nodded, his smile sad. "She is a marvel. Having so many mouths to feed keeps her very . . . occupied. Which is good. But I worry for her." Aust went on to explain briefly that his father had recently passed Behind the Veil and that Elora was grieving in the only way she knew how—losing herself in the needs of others. When Aust finished his story, Faolan laid her head on his lap and whined.

I could feel the depths of their sadness, but only time and distraction would ease their mourning. I knew that first hand. "Hey, how about we go stretch our legs? Last night, I believe you made me an offer to show me the castle."

Aust bowed his head and stood and Faolan bounded for the door, tail wagging. I put my dirty dishes back onto the tray and Aust collected the tray and followed me into the hall and toward the grand staircase.

It was nearly noon by this time and with the sun straight overhead, a kaleidoscope of light streamed from the stained-glass ceiling positioned above the great foyer. I stopped at the balustrade at the top of the stairs and cast an upward glance. There was an intricate depiction of a battle between a man and some sort of ugly Orc guy. If I wasn't mistaken the man bleeding violet blood into the soil was Castian.

Movement three stories below caught our attention as we began our decent.

"Is that Nash?" I asked Aust as a young man with a tribal tattoo and a mohawk jogged across the foyer and retrieved a football from beside the front door.

Aust nodded and Faolan ran down ahead of us.

When the wolf reached the bottom, Nash looked up at us and smiled. "Hey Aust. Good morning, Mika. Welcome to Haven."

How the hell does everyone know who I am? We continued to wind our way down the steps, passing the landing for the second floor. "Thank you . . . Nash, right?"

He nodded and crossed his arm in front of his belly for a bow. Cowboy barrelled out of nowhere and linebacker-tackled him backward into the lounge. The two of them slammed onto the carpet in a tangle of arms and legs, grunts and curses.

Nash coughed, laughing as he swore. "Can you say personal foul, Wolf?"

"Nobody dropped a flag."

The two continued grappling at the ball, one liners and insults filling the foyer.

I stood, watching them wrestle while Aust stepped away to dispose of the tray of dishes.

"Your stomach is growling again, Mika," Aust said right beside me.

I pressed my hand over my rapidly thrumming heart. I hadn't even noticed him return. "Aren't you a quiet one?"

He chuckled and turned me toward the double doors. That's when a poem mounted on the wall of the foyer caught my attention. "What's this?"

"A prophesy made a few months ago about the Scourge uprising. No one seems to agree on the meaning, but there is no shortage of theories." Once I had read it through a second time, I let him lead me out onto the front porch of Jade's mansion.

CHAPTER TWENTY

Standing outside the Hearthstone tavern I wasn't sure what to think. It was the kind of place you'd expect bikers to frequent, leathered-up men with chains wrapped around their fists and barmaids named Candy. In my world, off the rails was fine, bring it—Spankz, after all, was a favorite haunt of mine—but in this world . . . I just didn't have my bearings.

Faolan whined at Aust's side and rubbed against his leg.

"I'm with you girl. I'm not so sure either."

Aust knelt on one knee and kissed Faolan's muzzle. "She wishes to run with the wolves. She said nothing about eating at the Hearthstone." The wolf's head turned, her gaze locked on the rooftop of a building down the clearing. He nodded and patted her side, then gestured to the forest. "Enjoy yourself, girl. I shall meet you back here when you return."

Faolan bounded off to the tree line, her tail up and wagging.

"This world is unbelievable. I'm still not so sure about your choice of restaurants."

"It was Bruin who said for us to meet here for a mid-day repast. Besides, where is your sense of adventure, *neelan*? Lexi once told me the Hearthstone is like fungus on a rock . . . it grows on you."

"That is so not encouraging, Aust."

Aust arched a golden brow and tugged me toward the entrance. "Fash not, Mika, the food is delicious, and I shall protect you."

"I'm counting on that."

He laughed and reached for the handle of the oversized wooden door. "The tavern is owned and run by the Were-Lion Prime, Hugh, his foster daughter Bree, and his six sons. They are a landmark on this mountain and command a great deal of local respect."

"Oh, I met Hugh yesterday. He and two of his sons took custody of the orphaned cubs."

"Yes. I aided Bree with the cubs this morning. They are too young to shift, but they seem to understand me when I speak to them. I tried to ease some of their confusion."

"Do you think they'll be safe here?"

He took a moment to consider my question. "Verily, from what I have seen, nobody crosses Hugh or his cubs."

"Weres are a protective bunch, eh?"

Aust smiled. "They would tear anyone to shreds if they even considered making a move on those cubs. I heard, a few years past, a drunken traveller got overly flirtatious with Bree while she served him. Hugh snapped both his wrists without blinking."

My mouth dropped open. "Is that normal behaviour?"

Aust's ice-blue gaze fixed on me. "Yes. Were males are dangerous when it comes to protecting their family and more so when protecting their females. From what I understand that aggression becomes lethal when there is a mating involved."

He heaved open the door and escorted us in. As the door bumped closed behind us, I paused, waiting for my eyes to adjust. It smelled like the midway at a country fair crossed with sweaty dance club. *Yum.*

One of the lion cubs from yesterday sat between the double set of doors. With his arms crossed over his chest, his t-shirt struggled to cover the heavily banded bulges of his biceps. When he met my gaze, he tapped the side of his headset and nodded. "Afternoon, Ursa."

I stiffened but tried to return what I hoped was a regal look. "Afternoon, Lion. Please, call me Mika. You are . . . Liam, right?"

"Aye, I'm impressed. Most cannae tell one of us from the others. Good on ya, Ursa." He tipped his head and sniffed the air around us.

"Liam!"

Liam dropped his gaze as Hugh stormed from inside the tavern and glared at his son. "S'cuse the bairn, Mika. Yer scent is none of his concern, but he's a cub yet."

My scent? Really? Did I smell that different?

Liam reeled. "I'm no cub, Da. Dinnae we three turn twenty-one months ago?"

"Aye, I remember, but it seems just this spring past the three of ye were throwing mud-balls at each other and making the lassies scream."

Liam's cheeks flushed, and his dimples showed.

"That *was* this spring past, Da." A petite brunette came to meet us and patted Liam's belly. Tiny as she was standing next to the lion, I got the sense she could hold her own. When she settled in with the group, she dropped her gaze and bowed. "Afternoon, Ursa. I'm Bree. What a blessing our Alpha found you. Congratulations."

Bree kept her eyes lowered and didn't straighten. She was a Were, obviously . . . but not a lion, I could tell that much. Dark to their fair, short to their towering height, athletic to their strapping builds, and she didn't have the dark eyeliner look around her eyes like the lions did. What the hell was the protocol for finding out?

My cheeks burned as my empty stomach churned. "Forgive me, Bree, I realize I'm supposed to address your species, but I don't know what that is. I'm likely the worst Ursa in the history of Weres and I apologize."

Hugh stepped over to his daughter and laid two massive, scarred hands on her shoulders. "Nothing to forgive, Mika. You huvnae been born with the nose to tell who's standing before ye. And your bonding's so recent you huvnae learned it yet neither. Bree here, is a coyote."

"Well then, it's good to meet you, Coyote."

Bree straightened, smiled at Aust and flattened her apron against her jeans. "Would the two of you like a table?"

I nodded, and as Bree began to guide us to our table, I leaned close to the brooding lion cub. "Don't worry about it, Liam. I've been known to let loose and fling a bit of mud myself ocasion. You should see my truck after a warrior weekend."

Liam looked skeptical but smiled.

As Aust tucked my chair beneath me, Bree set menus down on the table. "Are you here to check on the cubs, Ursa?"

Aust picked up his menu, but never took his eyes of the coyote. "First, we shall nourish Mika, then we shall check on them. Are they upstairs or out back?"

"In the yard." Bree tilted her head toward a hall leading to the back of the building. When a whistle sounded from the corner, Bree excused herself and hustled off.

I had to remind myself yet again that I had fallen down the rabbit hole. The tavern looked like your average rough and tumble road-house. Booths along the back and side walls framed a wooden dance floor and stage, while pool tables sprawled across a mezzanine situated over the long bar with the usual tin signs displaying the meads and spirits the bar stocked. What made my heart thunder were the patrons.

A woman with glowing peach skin and sapphire eyes sat opposite a table of . . . what I could only guess were Centaur's standing around a highboy near the back, clopping their hooves to the music. There was also a tiny winged couple one-foot-tall kneeling on the table across from us, sharing a plate of something that looked like nothing I wanted in my mouth.

"Sprights," Aust said as he followed my gaze. "Those are Lightning Sprights, the largest species of their race."

What do you say to that? Nothing came to mind.

Aust didn't seem to notice my lack of focus, or if he did, he was gentleman enough not to mention it. He pointed to the stage. "It looks like the house band, Thunder Roar, is setting up for tonight. The band is made up of Hugh's three older cubs, plus Nash, and Bruin's brother Julian. Julian said the band is gaining quite a following on campus."

"Actually," Bree said, laughing as she set down two glasses of water with lemon. "He said the band might one day rival the Highbornes for groupies. Aust is just too modest to quote him."

Aust sat back in his chair and ducked his head. "Mayhap, my brothers attract that kind of notoriety, *neelan*, but not I."

Bree laughed again. "Please. Why do ye think yer nature expeditions and wildlife workshops are filled to capacity? Do ye really think that many women are interested in honing tracking skills? You and Tham are the only Highborne bachelors on campus. Yer a hot commodity, Aust. There's even a website."

I held back laughing as Aust's ears blushed right up to the tips but couldn't let that go. "Really? What's the site name, I'll have to check it out."

Bree licked her finger then made a sizzle noise as she touched Aust's shoulder. "HighbourneHotties.Fair."

After we teased Aust a little more, Bree left to put in our order. Aust watched her until the kitchen doors closed. When he caught me watching him, his ears flush pink. Again.

I patted his hand on the table. "She's adorable, Aust—"

Wooden chairs scraped the floor and I turned toward the door, the nape of my neck prickling. Three men wearing black fatigues strode inside and stalked straight toward our table. The tavern's social hum fell silent.

The leader, a tall, olive-skinned man with slicked, black hair and even blacker eyes offered me a seductive smile that had my senses reeling worse than ever. His smooth gate gave off the illusion of nonchalance, but his body language, and the way he assessed the room, said different. The closer he got, the stronger my urge to run grew.

The two brutes backing him up were—oh, god. The stench of fetid death hit me like a wall. My mind stumbled on the rotting features, the reek of the air, the unnatural energy—Scourge.

Aust drew a long knife from his belt, pulled me out of my chair and behind him.

Before I caught my breath, Bruin appeared in front of us both. He didn't step in front of us. He Flashed. The muscles of his arms and shoulders flexed as he clenched his fingers into fists. "That's close enough. Back the fuck off, asshole. And leash your mutants while you're at it."

The Scourge soldiers curled their lips and bared jagged teeth. A chill shot down my spine.

The leader moved to sidestep Bruin, but found his path blocked. His ebony gaze glittered with coy amusement. "I simply want to meet the new Ursa, Bruin. Won't you introduce us?"

I shook my head, his voice echoing in my mind. There was something *waaay* wrong with this guy. The cadence and tone of his voice seemed charming on the surface, but there was an edge to it. Magic maybe? Whatever it was, it felt invasive and I knew enough to fight it.

Bruin rolled on the balls of his feet and shook his head too. "Who the fuck are you?"

The sadistic current of the guy's laughter made my skin crawl. Bruin's too, judging by the way his body stiffened in front of me.

"Well, that's a blow to my ego," the guy crooned. "Welcome into the mix, *Miss Silverbrook.*"

The air crackled as a rumble tore from Bruin's chest. He seemed to grow larger . . . or maybe the room shrank around us. "You need to leave . . . I want you . . . gone, asshole."

The man crossed his arms over his chest and grinned as if something Bruin said amused him. The nauseating tingle on my skin ratcheted and when he spoke this time, I was thankful my stomach was empty. "Haven is a sanctuary, Alpha. A safe zone. My associates and I were merely passing through and heard the blessed news. We *are* welcome, aren't we Alpha?"

Claws grew out of Bruin's fingertips, long, hooked daggers that could tear a throat out in one swipe. I felt the rush of aggression as his bear surfaced, but something wasn't right. Bruin shook his head again and then fell still. "Of course," he said stiffly. "All are welcome at Haven."

The words were spoken as if dragged out of him and the man's grin grew. "Better. Now tell me, how is your mating progressing?"

Bruin growled. "Mika refuses me. She doesn't understand our world."

"Bruin, wha—?"

The man made a *tsk-tsk* noise as he waggled a finger. "Imagine. One chance to revive your heritage and reclaim your life and she doesn't even want you. That has to sting."

"Stop this." I stepped out from behind Bruin and grabbed his jaw. Neither he nor his bear were tracking. Aust was vacant too. I scanned the tavern. Whatever was happening had body-snatched everyone in the room. "Whatever you're doing to them, *stop it* and get out."

The two Scourge stepped closer, but the leader raised a hand and focused on me. "Relax, Miss Silverbrook, relax."

Did he really expect me to obey? Yeah, fat chance. Whatever coercion he was using didn't seem to work on me. It just made me want to throw up on him.

He took a step closer and Bruin growled.

"Hush, Bear," he commanded, and Bruin fell silent.

Earth Spirits, please help me. Not knowing anything about the magic in this realm, I had no idea how to protect myself from falling prey to this man's evil. But if he could ensnare a creature as strong and willful as Bruin, I needed help. Earth Mother responded immediately.

My perception shifted. Calm washed through me as my vision focused and the sounds of the world grew quiet. And as my connection to nature strengthened, I saw the sickly, puce strings of magic stretching from the man's throat, ensnaring Bruin, Aust and the other Weres. Long, strands wove a web of dark control, connecting everyone in the tavern.

Either he didn't notice or didn't care that I hadn't fallen under his spell. He only had eyes for Bruin. "What a shame, Alpha, to find your mate only to have her killed. Mundies being so fragile and all. Same terms you were offered a decade ago—a ring for a life. Do you have it or know where to find it?"

A violent rage rumbled from Bruin and vibrated in my chest. "No."

"Pity, then I guess you have some serious searching to do, Alpha. You understand what's at stake, yes? What will happen the next time we meet if you haven't got what I want?"

"Yes," Bruin said.

And with that, the three men walked out and were gone.

CHAPTER TWENTY-ONE

I slumped down in my chair as the hum and chatter of the Hearthstone resumed. A range of emotions surged through Bruin, his bear so lethally wound I wondered if he'd have to shift to work off his mood. In the end, he sank into the chair across from me, his hands clenched into white-knuckled fists, his eyes glowing amber.

"Are you all right," I asked.

When his claws receded, he used a napkin to wipe the blood from his fingertips and closed his eyes. "No. What happened?"

"You don't remember?"

He shook his head and winced as if his skull was splitting wide open. "It's there, impressions, a voice, my Bear raging inside me . . . but no. It's a violent, frustrating fog."

"Aust? What about you?"

Aust pulled his golden waves back and secured his hair with a leather band. "Apologies, *neelan*, I remember drawing my weapon . . . but I am unsure why. I am afraid my memory is no clearer than Bruin's. Do *you* remember what occurred?"

I recounted everything that happened from the moment the chairs scraped the floor until the three intruders strode out. Neither of them remembered any of it. Aust excused himself to speak with Hugh and Bree came over with a tray of drinks.

Bruin accepted the beer she handed him and downed it without pausing for breath. Then he pulled out his phone and held it to his ear. "Julian, something's happened."

After relaying my account to his brother, Bruin hung up. "I'm sorry. Whatever happened to me, I couldn't fight it. You were left you to defend yourself again. I'm sorry."

I shook my head. "Who was that?"

"I honestly don't know." But by the clench of his jaw I knew he had an idea. Fine. If he didn't want to speculate, I could let it drop. For now. He scrubbed rough fingers through his hair and grumbled. "No one should be able to do that. To make me obey a command like a cub."

After seeing how Bruin fought and how the other warriors treated him with both fear and respect, I believed the Were-King stood at the top of the food chain of this realm. And if not at the very top, then at least a long way up. Despite the bewilderment and fury bleeding from his pores, I had a feeling almost anyone would have fallen victim to that level of evil.

So why not me?

"What did he mean by . . . a ring for a life?" I asked.

Bruin scowled. "When my family was killed . . . when the Scourge came . . . father and I had been away. He'd Flashed me around the world and introduced me to the Primes of each species. We'd been gone over a week when he felt the first member of our sleuth die."

"Felt it?"

"Yeah, as the Bear Prime, his life source connected with the lives of all other Bears. When the slaughter began, he knew at once."

"But you're the Were-King, why didn't you feel when your friends were killed?"

His chair creaked in protest as he leaned back. "Lucas and Amy were Lion, not Bear. It's a Prime thing, not a King thing. Besides, I never assumed my role as the King."

"Why not? If you—"

Bruin rubbed his hand over his eyes and exhaled. "Mika, please, no questions. Let me get this out."

Shit. As a journalist I knew when to let someone talk, but my nerves had gotten the better of me and there was so much about this I didn't understand. "Okay, sorry. Go on."

He didn't look at me. As he spoke, he stared blankly across the tavern. "So, at the time of the attack, my father left me behind. It took me two days to find another Were and get him to Flash me to our den. When I got there, everyone was dead, but a raid party remained. They'd ransacked our lives and demanded Father's ring. Apparently, he didn't have it on him when they killed him, and they figured he'd given it to me before returning to defend the sleuth."

"Did he?"

He scrubbed his palm over his jaw. "No. He never took that ring off. Ever. The Scourge left me alive and told me to find the ring. Said that one day we'd try this again."

"Why would they want it? Is it magical?"

Bruin rapped his fingers against the wooden table and shrugged. "Not that I know of. I always thought it was symbolic of the Weres' commitment to unite under their King. I never understood why anyone would want it so bad."

"Never a dull moment." Bree placed my lunch and Aust's on the table. Smiling as she flipped the page of her crumpled notepad, she reached to the bottom of her apron from one corner to the other. Not finding what she was looking for she patted her pockets, then reached behind her ear and found her pen. "What can I get ye, Alpha?"

He looked over at me sinking in to my banquet burger and a little of the tension drained from his face. "Another dark ale, a salmon-burger with fries and a side plate of rings."

"Oh, this is fabulous." I wiped a gob of sauce off my mouth as Aust joined us. When my stomach growled, I dipped a fry and popped it into my mouth. "But I don't think it's going to be enough. All of a sudden, I am starving."

Bruin smiled for the first time in ages. "Bree is here with her wee pad and pen. Tell her what else you'd like."

My stomach growled again at having the carte blanche. "Can we get an order of the feta bruschetta . . . oh and everything nachos with extra jalapeños."

Bruin chuckled and raised a brow.

"Oh, and could we get a dessert menu to look at while we're eating, please."

Bruin's grin widened to full out delight.

After lunch, Bruin and I followed Aust down the back hall of the Hearthstone. Letting Aust go out ahead of us, Bruin stopped just inside the back door. "Hey, remember this morning when you asked if we could back things up a bit? Well, I was thinking that after I finish up a few things, maybe later this afternoon we could lock ourselves in my suite and have a movie marathon. You know, just relax and escape from the world for a few hours."

"And hide me away from the wacko creepy man and his goons?"

Bruin shrugged looking unrepentant. "Two birds. One stone. Besides, Julian will figure things out whether or not we're hovering over him. Besides, it could still be nice."

I nodded. "It sounds heavenly, actually, but I'll warn you, I don't like head-chopping movies or anything where things pop out at you."

"What about chick-flicks?" He scrubbed his hand over his jaw, but it didn't hide the blotches of scarlet bursting onto his cheeks.

"Are you saying you have some back in your room?"

Bruin scanned the hall and I couldn't tell if he was thinking or stalling. He stretched his neck from side to side, then just when I was about to give up, he nodded. "I . . . uh, have been known to OD on fudge-crackle ice cream and get sappy."

I forced a straight face. "You're lying."

Thankfully, he was the one to bust loose with a grin first. "Nope. For reals."

I gave up the fight and laughed. "Prove it. Gimme your top five."

He leaned back and counted them off on his fingers. "In the

cabinet below my wall-mounted plasma, behind the Star Trek box set, I have all my top picks. Pride and Prejudice is hands down number one. Some argue the older versions are better, but it's Kiera Knightley all the way for me. P.S. I Love You is a close second—I mean, please, getting letters of love from beyond the grave—How can you not mist up? Breakfast at Tiffanies, for sure. Then it's a toss-up between Dirty Dancing, It's Complicated and/or anything with Hugh Grant or Sandra Bullock."

"Wow, that's quite a list. No testosterone in sight. I never would have guessed."

He shrugged. "I can't explain it. I'll be totally myself, working out in the gym, just back from clubbing with the boys, or getting shredded in a battle, when suddenly I get hit with this overwhelming urge. It's bizarre. I used to fight it, but it's no use. Now I look at it as keeping in touch with my softer side."

"Well, your secret is safe with me—"

The *clop-clop* down the hall made me jump—a Centaur headed for the washroom. For the briefest moment I wondered how that would work.

"Is it a date?" Bruin asked, breaking that bizarre train of thought. "We'll forget what happened here for a few hours and spend some quiet time with a bowl of popcorn."

"Extra butter?"

"Anything you want."

"Sounds good. Thank you."

Bruin's smile fell short. "We can try to slow things down, Mika, but that's not exactly how bonding works. The sexual hunger, volatility and possessiveness between us will continue to grow until we claim each other."

"Hasn't anyone ever chosen *not* to be Mated?"

Bruin winced. "Finding your perfect other half is a gift, no matter how inconvenient you find it. If you try to remember that, I'll try to hold off my base instincts and give you space—but I warn you, your denial only makes my desire more intense."

I swallowed. "Like what happened on the plateau in Africa?"

Bruin pressed me gently against the wall as he reached for the push-bar of the back door. "My bear is a powerful part of me, Mika, and he wants you. *All* of you."

Bruin stepped out the back door of the Hearthstone and blocked the doorway until he'd surveyed the area and drawn in a couple deep, lung-filling breaths. I ogled him as he scanned the meadow and forest beyond. The way his black t-shirt molded to his lats. How his ripped jeans cupped heavily muscled legs and thighs. My palm stung, burning for his touch.

He canted his head and brushed back his hair.

"Do you hear something?"

He smiled back at me, dominance and possession glowing gold in his gaze. "Just making sure your new friends aren't hiding in a bush somewhere. S'all good."

We stepped into the mid-day sun. Bruin held my hand as we headed to a penned play area and the sting abated. Wild grass and sun-burnt weeds brushed my shins as we tromped on.

An old wooden jungle gym, a kiddie-pool and two sunning rocks sat behind a five-foot fibreglass fence scratched to the point of opacity. Even though the play area had seen better days, the cubs climbed, tumbled and splashed over every inch without objection. I eyed the two flat boulders basking in full sun and wondered when I had last paid tribute to the sun myself.

Faolan bared her teeth as a cub bit her bushy ebony tail and the other cubs barrelled over to nip her paws. The quads didn't seem intimidated by the wolf's annoyance. In fact, they quite happily used both her and Aust as extensions of their climbing equipment.

After fiddling with the latch for the gate, I let myself in to the circus ring. Before I could blink, they rushed Bruin's legs and shimmied up his worn, fitted jeans. I sidestepped the attack and joined Aust, bumping his shoulder as I settled cross-legged beside him.

"I don't think I properly thanked you for last night," I said.

Bruin glanced over, propped on all fours tussling with two of the male cubs while the other two rode his back and chewed his hair.

"Well, that's not what a man wants to hear his betrothed say to another man."

I threw him a droll stare. "Aust took me into the forest to meet the wolves."

"So . . . a moonlit stroll. Oh, please, go on." The corners of his mouth lifted.

I kept a straight face. "Then, he took me to the kitchen and his mom, Elora, stuffed me full of the best banana chocolate chip pancakes I've ever tasted."

"A meal and he introduced you to his parental unit. This sounds serious."

I chuckled. "Then he showed me to my suite and we said good night."

"Ah, the old love 'em and leave'em wanting more routine. Very effective, Aust. I've used it myself dozens of times."

I raised a brow. "Dozens of times? Do you really want to bring up past encounters, because I have a few stories that would make you—"

Bruin coughed and shook his head. "Absolutely not. For both our sakes and the safety of the men involved, I invoke a don't-ask-don't-tell clause in our relationship."

He scooped up Kiara and nuzzled her face against his. She was smaller than her brothers and her paws were noticeably less clunky, but she had more sass and knew how to use it. Bruin blew a long raspberry against her belly and laughed as she flailed and squirmed, growled and spat, trying to right herself.

Bruin set her down and laughed as she tackled one of her brothers. "As much as I love playtime, we have to head back to the house. Before we can lock ourselves away for our movie date, Lexi has Iadon doing last-minute tailoring for the big wedding. She's threatened pain of death if I bail. In fact, she's probably already tapping her designer boots wondering where the hell I am. Are you ready to roll out?"

Um, not in a million. "Can I pass? Lexi isn't a member of my fan club and I don't want a catty scene to take away from Jade's celebration. You go. I'll meet you."

Bruin straightened and looked into the trees. After a moment he nodded. "Okay. I shouldn't be more than an hour. Should I meet you back here?"

I turned to Aust. "Would you mind company for a bit?"

"Not at all, but might I make a change in your plan? Jade and Galan are to be out of the house while the wedding arrangements are underway. I am scheduled to meet them for a gathering of wildflowers and roots. We are attempting to mix some new remedies for Lia."

Bruin met my gaze, his vibrant turquoise stare flooded with sadness. "Galan's younger sister was kidnapped by the Scourge a few months back. They thought to use her somehow to release Castian's bat-shit sister, Rheagan from exile. We're not sure what they did to her, but she's been suffering from panic attacks and debilitating headaches ever since."

Aust brushed himself off and put on his Ray-Ban's. "Verily, Mika is welcome to accompany me, but we would be returning to the house closer to late-afternoon."

Bruin's clenching jaw made me smile. I could feel him fighting his bear for the control to nod his head. And after what just happened in the tavern I couldn't blame— "Be careful, 'kay?"

My mouth fell open.

Aust nodded. "We shall."

One of the male cubs leapt from the rock and clung halfway up Aust's back. Latched on, he shimmied higher and gnawed on Aust's wavy golden hair. Wrapping both hands around the cub's fuzzy chest I eased the speckled menace away.

"Aey . . . watch the claws, *neelan*, they are as sharp tipped as their teeth."

Bruin growled and lent a hand. The sound of the Alpha's rumble had the cub going limp and submissive. He gave him a firm pat on the nose and set him down to run off again.

Bruin lifted me off the ground and kissed me. When he pulled back, my heart was pounding. He affected me more than he should. I tightened my fingers in his hair and pulled him closer. Vaguely, I pitied poor Aust being subjected to our PDA, but I couldn't stop myself from sliding my tongue into Bruin's mouth and practically climbing up his body.

Bruin's low growl vibrated inside me. After another sweep of my tongue, he eased from my grasp. "I thought we were slowing things down?"

"Slipped my mind." I closed my eyes, imagining the two of us getting good and naked. Yesterday had been primal in Africa, but at the Stanley Suites Bruin had taken his time and been very thorough. My hands traced his muscled curves, broad and strong. My skin warmed to his touch, ached—

Bruin's nostrils flared, and his eyes widened. He moaned and set me back on my feet. "I gotta go or there won't be any stopping me. Be safe, baby."

He kissed my forehead before jogging off toward the main house and leaving me cursing everything I'd said about taking things slow.

CHAPTER TWENTY-TWO

$\mathcal{A}$fter twenty minutes wrestling with the four furry fiends, my shredded arms looked like I'd taken on a Ginsu ninja and lost —miserably. I ran my fingers over the worst of the damage as the back door of the restaurant swung open and Bree hurried out.

Aust put down a cub, adjusted his sunglasses and rose to greet her.

"You are officially off duty, guys. Sorry, we got hit with a late lunch rush. How are our tireless little monsters this afternoon?" she asked, scooping up Kiara.

"Behaving like the predators they are." Aust's head cocked slightly as his nostrils flared. "Are you well, *neelan?*"

Bree's expression became wistful and when Aust's eyebrow arched above the rim of his glasses, she sighed. "Damn, I forget you High-bornes can scent things almost as well as Weres. Fine. I've got a wee problem, but I'll figure it out."

"Could I be of aid?"

"Sweet, but it isna you who needs to step up." Aust said nothing, waiting until Bree set Kiara loose on the other cubs and brushed her palms against her jeans. "Well, ye know how I go to University in the Modern Realm three nights a week? I have a lab due tonight for my bio-chem class and nobody can watch the cubs. Da insists on escorting me to class, Rhys, Bram and Caelan will be on stage and we still need to cover the door, the bar and the floor. So, I'm stuck watching the cubs. If one of my brothers in the band would—"

"Faolan and I shall watch the cubs."

Bree shook her head. "I can't, Aust. You've been here for hours today already. Surely you have other things ye'd rather do?"

"It would be my honor to aid you. When shall I return?"

She bit her bottom lip and then sighed. "Is 5:30 all right? I'll help ye feed them and then I'll have just enough time to Flash to the portal gate and make it to class."

"I look forward to it."

Bree bounded forward, hugged Aust and kissed his cheek. "Gods, you are the sweetest, male. I owe you. Now, get out of here for a while and at least enjoy part of yer day."

As we made our way into the cool shelter of the trees, Aust's ears flushed all the way to their gentle Elven points. He caught me watching him and smiled. "Come, *neelan*. Jade and Galan will be waiting."

He fell into an easy jog and I followed, thankful for the view. Bonded or not, no warm-blooded woman could watch Aust in motion and not become one of the Highborne groupies. He ran with the grace of a deer in the wood, but even better was how he looked in tight suede pants. I'd bet if Bree saw him like this, she'd be on him like a coyote on a hare.

We left the main cobblestone walk and continued deeper into the forest on a well-worn path. Aust whistled a bird call and further up, his call was answered. We slowed to a walk.

"There you are," Jade said, as we rounded a wide rock. Damn, Jade could wear a burlap sack and other women would still take a hit to their self-esteem. Even with her hair pulled back in a ponytail and wearing a simple halter top and cargo pants she'd stop traffic. "*Mika*, I'm glad you're joining our little Lewis and Clark expedition. Look who else is here."

Galan stepped out from behind a stand of trees with Grandfather, chuckling and nodding about something one of them had said. I had to stare. Grandfather stood straighter and walked steadier than he had in the past decade. "How goes the chase, Rabbit?"

I kissed his cheek and answered as I always had. "It goes, Grandfather, fast and frenzied."

"Merry meet, sir." Aust extended his arm and Grandfather clasped his forearm the way the Elves greeted. "Gratitude for joining us."

"My pleasure son and please, call me Grandfather or Hawk."

"Are we ready?" Jade bent to pick up her backpack and pitched to the side.

Galan and Aust both moved with blurring speed. Galan caught her elbow and steadied her against his chest. Taking the backpack from her hand, he handed it to Aust. "Blossom, are you well? Thrice today your balance faltered."

With the gentlest of touches, Jade cupped his smooth jaw. "I'm fine, probably just an ear infection or something coming on."

"Can you heal that with your powers?" I asked.

She shook her head. "No. My healing affinity works on injuries, unnatural traumas and complications from those two things. I'm powerless against germs, aging and disease just like everyone else. Speaking of healing . . . were you the latest lion cub chew toy?"

I extended my arms and nodded when she asked to heal them. Two minutes later, I marveled at my perfect skin. "Thanks, Jade. And thanks for speaking to Bruin last night and bringing him home."

"My pleasure."

The men tromped off ahead of us, Galan with his bow strung and his quiver slung, Aust with Faolan bounding by his side and Grandfather plodding along with a walking stick in hand.

"I think they're giving us space for girl-talk." Jade chuckled. "How was Bruin this morning?"

I thought about the lilacs and how good his arms felt around me when I woke up. He'd been so hurt to think his bear had taken advantage of me. Then I'd twisted the knife by insulting him and his motivations. "This morning wasn't our best event, but we patched things up a bit."

"I'm glad." Jade stepped off the path and chopped the heads from a tall purple plant with silver leaves. She sealed the cuttings in a plastic container and pocketed her pruners. "I wish I could convince you this bonding is a wonderful thing."

I moaned. "Please don't. I don't think I can stand any more enthusiasm about me being the new Were Queen."

"Getting a lot of congratulations, are you?"

I frowned. "It's like it's a *fait accompli*. I'm Bruin's other half, his Queen. What I want has nothing to do with it."

Jade set the pace up the path, which turned out to be only slightly faster than standing still. I picked up a stick and tore off strips of bark.

"What *do* you want?"

I shrugged. "I know what I don't want—I don't want to be a brood mare popping out a bunch of cubs, no matter how important it is to Were-Bear survival. I don't want to give up my work or stop exposing the scum of my world when they hurt wildlife. I don't want a man who thinks he controls my future just because we slept together. And I really can't stomach the idea of being put up on a shelf for safe-keeping because he's worried I might get hurt."

"*Worried?*" Jade's voice rang of incredulity. "Worried doesn't begin to cover it. Bruin and his bear are out of their mind." She saw I was about to say something and pulled us to a stop. "Has he spoken with you about the slaughter of his sleuth?"

I tossed the stick into a patch of bracken. "He said everyone was killed when the Scourge raided their den and a raiding party was waiting for him and wanted his father's signet ring."

"And?"

"And what?"

Jade crossed her arms over her chest. "There's more to it, and if you knew the whole story, you'd understand him better."

"Then enlighten me."

She pursed her lips. "It's not my story to tell. Talk to Bruin."

"That's one of our problems. Either he doesn't trust me or he's protecting me, but whichever it is, I'm in the dark here. I don't under-stand any of this."

I lifted my gaze and scanned the trees a full 360 degrees. The tingle raising the hair on my arms wasn't danger, but I'd felt it outside the Hearthstone too.

"Jade. I know I'm not your favorite person and Lexi wants to slit my throat, but I really do care for him. We're not a perfect couple, but there are moments when I think we could be great together. We're just strangers that want different things. I want a productive, independent life and Bruin wants a woman who will follow his lead and smile while doing it. I can't live under someone's control like that."

"It's not about control."

I snorted. "Please, he's so Alpha it's ridiculous. He's the poster boy for testosterone."

"True. It's still not control." Jade pointed to the men just ahead and stepped away before I could argue.

I joined them at a railing overlooking the valley beyond Haven. Grandfather swept his hand out toward the horizon and smiled. "Rabbit, is the view not breathtaking?"

I leaned against his side and wrapped my arm around his waist. "It is."

After another hour and a half of weaving through the mountainside vegetation, Galan and I had learned a shitload about healing plants and remedies. Jade, Aust and Grandfather each held a mass of knowledge, but together they were a frickin' nature-pedia. Hopefully they could help Galan's sister with her headaches.

A phone call for Jade invaded our commune with nature. "One of the Academy's second-year students was injured in a wizardry class. I have to Flash back to the castle."

Galan grabbed both the backpacks and slid beside her.

"May I return with you two as well?" Grandfather asked. "It has been a wonderful afternoon, but I could use a rest."

My heart raced, but he looked good. Tired, but good.

Galan held out his hand. "Apologies, Hawk. Have we neglected your needs?"

Grandfather waved away the concern and blew me a kiss on the wind. "Not at all, after an hour's rest I will be as spry as a lamb. Rabbit, shall I see you at dinner?"

I nodded. "I hope everything works out with your student, Jade."

Galan's appraising gaze for his wife made me blush. "I am certain once she returns all will be well. Aust, will you bring Naith home when you come? He is exploring."

When they vanished, Aust held out his hand and gave me a mischievous grin. "Are you ready for another incredible adventure, Mika?"

"Sure. Where are we going?"

"The question is not *where* we are going, but *how* shall we get there?"

Aust turned and jogged down the forest path toward an open clearing. When he stopped, he tilted his head to the forest beyond. An angelic smile lit his face. "Ready yourself, *neelan*. You shall love this."

"Love wha—" I jolted to a stop as a massive black jaguar walked out of the trees.

Stumbling backwards I stepped on Aust's foot before he caught me and held me in place. "All is well," he whispered. I wondered if his words were meant to soothe me or the pony-sized jungle cat plodding toward us. Unbelievable. Its shoulders rose and fell in a lazy wave of strength as it plodded forward. The afternoon sun spackling the forest floor caught the patches of rosettes hidden within its ebony coat—wow, a melanistic jaguar.

A *reeeally* big melanistic jaguar.

Aust chuckled. "You are going to ride Naith home while I run alongside the two of you."

I stared almost eye-level into the golden gaze of the majestic cat. His lips curled up and he flashed long, white canines. *Shit. Dominance.* I dropped my gaze. He chuffed. The moisture of his breath on my face had me almost wetting my pants. "How will Naith feel about me riding him?"

Aust lifted my palm for Jade's cat to sniff. When we were acquainted, he walked me to Naith's side and slid my foot deep into the stirrup. With a grace I didn't possess, Aust vaulted me up and into the custom saddle which straddled the cat's broad back. "Naith loves the idea. He enjoys nothing more than an afternoon excursion."

I shuddered. "And has Naith ever been known to return without his rider? Maybe with his belly a hundred and twenty pounds heavier?"

Aust scowled, then chuckled at my expression. "Naith is a perfect gentlemale, a veritable kitten. Jade had your grandfather ride him earlier. Now stop your protestations and sit deep in your saddle so I can ensure it is tethered properly for you."

I must have completely lost touch with reality because a few minutes later I was swaying like a sailor on the deck of a ship, but I wasn't on the rolling sea, I rode the back of a giant jungle cat. As I got my sea legs, Aust jogged beside us, watching me with a dazzling smile. Faolan bounded ahead then returned in wide arcs obviously implying that I was holding things up.

"Are you well, Mika? You look as though you might swoon."

I didn't miss the male amusement in his voice. "Give me a chance to settle and then I'll race through the trees. You better get ready to watch the tail end of this beast 'cause I'm going to leave you in my dust."

He laughed, his voice deep and smooth as velvet. "I have no doubt."

CHAPTER TWENTY-THREE

My feet barely touched the marble inlay as I crossed through the foyer. *Could this world even be real?* I pulled the elastic from my ponytail and shook my hair free as I floated down the carpeted stairs toward where Nash told me I'd find the training center.

I stopped short at the first doorway and peered into the large rectangular room. Something as normal as the polished floor of a gymnasium with black padded mats stacked in the corner seemed wildly out of place in the context of my day. Rows of florescent lights hung above, caged to prevent breakage from wayward balls. The normality of it seemed bizarre.

I continued down the simple beige corridor and followed the faint *tink, tink, tink* of weights clinking together in rhythmic reps.

The training centre in Jade's basement crossed the wires of normal and mystical: cycles, steppers, elliptical and tread mills over against one wall, free weights and weight machines against the other and then a medieval wall of weapons mounted and hanging on the long wall at the back—a hundred or more—blades, spiked chains, battleaxes, flails, maces, daggers, swords, slings and several variations of whips I didn't recognize, but wanted nowhere near my backside.

Abrupt silence brought my attention back to the room.

Cowboy lowered the wall of weights he was pressing and swung his long muscled legs over the bench. After patting his face with his t-shirt, he tossed it into a laundry bin and stalked over. With his short brown hair slicked back and his brow drawn tight, he looked like someone who could kill as easily as he could light a cigarette.

"Something wrong, Mika?"

I eyed the weapons of mass dismemberment and swallowed. "I, uh . . . is Bruin here?"

He narrowed his gaze and drew a deep breath. "Nervous? Now what would a head-strong, opinionated woman like you have to be nervous about?"

Working with wildlife taught me many important lessons. Dominant creatures consider retreat a sign of weakness . . . and Cowboy was definitely a dominant creature. "Cowboy, why don't you call me Ursa like the other Weres?"

He smiled wide enough to let the tips of his fangs show. "You deny the Alpha, you deny my kind. Should I bow and call you Ursa for that? What do you think the Were Primes would do if they knew their Ursa is a Mundie who wants nothing to do with us? How long do you think you'd survive?"

The thuds of a Mack truck hitting concrete erupted from the corner. Nope. Just Savage versus a boxing bag. Another crack and I felt sorry for the bag. Wearing only a wide leather dog collar and workout shorts, I got the full effect of the artwork tattooed over his body. I tried not to stare, but the image of a dragon clawing and burning the man in its grips sent a chill up my spine. Drawn by my observation, the skin-head warrior turned a violent glare.

Cowboy snapped his fingers close to my face and I jumped. He leaned close. "Don't fuck with Bruin, Mika. He's not just my Alpha. He's my friend."

After a moment, the slamming of iron fists into the punching bag resumed.

Cowboy tipped the brim of an imaginary hat and stepped back. "Bruin's in there."

Right. I crossed the springy white floor and headed through the doorway on the side wall.

Suspended by his ankles on an inversion table, Bruin hung upside down as he crunched and released. The hard edges and smooth planes of his body glowed with a sheen of sweat, his cheeks coloured with a rosy-golden flush.

Holy hell. Gone was my pique at being threatened by Bruin's friends. One glance at the man glistening before me and every cell ripened with need.

"Hey baby," he said, "one sec, I'm just finishing off my core." With a wink Bruin continued and I took the opportunity to regain control of my hormones. I was more than my sex drive. More than Fates forcing me to accept a destiny I didn't choose. Deep breaths.

The exercise room had no windows but plenty of mirrored walls and black mats. On a hooked rail by the door, skipping ropes and tension bands hung waiting to be used. My hand burned, and an erotic inferno raged inside me.

Closing the door, I latched the lock and buttressed a plastic chair beneath the knob. If anyone came in, they were in for an eyeful. Cowboy and Savage probably wouldn't come-a-knockin' and I doubted, despite their hostility, they'd let anyone else bother us either.

Stalking toward Bruin, another surge of liquid heat exploded through me. It was either a physical side-effect of the Bonding, an after-effect of riding a giant jaguar through the forest, or some other nympho-effect that had me in its clutches.

It didn't matter. That glistening male was mine.

Bruin uncoiled from a crunch and sank toward the floor. "Did you and Aust have—"

I grabbed the bottom of my shirt and pulled it over my head, my clothes were an offense to my skin. My jeans slid down my hips and I stepped clear of the cotton pile gathering by my feet. My underwear went next.

Bruin's eyes widened. His heated gaze flicked to the barricaded door then back to me. "Uh, what's doing, Mika?"

"I just rode a gigantic jungle cat through the forest and I gotta tell you—I'm jazzed. I don't know if it's the bonding or what, but I really need to burn off some energy."

Bruin's husky growl filled the room and vibrated in all the right places. He reached up to unhook his ankles and I caught his hand.

"Not so fast, big guy." I tilted the table horizontal and set the locks. Bruin tracked me as I crossed the room, grabbed two skipping ropes from the pegs and folded them in half. "You're at my mercy, Alpha. Ready for a real workout?"

Bruin growled again. "Let the marathon begin."

Once Bruin's hands were secured above his head and bound to the frame of the table, I tugged down his nylon shorts and boxers. *Mine.* I shook my head. "This isn't natural. I've never been a prude or anything, but these bonding hormones make me downright aggressive. I'm one whip and corset away from being a Dominatrix."

Bruin's head fell back as his whole body stiffened against his restraints. "That's one image I'll never get out of my head."

The picture flashing in my mind's eye was hot as hell, me all leathered up, him naked and at my mercy, both of us writhing and insatiable with need. I moaned as another warm rush hit me between my thighs.

Bruin's nostrils flared. "So sweet. Gods, what are you thinking about, baby?"

I scanned all that bronze skin, running my nails from his shoulders, down the smooth planes of his pecs, over the tightly cut ridges of his abs to the outside of his hips. I avoided his erection and continued down the thick trunks of his thighs, around to his chiseled calves, I jumped past his clothes trapped around his ankles and finished my sensory experiment at his feet.

Damn. Even his feet were beautiful.

A rich, musky scent rose from his skin. "I love it when you look at me like that."

I massaged the flesh of his insoles, kneading at the tender parts of his arches before launching a fingers-do-the-walking return trek back up his body. "Oh? And how's that?"

"Like you're about to savagely devour me."

"And if that's what I plan to do . . . are you okay with that? No strings? No promises?"

Bruin's body twitched, his muscles rock solid under my touch. "Have at it."

I stared at his offering and decided, in the spirit of being thorough, I'd start at the top and work my way down. Bruin's shaggy brown hair was softer than it looked. Like his pelt, it was a little wiry on the surface, but silky soft as you ran your fingers through it.

His eyes rolled closed as I stepped to the top of the table and my fingers scrubbed his scalp. I pressed my lips to his and kissed him in slow sweeping strokes, tasting, teasing. With each invasion of my tongue I sank further inside him.

With careful attention, I kissed his throat, across his collarbone and blew a gentle breath over his nipples. They stood tight at the tips and I had to beat back the growl rumbling in my chest. Returning the favor on a little circle-and-suckle trick he'd used on me was *soooo* rewarding. And when his head kicked back, and he arched off the table, I nearly lost it.

He bit his bottom lip, his eyes wild, his breathing loud. But not as loud as the squeal and squeak of the metal frame of the inversion table under stress. He gripped the bars above his head and tensed.

Nipping my way further down the ridges of his body, I raked my fingers through the golden-brown hair of his navel and tested my teeth on the rise of his hip. "This is for you."

"Mika, you don't have to—"

I took him into my mouth.

He blew out a lungful of air, his whole body racked in spasm. "Never mind. Yes, yes you do."

Completely spent, I sprawled across Bruin's bed and watched as he leaned over the bathroom sink. He'd Flashed us upstairs after my bondage experiment in the training room and we'd spent hours lounging naked, watching sappy movies and talking cars, journalism and books. He liked biographies, of all things. The only biography I'd ever read was Jane Goodall's *Africa in My Blood*. He said he liked to understand how people are shaped by what happens to them through the course of their lives. I saw his point.

With his perfect profile highlighted by the overhead incandescence of his bathroom, Bruin drew an old-fashioned straight blade up the skin of his neck. As he removed each white strip of shaving cream, his gaze in the mirror shifted to me. He smiled, swished his blade, tapped it on the edge and took another scrape.

After he finished with the swish, tap and scrape, he removed the towel wrapped around his hips, blotted his face dry and netted the thing into the hamper with a weighty *thunk*. Whistling a quiet tune to himself, he pulled on a fresh pair of jeans and a slogan T-shirt.

I rolled onto my stomach to read it. 'It's *tourist* season. Why *can't* we shoot them?'

As the mattress dipped under his weight, Bruin grabbed the remote and clicked off Patrick Swayze just as he was pulling Baby out of the corner. "Mika, my love, get your perfect little ass in that shower. The grill is calling, and a hungry bear is a cranky bear. If I don't eat some*thing*, I might eat some*body*."

I flopped back down, so sated I didn't plan on moving. Ever. When he leaned closer, I tightened my grip on the quilt. "I think you broke me."

Bruin chuckled, his expression free of its usual tension. "*You* broke you. I was bound and tied remember?"

I blushed and licked my lips. "Not sure where that came from. I'm a little embarrassed."

He laid his palms flat on the mattress beside my shoulders and leaned close, the corners of his mouth turned up in a cocky smirk. "You can go grizzly on me any time but right now I need sustenance. Nourish me woman."

He was so damned lucky he was laughing.

I yelped as he nipped my shoulder. "Can't we eat in? We could watch Love and Other Drugs. A little Jake Gyllenhaal for me, a little Anne Hathaway for you. Win-win."

Bruin scowled. "We're going to the back courtyard to have dinner. Whoever's not on patrol is meeting up for a meal. I promise it'll be fun. Your grandfather will be there and Aust should be almost done watching the cubs. I'm sure he'll be along shortly. You seem to be getting along well with him."

"Yes. He's a wonderful friend, but . . ." I pulled the quilt over my head, "your warrior friends hate me. I'm the freaky side show at the circus. The Mundie your Fates saddled you with. The one daring to deny the Alpha. All I need is a beard and an extra three hundred pounds and they'd cage me and sell tickets."

"Not true, and *ew*." Bruin tugged the quilt down, his nose crinkled.

Orville scratched his back paws on the mat at the glass doors to the balcony. Bruin strode over and as the August breeze carried the scent of buttered popcorn into the room, my binturong waddled outside, climbed the railing and reached for a low hanging branch. His wiry grey coat disappeared into the foliage as the Heartbeat Drum Song rang on my phone.

"My cell's working?" I bounded off his bed and through the connecting door to my suite.

"Reign approved it this afternoon—with provisions. You can't tell anyone where you are." Bruin followed me in and yanked closed the drapes in my suite as I retrieved my phone.

Right. Still naked.

"Ms. Silverbrook, this is Assistant Crown Attorney Brantfield's secretary. He asked me to confirm with you regarding your deposition interview for the Nimithic Group trial? He wanted to ensure that you were still available, since you missed your appointment today and haven't responded to our emails."

I jogged over to the desk, pulled my laptop out of my backpack and booted it up. As my screen initialized, I noticed the date. *Damn this world is messing with my sense of time.* "I am so sorry. It's been a hectic week. When would you like to reschedule?"

"We have an afternoon opening tomorrow at 2 pm if you are available."

Bruin leaned against the jamb, arms crossed and shook his head.

Could he hear my conversation from across the room?

"That will be fine. And please extend my apologies to ACA Brantfield." I closed my phone, stroked the keyboard and pulled up my files to scan my notes.

Bruin prowled closer. "Just so we're clear, the answer was no."

I bit back my first impulse and smiled. "What was the question?"

"You're not making that deposition tomorrow."

"Eavesdrop much?"

He tapped his ear. "Heightened hearing. And the answer is still no."

I grabbed clothes from the dresser and slammed the drawers harder than I meant to. "I don't remember asking permission. Oh wait, that's because I *didn't*."

He met my smirk with his own. "You're not going to Vancouver with Scourge, mercenary bikers, and Jackals barking at your door. It's too dangerous. Call back and cancel."

I lifted my chin and headed to the bathroom. "*Mmm*, your dominant barbarian impression gets me seriously hot. Order me around again . . . slower."

He Flashed in front of me, his eyes burning gold. "You got the dominant part right. I am your Alpha—you *will* listen to me."

Something primal in Bruin's gaze quickened my pulse. His imperious command resonated in my skull and multiplied. His authority rippled through my nervous system and demanded I obey. It pressured every cell in my body to comply. It overrode my will.

He glared down at me and I fought to hold my ground.

He loomed closer.

My knees buckled, and my head bowed.

Tears blurred my vision as I sucked in a violent breath and struggled to my feet. With my clothes clutched to my chest, I shoved past him and stormed into the bathroom. "You *bastard*. Get the hell away from me."

CHAPTER TWENTY-FOUR

Forty-five minutes later, I stood alone amongst strangers, leaning against the railing of the back deck. The late summer air hung heavy with the day's heat and the rich succulence of summer blooms. As I watched the sun sink behind two violet mountain peaks I reached out and absorbed nature's strength from my surroundings. Haven Mountain was magical and, having grown up as a Vancouver native, that was high praise.

If only a perfect moment could be frozen, and its sense of serenity preserved.

Inevitably, though, the chaos of life forces its way back and shatters the fragile balance.

A cloud of mesquite smoke billowed by, accompanied by the hiss of flames sizzling the grill. The multilevel deck at the back of Jade's mansion sprawled along the length of the house and across the lawn towards the forest beyond. Built-in flower boxes followed the zigzag maze of tiered railings. Many of them overflowed with sedge, kale, verbena and coral bells, while others brimmed with ice and long necked bottles ready for the night ahead.

"What would you like, *neelan?*" Aust asked. He'd come home from cubsitting—arms scratched and a gleam in his pale blue eyes—and when I'd passed on dinner, he insisted on escorting me down. I hadn't gotten into the whole 'Bruin is an overpowering bully' thing, but after his nostrils flared in my suite, I assumed I didn't have to.

"There is mead, wine, whiskey and the ladies have a margarita bar on the upper deck if you prefer something more female and festive."

Wasting away in Margaritaville sounded great—until I caught a glimpse of the bartender. Lexi pressed down the lid of the screaming blender and mulched ice while still managing to toss a cold amethyst glare in my direction. *Nice.* Man, I missed my girls back home. If Paige and Meg were here, I might even enjoy myself. Mind you, if they *were* here, they'd be making one scene after another with all these finely tuned men strutting around in muscle shirts and leather.

"Beer's great, Aust, thanks. Got anything dark, maybe a honey brown?"

Kobi swiped the ice off a bottle and stepped over. I checked out the silver rings on his hand as he held it out. Skulls, demons and symbols I didn't recognize. What was his story? He caught me staring and for a moment his eyes flashed red. "Honey brown? A girl after Bruin's taste. Maybe the Fates aren't totally fucked after all."

I twisted off the cap and took a long draw. The chill eased the knot in my gut but didn't touch the suffocating pressure in my chest. Bruin coerced me. Turned me into a mindless puppet forced to do his bidding. No amount of sexual chemistry was worth that.

I took another drink. He'd tried to apologize through the bathroom door—

"Mika, *sweeting*," Aust whispered, brushing a finger against my cheek. "Your betrayal burns in my lungs. Half the men here have senses as keen as my own. If you wish to keep the household out of your affairs, you must needs tamp your emotions."

Good point. I tipped back my beer and searched the crowd. "Are Jade and Galan here?"

Aust chuckled. "They have yet to surface this evening."

"May we all find such passion in love." A sexy velvet voice announced the arrival of more Highbornes, two men and a woman carrying a baby.

The resemblance between these Highbornes astounded me—the porcelain skin, Prussian blue eyes and long golden hair. Dressed in doeskin pants, butter-cream tunics and elaborately embroidered dinner jackets, the toned, slender men lived up to their Highborne hottie reputation. And the woman with them exuded an air of Victoria's Secret supermodel in a sheer, blush gown.

"The honeymoon continues," the woman said and then met Aust's kiss.

"As it shall for some time," he replied.

One of the men set down the empty bouncy chair and pink diaper bag he'd been carrying. The intricate gold braid he wore in his hair brushed the side of his cut jaw. Galan wore one as well, though his braid blended the silver of his hair and the rich burgundy of Jade's. This one was a subtle blend of gold and flax. He straightened and winked at the woman. "When Nyssa and I Recognized we craved each other insatiably for decades."

"I well remember." Aust chuckled. "I warn you now, Mika, Highbornes have a fondness for making love in the outdoors."

"And a lack of modesty even an Incubus can respect," Kobi added handing the two men each a dark ale. "Prepare to stumble upon the loving couple every time you turn around."

The woman, Nyssa, gave her husband a wry smile and kissed the baby's head.

Aust laid his arm across my shoulder and introduced us. "Mika, this is Tham, Iadon and his beloved mate Nyssa, and the precious young in Nyssa's arms is Ella." He glanced around the courtyard and to the decks above. "Is Lia joining us for evening repast?"

"Mayhap later," Nyssa said. Her smile was warm though her tone seemed skeptical.

Aust, Iadon and Tham spoke privately in another language and by the looks on their faces, the mention of Lia's absence had them worried.

Ella's bright blue eyes and cherubic face peered up at me. Her little mouth stretched into a wide 'O' as she yawned.

"Wow, she is precious."

"Gratitude." Nyssa beamed and adjusted the baby against her chest. "Merry meet, Mika. Welcome to Haven."

I blinked as the men rejoined our conversation and Iadon pulled me into a hug and touched his lips to mine. "It warms our hearts that you and Aust have found a common bond. He deserves nothing less than true friendship."

"Merry meet, Mika." Tham slid in and kissed me next. Their lips were all as soft as silk and god, they smelled so good. Tham winked. "Bruin gaining you as a mate is most certainly a loss to all other males in Haven."

A musky outdoorsy scent on the air had me looking for Bruin. I didn't see him.

Kobi laughed at my expression and coughed behind his beer. "Highbornes are a touchy-feely bunch. Free love and all that. Get used to it."

"Help yourselves to food, y'all," Cowboy called from the grill. Another cloud of mesquite smoke wafted by and the sizzle of meat triggered a rumble in my stomach. I didn't need a second invitation.

Ignoring the stares of strangers, I tucked in close to Aust and picked up a plate. I pointed to a steak and noticed Cowboy's medallion shone turquoise once again. *Huh.*

Aust nudged me and we started down the thirty-foot, barbeque assembly line. Passing the fruit bowl, I pocketed an apple and a pear for Orville, sliced open a baked potato and spooned on the fixings. I added some radish-looking stuff with berries in it, passed on the green mushroomy stuff, despite Aust's insistence that it was delicious, and filled the only space remaining on my plate with a spoonful of baked brown beans.

When we reached the wrapped cutlery mountain at the end of the table a warm breeze caressed my face. Grandfather's touch drew my gaze toward the large gazebo above us on the main deck. I returned his wave and headed to where he sat next to the monolithic man with amazing brindled hair—Maximus Reign.

Had Bruin's father forgiven me for holding a gun on his girls?

Would he hate me for rejecting his son? Everyone else did. A wave of nausea sloshed and capsized in my empty belly.

After setting my plate and beer down at the table next to Grandfather I wiped my palm on my jeans and held out my hand. Dressed in a stylish, black suit with his hair just brushing his pressed white collar, the man looked deceptively urbane. Reign rose to his feet and enveloped my palm in a massive, scarred hand. "Mika, it's good to have you home. Welcome."

Home? I settled beside Grandfather and Aust took the seat beside me.

Bruin climbed the steps and stood across the table with two heaping plates and a couple of bottles of beer tucked under his arm. He made no move forward and I tried not to let the sick-fear I felt show on my face. His expression faltered. "May I join you?"

Reign looked from his son to me and his dark gaze narrowed.

I knew if I refused, Bruin would walk away. I couldn't do that to him. Not in his own home. Not in front of his father and his friends. I gestured to the seat across from me. After he set everything down, he shook hands with Grandfather and took his seat.

Knowing how hungry Bruin had been, I half expected fork-shoveling, but when I finally had myself reined in and raised my gaze, he'd lain his napkin across his lap and waited for me to start. He offered me an apologetic smile.

"This seat taken?" Lexi plopped down next to her brother and I cringed.

"Play nice and it's all yours, Princess," Bruin said.

Lexi rolled her eyes. "Have you heard any more about your missing Weres? Cowboy mentioned that a couple Bengal's didn't check in with your roll call."

Bruin picked at his potato salad. "They aren't really *my* Weres, and no, I have no idea where the Tigers are."

"Lot of drama in the air," she said, tipping her margarita glass. "Missing Weres, you getting shot, guns pointed at us, a bonding going nowhere—"

"*Princess. . .*" Reign didn't look up from his plate. He meticulously cut his steak as he spoke. "Mika and Hawk are our guests. Are we crystal?"

The hair on my arms stood on end.

"Crystal," she repeated, flashing me a venomous smile. "But besides whoring around with Bruin, why is she here—"

Bruin grabbed the back of Lexi's shirt and lifted her from her seat. The courtyard fell silent, all eyes on our family tableau. Aust laid a warm hand on my leg and squeezed my thigh.

Reign stood at the head of the table, towering, shoulders rigid. When he spoke, his voice sounded too quiet, too calm. "Alexannia Grace, apologize to Mika and her grandfather."

After a long pause she ran a rough hand through her ebony spikes and nodded to my grandfather. "I am sorry if I offended you, sir, but those I love have been offended too." She thrust her napkin onto the table and stormed across the deck and into the house.

Bruin eased back into his chair with an eerie stiffness, both his voice and his expression hard as stone. "I apologize as well, sir, for my sister's comment. I assure you, your granddaughter has done nothing to deserve her judgment."

Grandfather raised his hand. "Mika is my blood, young man. I know her spirit as well as my own. We need not speak of such things again."

I fought back tears.

Grandfather pat my hand and kissed the side of my head. "Only those who struggle greatly are able to achieve greatness, Rabbit. Be patient, in time the Earth Mother's plan will unfold as it is meant."

Head bent, I focused on my baked potato. Polite conversation droned on. Aust and Bruin—probably scenting my near hysteria—kept the discussion away from me. After cleaning my plate and bottoming a second beer I excused myself and retreated to the dessert table.

"I'm sorry," Bruin whispered close to my ear, stepping tight against my back. He wrapped his arms around my shoulders and rested his chin on my head. Against my wishes, his heat and musky outdoor scent calmed my nerves. "I'm sorry for what Lexi said *and* I'm sorry for what happened earlier. I never meant to use my command on you. I swear, it just happened."

I stepped from his embrace and gathered some cookies and sticky pastries onto a plate.

"Mika. Believe me. I'm trying to *build* this relationship, not destroy it."

I forced myself to look at him and the anguish in his eyes broke my heart. "You're trying. I get that. It's just . . . I'm not the woman for you, Bruin. You want obedience, someone to do as she's told and stand safely behind you in your crazy life. I'm not that woman."

Bruin cupped my jaw and wiped my tears with his thumb. "I want *you.*"

"In your bed, but as an equal?" I shook my head and pulled away. "I'm not a puppet. What you did . . . forcing me to bow to your will . . . I'm done whoring around with you. Lexi's right. It's time for me to go."

Bruin leaned closer, his massive upper body blocking out the world. "I'm sorry about what happened. I've apologized for that. The way I see it, we've got the sex part down. It's fabulous. Beyond anything I've ever had. If that's our base connection while we figure everything else out . . . then take as long as you need, I'm not complaining. But Lexi is *not* right. Don't give up on us. Don't walk away. Not when—"

Cowboy stepped behind us and cleared his throat. "Sorry, Alpha, that intel you wanted from Yellowstone came in."

Bruin scrubbed his palm over his face and turned to his friend. "And? Any sign of the missing Puma pride?"

Cowboy shook his head. "The good news is there are no pelts lying around, but the pride is nowhere to be—" Bruin tapped the wolf's bolo tie and frowned. The centre stone had turned solid black. "Nature's calling, Wolf."

"Shit. Catch y'all later." Cowboy dipped his head and fingered the brim of his hat as he turned away and jogged down the steps of the deck. At the edge of the forest he set his hat on a stone bench, pulled his white muscle shirt over his head and toed off his cowboy boots.

When his pants came off I stopped gawking and focused on Bruin's adorable scowl.

"What's that about?"

Bruin scrubbed his jaw and leaned heavy against the railing. The muscles in his shoulders stretched the sleeve of his shirt until I thought it would split at the seams. "Cowboy has a condition—something to do with his adrenal glands. If he's not stimulated or active, his hormones drop and his body doesn't produce what it needs. It messes with his heart and a half a dozen other things."

I turned back to see the form of the man drop to all fours and shift into a wolf's body. His deep caramel coat caught the setting sun and glimmered with a sheen of gold and silver. And like all the Weres I'd seen so far, Cowboy's wolf was large, much larger than Faolan or any of Aust's forest wolves.

"A few years ago, it got bad. We almost lost him before Jade figured out the problem."

"That's awful."

"Samuel, our best wizard, worked with Jade to spell that neck-tie as a monitor. Now we can usually correct the problem before anything happens."

"And the stone changes colour like a mood-ring kinda thing?"

"We all keep an eye on it," Kobi said. He joined us and handed Bruin and I each another beer. I already felt a little rubbery in the legs. Another bottle probably wasn't a smart idea. "Usually if we're on a mission or working on a hook-up at a club he's good."

Bruin lowered his beer from his lips. "It's because we're home and he's relaxed that he's having a problem."

I looked back to the pile of clothes by the trees. "So, is he all right?"

Kobi nodded. "He'll meet up with Aust's wolf pack and race across the mountain chasing deer and rabbit. In a couple hours he'll trot back, tongue hanging out and a spring in his step and fur in his teeth."

Um, gross. "Is this a genetic trait in Weres or an isolated thing?"

Bruin shrugged. "Impossible to know. Weres with weaknesses are put down as young. It's survival of the fittest whether in a pack or pride or sleuth."

I gasped. "His family would actually kill him?"

Kobi pulled the cigarette from his lips and exhaled a cloud of sweet, smelling smoke. "And almost succeeded. If it weren't for our Alpha Bear's big ol' heart, Cowboy would have been killed years ago."

It hit me then, Cowboy's comment about weakness and me being Ursa. "A human Ursa is as weak as it gets. The Were world will want to kill me because I'm human, won't they?"

Bruin pushed off the railing and drained his beer.

Kobi's pierced, ebony brow arced. "Ding-ding, give the journalist a prize."

Bruin's growl rolled low and long.

"She's not stupid, Bear. She should know what she's up against and we should assess her skills, ASAP. Let's see if she's got anything we can work with. I'm thinking gun range tomorrow afternoon and you should test her out with some hand-to-hand. See what she can do."

Bruin cursed. "Fine. Tomorrow afternoon—"

"—won't work," I said. "I have an appointment in Vancouver."

Platinum piercings flashed in the lantern light as Kobi turned to Bruin. "We're headed back to the Modern Realm? Have you cleared it with Reign?"

Bruin glared. I met his glare and raised him a scowl. "So, it's Reign I need to speak with. Good to know."

"Don't bother," Bruin snapped. "I'll take care of it."

The three of us stood there at the railing staring, until Kobi finally broke the silence. "*Soooo*, in the spirit of blatantly changing the subject, how about we head inside?"

CHAPTER TWENTY-FIVE

Kobi ushered Bruin and me through the French doors off the main patio and into the first-floor lounge of Jade's home. A full-sized stocked bar and mahogany stools ran the wall to the left, four billboard-sized plasma screens covered the wall to the right. And beyond the maze of leather sofas and recliners sat a pool table, an air hockey table, and a Foosball table. Yep. It was a testosterone temple. A gathering of a dozen men had kicked back with game controllers to enjoy a head-to-head slaughter.

"Wow, nice man-cave."

Aust patted the couch and offered me a controller. "Ready to have some fun, *neelan?*"

I laughed. It seemed so out of context to see Elves hunkered down playing video games. But play we did. I didn't realize how long we'd been at it until Cowboy strode in, his medallion brilliant turquoise.

"*Shiiit*, Aust," he drawled. "Look at your kill streak. You rock, my man."

Aust raised his fist and met Cowboy's bump. "Welcome back my brother. I have shred warriors from Jungle to Villa to Havana. Mayhap you might prove more of a challen—"

"What the—" Tham jumped off the other couch and Orville

dropped to the carpet with an indignant huff. He'd pay for that later, I was sure.

"What?" Bruin palmed the knife from his belt and pulled me against his hip.

Tham's ears flushed pink as he shifted. "Uh . . . well, it felt like a hot wave of energy pulsed through the room and went straight to my crotch."

I sat quietly, dazzled by that little tid-bit of sharing.

As if some invisible bomb detonated in the room, the men stiffened and cursed. Looking from one to another, a wave of throat clearing, position adjusting, ball scratching and skittering glances circulated throughout the room.

Tham leaned against the sofa and stared at his lap. "Without getting too personal, is anyone else suddenly . . .."

"Uh, yeah."

"A sledgehammer?"

"Throwing oak?"

Another tidal wave seemed to hit the shore and the men jolted again. Aust paced, shaking his legs as he stepped. Savage covered his lap with a pillow. Kobi retrieved his sunglasses and covered his glowing red eyes. Iadon strode to Nyssa, picked her up by her ass and pinned her against the lounge wall. Overtaking her mouth, the Highborne kissed his wife deep and hard. Nyssa uttered a feminine moan, laced her fingers into his flaxen hair and succumbed to the surprise attack.

The sexual tension in the room thickened as if someone had released an aphrodisiac in the air vents and they were all responding to it.

Bruin and I looked at Julian and Nash. The two of them were taking in the room with the same bizarre curiosity we shared. Bruin sheathed his knife. "Either of you ready to get busy?"

They looked at each other and shrugged. "No, we're good."

"Okay, so humans don't seem to be affected and I'm guessing I'm not affected because I'm bonded to Mika not because I'm a Were."

"What makes you say that?" I asked.

Bruin chuckled and pointed across the room. "Because Cowboy looks like he's about to hump the sofa—"

Another assault struck. Aust stumbled into a recliner and dropped his head between his knees. Tham's knuckles were white from the death-grip he'd taken on the edge of the bar. I couldn't help but giggle when he slid his hand to his leathers then moaned as he rubbed himself with the heel of his palm.

Iadon? Well, he was not to be disturbed. I averted my gaze, thankful that Ella slept and that Iadon's thigh-length, suede dinner-jacket hid everything going on.

"What is happening?" Tham groaned.

The scent of apple blossoms on a warm spring breeze filled the room. Jade sauntered through the doorway wearing a slip of silk. Her hair, long to her waist, swayed with her loose limbs. Tousled and mussed like she'd spent the afternoon being pleasured. Her lips, pink and swollen, highlighted the remarkable glow of her skin. No wonder we hadn't seen her and Galan at dinner.

Bruin cleared his throat. "Love the look, Blaze, but not the best time to be half-naked in front of this crowd."

As she drew closer, the hair on the back of my neck stood. Something was off. All male eyes locked on her. She was the magnet and their poles were pointing due north. The pull of desire seemed to grow as she approached, every step nearer brought more fidgeting.

"Bruin, it's Jade," I said. "I think the sexual energy is radiating off her."

His eyes widened. Slipping off the white linen, button-down he wore loose over his T, he started for his sister. "Hey honey, let's slip this on you."

While he buttoned her up, Jade's piercing emerald eyes locked on Cowboy. Lust flared.

Brushing past Bruin, she backed Haven's lone wolf onto the arm of the sofa and slid between his thighs. Running her hands up both sides of his neck she scrubbed her nails into his caramel coloured hair. "You smell good, Wolf."

Cowboy's eyes hazed over as he leaned back.

"Jade, how about you step away—" Bruin reached to grab her shoulder, but pulled his hand back just as Cowboy snapped, his canines long and sharp. "Shit. What's she doing to him?"

Jade whispered something into Cowboy's ear and Bruin cursed.

The wolf's arms wrapped tighter around her and they fell as one onto the couch. Cowboy covered her body, his thigh holding her down as his hand slid to cup her ass. Her very bare ass.

Bruin didn't move. Didn't seem to be tracking.

I rushed to the sofa but stayed out of reach of Cowboy's teeth. "Jade, where's Galan?"

"Sleeping." Jade mumbled against Cowboy's neck, nipping his collarbone.

I nodded to Nash and he bolted from the room.

Jade's hand disappeared between their bodies and Cowboy growled. "I claim you as my consort, Wolf. You have untapped skills I need to explore."

Cowboy's hands locked into her deep red curls and pulled her mouth to his.

"Okay, blossom." Galan's deep tenor sounded weary but not angry. I tried not to notice how the lounge pants he wore hung low on his hips. But damn, Highbornes really were hot.

He reached for his wife and Cowboy snarled, baring his teeth.

Bruin snapped out of it then and when he spoke, his voice rang with that Alpha command he'd used on me earlier. "Weylyn, come here to me."

Cowboy growled. I couldn't tell if it was because Bruin used what I guessed was Cowboy's proper name, the Alpha command in his voice or that he was forcing him to give up his hold on Jade. Whatever the reason, Cowboy's lips curled and a dangerous rumble vibrated in my chest.

"*Mine*," he growled.

"No. She's not." Bruin's gaze narrowed. "Wolf. Come. To. Me."

He didn't speak loudly, but somehow his voice spread through the space. It rolled like distant thunder. Threatening. Powerful. I wasn't immune. I stepped forward.

Cowboy obeyed too. He rolled off the couch with predatory grace and dropped to his knee before his Alpha.

Bruin patted the guy's back and pulled him close and then nodded that it was safe.

Galan lifted Jade off the couch. "Back to our suite, Blossom."

"But Galan . . . you're tired and I'm running hot. I'm recruiting reinforcements."

"I see that, darling, but a Were may not be the best choice to join us in private. They don't understand our mating laws. Plus, I am certain if you were thinking clearly, a sexual encounter with one of your fellow warriors might be awkward for you moving forward."

Her head fell back as she laughed. "Awkward? Have you seen him naked?"

"No, love." He sighed and offered us an apologetic smile. "How about we keep your consorts to the Highbornes, shall we?"

"Killjoy," she muttered.

Galan set her on her feet and kissed her glistening forehead. "I know, *mela mir*."

"What the fuck is going on, Galan?" Bruin asked.

The look in Galan's eyes was a mixture of worry and exhaustion. "Castian said she's in a traditional Fae procreation cycle."

"She's in *Yearning*?" Tham gasped. "That's Fae myth."

"Apparently not. Castian is her father and as Fae as one could be." Galan tightened his grip around Jade's wrist as she reached into his lounge pants. "The only way to keep her fever from raging danger-ously high is to keep her sexual appetite sated. I am a mere nine hours in, fell asleep for a moment and look what happened. Jade is right. We need assistance."

"How long will it last?" Bruin asked, scrubbing his face.

"Castian said anywhere from three days to a week depending on if she conceives."

Another wave of Jade's yearning rippled through the lounge. The Elves and Cowboy moaned and steadied themselves.

"By the gods, you need more than a consort," Tham chuckled. "A week nonstop? It is going to take several of us."

Galan nodded. "Lexi, have you any objection to Tham being Jade's consort?"

I hadn't noticed Lexi standing next to Nash. "To save my sister's life? Hells no."

Aust cleared his throat. "I shall teach her Herbology classes for the week and talk to Maximus about the rest of her schedule?"

Galan glanced to where Iadon was still very distracted under the layers of Nyssa's skirt. "When the opportunity presents itself, could one of you ask Iadon and Nyssa to come to our suite? And could someone take care of Ella when they do?"

"I've got her," Bruin said. "You take care of my girl and I'll take care of yours."

Galan nodded. "Very well, Blossom, how about Tham and I take you back to our suite?"

"*Mhmm.* This is hot."

Jade giggled as Galan threw her over his shoulder and headed for the door. "Yes love, I am certain it feels that way to you."

CHAPTER TWENTY-SIX

I stirred to life the next morning with Orville snoring his little rumbled wheezes into my ear. After fighting my way free from sheets strangling my legs, I reached for the fallen quilt on the floor and heaved it back onto the bed. Long, slow blinking brought the alarm clock into focus.

5:23 am. *Good god, that's obscene.*

My bleary gaze shifted to the closed door connecting my room with Bruin's and I couldn't help but revisit the death spiral of the previous night. After the drama in the lounge, Bruin totally shut down. He had gathered Ella's carrier and gone straight to his room to studiously ignore the awkwardness of Jade, Galan and almost every Highborne in the house participating in the sextathalon of the century.

He'd obsessively organized his closet, arranged the cologne bottles on his dresser in order of height and colour, and alphabetized a massive CD collection and then sorted by year of release. Ella waking up settled him a bit. He'd doted on her for an hour or so, but all too soon Nyssa came to pick her up, gave us an update and Bruin was lost again.

"Are you all right?" I'd asked.

He stepped around me and laid his daggers out to clean.

"Can you talk to me?"

His jaw clenched tight as he sat his cleaning oil and rag side by side, then adjusted the label so it faced perfectly to the front. He wasn't listening, and I didn't seem to be helping. He hadn't even looked up when I made my way to the door. It hit home then, Bruin and I were strangers. Mind-blowing, life-altering sex aside, if I evaluated our compatibility, we didn't have anything to check in the boxes for relationship or communication.

Moaning at the futility of it all, I rolled over and grabbed my laptop from the bedside table. Julian said in the lounge last night that I had Internet, and though I couldn't upload anything, I could download. Surely reconnecting with the real world would ground me and reinforce that I didn't belong here.

As I opened up my browser, I thought about Aust. I may not belong here, but I would miss him and Faolan.

My inbox downloaded twenty-nine email messages in the past week, seven since yesterday: four notices that my Facebook page had been updated by friends, one email from ACA Brantfield's office, politely reminding me of my appointment today, one from the World Wildlife Foundation about membership renewal and two from Paige, sent from her home email account, marked urgent. *Weird.*

I opened the first one from Paige:

Hey Chicklette, Where the hell are you? Tried to call...

Something happened today. Something bad. Your cubicle and my office were broken into. I'm assuming you have your laptop with you because it wasn't here. Right? Well, mine's been stolen along with some of your files from the main cabinet and a couple more from your ped.

Call me as soon as you get this.

P.

I read it over a second time. What the hell was going on with my life? Why would Bruin's enemies want Paige's computer? My computer I could see. It could have personal info and tons of ways to get to me, but Paige's?

I moved my mouse over the second message and inhaled deep before clicking on it.

Me again.

Haven't heard from you and have been trying your home and cell all day. Listen. There was more to tell you this morning about the robbery. I didn't want to do it in an email, but I have no idea how to reach you. Meg's hurt. She came in early and had the horrendous luck of walking in on the break in. She's at Vancouver General in ICU. She hasn't woken up yet and the doctors say they won't know what they're dealing with until she does.

Anyway. Call me. I'm losing my shit and it's not like you to be unreachable.

P.

I lunged to the nightstand and fumbled my phone out of the charger. Orville grumbled, squinting his tiny black eyes at me. "Sorry, baby, but this is important."

After scrolling through my contacts, I pressed SEND. Nothing. End call. I tried again.

Nothing.

I jogged to the connecting door to Bruin's room and clicked on a lamp in his suite. He wasn't there, and his bed hadn't been slept in. *Fine, I'll figure this out on my own.*

Barefoot, I ghosted through the maze of corridors and down the main staircase. The marble mosaic of the foyer was cold on my feet as I headed towards the kitchen. One thing I knew for certain—in my world or this one—if anyone was awake, there would be coffee.

Scuttling down the corridor, I rounded the corner and smacked into a seven-foot linebacker. There is no graceful way to land on your ass, so I took comfort that at least no one but the two of us had seen my back dive and sprawl.

Extra points for sticking the landing. Hard.

"Mika?" Strong hands closed around my upper arms and lifted me to my feet. Even this early, Maximus Reign looked like someone on the cover of Esquire magazine. Somehow, he managed to pull off incredibly dapper, yet frighteningly intimidating, at the same time. "Where are you going in such a rush?"

I looked up and shivered. "I . . . uh, need someone to help me make a phone call."

A crease formed in Reign's brow as he looked down to me. "Didn't we set you up yesterday?"

"You did, but I'm not getting signal this morning."

Reign held out his hand and took my phone. After opening the back and raising a brow he closed it up and sighed. "Who do you need to call?"

I explained my emails and how Meg had been admitted to hospital because of something Bruin and I started. "I have to help figure this out and make sure my friends are okay."

By the scowl on his face, he didn't seem moved.

"Please," I said, "You don't know me, but these are more than my co-workers, they are my family. I'll just find out what's going on and then maybe Bruin and I can check on them when we're there this afternoon."

Again with the brow lifting. "When you are *where* this afternoon?"

"In Vancouver." A sick feeling twisted in my stomach. "He didn't get permission to take me to my meeting with the Crown Attorney's office, did he? He said last night he'd take care of it."

Reign spun a massive silver ring on his finger. "I'm sure his requisition is on my desk somewhere. A lot happened last night. I probably overlooked it."

Yeah, I'm sure. "Well, I need to make this appointment. My career and my reputation are on the line, not to mention putting some very bad men behind bars."

Aust's mother, Elora, came up the hall carrying a large tray. Like all the Highbornes, she moved with an elegance and grace that seemed unreal. Her long blonde hair was plaited in an intricate braid and fell to one side of her face and reached the silk bodice of her dress. She wore the same wide black choker around her neck that Aust wore around his.

"Elora, I've told you before. You have staff to do the heavy work." In three long strides Reign met her and relieved her of her burden. He moved with more grace than I imagined possible for a man of his size.

"Maximus, I am well and capable," she said, seemingly unaffected by his censure or his tone. With straight shoulders she smiled up at him and then at me. As she looked me over, I realized for the second morning in a row, I'd run from my room in my pajamas. "Merry meet, Mika. Are you well?"

"Uh, yes, thank you."

Reign studied the contents of the tray he was holding. "Is this for me?"

She nodded. "I was preparing first repast for Aust and knew you would be heading to your office soon. I took the liberty."

"You're spoiling me."

Elora dropped her gaze, folding her hands in front of her. "I shall leave you to your day."

The hem of her delicate gown flowed and swirled over the hardwood like smoke in a breeze. When she turned the corner, Reign headed across the open foyer in the other direction.

Was I supposed to follow?

"If you want to make that phone call, you'll need to come to my office."

I jogged after him, his long legs increasing the distance between us with every stride.

On the other end of the house, he entered a large room with a bay window and a view of the front lawn. The grounds were beautiful at dawn. They almost made you forget this place was a fortress. The stone wall surrounding Jade's compound was of the two-foot thick and twenty-foot high, 'piss-off-or-die' kind of design, even before Julian added his laser security measures and Aust brought in the attacking wolves.

"I'll allow your communication, but it's imperative you say nothing to expose our realm."

I nodded and stepped further inside. The room didn't suit my impression of him. It was elegant, decorated with fine antiques, books and collectibles from around the world. He set the tray on a pristine walnut sideboard and leered at me. His charcoal eyes were almost black today.

"Do you understand the consequences for exposure, Mika? Has Bruin explained how our enforcement of justice works?"

"If I spill . . . you kill. Yeah I heard."

"Good, then we understand each other." He pointed toward the phone on his desk and picked up a piece of cinnamon bread from his plate. Leaning back against the cabinet, he crossed his ankles and took a bite. Privacy didn't seem to be an option, so I dialed Paige's number.

"Hello?" Her whispered muffle had me looking at the clock on the mantle. *Damn.* It wasn't even six yet.

"Shit, Paige, I'm sorry. I just got your emails and forgot what time it was."

"Mika!" A low ruffle of sheets was followed by what I assumed was the click of a lamp. "Thank god, where the hell have you been?"

A shadow of severity darkened Reign's eyes as he slowly shook his head. Could they *all* hear things from across the frickin' room? "I'm staying with friends out of town and just checked my messages, sorry. How's Meg?"

Paige sighed. "Better. She woke up late last night and the doctors gave her a once over. She's got a nasty concussion, but they think everything is intact . . . or at least as intact as it ever was for Meg. They're keeping her for a day or two for observation."

I fought the burning in my eyes. "Good. I'll try to go see her this afternoon."

"Are you home?"

"No, but I have an appointment with ACA Brantfield about the Nimithic trial today."

"Listen, Mika, is everything okay? It's not like you to be out of touch. I would have swung by your house to make sure you weren't dead, if I hadn't been stuck at the hospital and talking to cops all day yesterday."

I thought about the shape we left my home in. Paige would freak if she went there. "No, I'm good. I, uh . . . I just took your advice and spent the week relaxing with the sexy guy from the bar Saturday night."

"You're *still* with him? *Man,* I need details."

I laughed how my sex life sidetracked her. "I'll fill you in as soon as I can, but for now, we're kind of working on something. Any chance I can take a bit more time off?"

"Mika, honey, you're freelance, not a staffer. You're supposed to set your own schedule. You run yourself ragged. Take as much time as you need, on two conditions."

"And what are they?"

"I get dibs on any print rights and you don't fall off the face of the Earth again. Ever."

"Done. Forgiven?"

"Forgiven." She yawned into the receiver. "Okay, I'm going to get another forty-five minutes before my shower. So, we'll talk soon?"

"Yep. Soon."

I hung up and took a deep breath. Meg was going to be okay.

Reign walked over to his desk and set down his coffee and his pastry plate. The leather of his massive chair crunched and protested as he sank into the seat. "Sounds like you cleared the decks to stay a while."

Had I? No. I'm leaving. My breath caught at the thought. I didn't want to leave. *Or did I?*

I held his gaze and projected as much confidence as I could manage. "I need to give this deposition and then I'll figure out what's next."

"Well then," he said, with a devious smile. "Let's see if you and I can come to an agreement that's beneficial to everyone, shall we?"

CHAPTER TWENTY-SEVEN

With a shake of my hand, Reign gave me the green light to go back to Vancouver.

The deal wasn't all to my liking but was simple enough. I'd stay with Bruin until after the full moon a few weeks from now. I would keep an open mind and learn about his world, and in return, Reign would replace the SIM card mysteriously missing from my cell phone and make sure I got to my meeting this afternoon. I had pushed for uncensored use of phone and Internet but, apparently, trusting me to interact with my world on my honor was a deal breaker.

I took what I could get. For now.

When I got back to my suite, I found myself wandering to the open connecting door to Bruin's suite. Had he gone out warrioring? Was he still a mess about Jade? We weren't in a place where he was obligated to explain his whereabouts to me, but still.

He wasn't going to be happy that I went to Reign. Nope. The Were-Alpha was definitely going to go grizzly when he found out.

I pushed the upcoming fight out of my mind and considered what I would wear to my interview. Nothing fancy in case trouble hit and we needed to book it. Professional yet comfortable. I fingered through the drawers and snagged a pair of khakis, a copper, silk, sleeveless top and a comfy pair of leather flats. Accessories left a lot to be desired, but I'd deal.

After turning on the shower I hung two fluffy white towels on the heated rack and caught a glance of myself in the mirror. I leaned in for a closer look. *Huh.* I'd swear my hair seemed shinier than usual. And my teeth looked whiter.

I peeled off my clothes and flung them toward the hamper with my toe. My legs looked good too. I'd never been concerned with weight, but this morning I looked almost athletic. I snorted at that. I was as athletic as a three-toed sloth in a pair of Nikes, but there was no denying it, my muscles looked toned.

In the shower, I took inventory of my body. I *did* look good.

Dressed, I grabbed my brush and started pulling it through the lengths of my hair.

The *tap tap* on my balcony door had my heart racing. Before pulling back the drapes, I peeked out to see who was there. *Aust.*

"Good morning," I said, stepping back so he could enter. Orville took the opportunity to lope onto the balcony and climb his branch into the tree. "What are you doing up so early?"

Aust stepped in and looked around. "*Naneth* mentioned you were awake. I uh, I was having some difficulty finding reverie."

"I'm sorry, what?"

He raised his gaze and my skin tingled. His eyes were rimmed pink and bloodshot, his face paler than usual. He looked squeamish. "Our rest cycle is called reverie. It is similar to your sleeping. Of late, my meditation has eluded me—"

"Aust?" I stilled his milling hands and backed him up until he sat on the edge of the bed. "What is it? What's wrong?"

He closed his eyes.

I swept his golden waves back from his face and cupped his smooth jaw. "Hey, tell me."

He stood, paced to the bathroom door and whirled back around. "I need an honest opinion regarding something . . . of a personal nature."

"Okay, you have it."

"Sweet Shalana, help me," he gasped. The panic in his unusual, pale blue eyes had my heart tripping. "Other than *Naneth*, you are the only female who has truly seen to my soul. Jade and Lexi are sweet and very kind friends, but I feel *more* with you. A kindred *belonging*."

"I feel that too."

"You may not . . . once you hear me out."

He continued to pace, drawing quick shallow breaths, furrowing his fingers through his long golden hair. "My *gift*, as you call it . . . left me a pariah amongst my people. They shun anything of a magical nature . . . never accepted my abilities. To them I am . . . a miscreation—"

"Aust honey, you're hyperventilating." I rushed behind him as he fell to one knee and wrapped my arms around his chest. "Breathe with me. Come on. Earth Spirits, help us please."

The air around us stirred to life, warm as a stream in summer. I drew a deep breath, my lungs filling with the strength of the Earth Mother. Pressing tight to his back, I breathed for both of us. Slow in, then out, another monster breath in, and out. My hands on his chest registered as he matched my motion. More breathing. Now slower.

"You still with me?"

I felt his chest rise and fall in time with mine. After a moment, he straightened, drawing deep cleansing breaths. His cheeks were blotched red, his eyes moist.

"Aust, you're scaring me. Whatever it is, I'll help you get through it, I swear."

He kissed my hand and then, even though he didn't look sure, he stood, blew out a huge breath and untied the side of his tunic. Stripping his shirt from his shoulders he dropped it to the area rug by the bed, closed his eyes and did a slow runway turn.

"Oh. My. God."

Stripes.

Aust had stripes.

I gasped. Faint, gray and black tiger stripes had appeared on the surface of his alabaster skin. I stepped towards him, fingers out. No. Not his skin. They were hairs. Fine soft hairs swiped in wide brush strokes from his shoulder blades, around his ribs and down his chest.

"What am I to do, *neelan?*" The agony in his voice twisted in my gut. "The elders were correct. I am an *abomination.*"

"What?"

"Do you not see? Other males, like Galan and Tham were called upon constantly to pleasure females. It is honor I have never received. Not *once.* Not one time in the four decades since my coming of age has a female desired me or asked for my company."

His voice shook with emotion and he ran a hand down the stripes on his stomach. "Last night, when Jade needed help, all I could offer was to handle her schedule. What sort of male knows naught of pleasuring a female? I have nothing to offer."

"I'm sure Galan doesn't judge you, Aust. He's your family. You—"

"—shall never find a mate, never be loved or have young and I most certainly will never gain acceptance amongst my people."

"Aust stop." I cupped his jaw between my palms and held on tight. "Listen to me. If your community can't see that you're amazing, screw 'em. You are perfect. And beautiful. And sexy. You will find love because you are *you.*"

I pulled back and stroked my fingertips along the stripe running across his heart and down to his ribs. It was pussy-willow soft. "Trust me. No hot-blooded female could look at you and not want to rub themselves all over you."

He canted his head, looking wary. "In truth?"

"Oh yeah, these are so erotic I can't even tell you. My only question is . . ." I stepped behind him, tugged at the waist of his fitted suede pants and peeked down, "how far south do these stripes go?"

Aust laughed as he spun and wrapped me in his arms. He pressed a kiss to the side of my head and held me there. "Gratitude, *neelan.* Verily, you are—"

I felt the presence of Bruin's bear even before the violent rumble filled my suite.

CHAPTER TWENTY-EIGHT

He filled the connecting doorway, his body rigid.

My breath caught. "Bruin, before you freak . . . this isn't as bad as I'm sure it looks."

"Are you alone in your suite with a half-dressed Aust, telling him you find him sexy and wondering what he has underneath his leathers?"

"Yes, but—"

"Did you go behind my back and conspire with Reign to go to Vancouver even though you know you'll be a target of violence the minute you're there."

"Yes, but—"

"Do you wear another man's scent on your body, when the Fates have promised you to me?" He lumbered forward. His nose twitched as the muscle in the side of his jaw pulsed.

Aust scrambled to tug on his shirt. "Apologies Bruin, I assure you—"

Bruin snarled and lunged. Aust flew over the end of the bed and crashed to the floor. As I screamed, Bruin grabbed me and Flashed. The buzz in my head and tightness in my chest lasted only a second. I blinked. We stood on a precipice, high on the side of a mountain.

"Why did you do that?" I shoved him and stepped away from the ledge into a small, sparsely furnished cave. "You don't just get to push people around, Bruin. What if Aust is hurt? Take me back there, right now."

He raised a trembling hand, and I froze.

The air vibrated between us—the man fighting his animal side. I dropped my gaze and slowly lowered to kneel on the cave floor. Dominance in the wild is a tricky thing. Every gesture meant something, and I didn't mind taking a submissive position if it helped him regain control.

I looked out upon the valley and tried to calm my emotions. The morning sun blazed, a golden curtain drawing across the treetops far below. It crept along the banks of a stream, glittered in the cascading waters of a waterfall and chased the shadows of night away. The sky as far as I could see swirled flamingo pink, warm and soft like a Cosmopolitan with streaks of garnet laced through nature's cocktail.

"Mika," Bruin said behind me, his voice not yet his own.

I rose to face his fury.

His jaw clenched so tight he should have been spitting teeth. He seized me. I'd never complain about the way Bruin moved his lips. He wasn't gentle. His mouth covered mine, possessive and demanding, his bruising kiss a smoldering blue flame burning low and hot.

Trapped tight to his chest, strong hands ran over my back, my butt, under my hair to grasp the nape of my neck. He growled as he nuzzled against my cheeks and neck. As angry as I still was, I almost laughed when realization dawned. He was marking me.

Never a dull moment.

After a long while and a lot of stroking, Bruin pushed away from me and stepped back. "You will be the death of me, Mika, I swear you drive me to insanity."

"I don't mean to." I crossed my arms over my chest, suddenly chilled with the absence of his body heat. He threw me a skeptical glance and I sighed. "Well, not usually."

He strode around the cave, not looking at me, pausing to touch things as he wandered. "Okay. Tell me, why was Aust undressed with you in his arms? I'm calm now."

He didn't look calm. The last word I'd use to describe him was calm.

Even still, I relayed the story from the beginning, from how inadequate Aust felt with Jade needing help, to how he woke with tiger stripes, to how he panicked, thinking no one could love him. "All I did was comfort a friend."

He ran his fingers through his hair and continued to pace. "*Fucking Fates.* The guy can't catch a break from their twisted sense of humor. First his father, then getting kicked out of his village and now this?"

I shook my head. "He mentioned his father was killed a few months ago and that the black band he and Elora wear around their necks are symbolic of their mourning, but that's all he said. What happened?"

"Cameron was struck down defending their village when Abaddon and a Scourge raid party kidnapped Galan's sister, Lia. Then, without his father there to defend him, they exiled Aust because of his affinity with animals and because his eyes had changed. They said they didn't want his *evil* in their village."

That boiled through my body like a raging fire. "His evil?"

Bruin gripped my shoulder, surprise plain on his face. "Mika? You're growling."

I am? I released my fingers from the fists I'd made and sighed. "These hormones are doing a number on me."

He nodded, the copper highlights in his hair catching the morning light. "On me too."

God he was exquisite. Nipple-tightening, panty dampening perfection. *Annnd* the hormones were off again. I swallowed hard and tried to rein myself in. "What you walked in on—between Aust and me— was me teasing him a little, trying to make him laugh. That's all."

He scowled, closing his eyes. "In my head I see that. I know Highbornes have strict rules about intimacy, but—"

"But you still attacked him."

Bruin barked a throaty laugh. "Baby, if I had *attacked* him, he would have bled. I just needed him away from you." His shoulders straightened and stiffened, reminding me, yet again, how massive Bruin really was. "I'm trying to hold back the effects of the Bonding, Mika, but let me make one thing clear—Weres don't share."

I shivered as a chill shot down my spine.

"Shit, you're cold. Your hair's still wet."

Bruin stepped into the shadow of the cave, lit a long wooden match and began touching the wicks of candles. On a hundred little ledges—where stone jutted out enough to set one on—there were candles. They had burned often enough that the dried wax flowed down the stone walls like ivory waterfalls cascading to the floor.

"This cave gets chilly. I'm sorry, I wasn't thinking."

"I'm fine. Where are we?" I examined the oval cave behind us. Completely self-contained, it reached about twenty-five feet deep and was half that in width, the floor strewn with a large pallet and covered in lush, overlapping rugs. Along the right, near the opening to the ledge, a wooden table sat with some old-fashioned quill tipped pens and ink. On the opposite wall stood an old, southwest cupboard.

"Welcome to my secret place." Bruin finished with the candles, the two of us lit by a warm golden glow. After snuffing the match, he stepped to the edge of the ledge. My heart lurched. For all my many devil-may-care adventures, heights were not among them. No sky diving. No bungee jumping. I wasn't even a fan of ladders.

Bruin noticed my apprehension and stepped back to the chair and ottoman looking out over the valley. He sat on the front edge of the chair, pulled the ottoman between his knees and materialized a brush in his hand. "Mika, sit. Your hair will tangle if we don't brush it out."

I took my seat in front of him. "What does a Talon warrior know about tangles?"

He leaned against my back and spoke quietly in my ear. "In another life, I used to have a twin sister. Gemma's hair was lighter than yours, not quite as long, but crazy curly. As litter-mates, it was expected that we take care of one another. I didn't do a very good job."

The ache in his voice stole my breath. "Tell me. How did you find this place?"

With my eyes closed, I sat while he brushed. Starting at the crown of my head, Bruin worked the brush back, gently tugging through my tangles. "One evening, about six months after Reign brought me home, I watched the sun set over the valley. From the edge of the forest on the western ridge I saw the silhouette of a massive bird disappear behind this rock formation."

He held out his hands in front of me, his arms wide. "She was a beast. Her wing span must have cleared six feet, easy. She soared across the sky with a fox kit clenched in her talons. It made me wonder if she had a nest."

"So, you decided to climb out and see?" I looked down and shuddered. Jagged rocks snaked along the trickling stream, winding through the forest. "It must be a five-hundred-foot drop. Are you crazy?"

"I was thirteen and heartbroken. It seemed perfectly logical at the time." He leaned against my back and reached over my shoulder, pointing out a ledge where the thatched remnants of a long-forgotten nest still clung to stone. "When I edged my way over, I came around the bend and a golden eagle perched right there, eviscerating her kill. It was amazing."

I scrunched up my face. "Charming."

He chuckled, the vibration of his laughter penetrating my back.

"So, who knows about this place?" I asked.

The brush continued to move smoothly through my hair. "Just me. And now you."

I wasn't sure how to process that. "Not Jade or Lexi or anyone?"

"No. Well, Jade probably knows but I've never told her, so she's never brought it up."

"Then how—"

He placed the brush on his muscled thigh beside me and worked his fingers through my thick mane. His hands felt wonderful as they gathered my hair at the back of my head and pulled it into a ponytail. "When Jade heals people she sees bits of their thoughts and memories. Everything you never wanted people to know is open for her to absorb. She's very discreet. She'd rather not have that particular side-effect, but she does. I don't even think about it anymore. You see, Jade is . . ."

When his hands dropped away, I turned. The pained expression he'd worn last night had returned. I squeezed his thigh. "Granted, I don't know anything about your world, but I read people. Galan and the others love her. They'll take care of her."

He met my gaze and I was taken aback, his eyes far too glossy. "She should have a *choice.* The fucking Fates constantly mess with us. You and me, Gemma, Aust and now Jade."

"Galan said it's temporary. In a week she'll be back to normal and maybe she and Galan might be expecting. That's good, isn't it?"

He scrubbed a hand over his jaw. "That woman in the lounge last night—the one draping herself over anyone and everyone—that wasn't Jade. That wasn't my sister. You don't know her yet, but Jade is strength, tempered with sweetness. She's not a lusty vixen who struts in front of a room full of people and then takes a handful of consorts to her bed. She's passionate, but private. She'll be horrified when she hears what this fucking Yearning fever made her do."

"It's not her fault. Everyone knows that. She can't change it any more than we can."

He shook his head, a light dimming in his eyes. "No. We can't change anything. We're marionettes and the Fates pull our fucking strings to make us dance. Someone needs to get at those bitches and show them what it's like to lose the right to choose, to lose yourself a piece at a time, to be forced . . .." He froze, his hands balled into fists at his sides.

"Bruin. What happened? What are you really talking about here?"

He stood and stepped to the ledge, the distant rush of the waterfall filling the silence. "Too much to recount. Scourge raiders have taken a toll from everyone who lives at Haven—most of the realm, really. Abaddon, their evil master, promises immortality and strength beyond imagination to those who follow him."

"And does he deliver?"

"For a price. The Scourge are strong and, because they're no longer truly alive, they don't die. But he absorbs their souls. He takes their energy and the empty shells he leaves behind just become more vicious and viler."

"And they killed your people."

Bruin nodded. "Gemma and I were the second litter to my family. My sisters, Risa and Emma, were three years older. They were the sweetest girls ever to grace this realm. They were spirited and fun and never spoke an unkind word."

He swiped his fingers under his eyes and cleared his throat. "Abaddon is a monster, Mika, and the Scourge are just as bad. They'll hurt you because you belong with me. They'll hurt you because you are a female and they can. They'll violate and degrade you, just for the thrill."

I swallowed. "I'll be more careful. I promise. And I'll try to listen to you."

He smiled, but it didn't touch his eyes. "I believe you mean that, but please understand . . . I can't let you risk your safety."

The hairs on my arms stood on end. Can't *let* me? I took in the isolation of the cave again. *He wouldn't.* "Bruin, don't even think about leaving me here. I will never forgive you."

He nodded, the backs of his fingers brushing my cheek. "Maybe not, but at least you'll be alive to hate me. I'm sorry, Mika. I really am trying to do what's best for you."

"And you think abandoning me in a cave is what's *best* for me?"

He stepped closer to the ledge and waved his hand toward the table. A platter of food and drinks appeared. "I'll be back as soon as I can. If I'm right, the Scourge will know about your appointment and will have people in place to secure you. They won't know the difference between your scent and mine until it's too late. I'll use that to draw them out."

"Take me with you. If I draw them out, you'll have a better chance of getting them."

Bruin's golden glare flashed. "You're not *bait*, Mika."

"You'll protect me." And he would. Of all the things I was sure of, that was one. Bruin would protect me to his last breath. "If you're worried, get me a bodyguard. Keep me close, but don't take away *my* choice."

He winced. I saw his resolve falter, but only for a moment. "Julian came to me late last night and confirmed it. The man who threatened you in the tavern yesterday was Abaddon. The spawn of evil himself. Nobody on the Talon council can believe he outed himself. He's been so secretive, so intent on keeping his identity hidden."

"He would still be a mystery if I'd fallen under his spell. I helped. Now you know what he looks like."

"But why did he do it? After decades sneaking around like a rat, why take a stand and threaten you?"

"I don't know, but I'm a journalist. Let me help dig up the truth."

"*The truth?* The truth is, I've lost half a dozen lions, snow leopards, two packs of wolves, a den of hyena and a mated pair of Siberian tigers. They all held dominant positions in the Were community, all skilled and able to defend themselves, yet all are missing and presumed dead."

I cupped his rakish jaw and made him look at me. "That's horrible, I agree, but I've investigated the disappearance of wildlife for years in my world. This can't be that different. As long as I'm a part of this world, use my skills. I can be an asset, Bruin."

"You *are* an asset. That's what I'm trying to tell you. I won't put you in the middle of a slaughter. As King I may be a failure, but as your mate, I won't be."

"So, your plan is to lock me away when things get dangerous? I won't live like that."

"You don't have to." He paused and watched two hawks drift effortlessly beyond the ledge. They were graceful, floating mid-air on the thermals rising up from the valley.

"The Bonding Brand lasts one full moon cycle. In a couple of weeks, since you refuse to be my mate, you'll stop giving off my scent and can return to your life. I won't keep you here if you don't want me."

I rubbed my chest. It felt like my Humvee was parked on my sternum. "Bruin, I adore you. I just don't belong here. I want *my* life."

His jaw clenched. "Then wait it out. Keep yourself alive until it's over and you return to the other realm. You'd be smart to move and maybe write under a pseudonym, but the beauty of the Internet means you can submit stories from anywhere, right?"

Right. My head was spinning. "Why didn't you tell me this earlier?"

He stared out over the forested valley. "At first I didn't know. No one ever walked away from bonding. But then I spoke to Castian about your choices. I couldn't give you the out before you considered what it could be like between us. I guess . . . I hoped you might choose to stay . . . that somehow you'd fall for me."

He turned and lowered his face to within inches from mine. "Whatever happens, Mika, know this—I fell for you. I was a goner from that first night in the bar."

Bruin placed a kiss on my forehead and then disappeared.

CHAPTER TWENTY-NINE

I paced the candle lit cave. "Bruin, get back here! When I get out of here, I'm going to. . ." I couldn't think of anything bad enough. "Well, I don't know what I'm going to do, but it's going to be bad. You hear me? Bad. And it will involve your male parts somehow."

I envisioned all the ways to make a bear's life hell. That cheered me up a fair bit. Storming around the interior of the cave, I half expected him to flash back and say he was an idiot. Which he was. When that didn't happen, I tried to understand how I'd ended up here.

Part of me seized the idea of the out, knowing that after the full moon, I could go home and forget everything about Bruin and his world. Part of me felt paralyzed with the thought.

I stared at the waterfall on the far side of the valley. A silver sliver ran from the blue sky to the green of the forest below—beautiful, yes —but really no different from exotic locations in my world. Was this world really so alien? There were good guys and bad. There were families who loved each other and suffered when those they loved were hurt. Did loving my life and my world exclude the things I loved about this one?

Over the next hour, as the sun's warmth inched into the recesses of my prison, I thought about what I chose to go back to in Vancouver. I could come and go without anyone censoring my actions or communications. I could meet up with my girls and not worry about them getting hurt because they were standing too close to me.

Crossing the uneven stone floor, I scanned the spread of food on the table. Bagels with strawberry cream cheese. He remembered. *Damn you, Bruin.* Even given my recent hearty appetite, I wouldn't make a dent. "He likes me well fed. I'll give him that."

I thought about boycotting the whole eating thing just to piss him off. My stomach had other plans. After picking up a bagel and slathering on some spread, I poured a glass of juice. When I set down the jug, it clinked against the inkwell and almost knocked over the quill. I set it right again and rubbed my fingers together. Sepia stained the pad of my fingers. It didn't drip, but it wasn't dry either. *Huh.*

I looked around. "Why have ink when there's nothing to write on?"

My journalistic spidey-senses tingled to life. I bit off a bite of bagel and I opened the doors of the big-ole cupboard. Nothing. Okay, Bruin wasn't the kind of guy to leave things out in the open. After all, he hid chick-flicks within the covers of other movies. I scanned the Spartan furnishings and lifted the rugs. Still nothing. The walls were stone. Where could he stash things?

"Come on, big guy, give it up. I'm like a dog on a bone when I'm curious."

I rethought my search parameters while walking back for my glass of juice. *Hello.*

A faint arcing path marked the dust on the cave floor. I bent down and lost it, but when I shifted to look from a different angle, I followed the arc back to the wall. Inspired, I grabbed the end of the wooden cupboard, hefted and swung the cupboard away from the wall.

There, right along the floor, a hidey-hole had been chiseled out of the stone. I knelt down and found a dozen leather-bound journals stuffed inside. I reached for one, but hesitated. "If you don't come back, Bruin. I'm going to snoop in your books. Don't make me violate your privacy."

Nothing. Damn him. Damn him for leaving me here. Damn him for thinking he could make me stay . . . for being a bossy, insufferable, dominate—*Bear*. I grabbed the top journal.

Fine, if that's the way you want to play this.

With the rest of my bagel on the table next to my juice, I pulled the chair over. After brushing the crumbs and stone dust off my fingers, I picked up the top leather-bound book, settled in and flipped it open to the first page. I had to smile. The penmanship and diction in his journal weren't at all what I expected. The man had a truly elegant side . . . his *royal* side, I'd guess. Like if you bit through his hard candy shell you'd get to the gooey caramel centre I'd glimpsed a few times.

His entries seemed almost poetic, written in formal cursive strokes with curled tails and fancy, flourishing script. I ran a finger over the page then gazed at the old-fashioned quill and ink set out on the table. Would he have been schooled in this calligraphy-style because he was a prince or because this realm held onto the old ways? I flipped through the thick almond parchment, to the last entry. Yesterday.

My heart aches for Jade. Never have I seen her so out of her own control and character. Castian promises she will recover as long as the Highbornes keep her fever from climbing. Little comfort. Until then, my Blaze is someone she would never want to be. I pray the Yearning ends quickly.

Mika and Aust. In my mind I know they seek each other solely as companions of common interest, but the beast that lives within me, he writhes and claws at the stench of another man's scent on her skin. I am glad she found some measure of comfort here, truly, though it strikes a piercing blow that it was not with me.

Does she comprehend what she means to me...for me? The prospect of having her...as a woman and as a mate, consumes me. Would she ever share her bed with me as my true self? Would she be safe? Animal lust burns in my blood. My claws ache to extend past their sheaths and my cock throbs day and night. I fight to silence my instincts more each day but fear I may rut her if I let my guard down. For now, I must remain in the cave to sleep.

Come morning, I shall go to her, try to make her understand the dangers. Have I earned enough of her respect to keep her from harm? I laugh even as I write the words. She has far too much will and spirit to shy away from danger. If only she understood, what her loss would do to me.

The dreams are back. I can't shut them out. The ache and agony as debilitating as when I was a cub and lost everything.

I reread the entry, pulling to draw breath. "Oh Bruin. What happened? What are you carrying around inside you?"

I put that journal back into the wall and grabbed the one from the bottom. It looked to be the oldest. The leather binding wore through in places and the tattered parchment was yellowed with age. I opened the cover and read the first entry.

What am I to write on blank pages? Maximus says to use this journal as a healing tool. How will a book and well of ink mend what's broken? Will it chase the visions of father staked and skinned from my nightmares? Will it silence Gemma's cries, begging the monsters to stop? No. Nothing will. Her screams will echo in my shattered mind forever.

Galan said Bruin was only thirteen when his parents were killed. I skimmed the pages, the strokes and curls of the ink becoming a blur until an entry caught my attention.

Happy Birthday to us.

I had the dream again Gem. They yanked me back by my hair and forced me to watch as they held you down. I tasted the salt of my tears and heard the weakness in my pleas for mercy. I am sorry. I should have done more. With father slain it was my duty to protect you. I will kill them—for you. If it takes a lifetime. I swear it. I ache for you, my other half, blood of my blood.

Never will I feel whole without you.

I flipped toward the back. By my estimation months had passed and still the pain in Bruin's words ravaged my heart. Over and over he spoke of his inability to honor his father, to protect his mother and his sisters, to exact the type of justice he believed his family deserved.

Risa: I found myself thinking of you this morning. After waking from a troubled night, Jade and Alexannia sat and rubbed my ears for what must have been hours. Finally, after weeks of exhaustion while sleep slipped through the foggy recesses of my mind, I found rest. It took me back to how you used to run your fingers through my coat when I was sad or afraid.

Father would have been so angry with my weakness, but you insisted that even the mightiest prince needed a safe place. Risa, you were that for me.

My breath hitched as I closed the journal and replaced it at the bottom of the pile. So much despair. I slid the cupboard back into place and laid on the pallet in the centre of the floor. Bruin's scent clung to the fabric and I breathed deep. Every nuance of him combined to make that smell, the outdoors, his cologne, his clean sweat, the soap he used.

Pulling a blanket over my lap, I closed my eyes.

"Neither of us had the childhood we deserved." Even as I said the words, I knew there was a huge difference between a walk-away-father leaving a vodka-addled-mother and having your parents and three sisters slaughtered and possibly raped before your eyes.

Africa filled my mind—Luke and Amy flayed, their corpses set out for the wild animals to consume come nightfall. Their cubs would never be able to feel the love of their parents. Tears warmed my cheeks and clung to my chin. "What a harsh and brutal world. Everything I despise. Everything I fight against in my world is happening to your people."

I swiped my face dry and scanned the empty little cave. Bruin wanted so much—from me, for me—more than it was fair to expect. Yet, the more I learned about him, the more I understood his need. Without Grandfather even being there, I knew what he would say. "If you cannot imagine your life with Bruin, perhaps imagine your life without him. Maybe that will bring you answers."

I brushed my damp cheek as the breeze pulled back and I was left with my thoughts. A life without Bruin would be . . . *tranquil*—nobody growling at me to fall in line, *my own*—I could make my own decisions again, no one bossing me around or leaving me in caves. The thought of him gone almost stole my breath. I wasn't lonely before him, *was I?* I stroked the rich brown ink on my palm, tracing the scrollwork of my Bonding Brand.

I'd definitely miss the sexual connection. There had never been, nor would there be, another lover for me like Bruin. He said Were-couples share a closeness that goes beyond what humans can experience. Apparently, it got stronger once the bonding was accepted and stronger again with each litter or cub born.

The blackened brand I'd noticed on Hugh's hand flashed into my mind. After the death of his mate, he was left to raise six boys on his own. Bruin said he would never love another woman. Weres only got one chance to love and that made their love deeper than any I had ever seen.

Was it better that Luke and Amy died together? Imagine one partner killed, leaving the other behind, knowing the Scourge had skinned their mate and taken his or her pelt.

What would they possibly want with the pelts? Trophies? *Sick.* Some twisted satisfaction of killing a Were? *Disgusting.* I'd become accustomed to the answer being greed. Dealing in black market exotics was big business. Two lion pelts could bring in close to ten thousand dollars. Wolf pelts, twenty-five hundred each.

Hell, the haul of pelts and exotic animal organs I exposed in the warehouse of the Nimithic Group was valued at almost one-point-five million. The pharmaceuticals they were developing in their lab using the organs and by-products, another quarter mil . . ..

Oh. My. God. I sat bolt upright. It's all connected.

Why hadn't I seen it? What an *idiot.* My mind snapped with the bombardment of connections I'd been too blind to see until that moment. *Oh God, Bruin's going to Vancouver. He's going to get himself killed and he doesn't even realize why?*

I screamed to the heavens. Please, let someone hear me and come. I paced, waiting, knowing it was futile. No one would answer my call. *Nobody knows about this cave.*

Glaring toward the edge, I remembered how he found it and swallowed. There was still one way out. If I dared. I scanned the cave again and thought about Bruin heading off to Vancouver without me. Risking certain death was better than standing there doing nothing. At least my fate was once again in my own hands. And if I fell . . . well, I wouldn't have to worry about what to do with my destiny, would I?

I swallowed the bile burning up my throat, grabbed hold of a jut in the rock and swung my foot off the stony ledge.

CHAPTER THIRTY

"What the hell was I thinking?" The pounding of my pulse drummed in my ears, I pinched my eyes closed and panted for air. Fainting would be bad. Horribly, irreversibly bad. The soft leather toes of my flats wedged into footholds as my fingertips curled over juts of rocky stone. My palms cried out as my grip forced shards of jagged rock into my skin.

It would be far safer to maneuver back onto the ledge than shimmy my way across the remaining rock face to the forest beyond. But Bruin, a good man despite being annoying as hell, was about to launch into an offensive and he didn't have all the facts.

"Earth Spirits, I need your help." As the enchanted breeze lifted my hair, my chest eased a little knowing I wasn't alone. "Help me find the footing and holds to make my way to safety."

Cracking my eyes open, I focused on the grey-brown stone striations in front of me. *Nature is part of me. It offers me strength. It will keep me safe.*

I'd watched guys on adventure weekends climb rock-walls a hundred times. This was no different. Except the lack of a life-saving harness. *Annnd* the five-hundred-foot plummet to become a puddle of broken goo for a turkey vulture buffet.

Using only touch and my inner sense, I inched across the face of the mountainside making excruciatingly slow progress. "Keep talking to me spirits. Guide me." I swallowed hard, my face pressed so tight against the sun-warmed surface it scuffed my cheek. About half way across, my legs began to tremble, and my stomach lurched. Praying with all I had, I willed my body to obey me for once in my life.

Give me strength, keep my bagel right where it is and let me focus.

With my toes set for the next move, I stilled. Either by prayer, my connection with the Earth Mother's grace, or some bizarre twist of fate, a sudden sense of calm engulfed me. The rush in my ears silenced, my muscles coiled with kinetic energy, ready to spring. I would have sworn my fingernails stretched to strengthen my grip as a new sense of confidence took hold.

I can do this.

I reached into the small crevice close to my right shoulder and swung my left arm along the rock face. My heart leaped. I held my weight without strain and without fear. I moved my right foot to a small ledge and shifted my weight again. Where my hands moved, my feet followed, and after another twenty minutes, I stepped onto the grassy ledge of the forest, my pants filthy and my blouse ripped and sweated out.

Huzzah!

Under the damp umbrella of the forest, my body surged. This was my element, the earthy smell of the moss and bracken, the chirp of the chipmunks playing in the undergrowth, the whisper of the wind dancing in the canopy above. I sank to my knees while I caught my breath. "Thank you, Earth Mother. Thank you, Creator."

With no path, and all the forest looking alike, I wondered which way to go. Then a strange sense of déjà vu hit me. I considered the direction of the mid-morning sun and breathed deep. Lifting my nose to the breeze, my skin tingled as I caught a scent.

Somehow, I could smell that Aust was close by.

On a run, I pushed my way through the brush, startling two red squirrels scurrying over the forest floor. After their initial start, they kept pace with me, chasing one another, darting under brush, over fallen branches, and leaping from one tree trunk to another.

Where the undergrowth thinned, I manoeuvred through the branches and brush. Effortless. What was happening? In spots, where the growth grew thick or the ground gave way to steep crevices, I used overhead branches to span the distances. Without missing a stride, I jumped up, caught the branches and moved hand-over-hand to the other side.

I cleared another gap in the terrain and dropped down softly to the pads of my feet. Right behind my Highborne friend and the wolf by his side. Aust jumped and Faolan yelped.

"Did I startle you two?"

His ears flushed to the tips of their gentle peaks. "You are a quiet one."

I smiled as he teased me with my own words and ruffled Faolan's scruff. He looked none the worse for his encounter with Bruin earlier and that was a relief.

The small groups of students he was with were on some sort of horticultural outing—gathering plants, clipping leaves and dusting off roots—all of them studiously working with their partners and engaged in private conversations. "I don't mean to interrupt, but I need a favor. I need to get back to the castle. Bruin's in a heap of trouble and about to do something stupid . . . well, even stupider than the last stupid thing he did."

Aust looked up and I recognized the student with the Mohawk and the crescent shaped tattoo marking his cheek and temple. "Nash," he said, "might I ask that you escort the group back to the castle once everyone has their specimens gathered?"

"Sure, man . . . I mean, yes, sir."

Aust held up a hand and addressed the group. "Apologies everyone, but I must take my leave. Nash is in charge in my stead and should you have any questions about our lesson, I will be at the Hearthstone this afternoon."

Aust took my hand and jogged toward a sandy path. Faolan's silver coat caught the morning sun as she ran alongside us. With a sideways glance he looked me over. "Are you well, Mika? When Bruin Flashed you from your suite . . . he was very angry, and I feared . . ."

"Bruin would never hurt me, please know that. His temper is more about him being hurt and afraid than anything." I sighed, thinking about the eloquent entries in his journal. Jade had told me as much, but I hadn't listened. "I'm not saying he wasn't angry, he was, but he's desperate to protect me. Did you know his family was killed by a Scourge raid when he was young?"

Aust broke stride and faced me. "Has something happened? You seem different."

I bit my lip and exhaled. "I don't know. Maybe it's adrenaline, but my body seems stronger and my senses sharper. And I feel different . . . about a lot of things.

Our winding path met with a wide dirt trail and we altered course, making our way through the forest ahead. "How long will it take to get back to Jade's compound?"

"At this pace, I would estimate a good hour's time."

"An hour? Dammit, I don't have an hour. Can you Flash, Aust?"

"No. Apologies."

I hopped over a gnarled root jutting up from the ground and upped our jog to a run. "Where's a Talon when you need one. We could Flash there in two seconds."

After a moment, Aust pulled us to a stop, his jaw tight, the furrow between his brow pronounced. "I may have an alternative, though I'm not sure how long I can hold my form."

Form? "What are you talking about?"

Aust pulled his hair free from its leather tie and shook it loose around his face. "I believe the reason I have stripes is because of an incident a few months ago . . . it is a very long story which I will tell you at another time. The important point is that I now have the ability to change into a white tiger."

"And this is the first you thought to *mention* it?" I wished I had the time to go over all the reasons that should have come up earlier, but I didn't have the time. "Okay, we'll talk about that later. Let's see this tiger of yours and get back to Jade's place."

Aust released the clasp of the belt holding his thigh sheath. With a speed and gentleness that was unique to Aust and the Highbornes, he buckled the weapon around my hips and tied the tip of the sheath around my thigh. "If we encounter Scourge, I want you prepared. Oh . . . I must undress and given Bruin's mood earlier . . .."

Good point. I nodded and gave him my back.

"Would you carry the pack with my clothes as we travel, then set them out when we get to the forest surrounding the compound?"

I made out the faint rustle of fabric as he removed his clothes and heard him pack his rucksack. When the air around me surged with electrical energy, I couldn't help myself. I turned, catching a beautiful glimpse of Aust's naked backside right before his form shimmered and disappeared. In the flash of a moment, he morphed into a sleek, muscular white tiger.

"Unbelievable. Aust, you are the coolest friend I've ever had. I swear."

CHAPTER THIRTY-ONE

"Where is he?" I stormed into the main foyer of Jade's house and almost bowled Julian over as he came out of the dining room. "Your brother. Where?"

"I'm . . . uh, not sure, one sec." Julian set his plate on the round table in the middle of the space and pulled his phone out. After pressing a few buttons, he lifted his head. "Reign's office, but you should—"

I was down the hall before I realized I hadn't thanked him. *Damn.* The closer I got to Bruin the crazier I felt. My earlier fury about being abandoned was back in full force. As I pushed the office door open, I realized this was Reign's office. I should have knocked.

Bruin's eyes widened. "How the hell did you get here?"

"You mean, how did I escape the cave you abandoned me in? How do you think, Bruin? I scaled the fucking rock face back to the forest."

Bruin had the decency to look stricken. "You could have fallen. What the *hell* were you thinking?"

"I was *thinking* I figured out what the slaughter of your people and the attempts on my life were about. I was *thinking* I needed to tell you, but was left in the wilderness alone and with no way to call you. I was *thinking* there was no bloody way you were going to get yourself killed when I wanted the honor of killing you myself."

My vision had quite literally gone red. I stopped just inches before him. "How dare you cage me like an animal."

"It wasn't a cage. I left you with food and comforts."

I stared at him in complete disbelief. "You left me on the edge of a cliff knowing I'm afraid of heights."

He growled and loomed closer. "Well you seem to have conquered that fear."

"Never underestimate a pissed-off female, Bruin. That was your first mistake."

"And what was my second—"

A whistle pierced the office and I caught my breath. Reign lowered his fingers from his mouth. "Okay you two, back it off. This isn't going anywhere. This situation is difficult—"

"Difficult?" I snapped, my chest tightening as his glower zeroed in on me. I drew in a deep, hard breath and fought back the sting of angry tears. I would not cry in front of these two. "Your son doesn't value my arrangement to go to Vancouver and we had a deal. Could you please arrange for someone else to take me through the Portal Gate?"

"You're not going."

I whirled on Bruin, his eyes alight with the animal writhing within.

Reign tightened his lips and looked like he was fighting back a smile. "It's only eleven now. Why don't the two of you cool down and talk this out. We'll meet back here at one."

Cool down? Not likely. "I *will* make this appointment, we have an arrangement, right?"

Reign rubbed his eyes and sank back into his oversized chair. "I will honor my end. This office. Two hours."

Hot fury raged in Bruin's eyes as his fingers curled around my arm. "Make all the plans you like, my love, but you're not going."

Reign sat forward and leaned over his desk. "I made my call, Bruin. Mika goes."

The monolithic desk flew to the side and hit the wall like it was made of paper. Bruin lunged forward, dagger drawn and pressed against Reign's Adam's apple. His shoulders tensed. "You don't make those decisions, old man. She is *mine*."

Reign's lips moved in a silent curse. He waited, breathing, sampling the tension in the air before speaking in a slow and soothing tone. "Yes, my son. She is yours."

Bruin's claws extended past his nail beds and against the flesh of Reign's throat. "I am the Were-King, Alpha of those under my rule . . . and *Mika* is *my mate*. Don't you fucking step between me and what is mine—"

"Enough," I hissed, shifting so Bruin could see me. "You've lost control, Bruin. Get a grip. Reign is your *father*. You don't want to hurt him."

"It's not him, Mika," Reign crooned. "His body's laced with adrenaline and those damned hormones. His bear has ascended. Look at his eyes. I'm surprised he's holding his form."

His form?

The possession of his bear flowed over me and warmed my body. How was that possible? Whatever was happening with my senses, this pull between us, it wasn't real. The fact that he abandoned me in a cave was real. The fact that he glared at me like *I* was the one who'd crossed the line—that was real. Again, my emotions bombarded and almost choked the breath from my lungs. I fought. Struggled to stuff them deep and lock them away.

Bruin's lips curled to a cold smile and he turned, distracted from his hold on his father. "Tell me, Mika, what's your secret?"

"For what?"

He breathed in deep, his nostrils flaring as he leaned closer. "For cutting off your arousal. When you look at me like that, the scent of your desire hits me. It's sweet and hot, then, suddenly it shuts off. Tell me how you do it and maybe I can control my own hunger as well."

I swallowed. "I think about how you boss me around—how if we were mated, you'd protect me to the point of controlling my every move. You'd tell me I can't investigate any more. I'd do it anyway. You'd lock me in a cage. I'd be forced to shoot you."

His head canted to the side. "You've got us all figured out, have you?"

"I'm right. Your actions today prove it." God, he smelled good. I couldn't think so close to him. I stepped back, but he stalked closer. My heart pounded, my fingers aching to brush his skin. He lumbered slowly, pressing forward until I felt the heat of his body warm my skin.

Pushing away, I stomped out of the office, across the main floor and up the steps of the grand staircase two at a time. I felt him follow, his presence more animal than man. Stalking. Down the hall, past the grandfather clock, and to my door. I didn't look back. I didn't have to.

My hands trembled by the time I stepped into my room. I wasn't sure if I was about to be strangled or stripped and thrown to the hardwood floor.

"Mika?" The husky uncertainty in his voice stole my breath.

I spun, my hands landing flat on his chest. He didn't seem to register the force I used to push him back, which just pissed me off more. "Don't do this. I'm not your property."

"You are *mine.*"

I didn't object. This was his bear and Jade had said his bear had claimed me. No sense arguing semantics. "If you don't want me hurt you need to listen. Every time you lock me in a glass house, I'll throw rocks until I shatter it. You can't cage me. I won't live like that."

He growled. "I don't want you to feel caged. I try to keep you safe. You're so reckless."

"I'm not reckless."

His brows disappeared behind his bangs and his mouth quirked in a gesture that spoke of the man regaining control. "You scaled a rockface and climbed out over a lethal drop."

I caught his exasperation and glanced away to avoid smiling. "Spirited. I'm Spirited."

Bruin strode away and leaned against the door, arms crossed over his chest. As we stared at each other from across the room, the corners of his mouth twitched. "You drive me crazy."

"You mentioned that."

"There are moments I want to strangle you."

"Right back atcha."

We stood there staring at each other while the current in the air settled and I could see clearly again. It was Bruin who finally broke the silence, his voice once again his own. "Tell me what you figured out. What's this about the Were slaughters?"

I moved over to my desk and pulled out the folders tucked in my bag. This was my wheelhouse. This I could handle. "I think it's all connected. We assumed I've been under attack because of our bonding. What if I've been targeted because of my case against the Nimithic Group. The first men came at me at Spankz and that was before we had anything between us."

Bruin's brow lifted. "What has one to do with the other?"

Grabbing the thick blue folder from the top, I opened it and grabbed the photos. "Three weeks ago I tracked the sale of large quantities of pelts and exotic animal organs to a warehouse outside Abbotsford. At first, I thought the Nimithic Group headed up a highly organized black market, exotics ring working both sides of the border, but that's wrong."

I spread out the eight-by-tens. "You said that Abaddon coming here was out of character, right? That the Scourge raids are escalating?"

"I'm listening."

"So, how would Scourge sneak up on Luke and Amy and kill them in their own bed?"

"They couldn't. Luke and Amy would have smelled them coming the minute they neared the house. If they couldn't Flash, they would have at least called for help or fought."

"Right, but what if they couldn't smell them, or for some reason, they couldn't change form, or maybe they were drugged? That would change the odds, right?"

"Sure, but how—"

"A shitload of money and a pharmaceutical lab working with the knowledge of Were biochemistry." I fingered through the pictures and tagged one that had confused me from the get-go. Half a dozen scientists in lab coats and masks hovered over tables of pharmaceuticals.

"I think they're gathering DNA from the bodies of your missing species and selling the pelts as a way to fund their dummy corporation. I think the Nimithic Group fills their coffers to fund the creation of some pill or weapon that's going to give them the edge while they systematically wipe out Weres. It's not poaching . . . it's genocide."

Bruin looked through the pictures, then looked at me. "How did you figure this out?"

I threw up my hands and walked around the table to face him. "That's what I tried to tell you. This is what I do. And whether you like it or not, I'm damn good. My truck, the weekend rallies, my job. I like an adrenaline rich lifestyle."

"You are going to get hurt."

I sighed, trying to think how to say this without setting off his bear again. "I'd rather get hurt than be wrapped in cotton, hating you."

"Better to hate me than be dead."

"I *would* be dead, Bruin." I lifted his hand and pressed our brands together. The discomfort eased, and I laced our fingers together and squeezed. "Locking me away will kill me faster than a bullet ever could. I need to live, not just exist. If you want me to stay here for the next three weeks, I have to be a full partner or I'm nothing."

Bruin pulled his hand away and shoved it deep into his pocket. There was so much fear and worry in his expression it stole my breath. I didn't need the Earth Mother to tell me how his spirit struggled. He was just as lost as I felt.

I held my hands up in the air between us. "Let's try a compromise."

"Compromise how?"

"For the next three weeks I'll make every effort to let you keep me safe *if*—and this is non-negotiable—you promise we can work as a team. I'll take part in the investigation of what's going on with the Weres and then, when we find the bad guys, I promise to stay in the house under guard, all snug and safe, while you go get them."

He bit his lip and scrubbed a hand through his brown, floppy hair. Bracing his weight on his palms, he leaned over the table. The vein in his jaw clenched and twitched as he looked over the coloured photos. Shit. He was going to shut me down. Again.

It shouldn't have been a surprise, but it still stung.

"Fine. We work as a team," he said, his words more a curse than a statement. "But when things heat up, you do what I say. I don't want so much as a scratch on that pretty little body of yours. Deal?"

I shook his hand and nodded. "Deal."

He kept his hold on my hand and grew serious. "Now, let's discuss how you scaled that rock-face."

I swallowed, my mouth watering for his kiss. "Let's not. Let's mend some hurt feelings."

Bruin's lips dropped to meet mine, but he recoiled, his nostrils flared. Gold flecks appeared in his eyes as his bear ricocheted back to the surface.

"What?" I snapped. "What now?"

"You smell like . . . him."

The room blurred as Bruin threw me over his shoulder and marched toward the bathroom. "I'm going to lather you up, clean you off, then mark every inch of your body myself. For whatever time we have together, you will carry *my* scent. No other."

CHAPTER THIRTY-TWO

*B*ruin rolled off and tucked me against his side, his smirk far too cocky. After nipping my jaw, he released a low growl that sounded closer to a purr. "Tell me again how I rock."

I laughed, still struggling to catch my breath. "A woman can't be held accountable for things she says during sex. Besides, the last thing your ego needs is stroking. I can't live with you now."

His chest vibrated against my side as he swept my hair and nuzzled my neck. "Oh, I can always use more stroking. Or lip service. I love when you give me lip service too."

Warm breath brushed my collarbone as he chuckled against my skin. Falling for sexy, playful Bruin would be easy. The intense, controlling bear was who I needed to make peace with. I raked my nails through the light thicket of hair covering his chest and sighed. "Bruin, we need a little brutal honesty."

He rolled to his side and propped himself onto his elbow. And damn him, I felt it tingle right to my toes. "All right, what's on your mind?"

How was a woman supposed to concentrate? I pulled a sheet over his hips and cleared my throat. "I spoke with your father this morning."

"Uh, huh?" His voice was soft, and he nipped at my shoulder.

"We came to an agreement."

His brow furrowed, his bangs hiding a hardening gaze.

"Reign agreed to restore my phone function and grant access to my world when it's important—like my meeting this afternoon. I also get full disclosure on issues that directly involve me or Grandfather."

Bruin's lips pushed out as he nodded very slowly. "What concessions did he get?"

"Pretty much the same ones I gave you. I promised that until the moon cycle ended, I'd live in this world and remain as open minded as I can. But I need to clarify one point."

Bruin sat up, bent his knee and rested his elbow over it. "Okaaay. Shoot."

I traced the design of the quilt beside me. "You have to be honest with me."

His eyes grew wary, confused. "I have been."

"No. You haven't. What you've said to me may have been true, but you haven't been telling me everything. You keep yourself behind a barrier and I feel the evasions. Trust is my hot-button, Bruin."

His lips narrowed into a grimace. "Mika, I don't—"

"You hide your scars. When your powers were off-line in the cave, I saw them." I rubbed my thumb over his eyebrow and up his forehead. "Here. You had a gash through your brow and the mark of a through-and-through bullet on this shoulder."

"That's not me being dishonest. It's just private. I don't let anyone see them."

"It's all or nothing, non-negotiable." I curled my hair behind my ear and sighed. "My father kept secrets and my mother drank herself stupid imagining the worst. Was it women? Money? Was he just unhappy? It destroyed my family. I don't expect you to gush with every thought running through your head. Honestly, I wouldn't want to hear it, but I want the broad strokes. All the broad strokes. Show me the real you, Bruin. The whole package."

Bruin frowned, but the veil of perfection lifted. One by one, scars, burns and old injuries appeared. More damage than I'd noticed at first glance. "Where did you get these?"

He studied the ceiling over the bed and shrugged. "Just a bit of Scourge artwork from the attack. They wanted me to remember them."

When I raised my fingers to touch the marks, he recoiled. I froze, my hand hovering over his ribs. After the tension in his shoulders eased a little, I took a caressing inventory of what had been done to him. If these were from when he was thirteen, the Scourge must have had him quite a while. I swallowed the bile burning the back of my throat.

"All right," he growled, reaching for his t-shirt. "I've shown you mine, so in the spirit of full disclosure, what do you want to tell me?"

I took a deep breath. "Okay, I should tell you that I found your journals in the cave."

Bruin paled and the scar through his brow made his scowl even more intimidating than it had been. "What? You just stumbled upon them?"

"I'm an *investigative* journalist, Bruin. Always curious."

"Did you read them?" His jaw tightened. "Did you?"

"I read a couple of entries, yes." I pulled the quilt up and tucked it under my arms. A flimsy and insubstantial shield against his anger, true, but it was all I had.

"I read what you wrote yesterday about Jade, and worrying about my safety if we shared a bed at night and how your nightmares have returned from when you were young. Then I closed that one and picked up the oldest journal and read two or three passages before I put it back."

He vaulted off the bed and yanked his jeans up those gloriously thick thighs. "Why stop there? You had me by the balls, baby. Why respect my privacy at all?"

"I decided, if you wanted me to be part of your life, you would share your memories with me. I won't steal them."

"Well, you'll be sorry you didn't read more when you had the chance." He shook his head and bent down to scoop his socks off the floor. "I don't talk about what happened. Not to you. Not to anyone. It has nothing to do with you and me."

Flipping back the covers I got out of bed and met him in front of the dresser. "It has everything to do with us. Your fear of loss is tearing at you and I didn't even understand why you were being such a complete asshat. I had to read it in a book hidden in a cave. I get that you need your space, but it makes a difference to me that you locked me away because you are crazed about me being a target and not because you're trying to control me. You've got to tell me what you're feeling, or I'll never be able to trust you."

Bruin cursed and tossed his socks on the floor again. "I said I was sorry about the cave. I want you safe. I don't think I'll go so far again, I've just been so . . .."

"Crazy?" I set my hands on his hips and waited until he looked down at me. "I want to know that your bear hates Aust's scent on me. I want to know that you dream of sleeping next to me at night. I want to know everything you're hiding from me, even if you think you're keeping it from me for my own good. Either I'm your partner in this or I'm out."

"I don't know if I can do that."

"You haven't tried."

He strode to the window and crossed his arms, staring out over the grounds. After a long pause, he scrubbed his palm over his face and huffed. "And if I can? What then?"

"Then I'll be more than your partner in the investigation. You'll sleep in my bed, mark me with Eau-de-Grizzly and we'll give dating a real go. No promises. You'll probably want to strangle me by the end, but I'll try. How 'bout it?"

Bruin pulled me against his chest. With his hair falling in front of his half-mast eyes, a surge of hunger rose up between us. In a flash of a movement his jeans hit the floor and he lifted me against his arousal. If you can seal an agreement with a hand shake, Bruin made sure our pact was cemented and reinforced with steel and then encased in marble.

~

When we finally made it back downstairs, Reign's office had filled to standing room only. The dozen people shifting and milling around hummed with pent up let's-kick-ass energy. It looked like a freaking Goth convention, everyone draped from boots to biceps in black leather. Full and thigh-length slickers did nothing to hide the weapons bulging beneath, guns, knives, and I'd bet whatever head-cracking, ball-busting weapon they could slide in a side pocket.

All this for me?

Standing hand-in-hand, I relished the cool comfort of our joined marks. I was getting used to the incessant burn, but man the reprieve was nice. Palm to palm was so good it was almost orgasmic.

Bruin stiffened beside me, his attention captured by a sleek Asian woman leaning in the corner. She wore a charcoal silk jacket and played with two white chopsticks. Her slate grey eyes locked on Bruin, as she twirled those tiny ivory batons over and under her hands and between her digits as if they were an extension of her fingers. When her gaze finally released him and passed right over me, I knew who she was.

"Ex-girlfriend?" I whispered.

Bruin studied his boot laces and squeezed my hand tighter. "No one for you to worry about."

Who said I was?

Reign cleared his throat, went over the travel plans, the back-up contingencies and discussed the possible ways things could go south. When everything was mapped out he came around to the side of his desk. "You all know what's at stake. Make damned sure these two come back happy and healthy. We crystal?"

Everyone nodded.

"Good, then give me a minute with Bruin and his Ursa will you?"

With a low mumble of conversations, the room cleared. Well, almost. A certain busty Asian beauty with slate grey eyes remained. When it was just the four of us, Bruin gave Reign a what-the-fuck glare then threw another one at the woman.

Reign sat on the edge of his desk and shrugged. "It's not ideal, but the only way I approve Mika's excursion through the lion's den is if she has a guard. That's the deal. Take Katsu or sit-yer-ass back down and enjoy the view."

I swear the woman made her breasts perkier for Bruin. Her cleavage was impressive, but the curlicue tattoo disappearing beneath the silk-covered mounds made me grit my teeth.

"Fantastic," I said, "so, I guess you're my new BFF."

"Looks that way, Mundie-girl."

"Why Katsu?" Bruin asked his father. His head swiveled from Reign to his ex. "And why would you agree to this?"

"Where are the choices?" Reign checked his watch. "A female can go places with her a male can't. Jade is still out with the flu and Lexi is watching over her."

Translation: Jade is still getting busy with her Highborne clan and Lexi hates my guts and would likely kill me herself.

Bruin moved half a step in front of me, and growled.

I caught his wrist. "Bruin stop. Reign thinks I need a guard. She is available. End of story. I can live with this."

Bruin scrubbed his fingertips through his shaggy hair and looked to his father. "It's a bad idea—mark my words—but it's Mika's call. I won't argue . . . mostly because she'll kick my ass."

Reign chuckled and focused in on me. "I think you might scare me, little girl."

Bruin sighed, though his smile was tender. "Why couldn't my mate like to bake or something? Why does she have to put herself in the middle of cluster-fucks for a living?"

Reign snorted. "She's your mate, son. A perfect match, heart and soul, to both your bear and the man you are. Could you expect her to be any less of a warrior than you?"

"Aw . . . stop, you're making me blush," I drawled.

With a low growl Bruin led me by the hand into the hall and the Talon enforcers fell into step. The walk to the Portal Gate was uncomfortably silent, other than the odd snicker from Kobi, Cowboy, or the other warriors at Bruin's expense. I admit, I found his discomfort amusing myself. As we made our way through the Portal Mirror, I didn't miss how Katsu angled herself toward Bruin or how she flipped her hair.

"Your neck all right?" I asked her. "That's a nasty twitch."

She slid me a smile. "Oh yeah, I'm perfect."

I just bet you are.

"So, how'd you kids meet anyway?" she asked, her Geisha Barbie routine so sickly sweet I hoped I didn't barf in my mouth.

Bruin bent and kissed the top of my head. "Mika and I hit it off at a club. It's been a non-stop adventure ever since."

"Hmm." She squeezed his upper arm with far too much familiarity. "I know what a whirlwind adventure you can be, Bear. You think she's woman enough for you?"

"She's standing right here," I said.

My stomach flipped when Katsu looked Bruin almost straight in the eyes. I was vertically challenged even by First Nations standards. What I wouldn't give to have legs like that.

Katsu smiled and removed her hand, which was good, because I was contemplating my odds of biting it off. I heard the warning growl rumble softly through the air between us and turned to Bruin. It took a minute, but realized it was coming from me.

Bruin's brow arched as his smile grew. "You okay?"

"Peachy." I snapped. "Just freakin' peachy."

CHAPTER THIRTY-THREE

"Oh, I've missed you, big guy." I stroked the cool, metal dash of my Humvee as Bruin, Katsu, Cowboy and Rue piled in. I keyed in the code to the truck's gun safe and opened it.

"Everything how you left it?" Bruin slid into the passenger seat, the hollow echo of metal on metal sealing them in as he closed his door.

"Yep." I shut the safe and cleared the screen. Two of the three guns I confiscated from the Jackals lay safely locked away. The third was in my purse. "Any chance I can get my truck to your realm? This garage is nice, but—"

Bruin's deep chuckle filled the truck. "Your truck won't fit through the Gate. The Realm of the Fair is more a motorcycle, ATV or horse type place. Besides, what would we drive when we came to Vancouver?"

I breathed in deep and smiled. Just being back in Vancouver settled my nerves. The turn of the key released the throaty rumble of the engine. Kobi drove past our parking spot in a black Escalade and a second truck stopped, positioned to come in behind me. Assuming I was the monkey-in-the-middle, I followed. "Good point. I guess riding jaguars and Elf-tigers is fun too."

Bruin growled. Damn. It was unnerving how sexy he was when he scowled at me like that . . . like he wanted to pin me down and bite me, mark me as his own . . . again. I shivered.

Bruin's nostrils flared.

Great. Eyes forward, I pressed the gas and assumed my position in the convoy, studiously avoiding my rear-view mirror. Since Bruin could smell my desire, so too could Cowboy.

Stupid Were senses.

Bruin chuckled. "How long will it take us to get to the courthouse, baby?"

"Twenty minutes . . . half an hour if traffic's acting up." I exited the parking garage beneath the North Vancouver Haven Sanctuary and our little band of warriors headed downtown. "Did you get in touch with Detective Delgato?"

"Yeah. He'll call in a favor to review the property seized in the Nimithic case. He's hoping he can get us a list of what they were working on in their lab or, if he can manage it, maybe a sample."

"I'd bet Bree could break down the components and figure out what they're working on."

Bruin tilted his head. "I hadn't thought of that, but yeah. She's taking chemistry or something, isn't she?"

I rolled my eyes. *Men.* "She's finishing her Bachelors in biochemistry with a minor in neuroscience and is enrolled to start her Masters in September."

Bruin laughed. "How do you know that? I've known Bree more than a decade and I didn't know that."

"It's all about the details, Bear. That's where a good story is always found."

We continued on, the drive remaining uneventful, and by the time I parked under the courthouse, I felt more like myself than I had in ages. It wasn't until we hit the main lobby washroom that my stomach tightened up. What a mess. I knew who I was. After everything being forced on me, it eased me to be back in my element.

In this world—this Mundie life—I belonged.

My eyes lifted to the mirror and slid to meet Katsu's reflection. She stood down the gleaming granite counter, the perfect example of geisha meets ninja. When her gaze met mine, she didn't even attempt to veil her lack of enthusiasm. She took a brush out of her Coach purse and ran it through her shimmering black lengths.

"So, how are things going with our bear?"

Our bear? Like I would speak to her about Bruin. *Yeah, hold your breath, bitch.*

I found my lip gloss in my purse and leaned closer to the mirror. After unscrewing the silver top, I slid the sticky pad back and forth across my lips and pushed them out for final inspection.

"I bet it's tough," Katsu said, sweeping back her sleek hair. With an ease of familiarity, she knotted it into a bun and pulled the two ivory chopsticks from the pocket of her silk jacket. The slender lengths of bone crisscrossed through the knot in her Japanese-style up-do. When her hair looked salon-styled, she traced her pouty red lips with the pad of her finger and stared back at me. "It's kinda nice though, Bruin being given a chance to breed. He'd given up the idea of having a family of his own years ago. It's just too bad . . .."

Don't do it. I screwed the cap back onto the tube of my Foxy Sand lip gloss and kicked myself for walking into this. "What's too bad?"

"That he didn't get to choose."

I caught myself before I reacted, but she wasn't fooled. "So, what? You think he would have chosen you over me, if given the chance?"

She smiled, throwing a lobby of insults with her exotic almond-shaped eyes. "We'll never know, but how should I put this?" She held up her hand as if scales weighed her explanation. "I'm a sorceress and a Talon enforcer he's known and screwed for more than five years *annnd* you're a freaked-out Mundie who can't keep her eyes off the door. Who would you choose?"

I tossed the lip gloss into my purse and eyed the ebony slide of the gun Bruin insisted I carry. *Tempting.* "I suppose that would be filed under none-of-your-damn-business. But really, after five years if he'd found you worth anything more than a fuck buddy, he would have settled down before now, don't you think?"

Katsu tucked her brush into her purse and buckled it shut. "Well, the way I hear it, you might be using the escape clause and waiting things out, anyway."

Does everyone know my business? I zipped shut my purse and pulled it over my shoulder. "Well you can file that one between none-of-your-business and back-the-hell-off. Besides, if I opt out, you can start the line for the rebounders club. I wouldn't expect your pride would get in the way of being sloppy seconds."

Katsu bit her bottom lip and checked the black toggles of her embroidered jacket. "Nah, who wants a toy once it's broken? Sadly, Bruin's not on anyone's wish list anymore."

What did that mean?

Katsu tipped her head back and laughed. "You don't know, do you? Whether or not you reject him, Bruin will never love another woman. Bonding is a one-shot deal for a Were. His body will only ever respond to you and by the next full moon, if you haven't accepted him, he'll lose even that."

I wanted to smack the smarmy smile off her face. "Bull. Bruin would've told me."

She slung the shoulder strap of her purse over her head and then straightened it across her cleavage. "Stupid Mundie-girl. You don't know a thing about Bruin or what he'd endure for someone he loved. Is that how you justify hurting him?"

"I can't help where we are. This situation has been tough on both of us."

Katsu's cool façade slipped as her eyes narrowed. "You have no fucking clue. Imagine being rejected by the one person the gods say he belongs to—finally belongs to—after a lifetime of having no hope. He suffers day and night, so aroused that his skin burns on his bones and his cock feels like it will explode if he doesn't find release. The entity inside him, his bear, breathes in your scent and rages to claim you with a savagery that threatens the man's very sanity."

"Now I know you're lying. There's no way he'd tell you that."

She rolled her eyes. "He's not the first Were to be branded by the Fates, Mundie. Bonded males are dangerous men until a mating occurs. Until then, his animal side will gain dominance until his humanity gets eaten away, bit by bit. When that happens, there's nowhere you'll be safe, and Bruin knows it."

"And *I* know Bruin would never hurt me."

Her gaze narrowed. "No. He'd put himself down before he let his bear ravage you."

My mind spun. I fought the urge to lash out at her, to tell her to shut up, to tell her she didn't know shit . . . but it was me who knew nothing. "If this is true, why didn't he tell me?"

Katsu shook her head and pulled the handle for the interior washroom door. "You really don't know him at all, do you?"

Before she pulled the second door open, I stopped her. "Why tell me any of this?"

She sighed and shook her head. "Because I *do* know him."

Bruin stood directly across the hall from the washroom, shoulders stiff, and hands at his sides. He looked like the weight of two worlds pressed down on him and I knew if anyone even looked at me sideways, they'd be face-planting onto granite tiles.

As I followed Katsu out of the ladies room, he stepped away from the wall with a heavy exhale. He looked from me to her and back. "You girls finished freshening up?"

Katsu swung her hips as she stepped into the hall.

Bruin bent his head and nuzzled my cheek, the light scruff of his jaw prickled my skin, a soothing balm on raw nerves. "You okay? You look pale."

I forced my shiny lips to lift. "Fine."

In one coordinated move he reached across my shoulders and squeezed. "It's not too late to back out, baby. We can Flash to the Gate and be home in a matter of minutes."

Home? I looked into the expectant faces of my security detail. Cowboy and Rue had the mic communicators down and had squared off, facing opposite directions of the hall. Mirrored sunglasses made it impossible to tell where they were looking, but as each Mundie passed, their heads turned.

Katsu occupied herself by checking the polish on her nails. She could probably see trouble coming in the reflection of the luster.

What was her game?

Bruin would be rendered impotent if I left. How could he not tell me? How could I, a journalist, not have asked more questions? For shit's sake. Was I that self-centered that I only looked at the end of this bonding cycle for what it meant to me?

"Mika?" Bruin's timbre rumbled deeper than usual. "What is it?"

"Nothing. Really." I rubbed my forehead. Did I have any Advil in my purse? "Let's get this over with."

After a moment, Bruin stopped us in front of the elevators. "Okay, you're in meeting room 317, third floor, left out of the elevator, fourth door on the right. Savage is up there with Kobi and Sin and everything is secure. Remember. Just like we planned. You're in. You make your statements, log in your files and photos and then we make tracks."

I nodded.

He kissed my throbbing temple and whispered, "I'm with you, baby. If you get one of your feelings, give me a nod and we're nothing but dust trails and vapor. Got it?"

I blinked back the sting behind my eyes and pushed the button for the elevators. "Bruin, if everything goes well here, could we make one more quick stop?"

His scowl deepened. "What quick stop?"

"To see Meg at the hospital. Paige will be there, and I need to talk to her."

Bruin shook his head. Once Katsu stepped into the elevator, he pressed his hand on the small of my back and we followed. "You can call them when we get back."

"They know I'm in town today. It would seem very suspicious if I didn't visit. Might even start them asking questions." I could tell by his body language, Bruin didn't like being manoeuvred any more than I did. I laid my hand flat on his stomach. "Look, if anything hinky happens, you can Flash me out of there in a blink."

He flipped me an exasperated look. "If we can Flash. The whole reason we brought the trucks was because if Abaddon or Scourge attack, they'll likely have a Pulse to block a quick escape. Let's just finish here and get back to Haven."

We made our way out of the elevator and up the hall to the ACA's meeting room. "Please, we're working on compromising remember? I swear, we'll be fast. It's important to me."

Bruin's phone rang, and he shifted to get it out of his pocket. "Yeah."

As he scowled at the framed photo of Queen Elizabeth II hanging on the wall and listened, he rhymed off a series of nods and *mhmms*. As he wrapped things up, he looked at me, one eyebrow lifted. "Sure, D, we're heading over to Vancouver General in a bit, but we're only there for ten minutes, tops. I'll have Cowboy wait in the lobby . . .. Thanks man, you rock."

When he hung up, I kissed his tattooed palm. "I'll thank you properly later."

CHAPTER THIRTY-FOUR

*B*ack behind the wheel, with our armed contingent squished in the back seat, I hit my indicator. As Kobi's Escalade turned in front of me, we left the hospital parking lot. "I told you we'd be fine."

Bruin unsheathed his gun, checked the safety and laid it flat on his thigh. "It was a bad call, Mika, even if things went off okay. We took a strategically unnecessary risk."

"It was ten minutes to check in with my boss and to visit a friend who got knocked unconscious and nearly suffered brain damage. *Because of us*, I might add."

"Bad things happen to good people all the time. We can't change that."

I followed Kobi close as he turned at a set of lights and headed out of town a different way we came in. "Think what you want. You could have at least let me hit the bathroom before we left. No assassins were jumping out from behind tacky pink curtains and yet somehow peeing got deemed an unnecessary risk too?"

"We could have Flashed to the Gate and saved the stress on your bladder."

I snorted and stroked the metal dash. "And leave my baby in the hands of your warriors?"

Now it was Bruin's turn to roll his eyes. "I wanted you out of the line of fire. All those people, rooms, entrances and exits—it was a logistical nightmare."

Of course it was. As annoying and rigid as Bruin could be, it was kinda hot when he talked all military. "You met with Detective Delgato. If you ask me, it was win-win."

He held up the small Ziploc bag Detective Delgato had given Cowboy while we were upstairs. There were two little pills, one orange, one blue, and a little glass vile grouped in the corner seam. "In another twenty minutes we'll be at the Haven sanctuary and you can pee there."

"And what if I can't wait twenty minutes?" I scissored my legs, pressing my thighs together. Twenty minutes. Twenty . . . minutes. All I could hear in my head was Grandfather saying, *'You best go before we leave, Rabbit. It is a long time before we stop.'*

I adjusted myself in my seat and gripped my leather-bound steering wheel tighter. With a sidelong glance I noticed Bruin's chest bouncing. Bastard. "This is so not funny."

"Then pull over and I'll walk you to that stand of trees."

"Yeah, it's not quite the same for girls." I glanced down at my new leather flats and rolled my eyes. "I'll wait."

Bruin's chest bounced some more.

As we turned and headed west out of the city the setting sun blazed on my horizon. Perfect. Another day done and now it was burning white spots into my retina. I closed my eyes, but the silhouette remained. *Great, now I'm blind* and *I have to pee.*

"So, Bruin, how did your fitting go with Iadon yesterday?" Katsu flashed me a smile in my rear-view mirror. "When I had breakfast with Lexi this morning, she said you looked amazing."

Really? Breakfast with Lexi. Bitch.

"Good." Either unaware of Katsu baiting me or ignoring it, Bruin produced a pair of sunglasses and handed them to me.

"I swear Iadon could put Armani out of business," she said. "And the way he sews the little designs for detail, it's incredible."

"Embroiders," I said, passing two motorcyclists parked on the right shoulder.

"I'm sorry?" Bruin said, turning to me.

I lowered my visor and squinted into the highway ahead. "The little designs he sews on the cuffs and lapels of your wedding jacket. It's embroidery."

Katsu laughed. "How sweet, Bruin, the Fates paired you with the next Martha Stewart."

Between one thought and the next the sensation of an army of ants crawled up my neck. Was it just my urge to kill Katsu? Maybe. Traffic was light, the road two lanes both ways. An RV and a sports car drove side by side on the horizon ahead of us, and there were a couple of cars going the other direction. I checked my rear-view. The Escalade covering our butt was slowing and the two motorcycles we just passed were on the road and accelerating. Hard.

I rolled my neck trying to ease the sensation. Nope. My early warning system had definitely been activated. "Cowboy, have a look behind us. Do those bikes look familiar?"

Bruin stiffened. His comm beeped and he snapped down the arm. He listened to the voice on the other end and cursed. "Sin's having car trouble. He's falling back."

He pointed to two silver SUVs with tinted windows cresting the hill in front of us.

Cowboy shifted around behind me, drew his guns and lowered the window. "Car trouble, my ass. Not with those bikes moving up on our six. We've got two more coming straight at us."

Bruin swung around. "Watch your flanks, Mika. Don't let them crawl up our sides."

Duh. "Having to pee doesn't make me stupid."

The motorcycles raced up both sides of the truck before I could do anything. I gritted my teeth. The images in the side-view mirrors showed two guys riding bitch leaning toward us pulling semi-automatics out from behind their drivers. I slammed on the gas and cut off the access to the shoulder.

I swerved a few times forcing the bikes to stay back. "What are your rules of engagement in my world? Can I flatten them?"

"Go for it." Cowboy said.

Katsu took her chop-sticks out of her hair and started waving the ends toward the bikes. "They've got a Pulse blocking us. I can't affect them directly."

"What's the code for the gun safe, Mika?" Bruin asked, fingers poised over the keypad.

I told him and while he pulled out some extra firepower, I returned my gaze to the horizon. The two SUVs swung crisscross on the road in front of Kobi and blocked our path. The time to make a move quickly circled the drain. "Okay, what am I doing?"

Bruin tapped his comm. "Kobi's running juggernaut. We're going to hit that blockade and plow right through. Ready?"

I gripped my steering wheel. "Ready as I'll ever be."

The explosion boomed louder and threw chunks of automotive debris farther than any dick-flick action movie I'd ever seen. Focused on the bumper of the Escalade in front of us, I tucked in tight and prayed the front ends of the two vehicles would swing wide enough to let us pass. If we all ended up crushed and tangled together, it would be a massacre.

Thankfully though, after the scrape of steel on steel died down, we were still moving away from the mangled roadblock.

"Where to next?" I asked, adrenaline burning through my veins.

Bruin scanned the upcoming traffic and pointed to the landscape off to the right. "Off-roading, baby. Kobi, we're veering into that farmer's field coming up on the right."

I frowned. "Uh . . . Bruin? There's a four-foot culvert between the field and the highway. At this speed you're going to wreck my under-carriage and break my axel if we try to cross it."

Katsu leaned into the front between the seats and waved her chop sticks, mumbling a few words. "I got it covered, Mundie. I was getting bored anyway."

Bored? Just up ahead of the lead car, a simple wooden platform spanned the ditch.

"Great job, Kat honey," Bruin said, then froze and looked at me. "Fuck. I'm sorry."

Pain like I'd never felt before seared my chest. On a surge of hostility, I cranked the wheel, bit my tongue and ignored my urge to explode into a fit of hormones. *Honey?* Good thing the bitch had retreated without comment or I might have lost hold of the wheel.

"*Shiiiiit,*" Cowboy drawled, "this farmer's is going to be madder than a wolverine caught in a piss fire. Open the sunroof, Mika." The southern Were-wolf squeezed his shoulders in between the front seats and through the rectangular opening in the roof.

That's when the *tat-a-tat* of gunfire started.

"Hey, they're shooting my truck!"

"You said the truck's bullet proof. Cowboy isn't," Bruin said. "What's the worry?"

"It's *my truck.*" I snapped, banking right and bouncing over rows of summer wheat. "And these bumps aren't helping my bladder any."

Bruin handed another gun up to Cowboy.

Rue leaned out the window and targeted the bikes.

Cowboy's laughter carried on the breeze. "What do I get if I wrap this up before Mika pisses her pants?

I winced. I didn't want to be the Ursa known for wetting her pants. "Undying devotion."

One of the bikes jostled along my side and caught a rut. As it went over I banked left and bounced over the sucker like a speed-bump at Walmart. Cowboy returned fire and Bruin and Rue fired their weapons in intermittent bursts.

The constant *pop* and *ping* of bullets hitting steel made me cringe. "Get them the hell away from my truck you guys."

Kobi swerved onto a dirt lane between two fields and I followed.

The second bike zoomed up the crack of my ass. I slammed on my brakes and giggled at the *cathud* of Ducati versus tailgate.

Bruin got a crack shot off at the driver of one of the SUVs and sent the vehicle careening into a rolling spin. Over and over it tumbled, like a kid rolling down a hill. Just one left. Bruin cursed as a couple shots bounced off my driver's window. "What the hell are you doing up there, Cowboy, waving to the crowds? This isn't a fucking parade, Wolf."

After another couple minutes speeding through farmer's fields, Cowboy's assault on the front grill of the second SUV ended with a *pop* and *hiss*. Steam blew out the seams of the hood as the last of the attackers fell behind. "Oh and I got all gussied up and everythin'."

Geisha-bitch got us back on the highway and we hung a hard right. Two minutes down the road I saw exactly where I needed to go. In a screeching halt my truck kicked up gravel and I took the shoulder. I threw the truck into park and tossed Cowboy my keys.

On an awkward hop and run I reached down and pulled off my shoes. As I ducked behind the bushes, I pitched those leather flats as hard as I could at Bruin's stupid, gorgeous head. "If you think I've forgotten you called her *honey*, think again, Bear."

When the world came back in focus sometime later, I found myself standing knee deep in the stream, tossing food for the fish. It was early evening and though my stomach had been growling like a bear since we returned to Haven, I couldn't bring myself to go back to Jade's and face Bruin. *Honey*. He'd called Katsu, honey.

Yeah, and then I'd reacted badly and stormed off. Again.

As each handful of kibble rained down, gaping mouths broke the surface and gobbled up the feast. I'd gathered quite a ravenous crowd.

"Are you well, Rabbit?" With his hand firmly curled around his walking stick, Grandfather stepped from the treed path on the far bank of the stream and lowered himself to sit on an old stump. "Have you and your bear quarreled again?"

I tossed another handful of food and watched it disappear into the frenzied mouths below. "Fighting is all we do. Did he send you?"

Grandfather shook his head and propped his hands over both his knees. "Reign mentioned Bruin was *shredding* himself in the gym. I thought you might need a friendly ear."

I sighed. "He said something that upset me, and I insulted his pride . . . again."

His sad smile crinkled the weathered lines next to his eyes. "I see. It is not my place to interfere, but an old man can take liberties, I think. Pride and honor are fine qualities in a man. When the world turns on him, those are the things he has within his control. Bruin carries himself with an abundance of both."

"I *know*."

The wind picked up, my hair flinging wild. I drew a deep breath and faced Grandfather's censure "Grandfather, I apologize. It's not your fault I'm angry."

"So, tell me, child? What troubles you?"

"Is it totally selfish to want things to go back to the way they were before I met Bruin?"

"Selfish, no. Naïve perhaps." He bowed his head and fished in the pocket of his vest for the rabbit skin bag that held his old, bone pipe. With slow, deliberate actions, he retrieved his pipe, pinched the ground tobacco out of the baggie and pressed it deep into the bowl with his thumb. When everything was to his liking, he sealed the bag and found his lighter. After a few short puffs, he raised his dusky stare to meet mine. "Do you remember when you were small, and you left your baby goat in the outdoor pen after dark?"

"Yes."

"When he got taken away by the Great Grey Owl, you stomped your feet and demanded he be brought back. This is much the same thing. No amount of demanding will change what the two of you have set in motion. Release where you thought you were, accept where you are now, and decide where you are headed from here."

"But where *am* I headed?"

He shrugged and exhaled a puff of smoke. "The future reveals itself one moment at a time, child. The truth is, your destiny with Bruin has only begun to unfold. Only the Earth Mother knows the entirety of what is to come. Bruin is an honorable man, Mika. You could do far worse than to be loved for a lifetime by him."

"Aren't you supposed to be on my side?"

He chuckled. "Always. Have you prayed to the Creator or the Earth Mother? What have they to say about Bruin?"

"Nothing. Every time I ask the Earth Spirits about him the air is silent. The spirits have never failed me before and I don't understand what their silence means."

Grandfather exhaled a puff of smoke and smiled. "From the day my eyes fell upon your grandmother until the day she became my bride, she was the only one the spirits would speak nothing of."

Tears filled my eyes as grief tightened like a band around my chest. "Oh Grandfather, Bruin is so willful and aggressive. He's infuriating. We don't make a good match. We fight constantly. How can the Earth Mother think we'd ever be happy?"

"It is sometimes difficult to look in a mirror, child, but it does not change what you will see. He may infuriate you, but you give him the same in turn. Neither of you are weak spirits."

I swiped at the tears dripping off my chin. "Are you saying I'm difficult?"

He chuckled. "I enjoy every moment of loving you, Mika, as will the man you are meant to be with. That boy loves you beyond all reason. I know you don't wish to see it, but those of us watching from a distance do. It's as obvious as a train running straight at you . . . with the headlights on . . . and the whistle blowing shrill into the night."

"It's just . . . he's such an unbelievable . . . .." I clenched my jaw and tossed more kibble.

"He is not your father, child."

I stiffened. "I never thought he was."

"No? You mean you've taken Bruin at his word and never judged him for the actions of the man who left you behind? The man who you believe never truly wanted you or loved you or your mother?"

He drew on his pipe and released a sweet-smelling cloud into the evening air. "Rabbit, whether you want to admit it or not, Bruin is perfect for you. You never have to wonder what's on his mind and you never have to worry about him straying or losing interest."

Fabulous, just the conversation I want to have with my grandfather. "You know? About the whole mating one person thing?"

"I've been speaking with Castian and Reign, yes. I need to understand where your path is headed. The power of the Were-mating is such that it grows and strengthens over time. What the two of you feel for each other now is nothing to the power of your connection if you accept him. I am told, once mated pairs pass the trials of courtship, their love becomes its own entity."

"What if it *is* because he has no choice? What if he'd have preferred his ex-lover to me? She's tall and exotic and a warrior, like him. What if she's who he wants?"

"Have you asked him?"

"Yes."

"And what was his answer?"

"He said he and Katsu were only a physical distraction, nothing more. He said he loves me . . . and even if I choose to go . . . he'll make sure I'm safe."

"His instinct to protect you is strong."

"I can take care of myself."

His smile crinkled his face like a Shar-Pei. He placed his pipe squarely in his mouth and used both hands to get up. Orville ambled out of the trees and rubbed against his shin. Leaning on his stick, he took a moment to straighten, and then turned back toward the path. "It does not make you weak to trust in someone, Rabbit. In fact, you may find it makes you stronger. Perhaps it isn't about whether or not you are able to take care of yourself, but the blessing that you no longer have to."

CHAPTER THIRTY-FIVE

There were aspects of life at Haven I truly loved. Being met in the forest by a wolf friend and her escorting me back to Jade's . . . yeah, that was definitely one of them.

As Faolan and I made our way back from the stream and across the well-secured grounds, I fingered through the wolf's coat and marveled at how my connection to my gifts flourished in this world. I'd chosen to live in Vancouver partly because the spirits remained remote and elusive in the city. The noise, the technology and the processed living all kept my gifts at bay. In the city, I was almost normal. Just a Native girl living my life.

Hiding from my life might be more accurate.

The people here rallied in the face of the strange and unusual, embraced their oddities, their abilities, their gifts. Yes. I supposed they really were gifts, though I'm not sure I'd ever really felt that way about what I could do before. Why did I close myself off?

I wasn't the first person to lose parents. At least my parents hadn't tried to kill me like Cowboy's. And despite the loss of Lucas and Amy, the new surroundings and everyone around them being strangers, the cubs continued to thrive. It spoke to both Hugh's family—as well as Aust—that they were doing so well.

Bruin had been lucky to be adopted and raised by Reign. He'd had siblings and friends, learned values and responsibility, but was it like that everywhere? I'd been blessed to have Grandfather. The cubs had Hugh. I wondered, in light of all the recent killings, if Weres had a system in place to care for displaced victims of the Scourge.

Following the path, Faolan and I kept to the inside of the massive stone wall encircling Jade's property. The chill of the night was a little shocking after the warmth of the day. A shiver passed through me as we headed toward the house, the sky all but giving up to dusk. The light might have been fading, but I still spotted them.

Bruin and Katsu.

Before they noticed us, I crouched beside Aust's wolf and found cover in the adjacent maze of trees. Under the trellised arbor well ahead, Bruin sat on a bench, tucked in all cozy and snug with a certain Asian sorceress. As she leaned against his chest, his arm lay across her shoulder, her head tilted and resting in the crook of his neck.

I couldn't breathe. She fit under his arm perfectly. *Bitch.*

Their body language screamed sorrow and longing, their touch familiar. For the millionth time I wondered why I was there. "Earth Spirits, carry their conversation to my ears, please."

Faolan must have felt the change in the air because she canted her head and whined. One of the reasons I excelled investigating was due to my ability to gather information from great distances. After a moment my hair lifted, and a cool breeze circled my body.

"—and I'm sorry," Bruin said, stroking the length of Katsu's black shimmering hair. "I wish it could be different. If there was something I could do . . .."

"Fucking Fates," she sobbed.

"*Shh.* Don't cry, honey. I swear you're going to get through this."

"It's just—"

"I know. All we can do is decide where to go from here."

"I'm going to Boston." Katsu stood up and looked up at him. "Come. Come with me for a few days. You said you're not getting anywhere with your Mundie. She probably won't even miss you."

Bruin shook his head. "I can't."

"Why? Is your leash that short? I need you."

"I *am* sorry. I wish I could. I just can't."

She kissed his cheek, her hand lingering on his chest. "Think about it, Bear. I'll grab a bag and fill out the paperwork at the Gatehouse. If you change your mind, you know how to find me."

My vision blurred, and I forced myself to stop looking. I blinked fast and whispered, "Thank you, I've heard enough."

As the wind left me, the breeze blew back toward the trellis. I gasped. *My scent.*

Leaving Faolan behind, I ducked behind the hedge and bolted toward the house. Guaranteed my scent would blow back to him and he'd know I was spying. I ran on the balls of my feet trying not to let my shoes click on the cobblestone of the courtyard. I bolted through the back-patio door and dashed into the empty lounge. After a quick over-the-shoulder, I wiped my eyes and exhaled. No sign of anyone behind me.

Scurrying along the hall, I headed away from the usual flow of traffic.

Down the back stairs, my feet flew in a rhythmic patter; down another flight to the next landing. The carpeted corridor of the sub-basement stretched silently before me and I hustled along until I came to an open door. I stumbled inside and down the short dark passageway into a cavernous black room. Home theatre. Somewhere in the back of my mind I marveled at how cool it was to have a cinema-sized theatre in the basement of a home.

Climbing the staggered tiers of steps to the back row, I collapsed into the middle seat and buried my face in my hands. *Shit. I knew I couldn't trust this fairy tale.*

Nobody gets chosen by the gods to live happily ever after. *Stupid. Sooo stupid.*

"Mika?"

I gasped and launched out of my seat, grabbing my chest. "How'd you . . . never mind. What do you want, Bruin?"

"To explain what you saw."

And heard. "Don't bother. I get it."

"Do you? Katsu's a friend and a colleague. She's going through a—"

I threw up my hand. *"Don't.* Please don't expect me to sympathize with her."

"Let me explain—"

I shook my head, swallowing past the lump in my throat. "You should go. You know . . . to Boston. I think it's best if we keep our distance."

"How do you know about Boston?"

I winced. *Shit.* "I heard the two of you talking. You should go. Despite what she said, there is no leash. I don't want you tied to me. Go to Boston."

"But I want to stay here . . . with you. I want *this*. I want *us*."

"There is no us!" I sank back into my chair, my sobs catching in my chest. I turned my palm to him. "Love doesn't happen like this. The Fates can't make you feel something you don't. I'm tired Bruin. Just. Go."

The room fell silent and my heart broke wide open. I thought he'd gone, so I jumped when he spoke a few minutes later. "What happened to you? Who hurt you so badly that you can't trust in love? Who made you hate men?"

I scowled, swiping beneath my eyes. "I don't hate men. I'm fond of men. Tall. Good looking. Adventurous. I enjoy men—I just don't need one to complete me. *I* complete me just fine."

"But I want—"

"Go," I sobbed, shaking my head. "I can't take it. I'm sick of it. I'm sick of listening to your lies of love. I'm sick of everyone knowing more about my life than me. And I'm sick of you following me around like a stray dog hoping for me to take you home. I want out. *GO!"*

His eyes glowed cold in the darkness. Two icy turquoise stars that could cut glass. "I'm sorry that me trying to love you has been such a burden." His husky timbre quivered as he turned away. "Trust me. It won't happen again. Consider yourself out."

He Flashed. Left alone in the darkness, my brand sizzled worse than ever. I wanted it all to stop. I wanted to go home. I wanted my own bed with just me and Orville curled up with my laptop and a package of Pop-Tarts. I wanted to call Meg or Paige or any one of my girls to vent until any of this made sense.

I don't know how long I cried, there, alone in my misery. An hour? Two? Ten?

When my tears dried up and my breathing evened out, I headed upstairs. My head pounded like thunder and my eyes burned. My gut rolled at the thought of meeting up with anyone. Sympathy was not my friend. Eyes on the ground and hands tucked in my pockets, I trudged heavy-hearted all the way back to the main foyer.

If I could make it to the stairs, I'd be home free.

Deep male voices carried from the lounge, followed by a smack, roll and clunk of billiard balls. Those open double doors stood between me and the main staircase, and the odds of making it upstairs without running into anyone were practically nil. Stepping over to one of the main floor powder rooms, I decided to splash cold water on my face and assess the damage. When I reached for the handle, the door opened inward.

"Fabulous," a tiny voice said. I lifted my gaze and sighed as I was sized up by two cold amethyst eyes.

"Lexi." I moved aside. Ironic that even though I was taller than her —and that never happened—she didn't seem to notice. She exuded a lethal hostility that in no way matched her size. "Sorry, I didn't know anyone was in there."

"Whatever." She flicked her hair and pushed past me.

Her elbow glanced my ribs and my temper flared. "I'm *so* not in the mood for your bullshit today."

"You're assuming I care?"

On a normal day, in my normal life, I would have let it go. I may be stubborn, but I didn't consider myself outwardly difficult. This, however, was not that day. Trapped in a fantasy realm with the hormones of a horny, emotional grizzly raging through me, my hand stinging like I'd dunked it in blazing nettles and my supposed other half spending his time hiding away with his ex in the garden . . . enough was enough.

"What is your problem, Lexi? Is it that I blocked you in the cave or that I haven't swooned and fallen into Bruin's arms? Either way, I'm done with your tantrums, *Princess*. If you've got something to say, spit it out or fuck off."

Lexi laughed. Her gaze hardened until it pierced me, icy to the marrow of my bone. "Bruin told me if I have nothing nice to say, shut the hell up, so I guess I have nothing to say."

"Well, Bruin's not here now, is he?"

Lexi's eyes widened as a grin spread across her face. "You sure you want to do this?"

"Bring it."

"All right, Mundie." She stepped in close and looked up at me. "You are nothing but a stupid human who doesn't know what it is to live in our world. A spoiled prima donna who thinks your wants and needs are more important than those of anyone else."

Being called a prima donna by *her* left a bitter taste in my mouth. "Well, *Princess*, take a look in the mirror. Are you sure this is about me or are you worried about sharing Bruin's attention?" As her eyes flared, I leaned over her. "Jealous much?"

Lexi crossed her arms over her chest and absently played with the bear claw pendant she wore. Staring at me she laughed. "A week here and you think you know about Bruin and his life? You have no idea who the man is and you certainly can't comprehend all the reasons you're not good enough for him."

"Well, the Fates of your world seem to think I am."

Lexi laughed even harder. "The Fates are meddling twits who screw around with lives for their own perverse amusement. They don't give two shits about who belongs together. You're nothing but an experiment to amuse them, a fatal attraction for them to watch crumble for shits and giggles. The sad thing is . . . Bruin actually wants you."

Now it was my turn to laugh. "Yeah, well, that's hard to believe after watching him canoodle with his ex under the trellis."

"*Liar.*" That touched a nerve.

"Yep, he's a man of honor all right. Talking love and devotion to two women at a time . . . maybe that's where he Flashes at night when he's not with me."

She lunged. Despite her size, she hit me with the force of a semi-truck and we crashed backward onto the marble floor. She grabbed a fistful of my hair and cracked my head against the floor. Black spots clouded my vision as the wind hissed out of my lungs.

Damn, she's stronger than she looks.

I sucked in what oxygen I could and let my grizzly rage fly. All my frustration. All my aggression. Over and over we flipped. Elbows, fists and knees. I didn't hold back.

She didn't either.

When I thought she would kick my ass, a surge of stubborn anger erupted. I had the momentary satisfaction of seeing her eyes pop wide as I bared my teeth. Like a caged animal I swiped at her arms, my nails digging into her flesh.

"Get off me, *bitch*," I growled, flinging my elbow as she leaned forward. I smiled as her head snapped back and a spray of blood flew through the air.

In the next instant, the weight of her straddling me lifted and I was dragged to my feet like a rag doll. We'd gathered quite a crowd. The majority of the Talon looked amused. Galan and Tham looked horrified.

"I believe we'll call that a draw, ladies." Reign had one arm around Lexi's waist, holding her back from getting a second round at me.

I craned my neck and looked over my shoulder into the coal-black eyes of Savage. His mouth twitched in a snarl, making his lip piercings glint in the light. He raised a tattooed brow.

I nodded. "I'm good."

He let go.

The weight of the day washed over me, the cave, the trouble in Vancouver, the scene in the garden, the fight in the cinema and the cherry on top—my melon doing a slam-dunk into the marble tiles. I swallowed past the cold sweat washing over me and fought the urge to vomit in front of everyone.

The prattle of people talking surrounded me but I wasn't tracking.

My hands were shaking . . . bad. The salty iron taste of blood filled my mouth and my stomach flip-flopped like a fish out of water. Touching my lip, I felt for the gash and my fingers came away crimson.

"If you'll excuse me," I said to no one in particular, "I'd like to clean up."

I took a tentative step toward the washroom. When all I got back from my limbs were a few creaks and a couple aches, I stepped up the pace.

How long did I stay in that six-by-eight room? Could have been minutes, could have been hours. Luckily, I'd skipped supper, so nothing to expel. I washed the blood off my face and from under my tender nail beds. Were they sore from the fight or the hormones? Would I even know what normal felt like if I ever got back to it?

Taking inventory of the damage in the antique mirror, I straightened myself and loitered long enough to be sure the rubberneckers and Fight Club fans had moved on. My vision and focus were blinking like faulty Christmas lights and I was pretty sure, given the throbbing in my cranium, that my grey matter was about to start oozing out of my ears.

Cracking the door an inch and peeking out would be childish, so I swung the thing open and did a hi-how-are-ya. *Sweet.* The coast was clear. I headed to the main staircase, grabbed the post and swung up the first few steps on a gimpy jog.

"Hey."

My heart kicked almost out of my chest for the second time this afternoon. People really had to stop testing my ticker like that. Sitting on the first landing in worn blue jeans, bare feet and a cotton blouse, Jade looked pale and weary.

"You scared me," I said. "What are you doing sitting here all alone?"

"I heard I missed a hell of a throw down. Thought I'd check that you're all right." She studied me up and down, pausing on the points of highlight. "That's one ugly lip you're nursing."

My fingers grazed over the damage. I continued up the wide steps and passed her. "I'll live. Thanks though. I appreciate the thought."

Jade followed me up the stairs. "I like you, Mika. Regardless of what's going on with Bruin, I like you. If you need a friend—"

"Who me? But I'm just a stupid Mundie who doesn't deserve to be in the same room as the rest of you, aren't I."

Jade sighed. "Lexi sees things in her own way. Please don't let her speak for the rest of us. Bruin will be furious when he hears what happened."

I huffed and climbed to the next landing, my vision blurring more. "More likely he'll be jealous he didn't get a crack at me. I swear he wants to throttle me half the time."

I brushed the egg on the back of my head and closed my eyes. Bad idea. The ground shifted under my feet. I opened them quickly and put a flat hand against the wall.

"And mate you the other half?" Jade nodded, a smile tugging at the curve of her full lips.

I continued down the hall toward my room, my hand running along the wall, Jade right beside me. I never realized how far it was from the main foyer to my room. My feet felt like cement blocks dragging under me. I needed to get to the suite soon. Whatever might be left in my stomach from the cave was going to boomerang back from whence it came.

"Bruin and I . . . we've run our course." I shook my head a little, watching the silver braid in her hair splitting into three. "Look . . . I know you're his sis . . . maybe we shouldn't . . .." I tried to grab the wall on the way down, but my body just wouldn't listen.

"*Mika?*"

CHAPTER THIRTY-SIX

*I*t's funny how sometimes you wake up in total clarity, ready to take on the world and sometimes you're mired in a murky fog, not sure where you are and no clue how the hell you ended up there. This was one of the latter.

Lying in a bed—my bed at Jade's I assumed—the musky-cedar of Bruin's scent filled the air. It mixed with the soft melody of a guitar and someone singing. The voice—so unbelievably pure and deep it could only be an angel's—sang in a language I didn't understand.

Despite my drugged, happy haze, I forced my eyes to open.

Aust's soft smile widened, lighting his eyes. "*Neelan*, thank the gods. Are you well?"

I tried to sit up and answer, but my voice cracked, and the room spun.

Aust leaned the guitar against the chair and eased onto the edge of the bed. As the mattress dipped under his weight, he brushed hair from my face. He was the one who looked like hell. His eyes, dull and blood-shot, lacked their usual gleam and he had one heck of a shiner blooming on the left side of his face.

"Aust? What happened to you?"

He waved away my concern and shook his head. "Fash not. It is you who suffered injury, *sweeting,* a slow bleed inside your skull. You fell unconscious. Blessed be Jade accompanied you at the time. Had she not healed your injuries immediately, you would have been lost to us."

Ahhh. I remembered the fight in the foyer with Lexi and proceeded to take stock. My fingers and toes still wriggled, stomach was solid, head no longer threatening to explode but still drumming out a throbbing beat. "My skull's too thick to crack."

He grinned and took my hand. "Mayhap not."

I rolled to my side and tried to sit up. "Was Bruin here?"

Aust hesitated, then helped prop me up and get comfortable against the headboard. "Other than Jade, Galan and Orville, no other came through the door."

Right, I'd sent Bruin off with Katsu, hadn't I? I swallowed back the growl rumbling in my chest. "Where's Jade now?"

"Right here." She glided into the suite, followed by Galan carrying a tray. "Finally decided to wake up, did you?" She leaned over and smiled. "You look better. Are you hungry?"

Aust jumped to his feet and made room.

"Starving. How long was I out?"

"Almost two days. Here, Galan remembered what you liked from the Modern Realm and we sent Cowboy. You need to regain your strength, so eat, Healer's orders."

When Galan set the tray over my lap, I peeled into the Hamburger Mary's bag and pulled out a chili-cheeseburger and onion rings. My stomach was imploding, the rumble quickly becoming a 9.0 quake. I drew on strawberry milkshake, amazed it was still frozen. "Galan, you rock."

"My pleasure, Mika. If you will excuse me, I am meeting Castian and a few elders of the Fae court and need to change. Feel better, little one." Galan kissed my forehead and trailed a finger along the edge of my jaw. "I shall thank the gods you are well."

"Thank you, Galan." I offered Aust an onion ring. "Somebody thank Cowboy for his trouble. This is fabulous."

"I shall," Galan said. He winked, kissed Jade and then, running her braid through his fingers he said, "I shant be long, an hour or two at most, I expect."

Her smile as she walked him out made my cheeks flush. It was sweet how the two of them loved each other. Gentle and peaceful. Not at all like the collisions Bruin and I constantly found ourselves in. The two of us were drawn like neodymium magnets, smashing together only to ricochet off into oblivion. Then, ten minutes later we'd be sucked back together again for yet another crushing blow.

I couldn't deny I wanted him. Physically he encapsulated everything I'd ever wanted in a lover, but the push and pull wasn't doing either of us any good. Sadly, it was time to get off the ride before someone lost a limb, or died of a cracked skull.

It wasn't Bruin that needed to go. It was me.

I hadn't realized I'd spoken aloud until Aust's expression fell. "Reconsider, *neelan*. Let things settle before you make such a decision." Aust gathered the crumpled wrappers from my lunch, stuffed them back into the bag and removed the tray. "I spoke to Nash earlier and he is hosting a stargazing event at the observation centre tomorrow night. I thought mayhap you and your grandfather might enjoy it. Come as my guests. Please."

"I don't belong here, Aust."

"But you do. You belong with me. I just found you."

Avoiding the heart-wrenching agony in his ice-blue gaze, I swung my feet out from under the quilt and set them flat on the floor. I couldn't stand the idea of leaving him looking so haggard and lost. What was this connection between us? He knelt on the floor before me and peered up through red-rimmed eyes. I didn't have the strength to walk away from him. Yet.

"Tomorrow night sounds perfect. Grandfather and I were supposed to go out last week with my telescope but, with all that's happened, we didn't get there."

The relief on his face was staggering. "Then it is settled."

When he leaned in to kiss me, I cupped his jaw. My fingers brushed the black velvet mourning band he wore for the loss of his father. He put up a good front, but he was struggling in this world too.

"Aust, you look tired. I'm all right. Go get some sleep . . . or reverie . . . or whatever you Elves do to stay healthy. I can't rest if I'm worried about you."

Aust bowed his head and clapped his hand to the thigh of his leather pants. Faolan bounded to his side as he headed out the door, her ebony tail swishing like a sword, narrowly missing a vase filled with lilacs on the coffee table.

My noggin felt like scrambled eggs. I rubbed my head, wishing both my skull and my palm would stop making my life hell. At least my vision had improved and the world stopped swaying beneath me like the fun-house floor. Yippee.

I slid a hand down my front and took inventory. Everything seemed to be working. I paused to read the black t-shirt I wore. It was one of Bruin's. It said, *'Rogues do it from behind.'* My chest tightened and I pushed him out of my mind. "Jade, am I good to go have a shower?"

Deep red curls bounced as she nodded. "Don't overdo the bending and reaching for today and you'll be fine. I can't tell you how lucky we were." She frowned and rubbed a claw pendant wrapped around her wrist. "Bruin would have lost his mind if Lexi killed you. Even now I doubt he'll ever forgive her."

"So, he knows?" I raised my hand. "Never mind, don't answer that." She nodded. "I called him."

I couldn't help the stabbing pain in my gut that he hadn't come. Well, what did I expect? The last time I spoke to him I told him he was no better than a stray dog crushing on me. *Nice.* That was one of my more cutting insults. I pushed back the chili-cheeseburger-churn in my gut and swallowed. "We had another fight."

"I saw," Jade said. "When I healed you . . . I saw. Sorry."

I checked my balance. Fairly certain I wasn't going to ass-plant, I pushed off into an old man shuffle toward the dresser. "Right, Bruin mentioned that side effect to your healing. Don't worry about it. Thanks for the save."

"I'd say anytime, but I'd rather not repeat the drama."

I grabbed a pair of worn jeans, a tank and fresh bra and panties and closed the drawers. "Yeah. Wasn't my best moment. Come to think of it, that whole day wasn't my best."

"He didn't go." Jade said.

I lifted my head. "Pardon?"

"Bruin. In case you're interested, he didn't go help in Boston."

"None of my—What do you mean help?"

"Join the search for Katsu's brother." She lifted the tray off the bed and set it on the floor outside the door in the hall. "That's where everyone went, what Bruin told her in the garden. Her brother is missing."

"What?" I leaned against the wall and tightened my grip on my clothes. "Could you start at the beginning, please? I'm not tracking very well."

Jade looked as confused as I felt. "Okay, Katsu and her brother Tenkei run a jiu-jitsu dojo in Boston for street kids. The day before yesterday, while she was with you in Vancouver, a class showed up and the place had been trashed. The human police were called, but it was Scourge. We're pretty sure."

I shook my head. "I thought—"

"I felt what you thought, and rightly so. What you overheard had me ripping Bruin a new one, but then he explained."

Shit. He'd wanted to explain to me, but I wouldn't hear it. I rubbed a hand over my face. "I hate what this world is doing to me. I've turned into such a crazy bitch."

"Shake it off, Mika. It's a lot . . . the world, the hormones, the pressure. Galan and I were catastrophic at first and we didn't have to deal with half the stuff on your plate. You'll find your stride. It's tough, especially as a strong woman used to steering your own life. I get it."

I snorted. "*Please,* you and Galan are perfect together."

"You should have seen the black eye and split lip I gave him in the beginning." She laughed. "It takes work to sync up, but if you can . . . there's nothing like these guys."

"It's so complicated."

Disapproval grew thick in her voice as she stared me down. "After the week I've had, you don't think I know that?"

I gathered my braid in my hand and brought it to rest on my chest. "I'm sorry. I should have asked, how are you feeling?"

She shrugged. "Sore. Embarrassed. Exhausted. Furious. It's different hour by hour."

"I'm sorry. It sucks having everyone know more about your business than you."

Jade propped herself on the edge of the bed and exhaled. "It does, but the point is . . . life feels complicated when things are happening, but it's not. It's simple. Iadon and Tham helped Galan save my life. And when I healed you, I felt how you love Bruin. I also felt how terrified you are to admit it."

"But my work. My friends. My life."

"You can make those things work form here and you know it. You're making excuses. It's time to stop. You're hurting Bruin and you're hurting yourself. You demand truth from everyone around you and yet you lie to yourself."

That's not true. My mind swirled with images and memories and fears. Everything I'd worked for and wanted, my job and my life in Vancouver. That was the life I wanted. *Wasn't it?*"

Jade stepped in front of me and squeezed my arm. "There's nothing going on with Katsu and deep down, you know it. He loves you. And you love him. Simple."

A knock had me clutching my clothes to my chest.

Jade strode over and opened the door a crack. "Julian's here to get you wired up. You up for a little tech visit?"

I smoothed down the t-shirt I wore, thankful that Bruin was a giant and it hung half-way down my thighs. "Sure."

Jade ushered in her genius brother and remained in the doorway. "I'll get out of your way and check on you before bed. Call me immediately if you feel dizzy or off balance."

I laughed. "How will I know the difference? Dizzy and off balance is my new normal."

Jade's smile was sad. "Hang in there, Mika. Work on syncing up."

She meant well—I knew that—but I was glad when the door closed behind her. I hadn't regained the strength to fight yet. And as Bruin's sister, she pushed things at me I didn't want to think about. Julian was better company. Safer.

He set out his tools and a box of blue cable next to my laptop and swung his bag off his shoulder. Before he got to work, he pushed up the sleeves of his shirt and dug through his gear. The elaborate dragon tattoo on his forearm caught my attention. I thought back to the Gatehouse when we'd met. He'd worn a blue Polo shirt and I hadn't noticed the ink.

How had I missed that? Details were my thing.

"Why are you looking at me like that?" He checked his fly. "Everything all right?"

I snapped out of my thoughts and pointed to the table. "What's with the cabling? Don't I already have access?"

"You had limited, monitored access. This is full access, nobody watching."

"Why now? A few days ago, I begged Reign to let me work and he shut me down."

Julian rubbed a palm over his face and exhaled. The action made me smile. Bruin did that exact same thing. "Reign is majorly pissed about Lexi hurting you. He knows how strong she is, and he didn't think to have you checked out when he broke up your fight. It was a lethal error that almost cost you your life and Bruin, his mate."

"I don't hold Reign responsible."

He held a finger over his mouth and smiled. "Keep *that* to yourself. A Reign apology is a rare thing. Bask in the glow, sister mine. It got you Internet didn't it?"

I guess it did. "Fine. I'll take it. Thanks."

I set my clothes on the top of the dresser and moved so I could watch him run my line. "Have you gotten anywhere on the names and photos Bruin and I gave you from the Nimithic case? Do you think I'm right?"

Julian tilted his head side to side as he pulled tools out and set them on the desk. "I've been ricocheting from one dummy corporation to another but, when I follow the money trails, I always end up in some off-shore country with a shitload of cash stashed away. I've set markers on the accounts to notify me of activity and will keep digging, but that kind of money . . . it makes me think it's a lot bigger than you and Bruin thought."

I looked at those lilacs and wished Bruin was here so we could talk this out. I wished like hell I could go back to when we'd made our truce before leaving for Vancouver. We'd set ourselves on a path for a future and I said I'd give us a shot. He'd been crazy happy until his stupid slip of the tongue. And then I'd ruined everything.

Shit, Julian said something, but I missed it.

He smiled up at me from where he knelt against the wall. "I was saying, when I'm done, your connection will be as fast as anything you're used to. When you download though, there might be a latency of a few microseconds, but nothing that will affect you."

He set down his crimping tool and his smile faded. "Remember, tech support is available 24/7. I'd rather wake up at 3 in the morning than have someone messing with my system because they think they know what's what."

"Got it, thanks, Julian. Being unplugged is a scary thing. I've been getting the shakes, Jonesing for . . ." I noticed the leather straps bound around Julian's wrist held a large polished bear claw. Both Lexi and Jade had one too. "That is Bruin's, isn't it?"

Lifting his arm, he smoothed his thumb over the silky surface. Its deep luster set off the warm mocha colour of his skin. "Yeah, it's a Skirl. He gave one to each of us a few months ago. It's like a dog whistle, but it calls directly to him. No matter where he is in either realm, he hears it and knows which one of us needs him."

"It's beautiful."

Julian slid it from around his wrist, unwrapped the length of leather and hung it over my neck. "You should have one. If anything happened to you—yeah, well, you should have one."

"But he gave it to you."

"No. Keep it." Julian placed a strong hand over mine and pressed it to my chest. "I know you're struggling right now, but he'll like that you have a piece of him with you."

I rubbed at the ache in my chest and struggled to draw a breath.

God, the hormones had gotten way worse in two days of me lying unconscious.

Julian paused, set down his tiny screwdriver and ushered me into the bathroom. Leaning into the shower, he started the water and tested the spray. "Take a break, Mika. By the time you pull yourself together, at least your tech world will be restored. Maybe together we can go over a few things I'm working on."

"Thanks," I said blinking quickly, "I appreciate it."

Dropping my bundle of clothes onto the counter, I held on to my fall-apart until the door clicked shut behind me. With nobody watching, all bets were off. A second later, Julian cranked music in my room, probably so nobody could hear me. *Bless you, Julian.*

CHAPTER THIRTY-SEVEN

"Fucking A. I think I found it, Mika."

Sliding my chair around to where Julian set up camp at the table in my suite, I checked out his screen. A bunch of numbers and symbols floated on a page looking like nothing much of anything to me. "I don't read the Matrix, "Neo". What does it say?"

Julian snorted. "You were right. I think I just found the order slips for large amounts of DMSO, Ketamine and three of the other chemicals on Bree's ingredients of horrors and had them delivered to that warehouse you busted. There's one more though . . . a drum of liquid Succinylcholine chloride."

"That could be part of the liquid in the vial. Bree hasn't nailed that sample down yet."

Julian clicked through a couple more pages and exhaled. "Christ, Mika, how'd you know where to look?"

I took control of his mouse for a sec and scrolled to the next page. "Agencies keep close watch on the purchasing of medical-grade chemicals, but the restrictions on veterinary grade are way laxer. Once Bree figured out what we were looking for . . .."

"You're one smart lady."

I bumped his shoulder and smiled. "High praise, coming from you."

I opened a new window and pulled up a fact sheet on liquid Succinylcholine chloride, or Sucostrin, as it was called. "This is seriously nasty stuff. Used for immobilizing wildlife, Sucostrin isn't exactly a tranquilizer. It acts as a muscle blocking agent, essentially paralyzing the animal, leaving them fully awake, aware and able to feel pain."

Julian cursed. "That's disgusting. So, what's the delivery system . . . Tranq dart?"

I fingered through the photos strewn across the table and pointed to a glossy shot of a glass wall case housing dart guns and jab poles. "Yep, that would be my guess."

I glanced up from the screen and gasped. "*Damn*, Aust. I gotta get a bell on you."

Aust tensed, not two feet away. "Apologies. You both seem so engrossed."

Julian laughed and patted his chest. "Not a problem, my man. We could probably use the break anyway. Mika's supposed to be resting after all."

I laughed and let Faolan jump up and lick my face. "Are you kidding? I feel better after an afternoon hunting down bad guys than I ever would lazing around feeling sorry for myself. This was the best medicine I could get, Julian."

Julian bumped fists with me and returned his attention to our computer searches.

I stretched my neck and turned back to Aust. He looked no better. "So, what's new with you? Faolan smells like she's been in the river."

Aust nodded, pulled a chair out from my table and looked at my laptop. "I see you are up and running." He looked to Julian, who gave him a thumbs up.

I smiled. Colloquialisms sounded incredibly awkward coming from Aust's lips. "Yeah, I'm reconnected to the world."

"In that case, could you and I go for a surf on the Internet, *neelan*?

Lexi and Jade said they would help me, but with all the happenings of late, I hate to ask."

"Sure, what are we looking for?"

Aust settled in beside me. The mauve discoloration below his eyes a disturbing contrast from his pale skin.

"Did you get any rest at all?"

"Fash not, reverie is fickle. It comes as it wills." Aust made a visible effort to brighten and pointed to the screen. "I seek a design to craft a mating gift for the wedding. I thought a keepsake box or a—"

"Oh, Aust, your nose is bleeding." I grabbed a box of tissues from the washroom, plucked out a few and handed them over. "Do you get these often?"

"Verily, this is my first."

After only a few seconds blood soaked through the tissue.

I pulled the waste-basket out from under the desk and angled it so he could get rid of them. "Tip your head back a bit and put pressure here."

After handing him a second and then a third handful, I returned to the washroom. Flipping the faucet on full, I grabbed a facecloth and held it under the icy flow. "A cold cloth sometimes helps. I used to get nosebleeds as a kid. It's no biggie, just a pain in the ass."

Aust exchanged the next round of bloody tissues for the cloth and stared at me sideways. "It would seem to be more of a pain in the face."

Well-duh. I laughed.

Julian noticed the state of the cloth and frowned. "Gods, you're really gushing, man. Try pinching the bridge of your nose, buddy."

The facecloth hadn't done any better than the tissues. I grabbed another cloth and a sickening dread took root in my gut. My skin tingled. "Okay, I don't like this. I'm calling in the troops. You stay here with Julian."

Launching down the hall in my bare feet, I took the stairs down one floor, along the corridor to my left and jogged up the three steps leading to the master suite at the end of the hall. Faolan apparently thought we were having fun. She bounced at my side, tail swishing and cutting through the air. When I came up to the carved double doors, I knocked, hard and fast.

Please, Jade, be inside.

"One moment." Galan open the door, fastening the ties of his pants, a pink flush to his normally ivory complexion. "Mika, what a—"

"Is Jade here?" I leaned around him before my mind caught up to what I'd interrupted. "Shit. Sorry, Galan, but this is important."

"What is it, sweeting," he asked.

Jade came to the door pulling the lengths of tussled hair from beneath her knit sweater. "What's wrong? Is it Bruin?"

I shook my head and started to jog back up the hall. Faolan was even more excited by the addition of two more people running the halls. "It's Aust. He has a terrible nosebleed. We can't get it to stop."

Galan cursed something in Elvish and bolted up the stairs and disappeared down the hall.

When Jade gasped, my stomach dropped. "Translation, please. What did he say?"

Jade caught my arm and pulled us to a halt in the hall outside my suite. "*Scareg morttha* is Elvish for scarlet death."

My ears buzzed as the blood rushed from my head. *Scarlet death?*

I followed Jade inside. Galan squatted in front of Aust's chair, a melodic flow of Elvish passing between the two of them. The expression on Galan's face made my chest ache. In the minutes it took me to fetch help, Aust had gotten a shitload worse. The wastebasket was littered with a sopping red mash of pulp and Julian had taken to holding a towel against Aust's face.

Aust looked like he was about to black out.

Jade went straight to work. Spreading Aust's knees, she stood between them and splayed her fingers on his cheekbones. "Mika, grab me a damp towel so we can clean him up and see what we're dealing with. Galan, tell me what you know about this."

"*Scareg morttha*," he said, "is a mysterious infliction which comes as unexpectedly as it goes within the Highborne race. On the rare occasion someone succumbs to it, the victim exsanguinates within the hour of onset."

"What?" I froze, handing Galan the damp towel. "What the hell do you mean exsanguinates? I thought the name was dramatic. People actually *die* from this?"

Galan's ocean blue eyes burned against a face that had drained dead white. His voice spoke in my mind. *Always.*

Well, not this time. I thought right back at him.

Jade took the towel and wiped Aust's face. "I'm going to get this bleeding stopped. Were there any theories of what causes it?"

Galan swiped his fingers through his silver hair. "We believe, after an extended absence from a proper reverie, the blood vessels weaken and lose their structure. In every occurrence, someone close to the deceased mentioned the loss of reverie."

I gasped. "*Dammit,* Aust. You knew this could happen and you didn't tell anyone you haven't been sleeping?"

"I told *you.*" He hissed as Jade pressed on his sinuses. "Apologies, *neelan,* had I known my condition had reached this level, I would have sought aid."

"Don't *apologize* to me." I looked from Jade to Galan and shook my head. "He first mentioned it to me the morning the stripes appeared, but I'd guess getting kicked out of the village and his father's death was the start of it. He has nightmares. To avoid causing anyone to worry, he runs the grounds at night with the wolves. I assumed he was lying down through the day to catch up, but apparently not."

"Fash not, Mika." He held out a bloodstained hand. "Jade is a marvel. All will be well."

If Jade could help him. I squeezed his hand and shuddered at its icy touch. *Jade's healing doesn't work on natural health issues. Does it?*

Galan didn't meet my gaze but shook his head.

I stumbled back a few steps and strong hands caught me. Julian. There was more talking at that point, deep voices speaking while Jade's ethereal singing voice filled the suite. Sing as she might, she couldn't save him.

The thought of losing Aust made my gut seize. I grabbed the smudge stick from where Grandfather had hung it on the back of my door and struck a long matchstick from the fireplace. Settling on my knees beside his chair, I closed my eyes and drew a ragged breath. "Earth Mother, please hear me."

When the warm breeze picked up my hair and swirled it gently against my face, I continued. "Earth Mother, lend Aust your strength as he faces this trial. He is truly one of your children, a gift to nature and all your creatures. Touch his life with your love as you touch mine. In your name, we serve you, forever and always."

Jade cursed and slapped at his pale cheeks. "Aust? Aust, wake up. Don't you *die* on us. Open your eyes, sweetie. *Aust?*"

He'd lost consciousness, his body limp in the chair.

I lit the smudge stick and arched the braid in shaky sweeps. Grandfather did this much better. The scents of sage, cedar and lavender caught in my throat. "Earth Mother, I *beg* of you."

We waited. *Please.* The scent of spring rain filled the room and my heart raced.

"Okay, Aust. Earth Mother is here. Can you feel her power? Don't resist her. Give yourself over. Trust her. Trust me." He didn't stir. Could he even hear me? "Aust, *please*, I need you to try . . . *try* to let her in."

I continued to chant and smudge while Jade resumed singing. Earth Mother's power built until the hair on my arms stood on end. Still, Aust looked no better.

Come on, Aust. Fight this. Come on.

As the breeze kissed my cheek and receded, I searched Aust's face. Did it work? Time froze, suspended as if held in one long breath. Aust lay deathly pale beneath a layer of crusting blood. Faolan whined and I absently scrubbed her ruff.

"All right, we're almost stopped up here." Jade exhaled. "He's coming around."

Tears broke free and I realized then how badly I was shaking. Julian squeezed my shoulders and rubbed my back as I sobbed. "Thank you, Earth Mother."

Aust's eyes fluttered open.

Jade straightened. "Don't scare me like that again, Aust. Do you know how close you came to being beyond our help?"

His ashen face lolled to the side, his head too heavy to hold. "Verily, I believe I do."

Jade brushed back his golden waves, kissed his forehead and wrapped her arms around him. "Okay, let's get you cleaned up and into bed. You're getting some rest, even if I have to tie you down and knock you out myself."

"I've got it," Julian said, jogging for the washroom.

Aust frowned, but Jade pressed her fingers against his pale blue lips. "I'm putting you down for a healer-induced nap. I'll use my powers to hold off the dreams while you rest, and we'll continue to do this until you're through the rough patch and able to find reverie yourself. No arguing. I'm more than your healer. I love you."

Faolan pushed her head through the bodies and found Aust's hand. As he stroked her fur, they both seemed to settle a bit more.

"Mika, you don't mind if we all climb in to your bed, do you?"

I shook my head, stripped Aust's bloody tunic off and tossed into the wastebasket. "Of course not. I'll be glad to know he's getting some rest." *But God help us if Bruin smells Aust in my sheets.* Galan's head snapped up and he frowned.

Aust shook his head and struggled to get up. "I shan't impose on Mika. If you insist, on this course of treatment, let us return to my suite."

"Great idea," Jade said, brushing back her deep red curls. "And when Elora comes to check in with you, should we tell her how close to death her son got? Do you think she won't take one look at you and know?"

Aust's lips tightened into a fine line. Jade had him cornered and we all knew it. With everything his mother was going through, he would never cause her more worry.

I squeezed his shoulder. "I'm glad you have the strength to argue, but don't. Go get cleaned up and for once in your life, let us take care of you."

Twenty minutes later, Julian and Galan came out of the bathroom, helping Aust to my bed. He was shivering and his lips had turned a sickly shade of purple-blue. The guys made it seem as if their arms around his back were merely guiding him, but I knew better. Jade and I pulled back the sheets and the men laid him in the centre of the bed.

Faolan bounded up and curled into a ball at his feet.

Galan patted the wolf then met Aust's gaze. "Allow these ladies to comfort you for a few hours. No argument shall dissuade us, and you are far too weak to escape. Besides, Jade needs rest after a healing. You will do her, and therefore me, a service to join her in rest."

Galan settled Jade in beside Aust, drew the quilt over her and kissed her cheek.

"Actually," I said. "I'll sleep in Bruin's room. I'm close if you need me and . . . I think it's safer for everyone if I respect the needs of Bruin's bear. Just give Julian and me two minutes to grab our stuff and we'll be out of your hair."

Galan nodded, slid in beside Aust, and pressed his lips to Aust's damp hair. "Never again, brother mine. You mean too much to too many, to lose you."

CHAPTER THIRTY-EIGHT

*M*oving myself into Bruin's room had seemed like a good idea . . . until I tried to sleep. After lying awake in his bed for hours, with the scent of him filling my mind and tingling through my body, I realized something I think I'd known all along. He was part of me.

Whether I liked it, or not. Planned it, or not. I *had* fallen for him.

Bruin was part of me. It was more than hormones. It was more than sex. It was *him*.

"I'm sorry that me trying to love you has been such a goddamn burden."

I flung the covers off as his words ran a repeating loop in my head. He'd tried to love me . . . and I'd thrown it back in his face. Grandfather was right. I hadn't wanted to see or hear it. But, my stubborn refusal hadn't done either of us any good.

Part of me had blamed him for the bonding. Why? He had no control over it. Because he understood more about this world? Because he was happy about it when I wasn't?

God. I really was a nightmare. I stared out the window at the moon, floating in the star-smattered sky, blurring behind a wall of tears. A small slice of darkness on the one side of the lunar globe kept it from being completely round. The full moon marked the end.

I didn't think. Raising the bear claw skirl to my mouth, I blew.

Bruin materialized immediately, knife drawn and ready to fight.

"Shit. I'm sorry." I stammered, my voice quivering with tears. "Julian said this was for emergencies and I forgot. I . . . uh, wasn't thinking."

Bruin sheathed the wide silver blade at his hip and strode for the door.

My heart sank. "Don't go. Please, Bruin. I don't deserve it, but please hear me out."

His hand hesitated on the handle, his shoulders stiff. After a long silence, he turned and leaned against the closed door to the hall. He folded his arms over his chest and waited. He looked bad . . . like run-over-by-a-train-and-dragged-along-the-rails, kinda bad. The cold turquoise glare he pegged me with said I was indeed the locomotive in question and needed to talk fast.

"I'm sorry," I said, trying to tighten up my voice. "I got twisted up about the mating, and the pressure of being pigeon-holed as your other half, and I handled it badly. Very badly."

Didn't even blink.

I swallowed and tugged at the hem of his t-shirt I'd worn to bed. "Aust almost died tonight. Jade couldn't save him and . . . we almost lost him."

That stirred something in him. His jaw tensed and he opened his mouth to say something, but closed it again. Damn. He was really upset.

"He's all right. Jade and Galan are with him in my room."

Cold eyes narrowed as he glanced to the closed adjoining door.

I eased a step closer. Shit, my legs were trembling. "I moved myself in here, so you and your bear wouldn't misunderstand. He's only in my bed because he collapsed while in my room and Jade didn't want Elora to see him until he recovers."

His gaze shifted back to me.

My voice cracked again, but I kept trying. "It hit me tonight. Jade couldn't help him, and I thought he'd die. Julian held me . . . but it wasn't his arms I wanted around me. It was yours."

Still nothing. I was too late.

My vision got blurry again and I blinked fast, but my lids couldn't keep up. "And earlier, when Julian and I were sleuthing through the slaughter of your friends . . . I wanted to talk things over with you. I missed not being able to bounce ideas off you and have you listen to me."

I swiped at traitorous tears and tried to breathe. "You were right. I didn't realize it, but you were. You asked who hurt me so bad I couldn't trust love. My father. He . . . he hurt me."

A rumble rose from his chest and his eyes flashed gold.

"No. Not physically." I swallowed and tried to organize my jumbled thoughts. If I didn't get this right, I wouldn't get another chance. "My parents married because my mom was pregnant with me. I don't know if he loved her, but he married her. It was his obligation to accept his circumstances and man-up."

I swallowed past the lump in my throat and rubbed my aching chest. "As time passed, he spent more and more time away. Mom bought new clothes and changed her hair and I kept my room extra clean and minded my manners. But nothing changed. After a few years he dropped out of our lives and she dove head first into a bottle of whiskey. In a few more years, she'd drank herself dead and I went to live with Grandfather."

Bruin cursed and the rigidity in his shoulders eased a little.

"So, I grew up the child of a walk-away father and a mother lost in the bottom of a Crown Royal bottle. She died loving a man who settled for duty over love." I wiped my tears and moved until I was standing directly in front of him. "I know we're not them, but part of me is still that little girl waiting for you to realize that I'm not enough for you. What if you wake up one day and realize I'm just a stupid Mundie you got stuck with?"

The air around us surged as Bruin flipped his bangs out of the way. Both man and bear front and centre. "I'm not going anywhere. It's the opposite. Everyone left me too. I know the pain of being abandoned and alone."

"Your family didn't *choose* to leave you. They loved you."

He brushed my tears with his thumbs and frowned. "I'm sure your parents loved you too. They just sucked at showing it."

"What makes you think we'd be any better?"

Bruin opened his arms. "Because I'm the perfect man for you. I'm bound to you . . . mind, body, soul and bear. You hold the reins of my life and I love that. Just claim what's been yours from the beginning and I'll be whole for the first time in my life."

"Your friends think that you being saddled with an average-looking Mundie is the cruelest thing the Fates could have done to you."

"Do you think I care what anyone else thinks? The Fates got this one so right, it's a slam-dunk, baby. We could be great together. You just have to believe that."

He brushed a finger along the polished curve of his bear-claw pendant and smiled.

Another wave of tears threatened. "I'm sorry . . . the thing with Katsu . . . blaming you for the bonding . . . all of it. I'm so sorry."

He shook his head. "It doesn't have to be easy to be right."

I chuckled and swiped my cheek dry. "Well, in that case, we should be golden, 'cause not one thing about this has been easy."

Bruin pulled me against his warm, powerful chest and wrapped his arms around me. A sob ripped up my windpipe and I got pulled in tighter. He held me, strong arms loving me, protecting me, holding me. And when he picked me up and set me in his lap on the edge of his bed, all my anger and fear and rejection bubbled up and broke free. He didn't mind.

And that was the point, wasn't it?

CHAPTER THIRTY-NINE

It was amazing what a little heart-to-heart could do for a girl.

With our bodies entwined under warm, weighty blankets, Bruin and I claimed the morning for ourselves. For once, we didn't have sex. We lounged. We talked. We listened. We slept. It was a kind of intimacy I'd never experienced before. And each time I'd woken, Bruin's bear had been wrapped completely around me. Warm. Protective. At peace.

Turned out, his bear was as much of a snuggler as he was. And how wonderful was that.

When we finally tore ourselves away from our love-in, we checked on Aust's recovery—he'd moved back to his own suite before lunch—and recapped the info Julian and I had found on the chemical shipments. The idea that the Scourge might be able to tranquilize Weres and torture them or mask their rotting stench would upset the balance of Were defenses.

Bruin didn't like the implications at all.

While he poured over the photos once again, I hopped into the shower and got ready for a night of stargazing. Today we'd started to get our bearings. Tonight, we'd build on that. With Aust feeling better, the three of us were taking Grandfather to Nash's celestial gathering.

I braided my hair and wrapped a towel tight across my chest before fumbling through my dresser . . . sweats, jeans, khakis. Bruin wore black jeans—no holes—and a white collared shirt that high-lighted the golden tone of his skin and a black leather vest. This was our first outing as a real couple and I wanted to look the part.

"What do you wear for a romantic night out watching comets?"

"As little as possible."

I rolled my eyes. "When other people are going to be there too."

His playful growl had me running, but there was no escape. In two predatory strides, he closed in and caught me. Ignoring my protest, he caged me in his arms and nipped at my neck while I squealed. When I was out of breath, he kissed the end of my nose and set me free. "Why don't you check your closet? Maybe something in there might work."

I straightened my towel and headed into my suite "I didn't bring enough to need the closet. I haven't even been in—"

My breath caught as I stepped inside and flipped on the light. Sliding one hanger after another down the chrome bar I stared at the collection of clothes: blouses, evening dresses, designer jeans, leather jackets and *wow*, the lingerie. I ran my fingers along the skimpy silk teddies, leather corsets and fine French lace as my cheeks burned fifty shades of scarlet.

"When did you do this?"

He pressed in behind me and kissed the bare skin at the back of my neck. When he spoke, his voice was husky and deeper than usual. "The night Jade started her Yearning. I couldn't sleep and felt bad about ignoring you. I, uh . . . was thinking about you . . . a lot."

I held up an embarrassingly flimsy teal teddy and raised a brow. "I see that."

Firm hands splayed across my belly and over my towel. "Try it on. Go on. I dare you."

I stuffed it back between the others as quick as I could. While he continued to chuckle behind me, I slipped into a cute pair of embroi-dered blue jeans and a white Grecian top. Man, he had a keen eye for shopping. And he could accessorize too. I buckled a chunky leather belt over my shirt. It hung low on my hips and looked awesome with the pair of gladiator sandals I strapped on. With a couple bangles clamped on my arm, I twirled in front of the mirror.

"Stunning," he said, lifting me up by the rounds of my ass and pinning me to the wall. "It's even more beautiful on you than I imagined. Too beautiful to stay on you, actually."

Nice. Amazing what new clothes could do for a girl's outlook.

The knock at the door had Bruin cursing and me giggling. "Save that thought for later."

I wriggled free from Bruin's hold and rushed to the door. Aust stood in the hall as Faolan bounded in. He looked a million times better than he had. Better even than this afternoon. "Hey there, we're almost ready. Come in."

Aust inclined his head to Bruin and paused inside the door. He looked from me to Bruin and back again, the tension obvious. "Mika tells me you will be joining us this evening."

"If you don't mind me tagging along."

Aust's ice-blue gaze narrowed. "And if I did?"

Bruin stood to his full height as his smile grew wider. "I'd come anyway."

Why did men have to be such . . . men? I sighed. "Well this is shaping up to be a fabulous night. What's going on? You two are friends, remember?"

Aust closed the door and touched the shiner on his cheek. "Friends indeed."

I stepped back and looked at them both. "What? Tell me you two didn't fight?"

Bruin exhaled. "Faolan recounted what you saw in the garden to Aust and he rose to be your champion before I could explain. It's all sorted out now though."

Aust waved away my glare. "Let us focus on the night ahead. You look lovely, *neelan.*

"Thanks." I spun slowly so he could get the full effect. "Bruin picked the outfit for me."

He inclined his head to Bruin and swallowed. "You have wonderful instincts. Your choices suit her perfectly."

I thought about all that silk, leather and lace in the closet and wondered what Bruin's instincts told him when he picked those out. I excused myself to check my pony tail and finish the last touch-ups to my makeup. Leaning close to the vanity mirror, I brushed my cheek with extra blush to hide my flush. When I straightened, the air around me swirled.

Rabbit? The Creator is waiting for us to come and be awed by him.

I smiled at the excitement in Grandfather's gravelly voice and freed Bruin's claw pendant, so it rested on top of my blouse. Focused on the warm breeze, I answered over the wind. "Yes Grandfather, we're ready. Are you in your suite?"

No. I am by the pool drinking mead with Cowboy and his warrior brothers.

"We'll be right down." I snagged a cute jean jacket from the closet and Bruin shrugged on his leather jacket. Though it looked like a regular biker jacket, I knew from trying to move it earlier, that the thing weighed a ton and was stuffed with weapons.

Aust and Faolan stepped into the hall and Bruin closed the door behind us.

"He guys. I'm glad I caught you." Julian jogged up the hall, coins jingling in his pockets, his loafers quiet on the beige hallway carpet. I read the slogan on his t-shirt and smiled. Definitely a gift from Bruin . . . *Come over to the geek side. We have Pi.*

"Bree's been looking for you two," he said, scrubbing his palm over his short trimmed hair. The smooth, brown skin of his forearm brought me up short. Where was his tattoo? He seemed to notice me staring and crossed his arms over his chest. "She's almost nailed down the exact formula of the pills, and you were right, Mika. They are scent-repressing. She also has a few more questions and wanted to talk when you have a chance."

"Oh, okay," I said, "we can head right over—"

Bruin shook his head. "Tell Bree we'll swing by the bar in a couple of hours, after we're done at the observatory. There's nothing to be done tonight and we have a date."

The observation platform, five stories above the Academy astrology centre, was buzzing when we arrived. Nash had the group's attention, making his way around the 360 degree balcony, pointing out key elements of the meteor shower. "If you trace the paths of the Delta Aquarid meteors backward what will you find?"

"The star Delta Aquarii—also called Skat," a bookish girl with frizzy curls answered.

"That's right, Mercy. And what two species draw its power from the Delta star?"

"Well," she continued, "unlike Weres who draw strength from the moon cycles, it's Star Faeries and Fire-Drakes who are powered by celestial movements including meteors and stars."

Nash nodded and moved to greet us. "Hey, welcome. Thanks for coming. I saved an observation station for you over here." He bowed his head to my Grandfather and led us to what looked like a large view-finder on a pedestal. As Grandfather, Aust and Nash discussed the celestial events of the past few weeks, Bruin and I pointed into the northern night sky and talked constellations. His favorite, of course, were Ursa Major and Ursa Minor.

When the evening eventually waned, we were the last to step away from our telescopes and give up for the night. Every question had been asked and answered about legends and beliefs from my world, his, and Aust's. I hadn't even noticed the observation deck was almost deserted.

Grandfather stepped back, his eyes twinkling with contentment. "What a wonderful evening."

"Glad you enjoyed it." Nash said. "Will you stay for the reception downstairs? It's always a lot of fun." As if on cue, music wove its way up the stairwell and students and guests began flooding from the main floor onto the cobblestone patio below. From where we stood at the railing far above, the glowing luminescence of cocktails shone like neon lights of fuchsia, lime and tangerine.

Grandfather picked up his walking stick and started toward the door to the stairwell. "I shall leave the festivities to the young. Mika and Bruin should stay though."

"Don't be silly, Grandfather. We'll walk you back."

"Nonsense." He waved a weathered hand between us. "Aust and Faolan will see me home well enough, won't you son?"

Aust bowed his head and gestured toward the doorway. "It would be my sincerest pleasure, Grandfather."

I knew better than to argue with Grandfather once his mind was set. I kissed them both goodnight. "All right, then I'll see you in the morning."

He winked and patted my hand. "Have a good time, Rabbit. And remember, every new day is another chance to live your life."

"Thanks Confucius."

Grandfather laughed and tapped my calf with his walking stick.

When the remaining students moved downstairs, Bruin walked around over to speak with Nash and I strolled to the other side of the platform for one final look. What a night. My hand skimmed the cold brushed chrome of the railing as hundreds of stars glittered above. It amazed me that the grandeur of the universe could be lost in a night sky filled with city lights. But here, in this realm of natural and magical wonders, Earth Mother's power really came through.

"Mika?" I turned to the sweet smile of a young girl with blue mottled skin. She was tall and slim, with an unnaturally long neck loosely covered with a swath of colourful silk. Her hand was propped by her shoulder, balancing a tray of multi-coloured drinks. Lifting a margarita glass filled with a sparkling crimson liquid, she offered it to me. "Something sweet while you wait for your mate's return?"

"Uh . . . thanks." I stared at the concoction swirling in the glass, mesmerized by the candy apple scent. "Is this okay for me to drink? It's not going to give me gills or Faerie wings or anything is it?"

She giggled. "No, but stay away from the yellow shots the Faeries have downstairs. Bruin should avoid the swirly green ones too."

"Oh, you know Bruin?"

She smirked. "I think most every woman on campus knows Bruin."

The skin on my neck tingled and a gentle wind lifted my hair as the Earth Sprits whispered in my ear. *Run, Mika.*

Something sharp punctured my skin. I reached for the point of pain, blinked and tried to clear the hum of confusion. My vision clouded. The blue girl spoke. The unfamiliar language circled in my mind. Words blurred my senses. She plucked the margarita glass from my hand.

The smooth, seductive youth of the blue-skinned girl undulated in the moonlight like a mirage. Soulless, black eyes replaced gold, a twisted, pointed-toothed sneer instead of the girl's sweet smile. "Sorry about this, but the master found you weren't affected by his charms the last time he visited you."

My limbs buckled, and I crashed to the concrete observation deck, paralyzed. *Master?*

Long, clawed fingers fished a leather cord from the cleavage of her blouse. At the end of the cord, hung a small golden flute, etched with black runes. She covered the holes and poised the mouthpiece to her lips. The high-pitched tune sent a shiver up my spine.

I swallowed and tried to speak. No sound came. My gaze dragged across the platform.

Bruin—Bruin dropped to his knees, the golden fury of his bear glowing in his eyes as he gazed at Abaddon gloating above him.

"Now, now, my young lovebirds, you didn't think I'd forgotten about you, did you?"

Movement in the sky had me rolling my gaze as far as I could to follow. Something was coming. Something big. A silhouette against the brightness of the stars grew larger, flapping powerful wings as it drew nearer. The rhythmic *swoosh* of giant wings cut through air. I searched the sky for the incoming bird, only it wasn't a bird. My mind reeled as the brindled wings of an enormous golden eagle flapped above me, lowering the massive body of a lion, five feet from where I lay.

Abaddon's amusement rang in his silky voice as he stepped over to me. "Never seen a Griffon before? Magical, aren't they? Quickly. Get her onto the mount."

A kaleidoscope of colours flashed before my eyes as the blue girl's silk scarf blocked my vision. Strong hands plucked me up and slung me over the coarse, golden fur of the Griffon's back. Within moments I was bound and felt the pull of being lifted up and up, into the night sky.

I struggled against the magic and drug binding me immobile. I fought to scream or call to the wind whistling in my ears. Nothing worked, and I was losing consciousness. Being blindfolded for the flight was good though. The last thing I needed was to be staring at the ground below, dizzy and about to pass out. Tight ropes held me snug to the flexing muscles of the beast. Tight enough to keep me from falling . . . I hoped.

What were they doing to Bruin? Had they kidnapped him too? The thought both enraged and comforted me. We banked a hard right and I slipped. My body shifted several inches on the fine fur of the beast. I gritted my teeth and my world dimmed.

CHAPTER FORTY

I suppose it was naïve of me to expect that a massive flying lion-bird beast would land us in a massive lion-bird *nest*, but somehow it caught me off guard when I woke on a pallet and found myself locked in a modern-styled prison. The room wasn't massive, but still large enough to have several cells divided and self-contained, the windowless, chiseled stone walls honed to a smooth honey finish, the rough stone floors and ceilings pierced with black iron bars dividing the space. How welcoming.

In the space beyond my prison, large woven tapestries hung, flanked by broken sculptures and defaced art. It was like *Metropolitan Home* met Caverns and Cages.

If I wasn't being kidnapped the mystery of this place alone would keep me busy for days.

A baleful whine had me on my knees and shaking the fog from my head. In the next cage over an extremely agitated silver-tipped Kodiak reared off his haunches, threw back his head and roared toward the ceiling.

"Bruin," I hissed, scrambling forward. "Calm down, big guy. I'm all right.

I crawled to the bars and shoved my arm through.

In the split second my arm touched the iron bar, it singed and sizzled. I screamed as my flesh burned and threw myself back.

Bruin's bear went wild. Over and again he threw himself at the bars until the fur on his shoulders had singed and the pads of his paws bled raw. Being out of his mind wasn't helping either one of us.

"Bruin. Hey big guy, look at me." His head swayed on a violent pendulum as if he wasn't hearing me, but I knew he did. I also knew he hated feeling helpless. "Bruin. I need you to calm down. I'm scared, and I need you. I need my mate."

His massive, heart-shaped face tilted to one side as golden eyes froze in a haunted stare. "That's right, baby. Please. Come to me."

Carefully this time, I reached through the bars and wriggled my fingers. After a moment, Bruin lumbered over. The throaty huff and the solid colour of his eyes told me his bear still held complete control, but he'd stopped hurting himself. When he was close enough, I scrubbed my fingertips into the ruff of his fur. When my fingers sank deep into the soft, smooth undercoat, my tension eased a little.

"That's right. Come closer, baby, let me scratch your ears."

I locked my fingers into Bruin's fur and blinked my eyes clear. Think. I needed to—

"How heartwarming. Beauty tames her beast." Abaddon clapped his hands as he stepped into view. Deceivingly handsome, the man carried himself with an unmistakable air of someone accustomed to being admired. Dressed in black slacks and a black silk shirt, the guy would give Bela Lugosi the creeps.

Bruin's violent spin knocked my arm against the bars and again I screamed and withdrew. His bear raged, throwing itself against the doorway of his cage as Abaddon passed Bruin's cage and came to mine. He held up his palm and the door swung open for him and latched behind him once he let himself inside.

The agony in Bruin's growls hurt my ears as the smell of his burning flesh and fur raised my urge to gag. I breathed through my mouth until my stomach settled. "What do you want?"

Abaddon bowed his head, his icy gaze locked on mine. The nearer he got, the stronger my senses reeled. He oozed an unnatural energy, a power that countered the very fabric of everything the Earth Mother governed over.

Though the compulsion in his words didn't hold me captive, when he brushed my cheek, my sixth sense exploded. Every cell in my body crawled in revulsion. It was like being infested by a million spiders and having them scurry around on my insides.

I recoiled. "Don't touch me."

The man was unnatural. Evil. An abomination hiding in a pretty package.

He arched an ebony brow. "My gifts don't affect you, but you do feel my power, don't you?"

I reminded myself not to give him any more power over us than he already had and shook off the sensation. "My skin crawls when you touch me if that's what you're asking. But you didn't answer my question. What do you want? Is this about the ring again?"

Abaddon glanced at Bruin pacing madly in the next cage and scowled. "It slipped through my fingers once, and with you at my mercy, I'm finally going to get it. After being forced to watch what we did to his sisters, there's no way he'll watch me do the same to you."

I flinched. He spoke about the murder and rape of Bruin's family without a touch of emotion. Violence exploded inside me and with the speed and power of the Were hormones raging in my blood, I punched him in the jaw. I heard the pop of bone, unsure whether it was his face or my hand that had made the sound.

My cheek exploded as his backhand connected and I hit the ground hard. With bruising force, he yanked me back to my feet and pulled me against his chest. "I smell him on you." His mouth moved down my neck paused over the spot on my shoulder where Bruin bit me a lifetime ago. "You refuse his claim, yet you let him inside you. Wet and willing, I'd bet. Tell me . . . does he fuck like a king?"

Bruin's bear went mad behind us, but I couldn't help him.

Abaddon's tongue flicked over the tiny scars and my goosebumps speared across my body. My legs trembled beneath me. I couldn't pull away.

"What do you think, Bruin? Should I take liberties with your mate?" Abaddon's mouth closed over my skin, his teeth threatening to puncture. After a moment he released his bite. "Or I could call in a few of my men and we can watch while they all have a go at her."

Bruin was all beast, lost to insanity. He threw his massive body against the bars over and over, the growls and snarls and thundering of impact ringing in my ears.

"You see, Mika, I know the need of a male to protect the females in his life and in a Were that need is compounded. It goes beyond dominance. It's visceral. Primal. Bruin would never get over it. Everyone knows he never got over what happened to his sisters. What do you think it would do to him to know he couldn't protect his mate either? What do you think the other Weres would think of a King who couldn't even keep his female safe?"

The rumble of his laughter against my chest made my stomach roll. Rough hands tightened around my braid and against my back, yanking my face upward. His mouth was hard on mine and tasted of tobacco and whiskey. I fought his kiss, cursing and screaming into his mouth. When he drew back, his eyes were lit with something truly vicious.

I wiped at the rancid taste of him in my mouth and lunged. With all my weight behind me, my knee came up and only his reflexes saved his crotch from my fury. An inch more to the left or a second sooner and I would have connected with something more sensitive than his thigh. He recoiled and I tottered on rubber legs.

A deafening roar vibrated off the floor and echoed from the walls.

Hot, shooting pain sliced across my back and I pitched forward. The force of the strike slammed me head first into the bars of the cage. My cheekbone collided with iron and singed on contact. One instant, the room disappeared behind spotty blotches of grey, the next, it was a blur as he fisted the front of my shirt and hauled me to my feet.

"This could've gone better for you, Ursa." He tossed me across the cell. I toppled over a small wood cot and the frame buckled and landed on top of me. My leg bent at an awkward angle and another wave of the shakes went through me.

I shook my head, blinking past the pain. Passing out was not an option right now. I planted my hands flat on the stone floor and reached out. "Earth Mother, I need you."

Natural warmth filled my shallow breaths and let me draw oxygen deep into my lungs. I wouldn't call it a second wind, but I rallied a bit. My vision cleared in time to avoid his boot. I rolled clear as his foot slammed down where my ribs would have been.

When he unsheathed a knife, I knew I was dead. He was twenty times stronger than me, and not half dazed. I hated to play the gender card but, he was a hulking man and I was . . . well, me.

Screw it. If I was going down, it would be swinging.

He hauled me off the floor by my hair and raised the knife to my throat. I caught a glimpse of the blade and jerked my head back, connecting with something hard. His chin maybe. I thought so but couldn't be sure. He grabbed my wrist and twisted it behind my back until I was on my knees in front of him. The *snap* of bone made my stomach lurch and the world went dark.

CHAPTER FORTY-ONE

*D*rifting on the wind I let my consciousness float, swept along by the Earth Spirits. The forest surrounding me grew vast, the scent and sounds of nature soothing, calling. I slowed my travel and descended, stepping onto the soft grass below with a grace I'd never possessed in reality. I stood. Breathed in. My lungs filled.

The afternoon light was in the process of changing, the gold of mid-day swirling pink. How long had I been dreaming? Running my hand down the front on my white, doeskin dress, I fingered the fringe and twirled like a girl.

"There you are, Mika." The native man's voice was strong and deep. "Your awakening has been a long time in coming."

On a slow turn the golden-pink haze shifted. Now I stood in a clearing on the edge of a stream. The man who spoke sat perched on the edge of a tall wooden stool and paid little attention to my stare. He wore tan hunting pants, no shirt over his brown skin and bare feet. Long chestnut hair pulled back from his face, bound by a thick leather strap.

Leaning over a debarked, red cedar tree, he focused on the totem he was carving. "Mika is not a proper Aboriginal name. We shall have to find you a more fitting title." His tone held no criticism, simply an assessment of fact. "Then again, my name leaves little to the imagination."

When he looked up, the hair on the back of my neck stiffened. A great surge of power washed through me and I tingled with Earth Mother's magic.

"Do you know who I am, *She Who Runs From Bear*? He grasped his adze in both hands and drew it toward himself, planing off a curl of wood.

"You are one of the originals," I said, searching the mystical clearing. "Why am I here?"

He reset the adze, and pulled again. "I asked you first. Who am I?"

Focusing on his task, he left me to sift through all the Native lore I could remember. How many nights had I sat with Grandfather at the fire circle listening to the elders speak of the original powers. Coyote. Hawk. Wolf. Thunderbird. Sun. Moon. Raven.

"Bear," I said, not sure how I knew it. "You are Bear."

Another long curl of wood hit the clearing floor. "And why do you think I brought you here, *Wind Talker With Sharp Tongue*?"

"Am I dead?" An icy chill speared through my veins. "Did Abaddon kill me?"

He bent forward, blew bits of sawdust and debris from the left eye of the raven's head he was carving and then flashed me a quick smile. "No. Not yet."

I stepped closer until I stood across from him, on the other side of the tree. "Yet?"

"Abaddon intends to kill you. You and your Bear. It just hasn't happened yet."

The fury that rose inside me shook my whole being. I couldn't let Bruin be hurt. I wouldn't. Not when I'd just found him. "Surely someone saw two Griffons flying across Haven skies. Reign and the Talon must be on the way to rescue us."

"And if they do rescue you, what changes? Bruin will have his mate, yes, but the Weres still won't be united and Abaddon will still plot to enslave them. The danger will remain."

"I don't understand. What needs to happen to make this come out right?"

Bear set down his tool and picked up a chisel. He spoke in that same, calm, you're-gonna-get-this-sooner-or-later tone Grandfather always used when delivering bad news. "If either you or Bruin die now the Weres will be ruined. Not broken . . . ruined. The species—volatile, powerful and head-strong—floundered long before Bruin's father came to be king, but with his leadership they were becoming a united and powerful race. They have been without leadership far too long. They need their King and their King needs his true and proper mate at his side if he is going to lead."

"I don't know anything about being the Queen of Weres. It's beyond my—"

"Do you love him?" Bear asked, interrupting my rant before I got started. "I felt your fury when I spoke of the plans for his death, but compassion is not the same as love."

Why was everyone so interested in my life?

Screw it. "Yes. I love him."

"Good. Now, the bigger question . . . Will you accept him as your mate and your Alpha?"

I considered everything that had passed between Bruin and me, the good, the bad and the growly. He was stubborn, over-protective, possessive and bossy, but also the sweetest, most devoted man I'd ever met, by nature and by choice. I'd never find a love like his again in ten lifetimes and I wouldn't want it if I did. "Yes. I will."

Bear set down his tool and straightened. With his hands on his hips he stretched his back, first one way then the other. "Come, *She Who Drives Bear Crazy*. We have much to discuss."

We walked along the edge of the stream, sheltered from the afternoon heat by the woven umbrella of the trees above. He bent to the edge of the bank and scooped up a handful of dark, rich soil. "Weres are an amazing race. Not only are they strong and passionate, they also carry the Earth Mother's magic."

I nodded as he let the cool, moist dirt fall into my palm.

"They can dematerialize and rematerialize, and manifest simple objects, but one of their most magical gifts is something you cannot see. Bound mates are connected on a level beyond love. The DNA transfer, from male to female and back again, physically transforms both partners in such a way that they become something other than what they were before their mating. You've noticed heightened senses and strength?"

I nodded. "And appetite. I can't stop eating yet I haven't gained a pound."

"Weres consume huge amounts of food to fuel their powerful bodies. You will never have to diet." Bear smiled and sat on a large flat rock covered in spongy moss. He patted the surface beside him. "Lie back with me, Mika. Close your eyes and breathe deep. What do you feel?"

I did as he asked. Lying still, his energy tingled in my veins. "I feel your power."

He chuckled. "That is not my power, child. That is yours."

"Mine? How?"

Male amusement rang deep in his voice. "Look inside yourself. Envision a connection between you and Bruin. It will be there, somewhere within. It might be a chain or a rope or a ribbon of some sort, but it will be a tangible thing that tethers the two of you together."

I filled my lungs, let my mind drift and followed the energy on its path. Knowing Bruin, and me, it would probably be handcuffs or a skipping rope. I blushed, thankful to have my eyes closed. "I see it. An intricate cord woven from grass, leather, reed and willow . . . but it's slack. It's just lying on the ground."

"Pick it up, Mika. In your mind's eye, pick it up and secure it around you. This is your mating bond. This is what binds you and Bruin as mates and connects your power. Usually the tightening of the bond occurs during the reciting of your acceptance and consummation, but in this case we're going to cheat a little."

I was amazed at how steady my hands were as I bent and picked up the cord. Every moment that passed I was more certain. Bruin was mine . . . my mate. My destiny.

He probably would've preferred someone more agreeable, but—

"He wants *you*, Mika. Bears are gruff and growl a lot, but they love deep. And once that love is given, it is eternal. If this is to work, you cannot doubt his devotion."

I secured the cord around my wrist and pushed away my doubts. As my trust in our bond grew, the cord responded, coming to life, twining itself up my arm until it grew taut and glistened with strength. The hold wasn't restrictive as I'd expected. It was grounding.

Bruin's presence built inside me, his scent steadying my nerves, his power lending strength to my injuries. The man was distant, his bear in full ascension. Jade's words came back to me. *"It's a constant balance between two entities sharing the same space—the man's soul and the animal's instinct."* I finally understood. He really did have two distinct spirits within him.

Two brothers living as one.

"Now," said Bear beside me, "reach out to him, *She Who Brings Change*. You must complete your bonding, so you can go back and finish this. With your connection bound he will hear you, no matter the distance."

Bruin? Bruin?

Bruin's bear bellowed into my mind, his voice hurt and half-crazed. *Mika, wake up. You've been still too long. Wake up, baby.*

I blinked fast. The bear's emotions were raw and exposed. He was back in that cage staring at my unconscious body and there was no doubt—I was *his*. The scent of my pain was shredding his control. He needed to protect me. The animal within Bruin coveted my life more fiercely than I imagined. It was visceral.

Brother Bear, I love you too. Yes . . . I am yours. I'm sorry it took me so long to see it. But right now, I need to speak to Bruin."

Inside the construct of Bruin's protective walls, Brother Bear vacillated between his need to protect me and his need to give me what I asked for. He didn't want me upset with him anymore. His pain at being rejected ached in his soul.

I couldn't breathe. *I'm sorry, Brother Bear. I won't deny you again. Not ever. I swear.*

Bear's relief flooded into me as emotion shifted and Bruin's consciousness came forward. Bruin was much more tentative with his thoughts and emotions, settling himself behind the protection of the walls he'd built a lifetime ago. The fact that he protected himself from me, broke my heart. *Mika, are you all right? How are you speaking to me?*

Tears spilled down my cheeks. *I'm completing our bonding, becoming your Ursa . . . if that's still what you want.*

His growl filled my heart to near bursting. *What I want? I've never wanted anything more . . . but can you do it? Can you trust my love enough to love me in return?*

I took a deep breath and let him in. All my memories, the pain and sorrow of my childhood, my determination to stand alone, my insecurity, everything I never meant for anyone to ever see. I opened myself up and let him see.

There was a pause while everything hit and then he opened himself up to me.

The fire burning in my palm washed with a heavenly winter fresh chill. I gasped and turned it up to watch it transform. What had been blue darkened to an indelible black.

Thick. Solid. Permanent.

And Mika, I love you too.

White hot pain shot through my shoulder. It yanked me from my dream state and I was back in my cage. Abaddon seemed pissed about something. He shook me by my sore wrist and the bump-and-rattle made me want to throw up.

"Wake up, you stupid bitch," he growled. "This is your fault, Shavandra. She's been in and out of consciousness for hours."

"How was I to know she'd react to my spell? That incantation shouldn't have knocked her for a loop like this. It's because she's a weak little Mundie."

The distant rumble of what sounded like a Harley barrelling down the highway vibrated off the cave walls. I smiled, recognizing the low, violent growl of Brother Bear.

Abaddon hesitated as he pulled back to strike the blue bitch and noticed me glaring. "Ah, finally. Good, you're awake. Let's get this done."

After seizing me by the shoulder, Abaddon opened the door to my cell and shoved me at Shavandra. The evil of his touch scrambled my senses like my head got wedged in a centrifuge. My hand had swollen while I was out. Broken by the looks of it.

"Calm yourself, Bruin," he crooned, his seductive command ringing in my ears. He leaned close to the other cell and looked Bruin's bear square in the eyes. "It's time for you to change back to human so we can end this. The ring is here someplace, and you're going to find it."

Through our new connection, I sent Bruin all the help I could to fight the command. The wide heart-shaped head of Bruin's bear canted to the side as if he was considering the request. But then, his form flickered and shifted until Bruin stood vacant-gazed beside us.

I caught the way the blue bitch eyed his naked body and growled. "Clothes, Bruin."

Bruin manifested himself jeans and a plain, black t-shirt.

Abaddon scowled and leaned toward his cell. "You listen to *me*, not her. Got it?" Bruin nodded, and Abaddon's smug smile returned. "Good. Now when I let you out, you're going to help me search this place and figure out where the Were ring has hidden all these years."

CHAPTER FORTY-TWO

The silver bangles on my arm jingled a soft Gypsy song as the four of us left the holding cells and followed a well-lit stone tunnel to a winding stairwell. Abaddon and Bruin led, shoulder to shoulder, though I wasn't sure how much of Bruin was actually present. Shavandra and I followed close behind, her prodding me forward with a vice-grip on my arm and her wand tip poking into my spine.

The smell of his soldiers hung rife in the air the instant we exited the cells. We passed two Scourge standing at the base of the stairs, dressed in black fatigues and looming large. Man, they really were hideous beyond imagination.

As we climbed, I tried to clear the cobwebs from my brain and reconnect with Bruin. I could feel him, but I couldn't break through the fog of Abaddon's hold. I also couldn't hear his voice in my mind.

"What makes you think Bruin can find the ring?" I asked. "He already told you he doesn't know where it is. And I'm guessing he can't lie while you've got your psycho-whammy on him."

"No, he can't," Abaddon said, "but since he doesn't know where it is, it must be here somewhere. I have no doubts that with the proper incentive, we'll find it."

Here? The air was damp in the dungeon but grew warmer the further we climbed.

On each of the lantern lit landings we passed another Scourge standing guard. Abaddon searched the small vignettes accenting the space. Though the furnishings seemed modern, the space felt old and forgotten. By the time we hit the third landing I had a pretty good idea where we were.

"This is the Dens, right? Bruin's home when his father was king?" I ran my fingers along the honed stone walls as I climbed. The natural strength of the surroundings still tingled with the magic of his race. Their pain and suffering was there too, saturating the space. Sorrow and agony. It was suffocating. I sent up a silent prayer and called on my gift.

Shavandra winced when Earth Mother's power rushed to me, but Abaddon seemed too distracted to notice. As he had on each of the other landings, he searched. He swiped his hand in front of a wall cabinet and the hutch below. When nothing happened, he moved onward and upward. "Bruin swears his father wore the ring when he returned to defend his race. So, if no one found it, it must be here."

He stopped our group when we reached the main floor and I slid in close to Bruin.

Earth Mother's aid allowed me to see Abaddon's evil. Like he had in the Hearthstone that day at lunch, the sorcerer oozed his funky evil mojo and puke-green strings of magic stretched from him to Bruin. This time though, there was also a beautiful cord woven from grass, leather, reed and willow connecting us.

Abaddon snapped his fingers in Bruin's face. "Tell me, where would your father hide his ring if under attack?"

Bruin's jaw clenched as he strained against Abaddon's bond.

"Don't fight me, Bruin. You won't like the result." In a move so swift I almost missed it, Abaddon slashed at me with his knife.

I hissed as a scarlet line bloodied my brand new, white Grecian top.

Bruin growled as his words tore from his throat. "In his library safe."

Abaddon pressed the tip of the knife into the hollow of my throat and narrowed his cold, black eyes. "Try harder, Bear. We've searched all the obvious places."

"The compartment under the billiards table."

Abaddon sheathed his knife and raised his hand. And off we went again.

We moved through a great eating hall and past the library Bruin mentioned, passing three more of Abaddon's soulless soldiers standing sentinel.

Consumed with the search, Abaddon took the lead and Shavandra took the rear. That left Bruin and I walking close enough that I laced my fingers with his and pressed our brands together. His fingers remained straight and stiff.

Bruin, fight him, big guy. I need you. I can only stall him so long.

Nothing came back to me but fog and the anger of Bruin being locked behind it. I sighed and turned back to Abaddon. "How do you think you can rule the Weres? The ring is symbolic, not magical. It doesn't hold the Weres enthralled to obey their king. It's a symbol of trust."

Abaddon laughed, taking a left through a golden corridor and leading us into an open space littered with overturned sofas, broken barstools and shattered games tables. The entire space was lit with a magical light. We found what was left of the billiards table under a shredded tapestry and he crouched over the mess. "All symbols hold power, especially when given noble purpose. The Were ring was a gift, kissed and blessed by every Prime in the race. It will enslave its members and add to my noble army. Wait and see."

"Noble army?" I turned to look at the Scourge soldier guarding the doorway—the rotting flesh, the stringy, patches of hair, the violent sneer. "What's noble about it? You align yourself with the honorless men who trade power and longevity for their soul. Filthy mercenaries, the lot of you."

"I didn't *align* myself with the Scourge, little girl. I *created* them. If you're planning a mutiny you need an army. The Scourge are mine. They are strong and loyal. The Weres will add to that power. Bruin set his people adrift a decade ago. The Weres are vulnerable and when I hold the power of the ring, they will heel to my command."

"Heel? They aren't pets. They're people."

I'm not sure what my expression gave away, but he seemed amused by my reaction. "Weres are nothing more than animals, Miss Silverbrook. Strong, trainable mindless beasts. And all beasts need a master."

"So who's yours, crazy man?"

Lethal fury flared in his eyes, but as quickly as it came, it extinguished. *Okaaay*, the man didn't like to be called crazy. He stalked forward, and Bruin stiffened beside me.

"Just this once," Abaddon hissed, "I'll forgive your insolence and educate rather than eviscerate. No. I'm not crazy. I'm inspired. I am reinstating the Queen of our realm and I will stand by her side, eliminating the weaker races, ruling over the Realm of the Fair with my—"

The keening of metal on metal rang through the stone corridors of the cave. The sound of weapons colliding preceded an explosion of angry voices.

The Talon. The cavalry had arrived.

Abaddon scowled, and the glint of silver gleamed between us.

I flailed my good arm to block, but it was a weak attempt at defense. Scarlet heat flowed as I toppled backward. I landed with an unceremonious thud on the stone floor.

Bruin's roar echoed in my head and in the room as he caught Abaddon by the throat and slammed him to the wall. Bruin's mahogany claws extended and sliced at Abaddon's flesh.

When Shavandra aimed her wand at Bruin, my bear instinct unleashed. It wasn't neat of course, but in a frenzy of hands, elbows and knees, I threw myself at the witch, scrabbling for the shaft of her wand, growling, screaming, raging. "You don't harm what is mine, *bitch.*"

I fisted her hair as tightly as I could and slammed her head into the stone wall. She started spouting off some kind of spell and I grabbed her mouth, dug my fingers into her cheeks and shut her up with every ounce of strength I had. Her serrated teeth sliced my palm, but I held on.

The fighting beyond the room grew closer. A rising cacophony of grunts and growls and chinking steel. The room cartwheeled as Shavandra rolled backwards and we collided into another heap of broken furniture.

My hand ached and when I couldn't hold on any longer, Bruin's strength filled me. In a flood of energy, his strength fed my muscles and solidified my hold. He was there, or at least his bear was. Without realizing what I was doing, I grabbed Shavandra's chin and the top of her head and twisted with a force beyond my capability.

Crack. Ding dong the witch was dead.

Her blank stare reminded me of the horror I'd felt that day in the Vancouver parking garage when Bruin had snapped that pony tailed Jackal's neck to protect me. I got it now. I would do anything to protect my mate.

Scrambling to my knees, I saw Bruin thrown over the remains of the billiards table.

Abaddon staggered forward hand extended. The power of the spell amassing had the hair on my neck standing on end. The buzzing built to a deafening hiss, the sound of a swarm of killer bees gunning right for us. Bruin wasn't moving.

Just as Abaddon's spell let loose, Talon warriors stormed into the fray.

"Duck and cover people."

I screamed and threw myself over Bruin.

In the aftermath of the explosion, I lay in darkness, my head throbbing, something large and furry lying over of me. My eyes opened but I couldn't see anything beyond darkness. Dust rained down on my face like hazy mist. Dry grains of sediment crunched in my teeth and stuck to my tongue. Licking my lips did nothing to alleviate the cotton mouth.

"Bruin!" My hamster got back in its wheel and my synapses fired. Struggling out from underneath the dead weight, I ran my hands over Bruin's body. His clothes were torn, his skin slick and warm and coated with moisture. "Bruin, are you all right, big guy?"

He wasn't. His energy surged, and he shifted to bear. Unconscious. Not being able to see him made my panic worse. I sunk my fingers deep into his fur and reached for our bond. I sobbed . . . our connection was . . . solid.

Bruin and his bear were there, weary but strong. Unconscious but alive. *Thank you, Creator.*

"Mika, we are coming, *neelan.*"

"Aust?" The dark space filled with the sounds of stone shifting, metal clanging and growls of frustration. "Be careful of Abaddon."

"Abaddon is gone, *neelan.* You are safe."

I struggled awkwardly to make it to my knees just as the debris around me shifted. As I slid backwards strong hands caught my fall and I was scooped into a hug that crushed my breath from my lungs. I hissed and braced my good hand against his chest.

"Apologies, Mika, are you well?" Aust lessened his hold, his fingers brushing my hair away from my face and gently probing some of my more serious gashes and abrasions. It took me a moment to remember Elves had night vision.

Handy.

A whine came from beside my thigh and the muzzle of a large wolf rucked my shirt and pressed against my stomach. I ran my fingers through Faolan's coat and stroked her ears, comforted by the warmth Aust's wolf. She nuzzled me again.

Voices, grunts and low grumbling curses of men excavating grew louder from moment to moment. "Let's hear it, Alpha. Is everyone okay?"

"Bruin's unconscious," I answered, "but I think he's all right."

"What about Samuel and Cowboy?" Jade's voice was sharp and tight. "They Flashed in right before the explosion."

Aust shifted his footing a bit but kept a hold on me. "Cowboy is guarding his Ursa and is well. I cannot see Samuel though. *Samuel?*"

Nothing.

I stroked the long ears of the wolf before me and realized Aust was right. Cowboy's wolf was much larger than Faolan. It never occurred to me that he'd show me any kind of love. I leaned closer and he licked my face.

"Jade," Aust said, "could you send us in some light? Cowboy can smell Samuel but if he climbs on the debris in here, he worries he might crush him."

A moment later, a shuffle of bodies edged inside the room and someone clapped their hands. A second clap lit the room with the glow of fire. The fire ignited between Jade's palms and as she spread her hands wide, the blaze arched and danced brighter. Blues, reds and oranges burned bright within the flame and as they grew, sparks broke away from her palms and leapt to the extinguished torches mounted on the walls.

Blaze. Again, Bruin's sister left me speechless.

Kobi retrieved a torch and waved it over the mound of rock, steel and rubble that filled the room.

Jade frowned. "I don't see Samuel. Does anyone see him?"

Cowboy shifted, sniffing, his tri-coloured coat glowing caramel in the torchlight. He seemed to smell something, but then hesitated, studied my face, then looked at Bruin's bear and at Shavandra's blue corpse.

"She's dead," I said. "We'll be fine. Help find Samuel."

Without disturbing the rocks, Aust followed Cowboy's wolf as they bounded over a mound of debris and landed soundlessly near the back wall.

"Got him." Kobi dropped to his knees where Cowboy indicated and started shoveling bits of steel and stone to the side. Aust joined in and, within seconds, uncovered a tall, dark-haired warrior in a long, leather slicker. I was no doctor, but even I could see the man was messed up.

Cowboy changed forms and cursed. "Jade, we're gonna need you, darlin'. Your boy here's in a bit of a fix."

"What's wrong," I asked, trying to see around the mass of men.

"Well, I'm thinkin it's a bad thing if I can see his knee and the heel of his shitkicker at the same time. That is unless he's part flamingo."

Kobi cursed as he and Cowboy grabbed under Samuel's shoulders and Jade secured the leg. When they cleared the pile of rubble, they set him down on the floor and Jade went to work. "Hang in there Samuel, I've got you."

"Wouldn't it be better if ye could see what yer doing, luv?" Samuel asked through gritted teeth. "I've got all the faith in yer abilities, but ye need light to heal, no?"

Jade stopped humming then waved for Kobi to bring a torch closer. "Samuel," she said, passing her hand in front of his face, "what happened during the explosion?"

"Well, it was a fair bit chaotic . . . Abaddon was about to let loose on Bruin . . . I blocked the spell the best I could." He probed the side of his head with his fingers and hissed. "It had more kick than I expected. Why? What's wrong?"

Cowboy straightened and stepped back, scrubbing his hand over his chin and I saw the problem. Samuel's eyes were white and blank. The man was blind.

CHAPTER FORTY-THREE

I hit SEND on the article I wrote for Paige and lifted my eyes from the glow of my laptop screen. Life had a strange way of dragging you through knot holes just to get you to the other side. Officially, as far as Paige and my girls knew, I was in witness protection until the Nimithic Trial was over. It was the easiest explanation for my disappearance considering they knew about the attack at Spankz and what happened to Meg at the office.

They'd all been sworn to secrecy for my safety which would keep them from snooping around and getting themselves into trouble. In the meantime, I was free to continue to write and send my stories via email. Julian had my IP address bouncing all over the world and back, so no one would be any the wiser.

An ice cream sandwich dangled in front of my face and I spun my desk chair. *Mmm*, tasty treats offered by the sexiest man alive.

"A chocolate treat for my Ursa."

I sat back to read the slogan-T clinging to his landscape and laughed. *You are free to bask in my glow.* Peeling back the wrapper, I moved to the couch to lounge with my bear. "Any change with Samuel?"

Bruin flopped onto the couch beside me and shook his head.

"Nothing yet. His leg healed well enough, but his eyes still aren't tracking. Jade's convinced it's some kind of black magic in Abaddon's spell that's blocking her ability."

I set the wrapper on the coffee table and slid my tongue between the layers of chocolate cookie, gathering the melting ice cream. "They're not giving up are they?"

"Nah, Reign has Savage and a few other guys trying to find a sorcerer or dark wizard who can help. So far, no luck." He tucked me against his side, his heavy arm squeezing me close.

I glanced up at his profile and sighed. "That flat out sucks."

"Yep. I'm not sure what Samuel did to piss off the Fates, but he's been getting his ass kicked the last few months: he lost Jade, his home and now his sight. I'm praying he can still use magic. I know the guy. If magic is out too, he won't come back from it."

My brain spun at an uncomfortable churn. Samuel was in this condition because of us. "What about Abaddon? Has Julian had any luck tracking him down?"

"He's in the wind. We got some of his men and Reign will interrogate them himself. If they know anything, they'll spill it."

Yeah, Reign was intimidating when dressed in a power suit at the dinner table, I couldn't imagine how frightening Bruin's father would be interrogating the enemy. I shivered. "Hey, what's with Julian's tattoo? One day he's got one on his arm, another day it's gone."

Bruin shrugged. "That's his story to tell, but he likes you. I'd bet he'll trust you enough to let you in on his secrets soon enough. As long as you promise not to do write an article about it."

I slapped his chest. "And what about you? How are you doing?"

Bruin kissed the side of my head and sighed. "Abaddon stirred up a lot of my demons. My father. Gemma's death. Me being the Were-King."

"And?"

"And Bear is right. The Weres needed a King after my father was killed. I should have stepped up. I need to lead my race. No, *we* need to lead them."

I savoured the vanilla ice cream melting in my mouth and smiled. "Partners?"

"Yep. Partners." Bruin inhaled his treat in two bites and licked the chocolate off his fingers with a sinful grin. Finished, he leaned over, attempting to take a bite of mine. I squirmed, defending my chocolate yumminess and took a huge bite so I wouldn't have to share.

When the giggling ended, and Bruin had sucked my fingers clean, I asked him the question that had been bouncing around in my head for days. "You enjoyed living in those caves as a young bear, right?"

"The Dens. Yes. I'm sorry you didn't see it when it was filled with life and love. After the Scourge attack I couldn't bring myself to go back there, but I think one day, I'd like to go see what we can salvage. Did you know the mountain it's built into is actually called Mount Bear."

"You're kidding."

His chest bounced and jiggled us both. "Nope. Honest. It's in Alaska, just a few miles away from the Yukon border."

"Do you miss it? Living like that?"

Bruin shrugged and flicked his bangs out of his sparkling turquoise eyes. "Never really thought about it. Why?"

"Well, I was thinking about us, and the orphaned cubs, and Weres in general. I wondered if you wanted to make a place like that our home. Our own Dens. I always loved hanging out in the caverns on the reservation. And I'm sorry, but I can't imagine living here with your sisters and building our own lives."

Bruin licked his lips. "I hadn't really thought about it. Sure, we can look into it."

"Um . . . I kind of already did."

His graceful brow arched until it disappeared behind his bangs. "Well, well, my beautiful Ursa, spill it. What have you done?"

"Castian came by with Grandfather while I was resting, and we talked about the future and you being the true Were-King. I thought you should have a place where other Weres could stay, if they needed a home or somewhere to regroup."

I wriggled off the couch and pulled him behind me through the sliding glass door. August was over, and the smell of autumn filled the air. When we emerged onto the balcony, I pointed up the gold and crimson slope of the mountain. "See that cave mouth past the plateau on that peak?"

He squinted off into the distance. "Yes?"

"If you agree, Castian will make that our new Dens. We can come up with the plans and he'll create a network of rooms and facilities. He said we could start moving within a few weeks. We'd be able to take in the orphans, hold formal meetings with the Primes . . . Bree could even have a lab to continue with her research. It could really strengthen the Weres as a whole."

Bruin's shoulders grew rigid and I stopped rambling. He hadn't said he wanted any of this. Maybe he loved living with his family. The look on his face was completely unreadable.

"Oh man. You hate the idea, don't you? I'm sorry. If you want to live here, we—"

His tongue in my mouth silenced my rant as did his erection pressed against my belly. Greedy hands lifted my skirt and hoisted me by my butt and my legs locked around his waist. I giggled as the balcony flew past in a blur. Just inside our suite, he propped me on the window ledge and pushed my skirt up and out of his way completely.

"Aren't you tired?" I unzipped his jeans and he pressed forward— "Oh *god.*"

He chuckled and broke from our kiss. "No, baby. I know I seem godlike at times, but it's just me." He surged forward and slid back. "Just your bear, your very hungry bear."

I reached behind his neck and held on. He was the perfect combination of brute strength and raw sex. Irresistible. The intensity of his love boggled my mind at times. And god help me, I even loved his bossy, grizzly side . . . uh, especially at moments when Brother Bear got possessive and demanding.

When both of us were breathless and spent, he stilled and held me in a tight embrace.

I marveled at the turn of our conversation. "So, you like the idea of the Dens?"

"I love it," he said, his breath caressing my cheek. "I love you thinking about our future. I love you wanting a place of our own. I love the fact that I'll finally make my father proud."

He lowered his mouth to mine and chuckled. "And I love you, *She Who Brings Change*. Now let's get you cleaned up."

He scooped under my legs, carried me to the washroom and started the shower. With gentle hands he pulled my shirt over my head and tossed it to the hamper.

I undid my braid and loosened my hair around my shoulders. "I still can't believe that Bear . . . *The Bear*, came to me."

Bruin retrieved a couple of towels from the closet as I stepped out of my skirt and draped it over the back of my make-up chair.

He chuckled and peeled off his T. "I can't believe that *He* bonded us without the sex and the ritual. That's a highlight for a Were and now I'll never know."

I laid my brand against his chest and laughed. "Poor guy, I'm sure you'll make do."

He winked and I was certain we'd be making do again, very soon.

A quiet knock had us both turning to the bedroom. "*Shhh*," Bruin whispered. "If we're quiet maybe they'll go away."

I bit my bottom lip, trying not to giggle. The knock came again, and Bruin's shoulders dropped. On a huff, he shut off the water, tossed me a robe and bounded across the room. The way he stormed toward the door, I worried he might kill whoever was on the other side.

"Be nice," I whispered, securing the silk belt around my waist. "They know we're newlyweds. If they're disturbing us, it must be important."

Bruin grabbed the door handle and glanced back to me. "Somebody better be fucking dying." He growled as he swung the sucker almost off the hinges.

Bruin filled the whole frame of the door

I couldn't see who was in the hall, but when his broad shoulders stiffened and his body went rigid, I grabbed my purse and drew out my Taser.

His everyday growl expanded into a thundering rumble. "What the hell are *you* doing here?"

There was a long silence before Lexi's small voice rang through his snarl. "I came to apologize—officially—to her."

"Her name is Mika."

"Right. *Sorry*. I came to apologize to *Mika* for my behaviour . . . before."

"You can shove your apology up your—"

"Bruin." I hustled towards them. "Don't. It's okay. Let her speak."

"Fuck that. She almost killed you. She almost took my life from me."

"It was a fluke. Don't." I did my best impression of Mohammad moving the mountain. The only reason I got anywhere was because he let me tug him back out of the doorway. He wasn't letting her in though. He took a step back and let me slide between them, but that was as far as she was getting. Honestly, I was okay with that.

"Uh, hi . . . Mika." Lexi looked up at me and for the first time her amethyst eyes held no edge to them. "I wanted to make sure you were okay and tell you how badly I feel that my temper got away from me."

Bruin snorted and grasped my shoulders. "There you said it. Now go."

Lexi's big purple eyes blinked fast as she drew a deep breath. "I also wanted to give her . . . *you* . . . this." She held out an ivory card with an emerald green ivy design decorating the surface. My name was written on the front in a beautiful gold script. "I heard you weren't coming to the wedding celebration and I thought that was probably my fault. I wanted to bring you an invitation and assure you that you are a welcome part of this family."

I took the card from her tiny hands. Hard to believe that this little thing could take me down and bash my skull into the marble floor at the flip of a switch. Been there done that, got the scar tissue to prove it. Deceiving. Lexi was not what she seemed. "I appreciate the gesture."

"So, you'll come? Jade and Galan will be so—"

I shook my head. "I'll explain to Jade and Galan. I'm not ready to sit across the table from you and make nice. Sorry. Must be the stupid Mundie in me. You'll have to survive the wedding without me. Now, if you'll excuse us, we were having a moment, before you interrupted."

Lexi shifted her weight and opened her mouth.

Before she could say anything, Bruin stepped around me and swung the door shut.

As he turned from the door and locked us in together, I realized I'd never been more at home with anyone. It didn't matter if I lived in Vancouver or in a castle or in a mountainside cave. Home was where my bear was.

Bruin stalked closer, a quirky grin covering his face. "I like it when you look at me like that, *She Who Drives Her Bear Crazy*. I think I like that one the best."

I laughed. "I was thinking about our bonding ceremony. We may have taken a shortcut, but you're right. We should have the whole experience. I'd like to recite the ritual."

Bruin's gaze narrowed as he licked his lips. "And what if nothing more happens?"

"We'll have fun trying."

His smile grew wider. "I like the way you think, mate."

In the beat of a racing heart, we were naked and sidling closer to the bed. The surge of his magic as our clothes disappeared made me smile. "You got any other tricks you want to show me?" I burst out laughing as he lunged and we both flew through the air.

Landing on the bed, caged in his protective embrace, he pressed his brand to mine. "It's not about tricks, baby. It's all about the love.

AFTERWORD

THANK YOU FOR READING
I hope you enjoyed Ursa Unearthed, Book 2 of the Scourge Survivor
Series. I sincerely hope you enjoyed Bruin and Mika's love story. If
you'd like to share your thoughts on the series, please leave a rating or
review at your favorite retailer.
Reviews help other readers find books.

If you're ready for more sexy adventures with the Haven gang,
continue on with Book 3 – Torrent of Tears.

TORRENT OF TEARS

With her birthday approaching and her adoptive family angry with her, Lexi doubts her place in her own life. Where had she come from? Where did she truly belong? When her identical twin emerges from the surface of a frozen pond to reclaim her, Lexi abandons the security of Haven to go find out.

Unfamiliar with the customs, laws, and obligations of life in Attalos, Lexi's warrior habits and acerbic wit clash with everything in her oppressed homeland. At odds with her mother, the royal guards, and her arranged betrothed, Lexi finds a reluctant ally in Rowan, shunned Noble of the Fifth House.

Through their sexually charged pursuit of freedom, Lexi learns that family and love are two very different things.

Author Notes

Written on 09/09/2018

Thank you for reading Ursa Unearthed, and here you are, still with me reading this. As a novelist of many genres of romance—fantasy, paranormal, timeslip historical, and sci-fi—I love to twist Alpha heroes and kick-ass heroines into chaotic, hilarious, and magical situations, and make them really work for a Happily Ever After.

To have you enjoy it enough to gift me with your time and attention is a true gift.

Thank you. I hope my imagined adventures continue to live up to your expectations.

All the best to you and yours.
 Blessed Be,
 JL

ALSO BY JL MADORE

Find Me:

Social Media – Facebook, Twitter, Instagram

Web page – www.jlmadore.com

Email – jlmadorewrites@gmail.com

Reader Group – JL Series Updates

JL's Reverse Harem Titles

Guardians of the Fae Realms

Guardians of the Phoenix – Calli's Harem

Book 1 – Rise of the Phoenix

Book 2 – Wolf's Soul

Book 3 – Bear's Strength

Book 4 – Hawk's Heart

Book 5 – Jaguar's Passion

Darkness Calls – Keyla's harem

Book 6 – Dark Curse

Book 7 – Dark Soul

Book 8 – Dark Crown

Guardians of the Crown – Honor's Harem

Book 9 – Honor Restored

Book 10 – Honor Guards

Book 11 – Honor Bound

Book 12 – Honor Empowered

Rise of the Amberloq – Lark's Harem

Book 13 – Find the Fallen